THE MARK OF WU

BOOK ONE

HIDDEN PATHS

A Novel by

STEPHEN M. GRAY

HELU PRESS
San Antonio, TX

The Mark of Wu™ Series
Book One: Hidden Paths

Published by
Helu Press
San Antonio, TX
www.themarkofwu.com

978-0-9990071-0-5 (Print)
978-0-9990071-1-2 (E-Book)

Editor: Cliff Carle
Cover and Text Design: Mayapriya Long (Bookwrights)
Maps and Battle Diagrams: Lee Casbeer

Printed in the United States of America

To Lisa, my wife and partner in every battle.

CONTENTS

PARTIAL LIST OF CHARACTERS AND STATES

STATE OF CHU

Yuan – Son of Sheh and brother of Shang.

Prince Chien – King Ping's son and Heir Apparent to the Chu throne.

Sheng – Prince Chien's son.

Sheh – Prince Chien's Grand Mentor, father of Yuan and Shang.

Shang – Son of Sheh, older brother of Yuan and Prince Chien's Junior Mentor.

Commander Wei Yue – The State of Chu's Field Marshal at the Battle of Chi-fu.

Nang Wa – Prime Minister of the State of Chu.

Lan – Yuan's archer.

Fen Yang – Yuan's halberdier.

Ga – Peasant soldier from Chengfu.

King Ping – King of Chu.

Princess Mei – King Ping's wife.

Queen Ma – King Ping's first wife and Queen of Chu.

CHU'S SUBORDINATE STATES

Duke Chao of the State of Ts'ai.

The Duke of T'ang.

The Duke of Sui.

The Duke of Hu.

The Duke of Shen.

The Duke of Chen.

STATE OF WU

Prince Kuang – The State of Wu's Field Marshal at the Battle of Chi-fu.
King Liao – King of Wu and Prince Kuang's cousin.
Fu-kai – Prince Kuang's younger brother.
Kai-yü – King Liao's and Chu-yung's brother; Prince Kuang's cousin.
Chu-yung – King Liao's and Kai-yü's brother; Prince Kuang's cousin.
Kan-jian – A Wu prisoner who fought at the Battle of Chi-fu.
Ke-lu – A Wu prisoner who fought at the Battle of Chi-fu.

NORTHERN ALLIANCE STATES

Duke Ting – Duke of the State of Cheng.
Zuchan – Emissary from the State of Cheng, who later becomes Chief Minister State of Sung.
Duke Ching – Duke of the State of Jin.
Zhou – Prime Minister from the State of Jin.

"Warfare is of vital importance to a country, a matter of life and death and a road to survival or ruin."
— Sun-Tzu

ANCIENT CHINA
519 B.C.

PART 1

THE STATE OF CHU

1

A MATTER OF HONOR

*Y*uan threw back the tent flap and entered. Death was inside.

He nudged through a small crowd of armor clad men, then paused to view the General's body lying on a bed of fur hides.

The General's Taishi looked up at Yuan and said, "His ancestors called him to the next life and sent a fever."

Three servants knelt to finish dressing General Yang Gai. One reached across the body, combing the General's long, silver hair so that it flowed to a gentle rest over his shoulders. The servant then groomed the stringy beard, which hung thinly from the tip of the chin, and laid it down the center of General Yang Gai's chest. Next, he tugged on the white quilted death robe, at the shoulders, straightening the fringe and smoothing out the wrinkles around the fold with the palm of his hand.

Another servant folded Yang Gai's arms across the body and tucked the cold hands into the robe's wide sleeves. The silk robe flowed from the General's shoulders to his feet. The third servant finished the task of putting finely woven slippers over stiffening toes and securing them around the heels.

Commander Wei Yue stood next to the General's Taishi. The six Dukes stood watching and anxiously waiting to learn what the General's death meant for them. Yuan looked toward Duke Chao of Ts'ai, who glared at the Commander.

"Commander Wei Yue, General Yang Gai's death is a bad omen," Duke Chao declared. "Prime Minister Nang Wa demanded my presence in this battle against the Wu barbarians, but shouldn't we wait until after he appoints a new Field Marshal before we continue this march?"

"I am now the Field Marshal!" Commander Wei Yue said curtly. The coldness of his words rivaled as much the chill inside the tent, brought on by the General's death, as it did the wintry day outside.

"Chou-lai is fully fortified, and the Wu barbarians haven't penetrated its walls yet," Duke Chao argued. "The town can hold out until we receive direction from the Prime Minister, and waiting may allow the siege to deplete Wu's supplies and tire their resolve."

Commander Wei Yue shook his head. "Our troop strength will overwhelm them. And don't forget, they're merely barbarians. They don't possess our virtue. Return to your camps, all of you, and I'll tell you my plans later." Commander Wei Yue's manner was harsh and showed an awkward struggle to assert his new authority.

It didn't take long for the in-fighting to begin, Yuan noted. General Yang Gai had been dead only a short time, and already Duke Chao was resisting Commander Wei Yue and angling for a way out of the battle. Yuan stayed as Duke Chao and the others brushed past him. The servant working at Yang Gai's feet picked up a cloak of grayish-brown hides and handed corners to each of the other servants, who waited on opposite sides of the body. They stretched the cloak over the General, covering his body from head to toe.

Yuan watched the cloak cover the stone face and allowed a moment to pass. "Wei Yue, you'll need the Dukes in order to defeat Wu in this battle." Yuan and Wei Yue knew each other well. Both had served many times under General Yang Gai. Yuan was slightly younger at twenty-two years old, and stood in equal height to the Commander. They both possessed bodies hardened by the labors of military life, but their similarities were mainly physical. Yuan had proved the more effective leader.

"They have no choice but to follow my orders," Wei Yue rebutted. "Before he died, General Yang Gai named me as the Field Marshal." Wei Yue tapped his chest, emphasizing the point. "His sickness didn't hit until after we left Ying, and the severity of it took everyone by surprise. Once the General realized that he might not recover, he instructed me how best to proceed." Wei Yue paused to gather words. "His ancestors' pull was so strong, it didn't give him time. He wanted to talk to you in person." Wei Yue looked down, shaking his head. "He almost made it." He walked around the covered body, closer to Yuan. "General Yang Gai was convinced that Wu would see any delay as a sign of weakness. It would enliven them. So he chose me."

Yuan understood the deeper implication. Wei Yue and Yuan were the two obvious choices. Commander Po Pi was a possible third, but he lacked the experience needed of a Field Marshal. If Yuan had arrived in time, the General would have explained that Yuan's personal circumstances, not inability, made him an unacceptable choice to Prime Minister Nang Wa and, more importantly, to King Ping. Yuan also knew Wei Yue would never admit that General Yang Gai's decision involved anything but merit. "Yes, General Yang Gai was wise in many ways." Yuan acknowledged, hiding his angst. "Certainly, the Dukes played an important role in his plans for this battle and will in yours. But now, Duke Chao is spooked. How will you bring him to your side?"

"Everyone will do as I say, or answer for it if they don't." Wei Yue's cheeks drew taut. He knew of only one way to deal with those who questioned his authority, and that was with anger.

He doesn't know how to lead Chao or the other Dukes. More than battlefield skills are needed from him. "It's not enough to possess General Yang Gai's authority." Yuan refrained from saying everything he thought.

"I suppose you want to take my place," Wei Yue quipped. "Do you really think the Prime Minister will accept *you* as Field Marshal? Do I need to remind you of your family's fall?"

Why Yuan's family was no longer in favor with the King was something no one talked about, at least not to Yuan. Everyone knew that the reason wasn't a just one. They knew the schemes that had worked against his family were simply too great to control, and as a result, people within the Chu army generally showed Yuan the respect his skill and success on the battlefield justified. Yuan avoided snapping back at Wei Yue and instead bowed in feigned deference, then left the tent. Wei Yue's barb had struck at the headmost purpose that drove Yuan in this march to war, and confirmed that until he restored his family's honor, the overhang would haunt his future as much as it did his past.

Once out of the tent, Yuan saw Duke Chao with the other Dukes huddled away from earshot. Duke Chao waved his arms and leaned into his words, pressing some point. Although Yuan was too far away to hear, it was obvious what they were discussing. Duke Chao wanted no part of the fight with Wu. General Yang Gai's death foreboded an ominous future, especially for those on the front line who would bear the main assault. That meant the six States: Duke Chao of Ts'ai, the Duke of T'ang and the Dukes of Sui, Hu, Shen and Chen. All of them served Chu, and had been subservient since Chu defeated the Dukes' grandfathers and great grandfathers. The Dukes' only real power now was persuasiveness, and Duke Chao was enlisting the aid of others to help convince the ill-prepared Wei Yue to pause or even abandon the march to war. It would take the combined efforts of the Dukes to change Wei Yue's mind, and Duke Chao did not want to face the repercussions of being alone in that stand.

Duke Chao's longtime friend, the Duke of T'ang, stood next to him. The two were noblemen from adjoining lands, enjoyed seasonal hunts together and shared the hardships of frontline battle, including their stinging encounter with Wu five years earlier. It was that pang that drove Duke Chao's reluctance now.

The Duke of Shen stood across from Chao. He was shorter than the others, wide and frumpy. Duke Chao spoke directly to him.

Yuan closed within earshot and stepped into the group. His clever mind saw the world through calculating eyes, and he focused on the immediate need of determining the extent of the in-fighting. He listened. Yuan's eyes cut to Duke Chao, then to the Duke of Shen and back.

"Look at us," Duke Chao scowled. "Here we stand at the Gap, in this cold, wet wind, instead of in our homes tending to matters more important to us. Our lands and people are mere servants to King Ping and Chu. The King takes from us what he pleases and sends our men to fight in battles that have no meaning to us. What good will this fight with Wu bring us?"

Yuan recognized that Duke Chao avoided the obvious. Chu was a vast country. Its northern border was across the Huai River, which lay north of and parallel to the Dabie Shan Mountains. About halfway along the east-west axis was the Gap, a narrow basin that severed the mountain range, providing access to the river. It also allowed passage into Chu from the river, and if Wu forces were left unchecked, its new foothold would provide a staging ground to attack through the Gap and into the heart of Chu. The States would be called upon to provide a buffer against Wu's attacks, inflicting constant turmoil on them. Duke Chao knew this, too, but now was not the time Yuan wanted to speak of it.

"It's no different than the past, but our fate will not change today, or anytime soon, so what's your point?" the Duke of Shen postulated, looking over his shoulder, and showing little interest in Duke Chao's complaints. He whirled a furry cape around his back and onto his shoulders to ward off the afternoon chill. Whether during moderate winters or subtropical summers, the frowzy Duke always appeared ill adapted.

"My point is that even with General Yang Gai, we weren't certain to defeat Wu, and it's our blood that always stains the front line. We'll all be dead before Chu's regular army draws a sword. Yet we're forced to subject our men to a battle that has no bearing on our lands and no meaning to our people. Besides, aren't any of you concerned that Commander Wei Yue doesn't recognize he's not General Yang Gai? Not in strategy. Not in tactics. Not in virtue." Duke Chao's back straightened. "Do any of you really think he can lead us to victory? Now that Yang Gai is dead, we're left with a Field Marshal who is in no way capable of defeating Wu. Proceeding will be a waste of blood. Our blood!"

The Duke of Hu stood cross-armed and rubbed the flab of his aged body, warding off the cool air. With his chin raised in a snooty pose, he admonished, "Now is not the time to bring this up, Chao. Our people and our lands serve the King. That's our fate. We will not change that now by disobeying Chu's command." The Duke of Hu was the oldest among them and had reached his age by not bucking the King or risking offense. In following those simple rules, even when it meant taking the battlefield to serve a despot king, he had outlived Duke Chao's father.

Yuan watched Duke Chao bristle as if ready to pounce.

"Yes, we serve the King, and by the time we return, *if* we return, the moon will be in the next year. The King's demands on us are heavy. It's difficult enough to pay that burden and still leave enough for our people to survive the winter. This winter was no exception. To make sure we raise the piculs of grain required of us, our men should be working the fields today, spreading manure and preparing to plant. Instead, we march them to their deaths." Duke Chao threw out his chest as his biting tongue wagged. "Who will work our fields then? The women? The children? Perhaps we'll have to take plow in hand ourselves."

"Don't show your anger. You'll attract attention," the Duke of Sui cautioned. He stood across from Yuan.

Duke Chao turned toward the voice. "What do the Sui people think of this?"

"We feel no differently than you, but we all live under Chu's fist. Remember, Sui fell to Chu's might long before your lands bowed to it. Indeed, so long ago that too many of my ancestors never knew life without Chu's heavy hand. It's been that way with every king of Chu we've known. And this battle with Wu is no different than the previous ones we were forced to fight."

Yuan followed the conversation, studying each man. Chao didn't have them all on his side but neither did Commander Wei Yue. Yuan wondered how the new Field Marshal was possibly going to lead them.

Duke Chao turned to Yuan. "You know Wei Yue best. What do you think of him as a Field Marshal?"

"I know you're worried," Yuan acknowledged. "You doubt him, but his battlefield tactics are sound. We've all witnessed that in the past. Remember, our power is far greater than Wu's, and the odds in this battle are no different. Our chariot strength alone will be overwhelming." Yuan hoped to turn Duke Chao's dissent before he whipped others into a fury.

"Even so, the Chu army has never completely destroyed Wu. We've struggled every time without much advance," Duke Chao reminded the group.

"This battle is only about forcing the barbarians out of Chu. Nothing more," Yuan assured the group.

"That may have been possible with General Yang Gai, but I don't think it is with Commander Wei Yue," Duke Chao argued. "You should be the Field Marshal, not Wei Yue. He's not capable of leading us to victory, but you are, Yuan."

Yuan shot a look of caution to Chao. "You know why General Yang Gai could not choose me. Tell me," he said to Chao, "did you trust him?"

Chao nodded. "Yes."

Yuan reached out with a fist, pumped the air for emphasis, then spoke to the broader circle of Dukes. "General Yang Gai tapped Commander Wei Yue as Field Marshal, believing in his abilities. We should trust that judgment now, just as we always have. The battles with Wu have been on their soil. In this one, we will fight them on our own land, if Commander Wei Yue decides to proceed." Yuan looked past Duke Chao and saw Wei Yue heading for the Taishi's tent. "There's Commander Wei Yue. He's going to ask the Taishi for guidance. We can talk more tonight after we hear from the Commander, but for now, we should join our men." Yuan wanted to break up the group to deflect Chao's influence over the others. Chao's complaints rang true. Yuan felt the same way, but chose not to reveal it. *The fight with Wu is winnable, but a divided effort makes victory much harder. If I validate any objection, doubt may take hold of the other Dukes. Keep them focused on my path, not Chao's.*

"And if the tortoise shell omen sends us into battle?" Duke Chao asked while stepping away.

"Then we fight," Yuan said evenly.

There was much to do to direct the factions toward a common goal, Yuan's goal – to restore his family's honor – and he didn't like having to navigate the different personalities. He much preferred the direct approach, but circumstances didn't allow it. He headed for the Taishi's tent where Commander Wei Yue stood in front giving instructions to the General's servants. Wei Yue pulled back the tent's flap and stepped inside. Yuan followed. "Taishi, it's time for you to divine our future," he heard Wei Yue say.

Yuan also wanted to watch, and if he only observed, he knew the Taishi wouldn't object and Wei Yue would simply ignore him. It wasn't normal for Yuan to be included in consultations with the Taishi, but he used the General's death to involve himself. Yuan let the flap fall behind him, stepped to the side and paused while his eyes adjusted to the darkness. The glow from a smoldering fire provided the only light, except for the few rays of sunlight that pierced through the gaps in the tent's walls. Next to the fire pit, the elderly Taishi nodded to Wei Yue and knelt on a pallet of hides. The coals sparked as the Taishi stoked them with the tip of a poker. He picked up a tortoise shell and a sturdy green-copper needle. He twisted the needle back and forth working a hole into the underside of the hard shell. Yuan watched Commander Wei Yue pace back and forth next to the old man.

"Get to it, Taishi. You're too slow," Wei Yue snapped.

"Divining the future requires patience," the Taishi sighed heavily. He finished two more holes and poked the coals into a clump. After finishing another four, the Taishi laid the shell cup side up on the coals. With fingers spread onto the rim, he nestled the shell into the fiery clump.

While the heat worked on the tortoise shell, the Taishi prepared for the next step. Wei Yue continued to pace. The Taishi picked up an assortment of small animal bones and rubbed them between his hands, raising them above his head while singing an ancient chant. He rocked on his knees, first facing east, then south and so on. Once the circle was complete, he opened his hands and let the bones drop, bouncing flatly on the soft skins.

Yuan watched the Taishi stroke his long, wiry beard while studying the bones. If not for the seriousness brought on by the General's death, watching Wei Yue's lack of patience and the Taishi's abundance of it would have been laughable.

After the tortoise shell dried, the Taishi took it by the rim and removed it from the coals, then blew cool air onto the surface. He rubbed his fingers lightly across the tiny fissures that ran through the shell, studying the direction and path of each one. While the heat dried the shell, the hull shrank causing tiny cracks to twine across the surface, some crossing, some forking and yet others worming in different directions. The Taishi drew the shell closer to his weak eyes, ran his forefinger along one crack that wiggled between two holes drilled near the center of the shell and followed it down an abrupt turn away from the path. "Ah," he mumbled.

Commander Wei Yue could wait no more. "What is it?"

Yuan was also filled with curiosity. *What's my future?*

The Taishi took a breath and replied, "The lines in the shell reveal someone gaining power, a worthy man, but there's more." The Taishi shook his head in frustration and explained, "The bones show a cloud of deception."

"What do you mean?"

"I do not know. I cannot tell. The cloud surrounds the man but is also a part of him."

"That makes no sense. Keep studying it!" Commander Wei Yue demanded.

The Taishi returned to his contemplative pose, stroking his beard and looking for greater insight. He rotated the shell, bit his lip, then looked down at the bones, shook his head and turned the shell again. "It's no use. I just don't know."

"What good are you if you can't read them?" Wei Yue barked.

"These matters are never straightforward, Commander. Omens are never easy to read."

"All right then, tell me this . . ." Wei Yue turned away and renewed his pacing. "Does the oracle apply to this current battle with Wu or something in the future?"

"Both."

"Both? How can that be?" Commander Wei Yue rubbed his cheek. "A worthy man. It applies to our battle with Wu, but Wu are barbarians, not men of virtue like us. If the omen prophesized my enemy, you would see a 'barbarian' ascending to power, would you not?" Commander Wei Yue queried, not really seeking an answer.

"The omen describes a worthy man, yes."

"With General Yang Gai's death, do I not ascend to power?"

"Yes, Commander Wei Yue, you are now the Field Marshal, even if it hasn't been sanctioned by the Prime Minister."

"Don't I treat my men virtuously?" Wei Yue did not wait for a response. "Am I not, then, worthy?"

"I don't deny the similarities."

"I must be the man in the prophecy," Wei Yue concluded before the Taishi could say otherwise. "Yes, I'm certain my fate is to gain victory for Chu. Maybe even a decisive victory, something no Chu general has accomplished against those barbarians." Commander Wei Yue quickened the pace of his walk and speech, confidently adding, "Glory is in my fate, I'm certain of it."

Yuan listened to Wei Yue's self-serving interpretation but held his tongue. *Is this how our future is decided?* he wondered. *I prefer to rely on my sword.* Yuan finally spoke up.

"The noblemen will need forceful direction. Duke Chao, especially, will be reluctant. But if the Prime Minister names you as Field Marshal, the others will follow."

Commander Wei Yue stopped near the tent's doorway. "That will take too long, and Wu will certainly breach the walls of Chou-lai by then," Wei Yue said, rejecting Yuan's caution. "Waiting for the Prime Minister will be viewed as a lack of initiative, an act unworthy of command. I'll also be blamed for the loss of Chu territory. You know the history. Since Chu began conquering lands and peoples long ago, no Chu general has lost land to any barbarian. It will not happen first under my leadership." He jerked open the tent's flap. "I will follow General Yang Gai's wisdom and not show weakness."

Commander Wei Yue shouted to a servant waiting outside of the tent. "Call for the Dukes. Have them meet me at nightfall, and let them know that the Taishi has divined our future. Tomorrow, we leave to free Chou-lai. My decision is made."

The day had been bad for Yuan. It had started with anxious optimism, but ended with General Yang Gai's death and Wei Yue as the Field Marshal, whose decision was final. Yuan respected the chain of command. Virtue required it. But going into battle without unity among the States was a problem that, if not corrected, could spell disaster for not only Yuan, but for all of Chu.

2

A HAUNTING PAST

uan's family's troubles began a few years earlier when King Ping banished his oldest son and Heir Apparent, Prince Chien. That was the seminal link in the chain of events that led to Yuan's misery. The reasons for the Heir Apparent's fall from the King's favor were murky. Lust and power were certainly involved. Perhaps greed and devotion played a role, too, Yuan believed. He was not completely sure, but he knew that because his father was the Heir Apparent's Grand Mentor, their lives followed the fate of Prince Chien. That meant banishment to a life in Chengfu, a desolate town far away from the pleasures and amenities of Ying, Chu's capitol city. And that banishment required him to leave for Chengfu with a pregnant wife in the dead of winter. It was this arduous journey, Yuan was sure, that had caused the death of his wife and only child.

He had been a hopeful, expectant father and for months had prepared for either a boy or a girl. For a son, he had crafted a small bow of mulberry wood to hang on the left side of the gate to their home. And for a daughter, he had made a soft napkin to hang on the right. He had imagined the baby's look and cries and had envisioned the feel of the tiny fingers in his callused hands. He was even prepared for his wife's angst when he denied the baby teat for three days to make sure he was strong enough to survive the harsh world. His hopes and dreams had ended that cold, tragic night in the northern plains, with Yuan burning both bow and napkin.

While King Ping's act of banishment led to Yuan's misery, oddly, Yuan resisted directly blaming him, although that temptation was always present. Rather, Yuan saw only his duty to family and a chance to restore their honor. He shouldered that burden for his father and older brother because he was the only one in his family who could carry it. Yuan's father was a wise and noble man, and his brother, as Junior Mentor, followed their father's path. Neither were soldiers, though, and only the distinguished valor in battle could attain the favor necessary to turn their lives around. Bravery and cunning were required, and the Wu barbarians' invasion presented just the right opportunity. Yuan's fate lay north, through the Gap in the Dabie Shan, then east down the Huai River to where the Wu barbarians were laying siege to the Chu town of Chou-lai.

Fortunately, Yuan was not without allies. General Yang Gai, whom Prime Minister Nang Wa selected as Field Marshal to fight Wu, chose Yuan to lead one of three columns. It was not the first struggle between the General and Prince Kuang of Wu, and Yang Gai had wanted proven leaders in the fight with him.

It was in an earlier battle with Wu that Yuan's bravery and fighting skills caught General Yang Gai's eye. Yuan was seventeen years old then, and in a matter of three years afterward, he had risen in rank solely on his battlefield skills. During that particular clash, he had demonstrated an ability to think quickly and lead during the chaos of battle, albeit sometimes without waiting for orders.

What to do with a young soldier who was impetuous, but his judgment was sound and tenacity crisp, was then the

General's dilemma. He chose to nurture the young Yuan's talent, and in the years since, Yang Gai's tutelage had also included a harness on Yuan's impetuousness. Now, Yuan was a commander General Yang Gai had wanted in the fight against the invading Wu barbarians.

Yang Gai had known the personal importance to Yuan but was more concerned with confronting Wu. Yuan understood that, and it pained him that he would never be able to show General Yang Gai his gratitude. *Perhaps, making the most of the opportunity,* Yuan thought, *is the best way to honor my mentor.*

Whenever something pulled his attention to the past, as Wei Yue had done in the General's tent, Yuan fought to keep buried the painful memories of his dead wife, his baby who had never breathed life, and the haunting images that visited him many nights. This was a difficult task. Reminders were everywhere; some were more evident than others. From Chengfu to the basin near the Gap in the Dabie Shan where they now encamped, Yuan had led his men across the dusty plain. The path had taken them within distant eyesight of the place of that cold, winter night. He had tried to discern the exact location, but couldn't. It was too far away. That didn't keep him from trying, though, checking every now and then to see if he could make out the spot. He had searched the breaks where brush and undergrowth gave way to open ground, looking to pinpoint the rock fire circle he had built. It was probably hidden by wind-swept dirt and overgrown with weeds by now, he had surmised. Yuan's mood had turned solemn once his mind drifted to the past. His men's usual banter had gone silent during that part of the march. A few of them knew Yuan well, and the passage had given them an eerie reason to pause. Even those soldiers who were less familiar with him stepped into the mood, as if traveling through hallowed ground.

Despite the emotional tug that Wei Yue had triggered, Yuan

refocused on the present. Wu was laying siege to Chou-lai, and Yuan was there to help send Wu and Prince Kuang back to the sea. It was critical for Yuan to cut through the immediate tension between Duke Chao and Commander Wei Yue. There was time, but not much of it. That both men were acting out of self-interest was no surprise.

The Dukes of each State were allowed to lord over their lands and people free from much of the daily edicts that touched regular life in Chu. That autonomy made them at times hard to corral, but Wu's invasion struck at their need for self-preservation. *That will make them willing participants, if only they can come to believe in Commander Wei Yue,* Yuan thought.

Yuan left the Taishi's tent for his camp a short distance away. Camps of the six States were positioned in a semi-circle along the perimeter with the Dabie Shan Gap to the north. Chu's army filled the cradle, behind the arcing line formed by the States. The States of T'ang and Ts'ai occupied the perimeter, directly in front of Yuan's camp, with plenty of space in between for the column of Chu's regular army that Yuan would command. Commander Wei Yue was positioned next to Yuan, in equal rank within the cradle. And from behind Wei Yue, General Yang Gai had established his command. His Taishi's tent was the next one over.

The space in between Wei Yue's and Yuan's camps was bordered by unhitched carts, set front to back, which formed a large corral pinning inside the oxen that drew the burden of pulling them. Horses for the chariots also ambled about inside. Yuan reached the edge of his encampment where the two men who shared his chariot during battle, his archer, Lan, and Fen Yang, the halberdier, stood leaning against a cart that contained an assortment of armored tunics. Made of small rectangular pieces of leather fastened in overlapping fashion and hardened by a lacquered finish, the armored tunics were designed to cover the soldier from the neck down to mid-thigh region, which allowed mobility. An extra layer fitted over the shoulders and collar bone.

Fen Yang and Lan watched men from Chengfu load grain from carts at the end of the row. Oxen, whose daily burden had not ended, lumbered through their task. The grain was from Ts'ai, a consequence of being subservient to King Ping and one, Yuan was sure, wasn't lost on Duke Chao. A horse interrupted its grazing when Yuan passed between two carts and stepped into the makeshift corral. It ambled away from Yuan's path as he walked toward Lan and Fen Yang. Both men had been with Yuan since their first battle. Fen Yang was shorter than Yuan but had a strong build and sported a scar across the neck, left by a dagger-axe that came too close. Lan never let Fen Yang forget how an adversary almost brought him death. He poked at his friend for the humor of it. That was his way. But Lan always increased the barrage when leading up to a battle, for Fen Yang was formidable when wielding a dagger-axe, but well-nigh invincible when a foul vein focused his skill.

Fen Yang noticed Yuan approaching and was the first to greet him, blurting the very question that dominated conversations throughout all of Chu's encampment: "Did Commander Wei Yue make up his mind?"

Yuan nodded. "We leave in the morning for Chou-lai."

Always practical, Fen Yang said, "We have much to do." He frowned while pointing to a young peasant, who stood nearby. About one hundred men accompanied Yuan from Chengfu. Most were conscripted farmers, guards at the city's gates and a handful of merchants, all of whom would soon be soldiers. Among them, only Yuan's chariot team and closest complement of five foot-soldiers were seasoned. Most weren't battle tested, at least not to the extent necessary to be comfortable in the role. Each household had given at least one male to the cause, and no peasant family was spared, regardless of trade or craft. Fen Yang had motioned toward Ga, the youngest among them.

"Yeah, that one is long in the face, not in experience," Lan agreed. "He fights like he looks, and he looks like a gangly fawn. His tunic swallows him, skin and bones. If it weren't for his high-sloping head sitting on top of that long neck, I'd think the tunic stood upright by itself."

"No doubt, it's made for a fuller body, and that neck of his does present a nice target for a halberdier," Fen Yang added, not intending any humor. He tucked his fingers under the collar of his tunic, pulling it away from his scar.

"You should be so lucky to find easy prey like that among Wu's ranks, right Fen Yang?" Lan teased.

"That would be funny if it weren't so true," Fen Yang allowed.

"Go ahead and laugh. It's funny." Lan nudged Fen Yang's side. "Hey, you don't have to worry about being swallowed by your tunic, do you? You're just a few grains of rice shy of busting out of it, don't you think? Yuan, you may have to stop the battle in mid-stride to change horses because of this extra weight Fen Yang is carrying."

Yuan chuckled. Lan's barbs were a welcomed relief, but his description of Ga was right. Ga was a peasant who had never seen a battle, much less fought in one, and was about the same age as Yuan was when he had entered his first fray. There was a youthful, clumsy, unsure manner about Ga, and his gait did resemble that of a fawn, as Lan had said. *Fen Yang is right. Ga has much to learn.*

With spear in hand, Ga stood lost in a different world, passing the moment by lifting the blade slightly off the ground and driving the tip into the dirt, then twisting it back and forth. He did not notice Yuan's arrival or see his Commander's approach. Yuan grabbed the spear away and raised the tip for inspection. With a glance, Yuan's eyes could deliver encouragement or cut a sharp rebuke. Lan often said that Yuan need not speak for they could tell his mind just by the look of his eye. Yuan spun the staff, blade up, and handed the weapon back to Ga, whose expression showed the surprise Yuan expected.

"This spear will keep you alive. It's good to get comfortable with it, but know its purpose." Yuan's tone was calm but direct. Ga didn't even need to hear the words. He ducked his head and bowed silently in embarrassment.

Yuan continued, "Tell me, Ga, what were you thinking?"

Ga moved his head to the side, eyes down, but said nothing.

"Speak your mind," Yuan instructed.

Ga awkwardly allowed his eyes to meet Yuan's and asked, "Commander, do you fight the Wu barbarians like you would other men? I hear they're more like demons than men."

Yuan smiled at Ga's naiveté. "They still bleed and die like men. And they kill like men, too. Tell me what you've heard."

"I heard they have faces of demons and to not look into their eyes because they'll steal your courage," Ga said with alarm.

"They're not demons, Ga. They mark their faces because they're water people. But don't think of them as men like us. Remember, they seek your death."

Ga pondered Yuan's explanation. "Commander, why did Wu attack us?"

"It's not their usual way. In the past, they've only fought once Chu invaded Wu. Prince Kuang is a cunning man, though. He probably attacked so that he could choose where to fight the next battle."

"Chu is so much stronger." Ga rubbed his brow. "Doesn't Prince Kuang fear Chu?"

"He does. That's why he attacked." Yuan continued, noticing Ga withdraw to a puzzled silence, "Chu constantly struggles. It must conquer or be destroyed. It must grow or whither. That is the natural order. That sends us down the path of fighting Chu's neighbors, and this fight with Wu began long before our fathers were born. Do you know the history?"

"I think we fight Wu because that's the way it's always been," Ga surmised.

"King Ping wants access to the sea. Both the Huai and Yangtze rivers flow through Wu before emptying into the salty waters. The rivers and rain make Wu a land abundant with water."

Ga scratched his head. "I'd like to farm without the droughts we suffer."

"Yes, you would do well. The soil is fertile. The harvests are bountiful. And Wu's land produces rich ores. There is much King Ping desires of Wu, which is why we have fought in the past. This time, though, we'll fight to keep the middle Huai for Chu."

"And if we lose?"

"We haven't. Sometimes we've fought to a draw, but we've never lost territory."

"Can we win this one?" Ga looked to Yuan with hopeful eyes.

Yuan said confidently, "Yes. Wu is on our soil, and we're much stronger." He stepped to the nearest cart and retrieved a shield. "Take this." Yuan handed it to Ga, then motioned to Lan. "Ga, show me what you've learned."

Lan moved to the cart. He was taller than Yuan and had surprising strength for his slighter build. He grabbed a spear and shield and waited for Yuan's nod.

"Ga, take a position as if you're told to hold the line." Yuan turned to Lan. "Go ahead. You know you want to say it."

"The dash to clash," Lan chuckled.

Fen Yang rolled his eyes.

Ga readied the shield in his left hand, holding it tight to his body, not sure if it was alright to laugh. He stepped forward with his left foot and raised the spear in front of him with his right hand.

"How do you use the shield?" Yuan coaxed.

"I hold it tight against my body and deflect the blow, turning my body just enough so that the barbarian's weapon glances off my shield."

"Good! How do you attack with a spear?"

"I shove it into the body, where there is no armor. Eyes, throat, legs, feet, armpits."

"Give it a little twist," Lan whispered, imitating the motion with a turn of the wrist. "And wiggle it on the way out." Again, he mimicked the movement, chuckling through the lesson.

Yuan nodded. "Now, when the enemy is attacking, what do you look for?"

"If he's running toward me, he will shuffle his feet before stepping into the first blow."

"If he's inexperienced, he'll do that," Yuan corrected Ga. "The better skilled won't, but the first thrust will be while he's stepping with the same side foot. There is more power behind the blow that way. Look at Lan. He holds the spear in his right hand and when he strikes, he steps with his right foot." Yuan gestured to Lan, who stepped through the explanation.

"Make sure the opponent's spear glances off your shield away from your body, so you don't end up looking like Fen Yang." Lan shot a glance at his companion's scar.

"Ga, your mind has learned much, but during battle, your body must move without thinking about it," Yuan said with concern. "We don't have much time before we meet Wu. Between now and then, work hard every day teaching your body what your mind knows." Yuan turned to Lan and then Fen Yang. "Make sure that Ga, and the others who need the training, spar every day. Work them hard. We want them to go home with us. We will leave in the morning."

Yuan exited thinking, *Now the hard part: figuring out how to unite Wei Yue and the Dukes.*

3

INTERNAL RIVALRY

From where General Yang Gai had died, Yuan and the Chu army traveled north, through the Gap in the Dabie Shan, to the Huai River. Once there, they turned east and marched a long journey between the river and the mountains. They hugged the river's edge, snaking into the undulating hills that fanned outward from the mountains. Now, in the vague distance, Yuan could see where the mountains elbowed southward, away from the river.

The Chu army, 30,000 soldiers strong, when counting the States' contribution, marched in three columns made necessary because the undulations of the Huai River, squeezing toward the Dabie Shan, opening and pressing, constricted their movement. Four lines of soldiers, each five men abreast, formed the breadth of just one column. And each column contained one hundred companies. A company consisted of one chariot, twenty-five supply wagons and one hundred men, seventy-five of whom were soldiers. The others were servants, who cooked, tended to armor and weapons, gathered firewood and water, and groomed the animals.

Yuan was near the front of the review, close to the folded mountains. There was less dirt to eat, forward of the army's mass. That was the privilege of being assigned to the regular soldiers and not to one of the States that followed at the rear. Once the enemy's location was close, though, the States would move to the front. And to find Wu, advance scouts traveled far ahead. The reality of Chu's extent, combined with the narrow terrain, forced a long procession, which unavoidably produced low, broad dust clouds that stretched the expanse, interspersed with tall plumes shooting above the chariots. *Prince Kuang is sure to know of our whereabouts before revealing his own,* Yuan speculated.

The journey from the Dabie Shan Gap had taken more than a moon's cycle, and it was tiring, especially for those who traveled on foot. Although Yuan's chariot provided him with a convenient transport, he chose to endure the same hardships the men under his command suffered. And his full comple-ment from Chengfu benefited. Yuan rotated among them the opportunity to ride, while he, Lan and Fen Yang took equal turns as well.

Yuan had worked on each of the Dukes and Commander Wei Yue since entering the Gap. The distance had given him time, which he vigorously used, encouraging Wei Yue to invite the Dukes for food and drink each night, so that they would not seek the company of misery with Duke Chao. *The rice wine flowed freely, and it worked.*

Some had softened to Wei Yue and were more accepting of his new role. Duke Chao, though, was still a problem. He never missed an opportunity to throw barbs at Wei Yue, but Wei Yue had handled the insults well. There had been times when Yuan thought Wei Yue's temper would erupt, but so far it hadn't. Yuan was pleasantly surprised.

The previous night, they had camped within a day's reach of the town of Chi-fu, which was nestled against a knuckle in the Dabie Shan. The locals had sent word that Wu had abandoned its siege of Chou-lai, which Yuan expected; Prince Kuang would not want to fight on two fronts. Duke Chao's response to it hadn't shocked him either. Duke Chao took the opportunity to call, yet again, for Commander Wei Yue to abandon the march, but this time, instead of attacking Wei Yue's competency, he claimed victory for the new Field Marshal.

"Wu feared your strength," Duke Chao told Wei Yue.

Wei Yue didn't go along with it. *A wise decision*, Yuan concluded. *It is better to find Wu.*

At Chi-fu, the mountain's knurl jutted toward the river, pinching Chu's march. Once beyond the clog, Lan chided Fen Yang, "You've ridden for so long, your feet must be stuck."

FenYang ignored him.

Lan continued, "You probably need to ride more than anyone. Walking is hard, something you're not used to." Lan turned to Ga, who was on the other side of the chariot, and chuckled, raising an eyebrow to clamor support for his jab.

Ga snickered. Fen Yang snorted. Yuan hopped onto the platform, tapped Fen Yang on the shoulder and took control of the reins. The rectangular frame was made for three men to stand side-by-side. In battle, Lan stood, bow at the ready, to Yuan's left, Fen Yang, with his dagger-axe, to the right. Lacquered hides that stretched around the frame armored the chariot. And to ensure success, the exterior adorned earthly creatures, paying tribute to Yuan's ancestors.

"Get on," he told Ga. The new soldier looked weary from the journey and in need of rest.

Ga bowed. "I'm not tired, sir. I'm fine to walk."

"Get on." Yuan's tone was neither demanding nor invitational.

Ga didn't question again. He moved around the conical hub, brushing past Fen Yang, and stepped gingerly onto the back of the chariot. Yuan turned to the front and gave the reins a quick slap. The horses jerked forward. Ga reached for the frame to steady himself, not having mastered the chariot (such luxury of warfare was reserved mainly for the highborn and officers). He lost his balance in the initial jolt and fell to the carriage floor. His time on the chariot had proved to be more effort than the break from walking was worth. Ga reached again for the frame, but his hand thrashed about disjointedly, keeping him from taking hold. With every rock, bump and dip, the fixed-axle platform jolted, jarred and jerked Ga from back to side and around. His legs folded beneath him.

"Didn't anyone show you how to ride?" Yuan asked, after witnessing the platform jerk Ga's knee into his cheek.

Ga rubbed the side of his face, fighting against the uncontrollable jarring, then grabbed the sturdy wood frame; anticipating the next jolt, he managed to bounce to his knees. "No sir," he forced through a teeth-chattering shock.

"It's been more entertaining that way." Lan helped with a timely push, followed by a cheerful pat on the new soldier's back.

Ga held steady and upright, but in an awkward stance, bent at the waist with feet spread beyond shoulder width. He was surprised by Yuan's ease in riding the contraption. All charioteers learned that basic skill through extensive practice, but Yuan's ease appeared natural, almost unfair. *There must be some trick to this, other than the rope,* Ga thought, looking at the horsehair cord. Both ends were fastened to the front panel of the frame, but with enough slack to form a loop that fitted around the back of Yuan's waist, which he leaned into for stability.

"How do you swing a dagger-axe or use a bow?" Ga asked, shaking his head in awe.

"It's not so easy," Lan assured. "Why do you think Fen Yang looks the way he does." He snaked a finger down his neck, mocking the halberdier.

Fen Yang pretended to not see the gesture, even though Lan walked next to him.

Ga wondered aloud, struggling to demonstrate even minimum coordination. "We're moving no faster than a walk. At a gallop, standing seems impossible."

Yuan smiled inwardly at Ga's difficulty. "Stand next to me and wedge your feet, one against mine and the other against the frame." Ga stepped into place to the right of Yuan and grabbed the staff of the dagger-axe that rested upright in the hold of the frame.

"Ga, holding on to that weapon for life is how Fen Yang does it, too." Lan broke into laughter before he finished the sentence.

Fen Yang, annoyed, checked his shoulder into Lan, muscling the taller frame into the side of the chariot. "Don't get caught in the wheel," he chided.

The cycle was always the same with them. Lan would pester, tease and taunt; Fen Yang would shrug, at first, then ignore him. But Lan would continue nettling until Fen Yang exploded in some physical moment that said: *Enough!* Lan would wait for Fen Yang's temper to subside, then start anew.

Yuan cracked an eye to Lan that reinforced the unspoken message Fen Yang had just sent. *I need both of you in the fight.* He then turned his thoughts to Wu. *Where are they?* He nudged the team of horses down the gradual slope of a small creek and slapped the closest haunch, when the chariot's wheels broke below the crusted surface. It had been a while since the last rain, but the creek bed was soggy under the hardened cake. In the distance, Yuan saw a cluster of three hills that dotted the floodplain, running from near the mountain to the river's high gradient. *That must be Spider Mound.* The Chi-fu people called it so for its shape. Two distinct, rounded heaps made the thorax and abdomen, and crooked protrusions, resembling legs, completed the spidery image. It was closest to the Dabie Shan and spired over the other two hills. His eyes fixed next on the middle knoll, something drew them, but he couldn't discern anything out of place. His gaze swept the rise of the fingerling. The evergreen brush looked alike against the brown background of the winter season. But as he drew closer, the outline of men, scattered on the slope, emerged. He glanced, only briefly, to the smaller butte by the river, saw nothing unusual, then returned his attention to the center hill. A commotion toward the river drew his gaze away from the hills and to where his soldiers parted, allowing a man to run through from the opposite direction.

"Where's Commander Yuan!" an excited scout shouted, while struggling against the flow.

"What is it?" Yuan called out to make his presence known.

The scout's frantic look, combined with the glimpse of the men on the hillside, answered Yuan's question. Wu was there waiting for them. His heart began to race. The fight was near.

"Wu's camp is just ahead, on that hill!" the winded scout confirmed between breaths.

"Are they in battle formation?"

"No sir. They're at their camps, making fires. They haven't even put on their armor. I saw several thousand on the slope, right there, in the middle." The scout turned and pointed at the knoll. "And they're just sitting there."

"You didn't just come from the hills," Yuan said, while Lan and Fen Yang joined to listen. "Does Commander Wei Yue know?"

"Yes, he sent me to tell you. He said for you to meet him to look over the field. He also said for your men to pull back and set up camp. He wants the States at the front, and Duke Chao is supposed to set up Ts'ai's camp on the mountain side. You will be behind Duke Chao."

Yuan placed a hand on Ga's shoulder. "Go help our Chengfu men set up camp. Show them where, if they don't know."

"Yes, Commander." Ga unlatched the horsehair belt and bolted off the chariot, all too glad to be on firm footing.

"Are you a part of the scout team?" Yuan asked the messenger.

"Yes sir. Commander Wei Yue ordered me back to my post, once I deliver this message."

Yuan glanced at Lan and Fen Yang and motioned with a nod. Fen Yang hopped onto the platform first, wedged into place and hooked the horsehair belt to the frame. Lan did likewise to Yuan's left, and once both were ready, Yuan leaned into his belt and with a flick of his wrists, whipped the reins. The horses responded instantly with a jerk, as much to the sound of the slap as to the feel. The scout ran ahead and leaped over a narrow ravine. Fen Yang grabbed the staff of his dagger-axe, expecting the frame's tilt once the wheel jolted across the sink. After a little wobble, the wheels were back on level terrain.

Yuan's mind raced to the battlefield and how Commander Wei Yue would arrange the army. He imagined the initial attack and from it, how Wei Yue would use the chariots and soldiers in battle. The details took shape. Yuan felt excitement pump through his body. His grip on the reins never felt in greater command of the beasts. His purpose never more certain.

Fen Yang grunted, shaking his head. "The mountain and river narrow the field. How will Wei Yue deploy our full strength?"

"Crowds make for easier targets," Lan chuckled.

"So, missing your target and still hitting the enemy is how you claim skill," Fen Yang jested.

Lan turned in surprise. "You made a joke! Now laugh. It was funny."

Fen Yang didn't crack a smile.

Commander Wei Yue was in the open field, beyond the soldiers, talking to the scout, when Yuan pulled on the reins and brought the horses next to him.

Wei Yue waved toward the cluster of hills, where Wu's camp was visible, and asked the scout, "Are you sure there aren't more men hiding behind those hills?"

"Yes sir. They're pretty much as you see them, up on that long rise."

Wu's numbers are too few, Yuan thought. *Wu is not at full strength.* "That's all of them?"

"We haven't seen any others, sir."

"Where are our other scouts?" Wei Yue asserted his command.

"As soon as we saw Wu, we set up over there." The scout pointed across the river, near the bank, where three men sat leisurely. "They're still in place."

"Good, add four more to your group," Commander Wei Yue ordered. "Put them on the other side, between Spider Mound and the Dabie Shan, and have one from each post report back to me immediately after the sun goes down. And when the night is half gone. Then again at sunup. Now tell me what else you've seen."

"Sir, you see the group on the slope?"

"What about them?" Commander Wei Yue looked over Wu's forces.

"We got close enough to see they aren't wearing armor, and their bodies look sick."

"Probably peasants," Commander Wei Yue spat, dismissing the scout's opinion as unimportant. "Look at their chariots. Is that all they brought?"

"Yes sir, that's all. I counted twenty-five."

"That's all you've seen?"

"Yes sir."

"Return to your position, and make sure I get timely reports."

"Yes, Commander." The scout lowered his head, backed away, and turned.

"Wait. How far downstream did you search?" Yuan asked.

"We only went far enough to see behind the hills."

Yuan stared at the enemy's encampment. *Something's off. Where are you, Kuang?*

"They brought so few to the fight," Wei Yue bellowed. "Have I worried too much about Wu?"

"It's too early to know," Yuan cautioned.

"Prince Kuang must have sent them in advance to claim that high ground. His main force hasn't arrived."

"Maybe." Yuan would not jump to Wei Yue's conclusion.

"You heard the scout. This is all they have right now." Wei Yue pointed across the field. "Wu is not hiding behind the hills. You can see what they have, and they're not prepared to fight. Battle won't start today," Wei Yue declared. "Come. I sent word for the Dukes to meet me at my camp. Let's tell the others. Even Duke Chao can't be alarmed." Commander Wei Yue turned the team until his chariot faced the opposite direction, slackened the reins and slapped the horses away from what would become the battlefield.

Yuan followed. On the way back, he tried to make sense of what he'd seen, ignoring Wei Yue's arrogant boast about worrying too much. Prince Kuang was not a man to underestimate.

By the time they returned to Wei Yue's camp, his tent had been set up, and the Dukes were waiting. The Dukes of Ts'ai and T'ang had arrived first and were standing next to the Commander's aide. The others had filtered in until all stood waiting for Wei Yue. Duke Chao of Ts'ai appeared ill tempered, still anxious about the future and bursting with questions.

Commander Wei Yue brought the horses to a halt near his tent, dismounted and instructed the others to join him inside.

Yuan handed the reins to Lan and jumped off his chariot. "Ride back to our camp. After everything is set up, put Ga through more practice. Include anyone you think needs it, and increase the intensity. Soon, it will be for real."

Lan nodded.

Yuan let the others enter Wei Yue's tent first, then followed. He stepped inside, stood at the corner of Wei Yue's work table, where the others had gathered, and waited to see how Wei Yue would manage the nobles. A map made of silken cloth lay on the table. The familiar river, mountains and hills were clearly marked but without the detailed topography of their exact location. Commander Wei Yue dipped a twisted horsehair tip of a bamboo stylus and quickly sketched in Chi-fu, the creeks on either side of the town and their crisscross before dumping into the river. He dipped the tip again, then added the three hills, pausing to remember the distinct shapes of Spider Mound and the knoll. Wei Yue finished with a tap on the map. "This is the enemy's position."

"You are not prepared to take on Wu, Wei Yue," Chao quarreled.

"They're not ready to fight yet, Duke Chao," Wei Yue answered ignoring the insult. "There are only a few thousand of them, and they aren't even wearing armor. A victory before their main force arrives would be without virtue. I feel Chu's fortunes against Wu are about to turn. Look at this. They're positioned right here at this point." Wei Yue poked the drawing, holding the mark on the center rise.

"They occupy the heights!" Duke Chao couldn't resist the opportunity for another jab at Wei Yue's self-importance. "You should pull back, so we're not caught sitting around our campfires."

"Listen to me." The Commander paused to cast a stern look at the irritating Duke. "They've just arrived. They only have about twenty-five chariots. We have three hundred. Their men look more like peasants than the battle-hardened barbarians we expect to fight," Wei Yue said, matching Chao's challenge with calm. "Just one of our columns outnumbers them." Wei Yue looked around the table at the other Dukes. "They aren't preparing to fight today. They're not to be feared."

"Five years ago, I fought against Prince Kuang. He is cunning. He is fearless. He is a worthy opponent. And Wei Yue, you are a mere suckling in comparison." Duke Chao forced the words through angry teeth. "You may have had General Yang Gai's confidence. You may even gain the Prime Minister's favor." He poked at his chest and barked, "But you don't have either from me, and you will not lead me to my death."

"Commander Wei Yue?" Yuan interrupted. He'd seen the lines of anger cross Wei Yue's face. Wei Yue's temper was about to explode. "No doubt our numbers overwhelm theirs. We've known all along they would, but you've never been one to underestimate your enemy, and we shouldn't underestimate Prince Kuang here." Yuan tried to feed Wei Yue's ego, although he didn't have it in him to keep pace with Duke Chao's attempt to crush it.

"That's right. Wu occupies better ground, and our fight will be more difficult now because of it," Duke Chao spouted. He could not help but elevate his challenges to Wei Yue. "You should have waited for the Prime Minister to appoint a worthier Field Marshal. Prince Kuang chose this place for the fight, so the first battle, the one over terrain, goes to him, not you. You lack a Field Marshal's judgment. With you in charge, regardless of having a larger force, it's foolhardy to take on Wu. Surrender command to Yuan."

Yuan kept silent knowing that Wei Yue would never willingly relinquish control.

Wei Yue glared back at Duke Chao.

The Duke of T'ang stepped forward, and easing the growing tempers, he said, "Tomorrow is the last day of the moon's cycle, and tonight will be black. Attacking before the new moon would bring imbalance to the natural order, so Kuang will not want to face the consequence of such a bad omen."

"Of course," Commander Wei Yue snorted. "That's why

they aren't ready now, and I will not risk tempting such a bad omen either."

"Would you rather tempt death?" Duke Chao said, slamming his fist down on the table.

Wei Yue drew his sword, then thrust the tip at the belligerent Duke. "Enough of your tongue. Another word and I'll remove it!" Wei Yue had endured all he could of Duke Chao and would have no more. "And after I'm finished, the Prime Minister will make an example of you."

Duke Chao gripped the handle of his sword, drawing it as he stepped backwards, away from Wei Yue's sharp tip, and shouted, "Better to argue your incompetence before the Prime Minister than to lose my life because of it."

Yuan nudged into the shoulder of Duke Chao and pushed Commander Wei Yue's blade aside. "Let's choose the right enemy," he said calmly. *The enemy is Wu and our in-fighting is standing in the way of my goal.*

The Duke of T'ang grabbed Chao's arm, more to caution his friend than to restrain him.

Duke Chao's grip eased and after a long, silent pause, Commander Wei Yue continued, "They're taking their time to set up camp today and won't attack until after the moon's cycle changes, just as we won't. So they're gathering their forces to attack the day after tomorrow. Let's use this time to rest our men. They've been driven hard and need rest. By the time our camps are fully set up, the sun will be almost down. That gives us tonight and all of tomorrow to eat and rest before battle the next day. But to be sure, we'll be ready to move into battle formation after tomorrow. And there will be time to spare." Commander Wei Yue sheathed his weapon. "Go back to your camps, make whatever preparations you need, then join me tonight for food and drink. In the meantime, our scouts will report back to me at regular intervals. I'll let you know if there are any changes."

"You think of them as mere barbarians and boors, savages, who lack the virtue you claim of yourself. You somehow believe that virtue will decide this battle." Duke Chao whirled, scoffing, "Fool." He was the first to leave, pushing the Commander's aide away from the entryway in his haste. All but Yuan followed.

"Yuan, the Duke allows fear to cripple him," Commander Wei Yue said with undisguised contempt.

"No, Commander, I don't agree. I've fought beside Duke Chao before, and he's not a man easily given to fear. He is skilled, and we will need that skill to defeat Wu. We need support from all the States."

"If not fear or cowardice, then why does he resist me?"

"Perhaps his confidence must be won."

"I am the Field Marshal!" Commander Wei Yue barked. "There's nothing I need to win from him!" Wei Yue drew breath and looked away from Yuan. "I need something else now." Wei Yue began to pace as Yuan had seen him do with the Taishi. "I need the Dukes to obey my orders. Their obedience depends upon retribution, if they defy me. How do I tie those two?" Wei Yue walked around the table and came full circle. "How do I?" he mumbled. Wei Yue stopped at the edge of the table, ran his hand over the map, across the hills, then came to an answer, and turned to Yuan. "Do you trust your men?"

"I do," Yuan said resolutely.

"All of them?"

"Yes."

"How many men did you bring with you from Chengfu?"

"A company."

Wei Yue drew an invisible line across the map with his finger. He started at the mountain and wriggled it to the river. "You have influence over Duke Chao. He'll listen to you." Wei Yue stared at the map, as if looking right through it.

Yuan remained silent, not sure where Wei Yue was going.

Wei Yue renewed pacing. "That's why I want you behind Duke Chao. And so he won't be tempted to ignore my orders, I want half your men from Chengfu to fight under Duke Chao. No," Wei Yue interrupted his own thought. "Divide your foot-soldiers among the Dukes. They'll fight under the Dukes."

The thought startled Yuan. *In no way will the likes of Ga fighting under one of the Dukes increase the chance of victory.* "Commander Wei Yue, they are my chariot's complement, and many are new to battle. This will be their first fight, and their success is more likely under my direction."

"Their success doesn't matter." Wei Yue's tone was cold. "Those numbers aren't great enough to matter to the outcome. The column you'll command, though, does matter. Replace your complement from the 8,000 soldiers in those ranks, and don't worry about 72 foot-soldiers from Chengfu."

While correct about the numbers, in the purest sense, Wei Yue had missed the importance. Yuan added, "Certainly, their numbers aren't many, but we should put all of our men in a position to fight well."

"Better for Wu to tire against the unskilled before our regular army enters the fight," Wei Yue replied matter-of-factly. "Who was the soldier that rode on the chariot with you? Not Lan or Fen Yang, but the one swallowed by his armor."

"His name is Ga," Yuan replied tentatively. "This is his first battle."

"The Hu line will be closest to the river. At that distance, I'll need someone easy to spot. He'll do. I'll know him by the look of an old woman, whose skin no longer fits and sags to the dirt. If he lives, I'll learn whether or not the Duke of Hu shouted my orders during battle."

Wei Yue's reasoning puzzled Yuan. It made no sense. "He's not experienced enough. He won't make it past the first attack," Yuan interjected, hoping to change Wei Yue's mind. "He won't survive long enough to do you any good."

"Well then, I'll have to look elsewhere. My order stands, Yuan. You choose how you want to divide your other men among the States. But do it."

Yuan understood Wei Yue's warning. Wei Yue would not be concerned with a small number of soldiers, and he would not argue the point. *I am the Field Marshal,* Wei Yue had said, and now was reminding Yuan again.

"Yuan, don't worry. I'm sure you've taught your men well, even the new ones," Wei Yue said, feigning concern, then waved a dismissive hand. "Return to your men."

Yuan nodded, stepped backward, and retreated from the tent. It was obvious that Commander Wei Yue would not listen to an opposing view, and Yuan saw no benefit in forcing it. While the men from Chengfu were important to Yuan, they weren't to Wei Yue, and arguing about it was useless.

Yuan returned to his camp. Much had piled onto his shoulders since leaving Chengfu. The weight of restoring his family's honor was heavy enough, but added to the load were the loss of General Yang Gai and his wisdom, Wei Yue's untested leadership, and the dubious support of the Dukes. Now he also had the fate of his men, fighting under someone else, to worry about. Wei Yue was right about their numbers being too few to matter. But each one mattered to Yuan. No doubt, they would bear the brunt of the initial attack, and they would do so without the comfort of fighting by the side of those they knew and trusted. He feared what would become of them. Wei Yue had said not to worry because Yuan had trained them well. *But have I done enough for the new soldiers?* Yuan questioned, and that introspection tightened the knot that formed in his gut.

When Yuan reached the camp, Ga was standing next to one of the oxen-drawn wagons. Stacked on it were armored tunics and an assortment of spears and shields. A helmet rested crookedly on Ga's head. It was made of small pieces of lacquered leather that was meant to fit snugly on his crown and flare down over the back of his collar. Ga used the flaps, which hung over the ears, to pull the helmet tight, so that it covered his forehead down to the eyebrows. It was a peasant's helmet, not the green-copper headgear that provided noblemen, like Yuan, with a metallic shell, cushioned on the inside by a layer of soft leather.

Fen Yang stood beside Ga, who then picked up the blade of a dagger-axe. The new soldier ran his fore-and middle-fingers down the spine of the green-copper point, curious about the weapon's different parts. A spike, axe blade and hook were the primary deadly advantages. The spike was hafted to the end of a long staff, and two inward curving blades fastened the axe to the staff. Ga's fingers crossed the top arc, then turned down the edge of the axe blade, pausing where it joined the bottom counterpart that formed the weapon's hook. The long wooden staff rested on the cart.

There was something about the way the helmet sat that made Ga's neck look even longer than usual and exposed. It highlighted his inexperience and heightened Yuan's anxiety over where his men would fight. Yuan grabbed the staff and asked Ga, "Have you ever seen a dagger-axe used? Not just in training?" He shoved the tip into Ga's side, in between two plates of the armored tunic, just hard enough for Ga to feel it.

Ga jumped back, almost tripping. "No, Commander Yuan."

"You get too close to the chariot and the halberdier will drive the dagger through you. Turn and run," Yuan spun Ga around by the arm, swung the weapon's hook over Ga's shoulder and twisted it so that the blade curved around Ga's throat, just below the lump, "and he reaches out and rips your neck. Either way, you die. If you're lucky, you die before the horses trample you or foot-soldiers finish you off." Yuan's voice deepened into a serious tone, bordering on mean.

His change scared Ga and also caught Fen Yang off guard. Yuan tossed the dagger-axe to him and retrieved a spear and wooden shield from the cart, then held them out for Ga to take. "Do you remember how to use these?"

The muscles in Yuan's jaw tightened, scaring Ga. Still puzzled, Ga slipped his hand into the hold of the shield. Yuan drew his sword, raised it overhead and struck downward at the shield. Ga backed away, but Yuan pursued, striking again, pressing forward and delivering a flurry of blows until Ga tripped over his own feet. Yuan shoved the tip of his blade to Ga's throat. "That's how fast you'll die in battle. It's not friendly sparring. It's your life." Yuan took a breath. "It's your death."

By this time, a crowd had gathered wondering what the spectacle was about and if Yuan was delivering some sort of punishment. He'd put enough strength into the blows to be fighting the Wu barbarians, not simply training.

Yuan withdrew his weapon, held out a hand to Ga, and in a softened tone said, "Lan's funny saying about the initial clash is fine when joking, but when it's real, there is no humor. There is only life and death. Come, we have much to go over."

He turned to Fen Yang. "Put on your armor."

Fen Yang grabbed a full-length battle armor. The sides that held the breast and back plates together were fastened, and he untied the binds on one seam. Lan stepped out from the crowd and walked to the back of the cart, took the breastplate and held it up while Fen Yang slipped inside. Fen Yang pushed his fist through the arm hole, while Lan tied the shoulder and side straps.

"Study him," Yuan instructed Ga. "What's the difference between his armor and yours?"

Ga remained silent, looking at Fen Yang. The armor

covered the body from the neck down to the ankles, unlike the armored tunic he and the other foot-soldiers wore. The halberdier stepped toward Yuan. The skirt flared from the hips down to the ankles but only enough to allow a shortened step.

"Watch him struggle to move," Yuan instructed. "He can't run. If he's knocked out of the chariot, he's vulnerable." Yuan laid his sword on Fen Yang's shoulder, then slid the blade to the neck. "Aim for the neck or face, just like you would against any foot-soldier. Same for the armpit when your enemy's arm is extended." Yuan grabbed Fen Yang's arm and nodded for Lan to do likewise on the other side. Together, they eased Fen Yang to the ground, where he lay prone. Yuan turned back to Ga, "Once you get him on the ground," Yuan grabbed the edge of the skirt and shoved his sword into the opening, but only far enough to illustrate, "Ram your spear inside, until he can't get up."

Yuan stood upright, looked over the crowd and said, "If you've never been in battle, step closer." He braced himself on the wheel of the nearby cart and hopped onto the platform. He paused, considering how best to deliver Wei Yue's order that his Chengfu men would fight under the States, and not him. Yuan raised his short sword. "You know by now that Wu is on that hill." He pointed his weapon at their adversary. "Soon, we fight. No Field Marshal reveals his full plan before battle, but Commander Wei Yue has shared pieces to let us know where we'll be when the fight begins." He avoided Lan's and Fen Yang's eyes while he spoke, fearing that he would not be able to keep his disbelief in the order hidden. "You will fight with one of the States. Tomorrow, I'll visit with each of you to go over exactly where, but for now, continue training, get plenty to eat and turn in early tonight."

He dismounted from the cart and walked over to Lan and Fen Yang. Ga stood with them. Yuan delivered a look to both Lan and Fen Yang that meant not to ask.

"Commander Yuan . . ." Ga said, looking bewildered, "what does this mean? I won't be with you and Lan and Fen Yang?"

Yuan placed his hand on Ga's shoulder and squeezed reassuringly. "No. You will fight with Hu. We'll talk more tomorrow. For now, go train. Remember, you want your body to act without having to think about it."

Ga bowed to Yuan, gathered his spear and shield and trotted toward where the Chengfu men had gathered to spar.

Lan shook his head in consternation. "What was that all about? Was Wei Yue drunk when he gave that order? I thought he was smart, but that order is *baichi*."

"It doesn't make sense for the battle," Yuan concurred.

"It makes perfect sense," Fen Yang interjected.

Lan cast a puzzled look. "You've fallen off the chariot too many times, my friend."

"It's not about the battle. It's about you." Fen Yang gestured to Yuan. "He knows that you make a better Field Marshal. Tactically, strategically, he knows you outmatch him. He also knows that the States will follow you without question. He's struggling with that, so he's asserting authority over you. He doesn't dare do it out in the open, so he attacks your control over the Chengfu men. He's showing the States that he's in control."

"He's showing everyone that he's a fool," Lan added.

"You may be right." Yuan nodded sadly. "It's not going to affect the outcome with Wu, but we won't return home with as many of our men as we should. Let's not discuss this with anyone else. It's better for our men to enter battle confident, rather than focused on Wei Yue's blunders. Understood?"

"Understood," Fen Yang echoed his agreement.

"I'm going to check on Duke Chao," Yuan said. "Help with the training and keep pushing the basics. They need to survive the initial strike."

"Unless he changes, Wei Yue is going to be the death of too many of us," Yuan heard Lan say to Fen Yang while his chariot team walked off.

~❧~

Yuan gathered with the Dukes and Commander Wei Yue, before the orange sky turned black. His mood lacked the excitement he normally felt in the lead-up to battle. And what he had seen of Wu's forces earlier in the day didn't fit with what he knew of Prince Kuang's skill. He was certain he had missed something, and Wei Yue was too sure of himself to second guess what his eyes told him. That made Yuan even more nervous. And the harder he worked to resolve the question, the more his mind drifted to the personal significance behind his drive and the reason why restoring the family honor was so important.

He found it difficult not to think of the short time he'd had with his wife, and why she and the baby were no longer with him. Most men of nobility had added their second wife to the family by his age, but the memories were painful; so painful in fact that it had taken years just to think of life with another woman. His sorrow was something he kept to himself, sharing it with no one, not even his father or brother, although they knew of his torment. It was something he buried beneath his rough exterior. But inside, the memories haunted him, so much that he could not bring himself to mention her name.

Their life together had begun awkwardly as arranged marriages tend to do. He remembered the first time he saw her face. Her soft skin flushed with color when he first spoke to her. He didn't recall his exact words, but she had answered in a blushing whisper. Her manner was refined. Yuan's father had thought her gentleness would be a good counter to his ruggedness, and he was right. Yuan remembered his excitement when she had begun to show signs of a baby and her smile of contentment when she rubbed her tummy expectantly. Life in Ying was good. Life with her made it better.

Since his family's fall, many among the nobility thought Yuan was no longer worthy to be a husband. The Shinyin family felt differently. Yuan had chosen his brother as Intermediary to negotiate the marriage arrangements and shoulder the burden of proving Yuan's worth to justify the Shinyin family's decision. And just as during the period leading up to his first wedding, Yuan did not now know the woman he was to marry. He knew only of the family and had never seen her.

When Yuan thought of all that had happened, he experienced a range of emotions. The memory always started with sadness and ended in anger, and it was that anger that fueled him now. How best to funnel that emotion was a question that was always at odds within him. There were times when he wanted to direct his anger toward King Ping, and others perhaps who were responsible for the banishment, but that would be without virtue. No, that emotion was better directed down a noble path. That meant distinguishing himself in battle – this battle with Wu.

He entered Wei Yue's tent without speaking to anyone and took his usual seat at the end of a long table. The Dukes and officers intermingled along the sides. Commander Wei Yue sat at the other end. Yuan was the last to arrive, except for Duke Chao. Chao's place was the empty seat next to the Duke of T'ang. A servant placed a dish of rice and chicken in front of Yuan and a goblet of rice wine to the side. Yuan drank the wine first.

"I know some of you are not pleased by having to join in this fight," Commander Wei Yue opened.

"Apparently, Duke Chao is so displeased that he deprives himself of good food," the Duke of Hu laughed, tipping a goblet to the empty spot. His nose remained high while others joined in the laughter. He downed the rice wine, then continued, "Let him eat gruel if he lacks the good sense to accept your invitation, Commander."

Commander Wei Yue chuckled. "Still, the barbarians invaded Chu and threaten your lands. I'd rather discuss, as right-minded men, what you think."

"Commander Wei Yue? The scouts have arrived to report," Wei Yue's aide announced. "You asked to be interrupted, sir."

Wei Yue turned toward the tent's door and his aide's voice. "Yes, tell me. Are there any changes?" Commander Wei Yue motioned for the two scouts to step forward.

Yuan paid close attention.

"There has been no change, sir," the older of the two replied. "They are as they were earlier."

"Their fires still burn in the same places?"

"Yes, sir," both scouts responded.

"No new fires?"

"No, sir. It's been quiet so far. Their camps are still on top of the hill and on the downslope as you saw them earlier," the older scout said, looking over at Yuan.

"Their bones still in need of a good meal?" Commander Wei Yue quipped, receiving the expected laugh from the noblemen.

"Yes, sir. I even moved to peek at the back side of each hill and saw no campfires. There are no new troops. Nothing was unusual."

"They haven't passed out weapons or armor, have they?"

"No, sir. They're just resting for the night."

"Very good." Wei Yue smiled his satisfaction. "Return to your positions, and report back when the night is half gone and then again at first light. Let me know immediately if their status changes."

The two scouts bowed, then backed through the doorway.

"Well, it looks like Chao doesn't have to worry about the barbarians interrupting his sleep." Commander Wei Yue chortled, motioning to a servant to refill his cup, then opened the floor to the evening's conversation. "With fewer chariots and fighters to put into the field, what strategy do you think Wu will employ?" Wei Yue motioned for the servants to refill the Dukes' cups as well.

To Yuan, Wei Yue's manner appeared familiar. It was a step General Yang Gai had danced many times. Wei Yue had asked the question not only to stimulate conversation, but to determine whether or not he had their full and unquestionable cooperation. Yang Gai had often said that the true purpose for filling the noblemen with food and drink was so they'd ease their guard. It was not enough, especially during the fury of battle, to rely on a sense of duty owed to the King, even though the obligation was supported by a fear of retribution. They had to be properly stroked, maneuvered and massaged, with the occasional reminder of harsh reprisal, as well as of glorious reward. *Not by imbedding Ga with Hu.* Yuan winced at the thought. The General had been an old hand at it, and now Yuan watched to see if Wei Yue could master the move, too. Much was riding on it. That bothered Yuan. He hated to rely on Wei Yue to make the right decisions in a battle, but there was no choice.

"Prince Kuang will wait on the hilltop for you to attack," the Duke of Chen volunteered, deviating from his usually quiet demeanor.

"He picked this fight by invading our land. Surely he didn't come all this way just to wait for us to strike first," Commander Wei Yue opined.

"Our 300 chariots will annihilate Wu on the flat terrain. He knows that, and he knows that our chariots can't traverse the hillside. That's why he's perched up there on top. So, I think he'll stay on the hill," the Duke of Chen concluded. "Maybe that's why he brought so few chariots."

We don't know Wu's full strength. We don't know what Prince Kuang has planned, Yuan worried. The exercise of this night's conjecture amused him less than it worried him.

The Duke of Shen stood, removed his furry cape and tossed it past Wei Yue to a servant, then said, "And when he's lost, he'll make a hasty retreat down the backside to the river, hoping to get away before we can catch him. I've been apprehensive about this battle, but now that I've seen their numbers, I'm not worried, no matter how many other savages trickle in."

"If we attempt to fight them on the hill, it will be a battle we'll win because of our numbers, certainly, but at what cost?" Cheng, the Duke of T'ang reminded the other noblemen that it was they who would suffer the initial onslaught.

Yuan went through the same mental tap as Wei Yue. The key was to correctly size up the parties from the beginning. Only then would he know how to influence their thinking. Where in the spectrum, ranging from full cooperation to complete subterfuge, did each one fall? Duke Chao was easy. His open and terse objections toward Wei Yue placed him in a category to be watched and not trusted. In the Dukes of Hu, Chen and Shen, Yuan found cooperation. Wei Yue's other commanding officer, Po Pi, who was the grandson of the Chief Military Minister, was of no concern as well. That was why he positioned Po Pi's column along the river, to Wei Yue's left flank. The Duke of Sui, Yuan figured, would also be no trouble, but what of Duke Cheng? His regard for Duke Chao put his motives in question. But he had interceded when Chao's belligerence grew, probably to save his friend rather than to show favor toward Wei Yue. Regardless, Duke Cheng was someone to watch as well as Duke Chao.

How does Wei Yue see me? Yuan wondered. *I have no subjects to govern and no lands to administer. I serve the Heir Apparent, which makes my motives different.* Although the Heir Apparent was not in the King's favor, Yuan had a direct path to the monarchy. *Wei Yue will see that political reality and fear that his performance will be reported back to the capital, filtered through my eyes.* He also thought it was interesting that Wei Yue placed Yuan's camp behind Duke Chao, and mused, *Does he think I'm a danger to him or am I there mainly to watch Chao?*

The evening wore on, and Yuan was the first to depart, leaving others to drink into the night, with Wei Yue encouraging their liberal intake. But Yuan didn't head immediately to his camp. He chose a detour instead, to check on Duke Chao. *Is he still brooding?* The night was black, as the Duke of Hu had surmised, and only fire pits illuminated the way to the other side of the long encampment. Yuan paused occasionally and looked at Wu's hillside campfires, still uneasy about Duke Chao's lack of commitment and Wu's hidden plans.

Duke Chao was outside his tent, talking to a Ts'ai soldier, when Yuan arrived. "I suppose Wei Yue's rice wine only fed his arrogance," Chao spat, then walked inside his tent.

Yuan followed, ignoring the dig at Wei Yue. "When we talked this afternoon, I didn't think you would accept Wei Yue's invitation. We missed you, though. Scouts reported during the night, and there is nothing new or unusual about Wu."

"Prince Kuang won't fight with so few men. Has Wei Yue found Wu's main force?"

"No, but one of the scouts moved upstream to check behind the hills and saw no campfires," Yuan assured him. "Does this give you any ease?"

"No. When the fight begins, no matter the day, I'll be with my Ts'ai soldiers on the front line, led by an incompetent Field Marshal." Duke Chao took a seat by a table and pointed to a pitcher of rice wine. "Help yourself."

Yuan pulled a small, round bench nearer to Chao and sat. "I've had enough for tonight, but thanks. Certainly, you will be at the front. You've been there before. It was no different under General Yang Gai. He knew you are effective and counted on you." Yuan leaned forward. "We all have counted on you. You know what you're doing in battle, and we need you in this one."

Chao shook his head. "This time is different. Yang Gai moved us tactically and strategically, but Wei Yue doesn't know what to do. His only plan is to throw bodies at the enemy; my people first."

"We don't know Wei Yue's plan," Yuan countered. "We never knew General Yang Gai's plan before the gongs sounded and the banners waved. This is no different."

"This is different. Very different," Chao spoke somberly. "Wei Yue doesn't care if we live or die."

Those words jolted Yuan back to the moment when Wei Yue had ordered him to place Ga on the Hu line and divide the other Chengfu men to fight with the States. He cringed in silence, though.

"Because to him, we are expendable. I don't trust Wei Yue," Chao finished.

He will question Wei Yue's every order. But will he follow them? "I'm concerned that if you disobey Wei Yue during battle, you and the Ts'ai people will suffer afterward." Yuan paused, rested an arm on the table and wrapped his fingers. "Tell me. Do you trust Duke Cheng?"

"Of course. He's an old friend." Chao withdrew to the pleasantness of a fond memory.

"And we've known each other for many years. Do you trust me?"

"Absolutely. If you were Field Marshal. I would follow you without a second thought."

"You trust Cheng. He will be to your left. You trust me, and I will be behind you, ready to help if you need it. Chao, I will lead a full column into this battle, and I promise, you will have whatever support your men need. Some in your ranks will be my Chengfu men, too," Yuan assured him.

"What?"

"Wei Yue decided to place my Chengfu men among you, Duke Cheng and the other States. I won't abandon you."

Yuan looked squarely at Chao, leaving no question about his commitment.

Duke Chao stared into space, but did not respond, except to mumble, "More stupidity, Wei Yue."

"Unity among us is critical for victory against Wu. You can rely on me. Can I count on you?"

Chao returned from his distant thoughts, but only to wave a dismissive hand.

He's not ready. "Think about this. We'll talk tomorrow." Yuan stood, replaced the bench and turned to leave.

Chao broke his silence. "You don't want me to defy Wei Yue."

"No. I don't."

"You think he would retaliate afterward."

"I do."

Chao nodded. "If Wei Yue orders you not to come to my aid, if he sends you elsewhere into the battle," Chao rose to his feet and cast a stern look, "if he directs you to sacrifice Ts'ai, will *you* defy him?"

Yuan did not confirm or deny. "We must wait and see how the battle plays out."

4

THE BATTLE OF CHI-FU

The next morning, the day before the moon's new season, a chaotic uproar jolted Yuan awake. It came from outside of his tent. *What's all the commotion about?* Yuan pushed through the closed flap, searching for the answer. It was early. The sun only peeked above the horizon. He looked across the floodplain, in the distance, and saw Wu barbarians advancing across the battlefield, paced to the deep rumble of a drumbeat that pounded a steady walk. *Only about a thousand,* Yuan estimated. Others remained on the center hill. Their numbers had grown during the night, but only by half again, Yuan guessed. *No more than five thousand.*

Among the tents and fire pits of the Chengfu camp, soldiers rushed about, putting on armor, grabbing spears and seeking direction. The same flurry existed across all of Chu's different encampments.

"Get my armor!" Yuan shouted to an Armor Servant. "Where's my Groom?"

"He went to hitch your chariot! Lan and Fen Yang are with him." The Armor Servant hurried to say, then scampered into Yuan's tent.

The camps of Yuan's column of eight thousand soldiers stretched along the Dabie Shan, toward Chi-fu. Commander

Po Pi's men were equally positioned, adjacent to the river, spanning the same distance. Commander Wei Yue's soldiers were in between, although he and a smaller force were at the rear. Lanes divided each column, and a break to the fore separated Chu's regular army from the States. Wei Yue had wanted the avenues for troop movement. The whole of Chu's soldiery bustled with agitation, uncoordinated in their individual efforts. Wei Yue emerged from his tent, rubbing away the sleep.

Time is running out, Wei Yue, Yuan thought.

The Armor Servant emerged from the tent, holding Yuan's battle armor. "Commander Yuan . . ." he started to say.

"Wait!" Yuan interrupted. He grabbed the arm of a confused Cook, who darted nearby carrying a hempen sack of rice. "There's no time for that. Get my Signalmen."

The Cook shifted the sack into the opposite arm, cradling it, hesitating from uncertainty. "Yes, sir."

Yuan jerked the sack away and let it drop to the ground. "Now! Go . . . go . . . go! I said, go!" He spun the Cook around, aiming him in the right direction, then delivered a helpful push to the shoulder.

Yuan felt blood pumping through his veins. The days of maneuvering the Dukes and Wei Yue were behind. Now was his time to fight. *Today is for family honor.*

"Yuan!" came a shout from behind. Lan pulled on the reins of the chariot, bringing the horses to a stop. Fen Yang was next to him, both dressed in full body armor. "What do you think about Wei Yue's omen, now?" Lan asked.

"About as much as I think of a tortoise shell foretelling my future."

Fen Yang extended a hand, helping Yuan onto the chariot. He stepped to Yuan's side, and grabbed the armor from the Armor Servant, then held the breast and back open, at the side. Both halves were already fastened, down one seam, so that Yuan had only to slip inside. He pushed his fist through the arm hole, nuzzled the shoulder plates into place and steadied the front piece to his chest. Fen Yang tied the shoulder and side straps.

"Fen Yang," Lan called. "I now see your true worth – dressing Yuan. I have a knot loose when you're finished." Lan strung his bow, not bothering to watch his friend's reaction.

Fen Yang didn't respond but finished the last strap with a disagreeable tug.

"Look," Lan shouted, directing their attention with the arm of his bow. "A second wave." More barbarians poured off the hill. The first was only about a quarter of the way across.

"About a thousand in each one." The percussion's timing clipped a casual march. Fen Yang observed, "They're not in any hurry, are they?"

"What happened to the scouts? Did they fall asleep?" Lan shook his head in disbelief. "Our enemy grew overnight."

"But still, far too few of them," Yuan assessed. He snatched his sword from the Armor Servant, then secured it around his waist. *Where is the rest of Wu?*

Chengfu soldiers, who made up Yuan's company, hurried into position, thirty-five on each side of the chariot. Four Signalmen gathered at the right wheel, holding an assortment of banners and pennants.

"Flag the column. Put them in formation," Yuan commanded. He paused, looking right, over the short distance to the mountain, then left at Wei Yue. "Then move them forward." *It's critical to get the chariots quickly into the fight,* Yuan thought. "Line the chariots on the outside." *What are you going to do, Wei Yue?* The attack was imminent, and Wei Yue hadn't taken charge. *Make a decision.*

He stepped into position, front and center of the carriage box. Lan and Fen Yang took their places on either side of him. Each man looped a horsehair rope around his waist and fastened it to the frame, then wedged their feet. Yuan caught the toss of his helmet from the Armor Servant and fitted it onto his head.

He slapped the reins, cueing the horses forward, and steered them around a tent and fire pit. Once clear, he turned the team onto a track to Ts'ai's formation, then brought the chariot to a halt, maintaining the distance between his column and Ts'ai and T'ang. *The camps are in the way. Move the States forward, Wei Yue.*

Fen Yang nudged him. "Are you going to send our Chengfu men to fight with the States?"

Yuan had forgotten about Wei Yue's order. The thought still sickened him. *Use the surprise as an excuse to keep them with me,* he thought. "Change of plans. Today, they fight with us." The two shared a mutual look of relief.

Lan wasn't quiet about his thoughts. "Good."

Yuan studied the field, watching the march progress. It was always a part of the early battle of wits, one side trying to coax the other, while hiding true intentions for the last moment. A steady bang on a gong from Wei Yue's camp interrupted his thoughts.

"Wei Yue finally issued an order," Fen Yan noted, pointing to the change in banners held by Wei Yue's Signalmen. "Form the line."

"But why order only Hu, Shen and Chen into formation? Why not all of the States?" Lan didn't expect an answer. "It sure is virtuous of Prince Kuang to give Wei Yue time enough to wake up. Kuang awoke us with this surprise attack, on an ominous day, only to allow us to gather swords and shields. That's odd."

"Indeed," Yuan agreed. *What are you up to Kuang?*

The first of the Wu barbarians reached the midpoint. "Look how they veered." Yuan mentally extended the angle. "They'll hit Hu's line first."

The States stretched across the floodplain, from the Huai

River to the Dabie Shan. Hu was nearest the river, positioned well in front of Commander Po Pi.

"That makes three waves," Lan counted. He motioned toward the hill, watching another launch. "About the same strength as the first two." Lan turned to Yuan. "They have enough only for one more."

"After Hu, they'll hit Shen, then Chen, but won't reach the other States." *Ts'ai won't be tested first,* Yuan surmised. He glanced over to Duke Chao. *Good, let him see success before he's ordered into the fight.*

Yuan's eyes darted back to Hu's camp and its mob of soldiers, scurrying about. The Duke of Hu was standing next to his chariot, pointing at the oncoming assault, barking commands. But the distance and roar of confused shouts made it impossible for Yuan to hear. Out of the ferment, a barrier line, two men deep in some places, three in others, began to emerge. And behind it, Hu chariots formed make-shift support.

He's getting things in order, Yuan thought. A volley of Hu arrows flew into Wu's assault, then a second.

"Did Wei Yue order that?" Lan looked at the banners for an answer.

"No. The Duke of Hu called it on his own," Yuan replied.

Wei Yue's Signalmen beat the gong again and raised other banners, telling Sui, T'ang and Ts'ai to extend the front line to the mountains.

"Why doesn't Wei Yue order an attack?" Lan wondered aloud.

"The first wave is getting close." Yuan's imagination calculated combinations of troop movements to obliterate the enemy. *Don't be strictly defensive, Wei Yue. A full charge is coming.*

The Duke of Hu took to his chariot and howled more orders. He was ready. Yuan glanced over to the Duke of Shen and then to the Duke of Chen. They weren't. Infantry and archers intermingled at the front, still muddled with uncertainty. Yuan watched the Wu's forward roll, while sporadic volleys from archers were ineffective. Additional Hu soldiers scampered to the line.

"They need to form tighter," Yuan said.

"What is Wei Yue doing?" Lan asked.

Yuan didn't respond. His attention bounced back to Wei Yue, then to the Wu's advance and over to the Hu line, gauging the tip of the initial clash.

"Oh, no!" There, at the nib, to Yuan's horror, he saw Ga. Until that moment, he had forgotten that the young soldier was the only one, among the Chengfu men, whom he had told where to fight. It was a casual response to Ga's question the day before. One, he now regretted. "Ga's at the Hu line." Yuan grimaced.

Ga bent over to pick up the shield he had dropped, then spurted gangly to the Hu line, showing all the eagerness of naiveté. He filled a gap, next to a Hu Squad Leader, then put his shield between his legs, holding it with his knees, and tugged on his helmet.

"That neck of his is too easy a target," Lan said, shaking his head. It was no longer funny.

A change in Wu's drumbeat turned their attention.

"There it is! The dash to clash," Lan shouted.

Yuan drew a breath. The slow roll of the barbarians sprang into a full assault. Ga turned toward the Hu Squad Leader, listening to orders. *He probably said to remember their training,* Yuan surmised. The Hu soldiers looked young, like Ga. Yuan feared that seeing the enemy's sprint would give his green conscript reason to pause or cause him to freeze.

"It could be worse," Fen Yang said for reassurance. He grabbed the staff of his dagger-axe, bracing mentally for the inevitable. "Their attack is thin. If Ga lives through the initial assault, he has a good chance."

One of the barbarians was slightly ahead of the others and on a direct line to Ga, ensuring him to be among the first who would exchange blows. The Hu Squad Leader steadied a wooden shield to his front, pointed his spear's tip toward the enemy, then yelled something else. Ga did the same. The boor closed on Ga, almost within striking distance.

If . . . Yuan thought.

5

GA'S TEST

*L*ike Ga, the barbarian who barrelled straight for him was also armed with a spear and shield. *Deflect the spear,* Ga remembered. *Don't think. React.* The foe pulled up, aimed his weapon at Ga's chest and shuffled his feet, just as Lan had said to expect. Sound faded into silence, it seemed to Ga, and time appeared to slow. He lost all sense of the present, except for the green-copper point that threatened his life. He raised his shield, stepped forward, then turned his body, glancing the menacing tip off his shield. Ga thrust his own spear, upward into the exposed throat of the enemy. He twisted and wiggled the blade downward and out. It was a single motion, with one shoulder moving the shield back and the other rotating the deadly weapon into his enemy. Lan's instruction had become instinctive.

The Hu soldier beside him proved less successful in the clash. Ga scooted to the side and shoved the tip into the open armpit of the Wu assailant, who had lingered too long in extending his spear into the soldier.

Ga's chest heaved, breathing life. His perception, though, returned to the moment, jerked there by the horrid shriek of the injured Hu soldier, who cried such agony, clutching the side of his neck. Blood squirted from in between his fingers, first in pulsating spurts, then diminishing to a steady stream, while his screams waned to a whimper. The silent stare of death followed. It was something for which Ga was not prepared.

Ga turned to the two barbarians he'd slain. *Why didn't I hear them scream?* he thought. Their ripped and bloodied flesh spelled a painful end for them, Ga was sure.

"Get ready!" the Hu Squad Leader shouted.

The next rush was almost to the Hu line. He felt a nudge from the Squad Leader, reminding him that there was no time for distractions. Ga picked out the specific man who posed his next threat and waited for the distinctive shuffle. The savage raised his weapon, then stopped, turned and ran into the fiend behind him. Both tumbled to the ground, picked themselves up and fled.

What just happened? Ga wondered. The Wu fighters Yuan had described were fierce. Fear was not something they showed.

Their flight took them against the flow, turning the surge. Without the beating of Wu drums and the sounding of Wu gongs, others among the enemy lost their courage and fled afterward.

The Hu Squad Leader shouted, "Wu turned! The inspiration that carried those cowards off the hill left them, once they saw their comrades fall so easily by our hand."

A well-organized movement, be it a retreat or an advance, resembled a flock of birds suddenly changing directions, moving in unison. But this flight was different. It was disorderly, nothing resembling coordination. The only semblance of unity was their common fear, and sight of the rippling withdrawal charged the Hu soldiers, who gave a brief shout of victory. Shen and Chen soldiers joined the celebration.

Despite the jubilation, the results along the line were mixed.

Wu barbarians and the States' soldiers, alike, fell quickly and in similar numbers. But the Hu, Shen and Chen lines had held.

Ga thrust his spear overhead with his shout, then proudly looked toward the Chengfu men. *I did it!*

"Move behind the chariots," the Duke of Hu shouted. He tapped the top of his helmet, fitting it snugly on his crown.

Ga, unsure of what to expect next, followed the Hu Squad Leader to the rear of the Duke's chariot.

The Duke of Hu waited for the soldiers to clear a path, then slapped his horses into the chase. There were no orders from Wei Yue. There was no sound of gongs, no beat of drums and no change in banners. Rather, he raced on his own decision to seize victory. He whipped the reins, charging at the fleeing barbarians. One straggler, in particular, made an inviting target. The Duke of Hu steered the horses straight for him. The crack of the leather reins, slapping against hide a second, third, then fourth time, spurred the horses faster. The beasts powered over the stray, whose death cry was cut short, not lasting beyond the first clomp. The trio on board steadied themselves as the chariot's carriage bounced over the body, the thud clapping against the undercarriage. Another Wu combatant veered away from the trampling hooves.

The halberdier waited for the wheels to steady, then raised his weapon. The horses responded to a left tug on the reins, which brought the stray within the deadly reach of the dagger-axe. He stretched the blade over the savage's shoulder, then sunk the hook. The victim's head and neck jerked backwards, while his feet ran out from under him. His body slammed to the ground, landing hard on his back, and on impact, the hook dug deeper into flesh and muscle. His screaking howl didn't last long. Drag, combined with the power of the horses, ripped the hook free, and the body rolled to a lifeless stop.

Stay away from the halberdier, Ga remembered Yuan having warned.

The Duke's archer felt to make sure his arrow was firmly nocked, drew his bow, then took aim. The wheels bounced over a dip in the ground, jostling his outstretched arm. Between bumps, the archer swung the bow from right to left, held steady on his target, then let the arrow fly. The sharp arrowhead pierced the savage below the shoulder blade, burrowing into the cavity, and sent the barbarian tumbling to the ground.

Ga rushed after the Duke of Hu's chariot. He jumped over a body and sprang for the archer's wounded prey. The mark, racked by pain, struggled to gather to his knees. He clutched his chest. His breathing quickened, bawling with each exhale. Ga leaped onto him, planted a foot squarely on the man's back and stomped his enemy to the ground. The finishing blow was swift, but the barbarian's last wail stretched to the Dabie Shan.

The Duke of Hu's chariot continued on toward Wu's center hill. It was well within Ga's sight but leaving him behind. The chase had led the States' soldiers in all directions, and now, having lost the security of the chariot's presence, Ga paused, wondering if he should follow. His untrained instincts urged him to do something other than stand frozen in place. He sprinted after the Duke of Hu.

The Duke's halberdier swung the axe of his weapon at, but missed, another boor, who rolled under the halberdier's reach. Ga closed on him. The man appeared uncomfortable with a weapon. *A farmer like me,* Ga realized, once the peasant gathered to his feet. He took measure of his adversary's planted feet and steadied shield, then bolted, full gait, swatting the savage's spear with his shield, then crashing into the foe, shoulder first, the way Yuan had done to him the afternoon before. He stomped on the lone opponent's chest, pinning the weapon hand, then drove his spear through the throat. Blood spewed at the gash when Ga worked the blade loose. The gush drenched his shin. A shrill followed, and for the first time since the fight began, he saw not a barbarian, but a man, someone who felt pain, blinked back tears and bled, just as he was capable of doing.

But the man looked different than him. His hair was shortly cropped. His armor wasn't the same, either. It was more like a padded cover, pulled over a hempen tunic, than the lacquered, leather plates that Ga and the other soldiers wore.

The creature! Don't look at the face, Ga thought, but he couldn't resist. The head was turned away, hiding the mark. Ga used his spear to turn it until the dark, shadowy figure appeared. *It didn't steal my courage. Yuan was right. He's just a man.* And this man's life ended with the gurgles of a last gasp. Yuan had told him not to think about the enemy in any way other than as fierce barbarians who sought his death. Ga didn't allow himself to dwell for more than an instant. The strange markings on the man's face held his stare a little longer. *Are those scales?*

Up and down the line where the Wu assault had struck, the result was the same. The Shen and Chen soldiers, also enticed by the anticipation of an easy victory, joined Hu in pursuit. The three-pronged assault of the chariots, twenty-four in all among the pursuing States, accelerated the rate at which the savages fell. The horses trampled over all who were caught in their paths, and the archers and halberdiers reached out even farther. A field of broken and battered enemy bodies was left in the wake, and the foot-soldiers were no less successful. But in short order, that success had scattered across the battlefield the armies of all three States.

From the center hill, a thunderous drumbeat, followed by the fainter ring of a gong, signaled a change. Ga recognized it to be a message but didn't know the meaning. Nothing, though, was different, at least not that he could see. Barbarians, who had started the battle atop the hill, remained there, behind about twenty-five chariots. It was still an unimpressive force.

Then he heard a cascading rumble. It was the unmistakable hurl to battle of chariots and infantry.

Barbarians swept into the fight, from between the long hill in the middle and the one nearest to the river. Strike chariots bounded straight for the battlefield, followed by infantry, who hustled on the speed and strength of fresh legs. And transport chariots skirted the outer edge, aiming for a deeper launch.

What now? Ga worried, looking around the battlefield. In front of him was Wu's hill. In the direction of the mountains, he saw fellow soldiers scattered across the field. Toward the river, the same, but now, more of the enemy. The soldiers weren't together, none were nearby, but from a little ways off, he saw one from Hu's ranks, running toward him. Ga straightened his helmet and stepped his way, intending to join him. But on a hard pivot, the soldier turned and readied to fight. A Wu squad had marked the soldier. *Five,* Ga counted, closed the distance. The soldier lunged his spear at the first barbarian to reach him, but the blade glanced upward, off the shield. The next member of the squad, who towered over his prey, drove his spear into the soldier's exposed thigh, while another aimed higher.

The soldier's painful clamor hadn't stopped Ga, but sight of the bloodied tip of a blade, poking through the back of the soldier's neck, did. The rest of the Wu squad stepped into the skirmish and quickly rolled past. They then eyed him. Their speed, combined with the sudden turn of danger, startled him. And there was something very different about these barbarians. *They must be the warriors Yuan talked about.* Ga searched for the Hu Squad Leader, who had begun the battle beside him, but didn't see him. He looked for anyone familiar, but saw none. Instead, he witnessed a fresh Wu onslaught enter the battle, sweeping from the direction of the river, and the States' soldiers falling to that tide. Fear spiked through his body, unlike any he had ever felt. The initial onslaught had scared him, but it also excited him, and that was nothing like the terror he felt now. This time, his legs felt wobbly; this time, the strength in his arms weakened, instead of growing; this time, the enemy looked demon-like, wild and unwavering, and their numbers only heightened his angst. Ga's body stiffened. He stepped backward, then turned and ran in the opposite direction, not knowing where to go. He careened past a dead foe and jumped over another combatant, who hunched over clutching where his neck and shoulder met. Screams accented the wicked damage done from the weapon's hook.

Hu and Shen soldiers, from the direction of the mountain, were headed his way. *They're coming to fight,* he thought. *They will help me.* He veered toward them, away from the footsteps he heard chasing him. The sound appeared not to gain ground, but he didn't dare look back for fear of losing a step.

On top of the hill, another drumbeat thundered. *Oh, no!* Ga knew the signal did not portend anything good for him.

From in between the center hill and Spider Mound, more strike chariots and fresh infantry entered the fight for Wu. Additional transport chariots sped around the battle's edge and joined barbarians from the earlier pinch, cutting off any hope of retreat for the soldiers. Prince Kuang's plan was out. He had baited the Dukes of Hu, Shen and Chen into a trap, and the snare was complete. Only the final squeeze remained. A battle that had earlier favored the chariot strength of the three States now tipped heavily to Wu, and so did the pending slaughter.

Ga hadn't realized how close he was to the base of Wu's hill. A loud yelp came from atop, reaching a fevered pitch. He glanced in that direction long enough to see the middle chariot flash down the incline, leading the rest of Wu's savages into battle. The swooping wedge angled toward the center of the battlefield, directly at him. Ga wanted his legs to move faster, but they couldn't. He turned sharply away from the hill, searching for some place to go or someone to help. His fright spiked again when he saw the Duke of Shen's chariot drumming a line that would pound over him. The snorting, bolting horses grabbed his attention first. *If the horses don't trample you . . .* he had learned. *They don't know we're on the same side!* The risk spurted through his mind. *If I slow, the boors will catch me. Can I beat the horses?* One step, then another; the rumbling hooves shook the ground. Ga stepped into their path. He could smell the horses' sweat, but he didn't dare look at them. A third step, and he leaped, landing one foot beyond the other side of the team, but the last steed's leg caught the trailing staff of his spear, spinning Ga to the ground. The spear snapped under the weight of the hooves. He rolled to a stop, feeling lucky that the sound was of his spear breaking, not his bones. His chest pumped harder, expecting to see barbarians closing in. Instead, he saw the Duke of Shen slap the reins and the chariot drive in between him and the chasers. The Duke's furry cape hung over his armored tunic and flapped behind him.

Ga lifted his butt off the ground and crawled backward like a crab. The horse on the farthest side of the chariot's team reared up and faltered into the next one. A spear flailed from the haunch, causing the horse to fight against the others. The struggle among them sent the nearest horse rearing up, which set off a chain reaction that rippled through the rest of the team. The chariot tilted, then toppled. The Duke of Shen let loose of the reins and grabbed the chariot's frame. When it rolled to the side, the jolt knocked the Duke into the halberdier, then the archer into both of them. All three tumbled over the edge. The archer flipped backward, over the frame, and alighted on one foot, then the other. He was the only one lucky enough to land standing.

The horses dragged the overturned chariot, opening Ga's

line of sight. The Duke of Shen had hit the ground, shoulder first, and there, hovering over him, a cutthroat pressed his spear to the Duke's forehead, not to kill him, but to hold him captive.

Although the assailant cropped his hair short and marked his face, both in the Wu custom, he was much different than the peasants Ga had battled up to now. The contrast started with the armor. It was made of plate construction, not padded covers pulled over hempen tunics. But the greatest dissimilarity was his war-like manner. A cold, hardened bloodthirst lurked from within. It was no different with the others in the squad.

The Duke's halberdier sprawled next to him. A coarse savage picked the dagger-axe off the ground and tossed it aside. He then crouched at the halberdier's feet and raised the bottom of the full-length armor. In full view of the open skirt, a towering barbarian stepped forward, then shoved a spear into the exposed cavity. The halberdier shouted and attempted to sit up and grab at the weapon, through the armor, before it did the intended damage. He wiggled in anticipation of the impaling blow, but unable to move, his effort was useless. Ga flinched when he heard the chilling scream.

The Duke of Shen's archer backed away. He didn't run, though. He couldn't. The skirt of the full body armor restricted his stride. Two peasants joined the Wu squad. Both had the look of those in the initial attack. They hurried straight for the archer, who stumbled on the stiff skirt, when he tried to take a full step, then caught his balance. The archer's bow had broken in the fall. He tossed it aside and drew his short sword. The two barbarians, one of whom showed lines of age, closed the distance. Both had shoulders and arms produced by a life of manual labor. The older, who wore a confident face, reached the archer first and drove his spear below the skirt, into the foot. The archer squealed and swung his weapon downward, hitting the spear's staff. The dull impact caused the shaft to split at the haft, where years of use had weakened the joint. Duke Shen's archer collapsed from the piercing pain, but on his way to the ground, he slashed his sword upward, in a desperate counter. The peasant dropped the broken staff and jumped back, avoiding the blow, but not before the blade ripped through his padded jacket. The younger of the two Wu attackers shoved his spear above their prey's armored collar, into the neck.

Once the archer was dead, the older foe picked up the archer's short sword, gave a curious look and tossed it aside. He then eyed Ga.

Ga had felt momentary comfort when the enemy turned their focus toward the Duke. But it was now gone. His chest heaved, gasping for air. He struggled against a frightful weakness to gather to his feet. *Get up,* Ga told himself. *Run! To Yuan.* His foot slipped on the first step. Ga stumbled, bounced up from the ground, then scrambled away, leaving weapon and shield behind.

He veered away from the swoosh and thud of an arrow that flew by and landed in the dirt in front of him. A second arrow tacked him back on course, and the thunder of more trampling horses pushed him even faster. A mix of soldiers who ran toward him equaled his fear, and like him, they too fled from Wu's pressing death. Ga wheeled toward the mountain to avoid colliding into them, but he faced the same corral of soldiers in that direction, as well. The trap's squeeze surrounded him. He slowed, not sure where to go. The body of soldiers thickened with every few steps. Ga turned again, and in that instance, collided with another soldier. Both fell to the ground. Soldiers scurried away from a charging chariot, and once the path opened, Ga saw the horses heading straight for him. He clawed at the ground, but the rest of him froze. *Stay away from the horses!* Sweat slung from the manes, and their snorts spewed into the cool air. Ga braced to be trampled, then raised a trembling hand to stop death. Not that he could. It was simply a reflex. The ground shook from the pounding hooves. He couldn't roll to the left because a heft of soldiers blocked him. It was the same to the right and behind him. *I'm dead!* He squeezed his eyes shut, tightened his muscles, stiff as a corpse, wanting to be back in Chengfu. And at the moment he expected to be under hooves, the chariot creaked and clapped to a stop. Ga sat there, stuck in place with four pale beasts snorting heavy breaths, their slobber dripping onto his forehead.

What do I do now? He peeked between the horses' legs and beyond the chariot. Barbarians stepped closer. Ga felt a hand tug at his collar. He looked up to see the Hu Squad Leader standing over him. He had no idea what his name was but knew they were on the same side. That brought some comfort. Ga stood up to join him, but a slobbering horse jerked its head, then stretched its nose downward and butted Ga into the Squad Leader. They stumbled backward into other soldiers.

Ga heard what he could only surmise was an order from someone on the chariot. He didn't understand the language, and the high-pitched chatter sounded more like gibberish than meaningful words. But once the man finished, his savages raised the tip of their spears and stepped closer. Ga looked around and saw the same in all directions. There was no place to go. The Hu, Shen and Chen soldiers clustered, completely surrounded. The Wu menace tightened its snare, herding the soldiers until they bunched together, penned. *What now?* The two barbarians, who had ended the life of the Duke of Shen's archer, stepped toward him. The older man, who wore the ripped, padded jacket, aimed his spear directly at Ga, head high.

The Hu Squad Leader nudged Ga, stepped in front of him, then tossed his spear to the ground. His shield followed, and just as the first barbarian to turn and run had sparked a massive Wu retreat earlier in the battle, so did the first spear thrown down in defeat trigger a mass surrender by Hu, Shen and Chen. One-by-one each of the trapped soldiers disarmed.

The charioteer shouted something else. He was a strongly built man with a hard manner, who showed a decisive gaze and a commanding presence. A shadowy creature marked the man's face.

"That's Prince Kuang," the Hu Squad Leader whispered. The creature on Kuang's face was different than Ga had seen on the other men from Wu. It looked alive.

"What is it?" Ga asked.

"Don't look at it," the Squad Leader instructed. "The creature is looking for courage to steal. Don't let it take yours. And don't look directly at Kuang. If he catches your eye, the manner of your death will be worse than death itself."

The angle wasn't right to see the demon's details, until Kuang turned the chariot and walked the horses down the line. *How can I not look?* On Kuang's profile, the menacing creature snarled through jagged teeth. Its piercing eyes glared. The creature blended into the details of Kuang's face, as if it and Kuang were one and the same. Its massive open jaws extended on to Kuang's chin, and sharp teeth rimmed both lips. Kuang's eye formed the creature's eye. It blinked when Kuang did, and sometimes on its own. The ribbed crown grew into the hairline, and throughout the shadowy figure, scaly armor protected the creature's body that continued down the neck, disappearing underneath Kuang's collar. The other half of Kuang's face, the man's side, was marked only by a scar that started above the eyebrow and curved down below the cheek.

Ga's momentary fixation with the markings disappeared when the Dukes of Hu, Shen and Chen were brought before Kuang and forced to kneel, facing their subjects. Prince Kuang nodded to one of his men. A boor forced the Duke of Hu's body to the ground, in front of Ga. The older Duke put his hands out, trying to resist the foot planted in his back, but his strength gave way and he bent at the waist until his forehead touched the ground. An extra shove for emphasis caused the flab on the Duke's arms to wiggle with the jolt. Another Wu man, an Executioner wielding a heavy axe, leaned over the Duke of Hu and said something in an instructional manner. The Executioner raised the axe overhead, then with a powerful downward blow struck the back of the Duke's neck.

Ga gasped. He wasn't the only soldier who heaved at the sight of blood spewing violently from the severed neck. The gruesome spray drenched Ga. He jerked his head and tightened his lips, but not before the gush reached his tongue. He gagged at the acrid gore, spat, then tried to step away, but the wall of captive soldiery blocked him. The Hu Squad Leader pressed backward, as well, but to no avail.

The reaction was quite the opposite for the savages. They cheered when the Executioner finished the job, then lifted the head by the hair. The Duke's lips moved, opening and closing, as if trying to speak, which turned cheers into laughter. The Duke of Hu's Executioner mocked the slain victim, then fixed the head to the end of a spear.

The Duke of Shen was next. He removed his cape, laid it on the ground in front of him, then bent forward until his head rested on the soft, furry cloak. He expected an immediate end. His eyes squinted shut, his teeth gritted tightly, and his lungs held one last breath. The Duke of Shen's Executioner stood over him, yapped and laughed, then jerked the cape out from under the Duke's head. The Executioner held it up, showing the others, and stroked the cape while chuckling. With his foot, he nudged the Duke back into position, then felled the axe.

Again, Ga turned away, not wanting to see the grisly sight. The body was farther down the line, and he felt lucky that he was too far away for the ghastly spray to reach him. The barbarians bellowed another round of cheers when, again, the Duke of Shen's Executioner raised the head for all to see, then skewered it.

Ga looked over his shoulder, across the field at the Chu army, which remained exactly where they were when the battle began. The sound of a chariot moving closer pulled his attention. Prince Kuang had turned the chariot around. Ga looked at him, and to his horror, the demon stared back. The creature blinked at him, not the man's side, only the living fiend. The eye's focus penetrated into Ga. The young conscript ducked his head.

"Aren't they coming to help?" Ga asked loudly. No one answered.

The Duke of Chen's Executioner completed the task, at which point Kuang shouted something. All three Executioners raised the skewered heads over the soldiers. The boors yelled again, pumping their spears overhead. They worked themselves into a fury, jumping up and down and paying more attention to the gruesome celebration than their captives. Each Executioner taunted the soldiers, swinging the Dukes' heads over the crowd.

Ga looked at the Hu Squad Leader and whispered, "Who will be next?" He turned back toward Kuang, and at that moment, his face met the bloody slap of Duke Hu's head. From the initial surprise of the early morning attack, to overwhelming confidence at the sight of the fleeing attackers, to complete and total defeat, Ga lost all hope.

Prince Kuang drew his sword, aimed it at Ga and yapped a command. It wasn't Kuang's man face that scared him most, though. It was the creature. Ga froze at the menacing gaze. *It's true! The creature stole my courage!* What bravery he had in reserve left his body, replaced by a cold chill that rippled down his spine. He fought to keep his bowels from dumping.

The Duke of Hu's Executioner lowered the head and poked Ga in the chest, then slid it up to Ga's chin and over his mouth to his nose, rubbing and grinding the blood-matted head into Ga's face. Ga shivered from fright. *I'm next!* He pressed against the soldier behind him.

The Hu Squad Leader whispered something, not loud enough to understand. Ga felt a gentle tug on his collar. He moved in that direction, a slight step. The bulk behind him gave way, and Ga moved a few more steps. They weren't big strides. They were more like shuffles, but Ga followed as far as the human wall allowed. He welcomed putting distance between him and the demons, even if by only half a step. Ga felt the Hu Squad Leader tug harder on his arm.

Ga pushed harder, stepping away from the threat. The soldier behind him gave more ground, and Ga pivoted, then fought his way into the crowd. To his amazement, after only a couple of steps, the soldiers moved with him, accompanied by shouting cries that urged flight. The soldiery heap, loaded with fright, broke through the enclosure, and the mob of Hu, Shen and Chen soldiers bolted for Chu's army and the safety of its numbers. Ga hurdled a soldier who had fallen in the mix. He didn't stop to help. No one did.

6

THE PLAN REVEALED

*Y*uan was astonished at the brilliance of Wu's feigned retreat, at the three Dukes' foolishness in pursuing it, and at Commander Wei Yue's failure to move. He understood Prince Kuang's strategic deception and predicted what would come next.

Across from the battlefield, Yuan saw the panicked captives break free. He was too far away to know how it had happened, but the burst was sudden, like a spooked herd forced through a narrow breach. Wu made no attempt to regain control. Odd, Yuan thought. Rather, its army waited until Prince Kuang released them into fast pursuit. Kuang didn't hold them for long, but his chariots remained behind, side-by-side, waiting for orders.

Barbarians on foot pressed the herd, threatening soldiers at the rear, one of whom fanned to the edge. Two others followed, while another challenged to pass even farther to the outside, stomping a path to the front. No one wanted to be last in the flight.

A strike chariot launched into the chase, racing for the stray soldier. Its charioteer whipped the horses with the reins, and slapped them again, then tugged on the right two beasts, bringing the team to within the dagger-axe's reach. The halberdier readied his blade, extended the staff, then lunged the weapon's spike into the soldier's back, letting the force of the horses' speed deliver the thrust.

"Did you see that?" Fen Yang asked, though certain that Yuan had.

The soldier tumbled to a lifeless stop, which forced his closest companion back into the throng, lest he suffer the same fate. Yuan nodded. "Kuang is steering them."

The retreat had started, in the distance, with a mere rumble, but once the chariots entered, the pounding of earth turned to thunder that echoed against the Dabie Shan. On the other side of the rabble, a Wu chariot barrelled over another soldier who had ventured too far afield. Kuang's plan was in the open.

"Straight for T'ang and Ts'ai," Lan noted. He pulled an arrow from his quiver, then spun the shaft between his forefinger and thumb.

Wei Yue, Kuang's full force is right before you. Attack! Now! Sui to the left, Ts'ai to the right. Yuan's instincts told him to charge into the fight, but the soldier in him, the one General Yang Gai had forged, held him at bay, respecting the chain of command. His impulse was further checked by more practical means, as well. The armies of Ts'ai and T'ang, along with the Dabie Shan, made advancing onto the battlefield impossible before the full vigor of the retreating stampede reached the States' line.

Wei Yue's drum beat and his gong sounded. "Finally," Fen Yang said. Wei Yue ordered Po Pi forward to fill the gap left by Hu and Shen. A column then separated from among Wei Yue's soldiers, moving forward behind Sui and the terrain Chen had left vacant.

"He better do more than just hold the line," Lan barked. "We've lost many soldiers waiting on him."

Wu chased the soldiers, matching them step-for-step,

neither gaining nor losing ground. Chariots patrolled the outer edges, controlling the flock, directing them, and the remainder of Kuang's chariots hurled into the chase to the rear. Yuan fought the urge to slap the reins. *Get me into this fight, Wei Yue!* His heart raced, the adrenalin surged; this was the moment he had been waiting for. *I want my sword bloody!*

"He is too defensive." Fen Yang looked toward Wei Yue, lifted the butt of his halberd slightly above its rest, then tapped it back down twice.

"He only intends to stop Wu's advance. Are we led by a dunce?" Lan placed the arrow on the bow's shelf, itching to let it fly.

"Yes, today we are," Yuan forced the realization through clinched teeth.

"Wei Yue fell for Kuang's trap, but we still have the numbers," Lan affirmed.

"Damn it, Wei Yue, move Ts'ai and Sui to meet Wu's flanks. Send us in between to stop the advance. Let me fight!" Yuan's controlled reserve let loose. He didn't care who heard his shout.

The first retreating soldier, who entered Duke Chao's line, grabbed a member of Ts'ai's troops, paused to say something, then bumped his way deeper into the formation. Yuan watched him knock into the next soldier in line, and bounce off yet another. *What's he doing?* An arrow pierced the man's armor, and the jolt from the back sent the escaped soldier to the ground.

Yuan shook his head in disgust. "And that stampede will keep Ts'ai and T'ang from fighting in full force." He turned to Lan, "Can your arrows reach far enough to provide cover?"

Lan stroked the feathers of his nocked arrow and shook his head. "I'm likely to hit our own men."

Yuan surveyed the horde. "Do you see Ga?"

Others in retreat poured into Ts'ai's front line, mixing

deeper into the ranks, jumbling together and obstructing the Ts'ai soldiers. The congestion made impossible Ts'ai's movement forward, even if ordered.

"There!" Lan replied, pointing the arrow toward a Ts'ai soldier who swayed to the side, trying to see through the crowd at who gave chase. He teetered the other way, letting another panicked soldier brush by. "There he is. It looks like he's bathed in blood, but that lanky neck is unmistakable. Ga is still alive!" He nudged Yuan.

Yuan leaned on the carriage and squinted, straining for a better view. He felt a moment of relief, knowing that Ga had survived. But the ease turned to knots in the stomach when he saw Ga fall face first, a spear sticking out of his back, then disappear underneath the trampling mob. *It's over for him. Damn, Wei Yue. You didn't give him a chance. You haven't given victory a chance.*

Lan sank his head, saying nothing.

A rapid *tap, tap* rang from Fen Yang's halberd. He gripped the staff tightly, then banged it again, muttering something inaudible.

The smell of blood and the sounds of battle filled the air. Yuan's horses tugged at the reins. His callused fingers tightened around each strap, keeping the team's spirit in check. He watched the same confused clash take over T'ang and Sui. The captives in flight ran into, bunched up, and obstructed the soldiers. Wei Yue had bungled the opportunity, Yuan's opportunity, but Yuan wasn't ready to give up. He couldn't save Ga, but believed he could salvage the day. Yuan ordered his men to sweep around Duke Chao to the right. "Push. Squeeze through," he yelled. He intended to ram Wu into Po Pi's soldiers, who were filling the gap. That would take pressure off Duke Chao and let his forces get into the battle.

The thud of spears hitting shields and the clang of swords grew. "We're not waiting any longer. Move the column forward, to the right, around Chao," he bellowed. His order traversed through the ranks, then the massive column began to move. Wu had pushed Duke Chao's soldiers into the wall of Yuan's men, though, making movement at the front painfully slow until the advance stopped all together. "Push right! Push through!" Yuan shouted.

"What's Chao doing?" Lan asked with exasperation.

Duke Chao turned his chariot, hard right, until he faced in the opposite direction, away from the battle. His complement accompanied the about-face, then all of his ranks followed, clashing into Yuan's column. Yuan's sweep, made difficult because of the pinch of the mountain, was now impossible.

"Turn and fight! Turn and fight!" Yuan yelled, but only the nearest soldiers could hear him over the roar of battle and shouts from his own men.

Duke Chao's attempted flight opened a crease between his position and T'ang's army, exposing T'ang's right flank to Prince Kuang's horde. Wu's drums sounded, and on that signal, Wu barbarians struck into the breach. T'ang was now fighting Wu, both in front and to the right flank. Yuan saw an opportunity. If he could get Chao's men turned, they could squeeze Wu against T'ang, then surround the enemy. "Turn and fight! Turn and fight!" he yelled, but his words went unheeded. Chao's men, working counter to Yuan's soldiers, felt like a stranglehold to Yuan. His soldiers were bogged down with Duke Chao's, neither group able to let the other pass. Yuan was stuck.

Then he saw something that spelled the end of the battle. The Duke of T'ang steered his chariot around and fled, yelling retreat.

"Wei Yue is too late. T'ang gave up." Fen Yang picked up his dagger-axe from the hold, then slammed it back down in disgust.

The T'ang soldiers, also anxious to leave the battle, turned and followed their Duke straight into Wei Yue's column. Wu's aggressive pursuit pressed them further into a heap, and with little resistance, the barbarians picked off those trying to flee. Down the line, the same was repeated with Sui's men retreating into the column under Po Pi's control.

"This day is done." Lan shared Fen Yang's disgust. "Wei Yue is *baichi*."

The rippling wave of retreat into their own forces prevented Chu from moving superior numbers into battle. Yuan looked back at Commander Wei Yue, who was frozen, not believing his eyes. The confidence Wei Yue had shown the night before was gone; Yuan's quest, still beyond reach. The battle was a total loss.

Wei Yue's drums pounded the sound of retreat. Fen Yang put his hand on Yuan's shoulder. "Wei Yue isn't up to the challenge. Let's live through this day and have another chance."

Fen Yang was right, and with that bitter reality, Yuan nodded. "Give the order." He waited for his men to turn about and begin a hasty retreat, yanked hard on the reins, then turned his chariot around. An agonizing rush of emotions seized him. Anger, frustration and disappointment all swept through him. He had failed to restore the family's honor, and he had failed Ga. His heart sank. The foul taste of defeat made him spit. Worse though, was the fact he never had a chance to fight. He never had a chance to succeed. In the distance, he saw Wei Yue leading the retreat. *That's the only thing you've led today,* he thought. To the rear, he heard Wu's shouts of victory. *Prince Kuang, you won the day.*

PART 2

THE STATE OF WU

7

THE SPOILS OF WAR

*W*u pressed past the encampments, wagons and food Chu's army would need to sustain the fight into the following days. Prince Kuang led them beyond Chi-fu, cutting off that town as a depot. The next city, having stores sufficient to replenish the defeated soldiers, was days away. *The village in-between won't have enough to feed them. This battle is ours.* Prince Kuang halted the pursuit and ordered his men back to Chi-fu.

He wasn't quite ready to relish the victory. Outside of Chi-fu, his men encircled their leader and pumped their spears to the beat of a rhythmic chant, intoxicated with victory. It was a feeling Kuang continued to feed. He handed the reins of his chariot to his halberdier, turned to face his troops and raised his sword to the sky. His commanding voice shouted for all to hear, "Warriors. Look at the mighty Chu. Their vast lands, their great numbers can bear your spears no more." Cheers followed. "Now, I ask one more thing of you before the day's end! Look at Chi-fu," he said, tipping the point of his weapon toward the town. "It's now a part of Wu." The shouts grew. "But they don't know it yet. They remain perplexed, and I need just one volunteer to lift their fog of confusion. Will someone step forward?"

Together, they all advanced, yelling, "I will! I will!"

Kuang smiled and sheathed his blade. "Let's tell them together," he shouted. Cheers rang again. Kuang jumped from the chariot. His men parted, allowing him to trot through.

The warriors stepped into Kuang's pace, each foot moving in unison. The warriors' tramp pounded a methodical beat to the town's gate. A tall wall ringed the city, adjoining the Dabie Shan on both sides. Kuang placed a hand on a young warrior's shoulder, then extended the other toward his aide, who placed in his hand a spear with a head affixed to the tip. Kuang allowed the crowd to quiet. "Will you do me a favor?" he asked.

"Yes, sir," the warrior replied, brimming with pride for having been chosen. It didn't matter what the task, he, like the others, was willing to follow Prince Kuang no matter where. At that moment, he beamed.

"Take this spear, and this head," pausing for a moment, Kuang turned to his younger brother Fu-kai, "Who is this anyway, the Duke of Chen?"

"I think it's the Duke of Hu." Fu-kai laughed. "He looks so puny without the rest of his body, doesn't he, Brother?"

Prince Kuang turned back to his chosen messenger. "Take this Duke's head to Chi-fu's Overlord, and extend my personal invitation for him to meet with me tonight, so we can discuss the terms of his city's new relationship with Wu and our King Liao." He waited for the collective chuckle to subside. "Tell him that if he refuses my invitation, his head will decorate a spear by morning."

⟫⟫

Later that afternoon, Kuang walked across the battlefield and among the post-battle chores being worked. A man who was in the initial assault paused, holding an armful of spears, and bowed to Kuang as he and Fu-kai passed. The younger brother's step still bounced from the euphoria of the battle, but to Kuang, such emotion was for the naïve. Instead, Kuang took a moment to reflect.

For years, Wu had suffered the King of Chu's ambition for its land. Although Wu had successfully fended off those desires, thanks in large part to Kuang's genius, it had always waited for Chu to invade. This time, though, Kuang had convinced his cousin, King Liao of Wu, to let him set the time and place of the next attack. From deep inside Wu territory, where the Huai River meandered through the coastal lowlands, Kuang's naval fleet had sailed up the river, entering Chu territory at night. The fleet had gone undetected to the place near Chou-lai, where infantry and strike chariots were offloaded. From there, they marched overland to hit the unsuspecting city, while the remaining naval force attacked the town from the river's edge. Kuang had deployed chariot-mounted catapults to attack two gates in the city's walls. Archers, packed into three-story towers that were built into the middle of the vessels, added additional destruction, raining arrows down on anyone careless enough to expose himself.

His strategy had lured Chu to the field of battle he selected, at the time he chose and into the trap he constructed. Fu-kai had led Wu's right flank that closed off the enemy's escape and was now bursting with talk. "Brother, about the battle. When you opened the prisons, I didn't know what you intended to do with the convicts. But now I understand. You perched them on top of the hill with only a small number of warriors. Chu must have thought we weren't prepared to fight. They believed we were weak. But how did you know your trap would work?"

Kuang didn't answer. Instead, he saw an opportunity to teach his youthful brother. "Why do you think it worked?" Kuang asked.

Fu-kai smiled. He was used to his brother's lessons. "Last night was black so it was easy to hide our warriors behind the hills, so long as we didn't light fires. It was a cool night, too,

Brother, so they must have believed all our warriors were on top of the hill around the fire pits. Maybe they thought we were waiting for more men to arrive. But they probably didn't expect us to attack with so few warriors."

"Good. What else?"

Fu-kai thought for a moment. "I know their General's death helped. Their new Field Marshal isn't as resourceful. Brother, how did you know he couldn't rise to the challenge? Chu's General Yang Gai must have appointed him Field Marshal for a reason."

"Remember what our spies told us," Kuang continued the lesson. "We learned that their new Field Marshal relied on a Taishi to sanction the role and that the Duke of Ts'ai was open with dissent. You know that the Dukes of Ts'ai and T'ang are close friends. Dissent is like poison, poured into a well. It spreads, even if it can't be seen everywhere it exists. Wei Yue showed inexperience. He didn't have unity, and he was too anxious to prove himself."

"If he was so anxious, why didn't he attack us first? We gave him reason to believe he could easily defeat us."

"You must learn everything about our enemy, Fu-kai. Do you know what this day is?"

Fu-kai shook his head. "No, Brother, except a day they should get their fields ready for planting."

"This is the first day of the moon's new season. Chu would not attack us today for risk upsetting the order of nature. Chu people would not chance altering that balance. And they did not expect us to tempt fate either. Remember Fu-kai, you control your future. Taishi's, tortoise shells and omens don't."

"So, they didn't bother moving into battle formation, because they didn't expect us to attack today." Fu-kai nodded, contemplating another question. "Why didn't you send the convicts charging fast into the fight? Why walk them across the field?"

"What was their purpose in this battle?"

"They were bait for the trap. I get that. But why not rush them into the fight before the enemy had time to react? They would have killed more soldiers before retreating. And how did you know our convicts would turn and run?"

Kuang eyed his brother. "Do you remember what I told them?"

"I think you said, 'fight, live and earn freedom, or disobey and die by worse means'?"

"That's right, and I gave them spears and pointed them in the right direction. They are criminals, not trained warriors. They easily accepted the incentive while they were on the hill. They knew that some would perish in the fight. But each man thought it would happen to someone else. They also understood that the sort of death, resulting from disobedience, would be far worse. The choice was simple, stark and easy to make."

"Then why did they flee from battle?" Fu-kai shook his head.

"Self-preservation. It's simply the nature of men. Initially, they saw Hu, Shen and Chen as unsuspecting prey, and every man left the hill believing they could fight and live. The slow pace across the field, though, forced them to see their enemy gather together and prepare for battle. The risk of death grew step-by-step." Kuang marched his hand out from his body, chopping the air to underscore each pace.

"The overwhelming numbers must have sunk in, too," Fu-kai deduced.

Kuang nodded agreement. "And better trained. Each convict, at some point, realized that death was likely, and once the untrained believes he is going to die, his mind seeks a way out. When retreat is open, that is the most likely choice."

Fu-kai looked at the ground and scratched his chin. "But wouldn't they have done the same by striking before the States were ready?"

"Yes, but when do you want them to react to that conclusion is the question you must ask yourself. If they had attacked before the States formed a barrier, they would have penetrated too deeply into the enemy's camp. And probably scattered, making it difficult to see others retreat."

"I understand."

"Once they saw their friends die in front of them, doubt set in. Their minds turned in the blink of an eye." Kuang tapped his temple.

"Okay, that's why you sent them in waves. Retreat was inevitable, but how did you know Chu would break formation to pursue? You didn't direct that at all."

"They pursued because the convicts scattered and offered tempting targets. Remember, the convicts fought and fled as individuals, not as a unit. They each cared only for themselves and gave no thought to fighting together. They weren't trained to do so. It's just that simple, and because of it, they each fled where their own fright took them. That made them enticing targets, teasing the enemy." Kuang allowed the lesson to sink in. "I have a question for you. Once we let the soldiers escape, why did we drive them into Ts'ai?"

Fu-kai scratched his brow. "Is it because Duke Chao was reluctant to fight?"

"Right. He was less likely to take the bait, so it was better to use his reluctance, and when he turned away from the battle, his men ran straight into Chu soldiers. Their great numbers didn't matter because they couldn't get into the fight."

"I see. And now we get all that Chu has left behind." Fu-kai chuckled. He motioned, indicating Chu's tents, felled during the soldiers' retreat.

Wagons, carts and supplies were strewn in all directions. Newly freed convicts, tasked with collecting weapons, armor, supplies, beasts of burden and any other useful spoil, worked through each task. They were not yet warriors who enjoyed the privilege of looting the leftovers for whatever pleased them. Kuang focused on two in particular. They had drawn the unpleasant duty of dealing with the dead, removing armor and stacking bodies onto burn piles. Although they were within earshot, they hadn't realized that Kuang was near. "Fu-kai, come here," Kuang said. He saw another opportunity to teach his young brother an important lesson from the battle.

Fu-kai stepped closer.

Kuang nodded toward the two convicts, who worked beyond a pile of stacked bodies near an armor wagon.

"That one got a little too close to a Chu dagger-sword, don't you think, Brother?" Fu-kai chuckled, hoping for a laugh at the convict, whose ripped, padded jacket bared his chest.

"Those were the two convicts who were first to turn and run during the battle," Kuang pointed out. "I paid close attention to who would start the retreat."

The older of the two convicts pulled the shoulders of an armored tunic over the head of a stiffened body and shouted in frustration, "This is disgusting!" He didn't know that Kuang was nearby. "The stench. The mess. Pulling armor off the dead is bad enough, but the mangled ones are awful. And now we have to stack their bodies."

Fu-kai shouted, "Would you rather be one of them? Come over here."

The convict covered his chest with the tattered remains of his jacket and pointed to himself, hoping Fu-Kai's command was for someone else.

Fu-kai nodded. "What's your name?"

"Kan-jian, sir." The convict bowed, keeping his head lowered.

"And you," Fu-kai said to the other.

"Ke-lu." The younger convict bent hurriedly, wanting to be forgotten.

"Chu had scouts across the river. Did you get their armor

and weapons?" Fu-kai asked. Before the morning battle, while the sun was still below the horizon, Kuang had dispatched two teams to remove Chu's eyes and ears. After eliminating the scouts, Kuang moved his men into position, transporting them from downstream.

"Yes, sir. We did that earlier," Kan-jian answered.

"What about the ones toward the mountain?" Fu-kai asked.

"We did that as well."

Kuang folded his arms, observing the two convicts.

Fu-kai smirked.

"Come forward and explain," Prince Kuang instructed.

"Forgive me, My Prince, but I don't know what explanation you seek," Kan-jian responded.

Ke-lu was glad to remain silent. In no way did he possess the mind of a warrior. Rather, he was only comfortable with the less serious days of lake life. He kept his head low, his eyes from making contact, but his body swayed, back-and-forth, unnerved by Prince Kuang's attention.

"Sure you do." Kuang didn't let Kan-jian off with a simple denial. "I want to know about the battle."

"The battle?" Kan-jian was reluctant to say too much.

"Yes. Remember the battle?" Prince Kuang paused to see how the convict would respond.

"Yes sir. Well, we followed your order and attacked Hu," Kan-jian offered.

"I saw that. Which group were you in?"

"I was in the second, sir."

"What next?" Kuang asked.

"Well, our strike was ferocious, sir," Kan-jian said earnestly.

Fu-kai's eyes rolled. "Ferocious, you say? You wouldn't lie, would you?"

Kan-jian thought. He took a long breath. "Oh, no sir. We charged hard."

Ke-lu shifted again. *Did they see us run? The manner of death will be worse,* he remembered Prince Kuang instructing. *Should I say something?* He looked at Kan-jian, then succumbed to the uncontrollable desire to race through his own version, taking no breath, "And then he turned around and ran right into me, knocking both of us to the ground, and by the time I made it to my feet he was already up and running away, so I only ran after him thinking he'd just been mistakenly turned around."

"Mistakenly turned around?" Fu-kai repeated, laughing, both at the speed with which Ke-lu spat his explanation and at the substance of the excuse. "Yes, it's a mistake to run from battle, unless ordered. And I don't remember the drummer beating the sound of retreat, do you?" Fu-kai was enjoying putting Kan-jian on the spot.

"No, Prince Fu-kai, I don't," Kan-jian shot his friend a glance. *Shut up!*

"Is it true? Did you retreat?" Prince Kuang asked evenly.

"Well, uh . . . sir."

"Perhaps you saw Prince Kuang still on the hilltop and just misunderstood his order?" Fu-kai said with a serious face.

"Well, uh."

"Kan-jian," Kuang said interrupting Fu-kai. He wanted his brother to get the lesson.

"Yes, My Prince."

"In a battle where all your friends lose courage and run, it's better to be among the first to lose your spine, isn't it?" Kuang offered.

"Sir?"

Fu-kai explained, "Those who are last to turn tail and run provide a buffer for those who are first, don't they?"

"Uh, yes sir."

"Relax. You've both won your freedom, but not for your

courage." Prince Kuang ended the misery of the newly freed men, as well as Fu-kai's fun.

Kan-jian shared a look of relief with Ke-lu.

"But tell me," Kuang said, "When your retreat reached the base of the hill, you turned and attacked the Duke of Shen's chariot. What caused you to suddenly find bravery?"

"They caught up to us." Kan-jian shrugged. "There was no way to outrun them."

"I saw you throw aside the soldier's short sword, instead of using it. Why?"

"It was bent. I guess it happened when he struck my spear. Those Chu people don't know how to work metal," Kan-jian offered.

Kuang stepped to the wagon and retrieved a short sword and responded dismissively, "All metal lose some shape during battle. Look at this." Kuang ran two fingers along a twist in the blade, starting at a bend near the midpoint. "What was your trade before prison?"

"I worked metal, Prince Kuang. And they don't have to lose shape. Our weapons are superior, because we are better at making them. May I see the blade, Prince Kuang?" Kan-jian lifted his head for the first time, but still avoided eye contact.

"Here." Kuang handed it over.

Kan-jian took the blade by the handle and at the tip. He focused on the defect and explained, "Chu can only make a dagger-sword, a blade that is no longer than twice the length of the handle, because their attempts to make a full-length sword like yours, Prince Kuang, results in a blade that deforms even easier than this one. They have to shorten the blade to get it to this strength." Kan-jian moved his hand back-and-forth across the defect. "We don't."

"You know how to make a stronger weapon; one that won't bend in battle?" Kuang's interest grew.

"I believe I do, sir." Kan-jian nodded.

Fu-kai interrupted, "What do you mean? Either you do or you don't."

"I was once asked to make a plow, but didn't have enough green-copper, so I made it by mixing different things. It turned out lighter and stronger."

"A plow is very different than a sword, but then your fighting ability explains your confusion," Fu-kai scoffed. "Brother, our smiths are the finest. No one can make a better sword."

Prince Kuang let silence hang, then instructed Kan-jian, "Continue."

"I was arrested shortly after that. I never had a chance to figure out how to duplicate it. But I know the metal would make a better blade."

"Do you think it's just a matter of experimenting?" Kuang asked.

"Not all, sir. First, I have to find the same rock as last time, then experiment with the mixture." Kan-jian shrugged, then surmised, "I may have to tweak how I work the mix."

Kuang reflected on the answer, while Fu-kai stood silently, not fully understanding the importance of his brother's focus. "What crime did you commit?" Prince Kuang asked.

"I was accused of charging more for that plow than the price the Director of Market set, and for not using green-copper."

"And, of course, you didn't," Fu-kai scoffed, cutting the answer short. "They're never guilty, are they?" Fu-kai turned to Ke-lu. "And from what crime do *you* claim innocence?"

Ke-lu rocked in his stance. *My turn!* "I offended the Jade Baton Holder."

Fu-kai eyed him warily. "There must be more to it. Tell us."

"He hired me to ferry him and his concubine across the lake."

"It's difficult to be arrested for that, so what did you do?" Fu-kai pressed.

"Once we were out in the lake, he was speaking softly to her and uh . . . became . . . well, focused on her. I asked him to keep still, but he ignored my plea. He's a portly man, and when he rolled too close to the edge, the boat took on water. I couldn't bail and scull at the same time, and well, they didn't help. He just sat there with his head buried in her, uh . . . affectionately. He paid no attention to my pleas."

The imagery was too much to hold back for Fu-kai, but the storyteller held steady. "You sank?" Fu-kai chuckled.

"We had to swim back to shore, but the young woman was not a good swimmer, and the Jade Baton Holder didn't know how to use his unusual girth to float. Instead, he struggled against it and couldn't help her. So I tried to. It was my duty," Ke-lu said, straightening his spine and bowing his chest to accent the purity of his motives. "But he wasn't angry until after we reached shore. Then he got mad. Real mad."

"So what happened?" Fu-kai beckoned him to continue.

"Her hair was kind of messed up."

"Messed up?" Fu-kai was thoroughly enjoying himself. Kan-jian, too, struggled to keep a straight face, but Kuang showed no emotion.

"It wasn't that bad. It just needed to dry. Her clothes, I guess, kind of clung tight to her, in certain places. You know. The curves."

"When did you notice her curves?"

"I thought it was appropriate to carry her out of the water, so that she wouldn't get bogged down in the mud," Ke-lu said with a flighty nod.

"You touched her?" Fu-kai chuckled in disbelief of such offense.

"I tried to explain to the Jade Baton Holder. I just let her sit in the cradle of my arms, while I walked out of the water. I didn't actually touch her."

"You didn't touch her?"

"Well, not exactly. I think he didn't completely lose control until after I fell."

"You fell, with her?"

"It was hard to walk in the mud. My foot got stuck, and I just lost my balance, and fell onto the bank, on top of her."

"Brother, we should always bring him along, just for entertainment," Fu-kai snorted. "Go on."

"I tried to wipe the mud from her clothes, but the Jade Baton Holder believed I was doing something else, I guess. The smile she wore, I thought, meant that *she* didn't mind. But, apparently, her good spirits did not last the rest of the evening. At least not long enough to please him."

"So, what actually were you arrested for?"

"He returned that night, not at all in good humor, and had me arrested for touching his concubine, and, oh yes, not keeping the boat according to regulations."

"I don't want to hear any more," Kuang said, finishing an unusual chuckle. He turned to Kan-jian, "Which market were you assigned to?"

"The Northern Market."

Kuang nodded. "Obey the Director of the Market, and next time, bring your experiment to me first, before trying to sell it. I want to see this metal."

Kan-jian returned the short sword to Kuang and bowed, as much from relief as for the recognition.

"We all have work to do. Fu-kai, come with me." Kuang turned and walked toward Chi-fu. His brother moved alongside him. "One last thing, Fu-kai. Most everyone has some skill or talent that can be of value to you, even people you least expect. That convict, the metal worker, may be a good example."

"Brother, do you really think he can make a better sword?"

"I don't know, but look at this." Kuang handed over the bent dagger-sword. "This is typical. In every battle, weapons bend and lose shape and edge. If anyone can improve on the green-copper blade, I want to know about it." *And now, I have eyes and ears inside one of King Liao's foundries.*

"And the other one? Ke-lu. What's his value?"

Kuang paused. "I said, most everyone." Prince Kuang and Fu-kai finished with another laugh at Ke-lu's expense.

⬩⟫⟫⬩

Six days had passed since the battle. Each night after Chu's retreat, Wu scouts reported to Prince Kuang about Chu's movement. Ts'ai and T'ang didn't stop to camp with Commander Wei Yue, avoiding a second day of fighting. Two days later, Sui broke away, as well. Chu's army would not be back, at least not before orders directly from Ying.

On the seventh day, a large wing galley withdrew its anchor and turned downstream, near Chou-lai. The double decked warship was seventy-five feet long. On each side of the lower deck, twenty-five oars propelled the ship into the Huai River's current.

Prince Kuang stood alone, forward on the upper deck. Warriors sat nearby, packed neatly in rows and columns, feeling the glory of victory. Each stroke of the oars, reminiscent of sweeping, outstretched wings, sent the ship downstream like a giant crane, flying effortlessly, barely above the water's surface. The heavy timber of the ship's ramming beak spiraled outward, pointing eastward toward home.

Kuang remained visible to the people of Chou-lai. The menacing creature on his face was there to strike fear in the water demons, but it had also worked against his enemy. Other ships in the fleet followed like a great migration, one by one, pulling anchors, dropping oars and turning downstream, each to a steady, easy-paced drumbeat. Kuang's gaze fixed on the horizon. He thought about the battle and Chi-fu and Chou-lai, while the fleet gained ground against the landscape. The battle at Chi-fu was one of many firsts. It was the first time Wu invaded Chu; it was the first time Wu captured Chu territory; and with that territory, it was the first time Wu possessed a meaningful avenue to reach out and strike at Chu's belly, using the Dabie Shan Gap. The conflict with Chu had entered a new era.

The immediate benefit for Wu, however, was defensive. Chu could no longer use the region to stage further attacks in its quest to conquer Wu. The momentum had changed. *Times are different now!* Kuang thought. But times weren't different back in Wu. There, the thirst for power among Wu's royalty presented Kuang with different problems; there, his enemy was unknown, not out in the open field of battle, like Chu. *What surprise awaits me?*

8

A VICTOR'S RETURN

*P*rince Kuang returned home to Wu's capital city, Meili, beyond the hills and near the mouth of the Yangtze River where it opened to the sea. King Liao, Kuang's cousin, had summoned him to Court. The morning fog had burned off, and the midday sun caked the mud Kuang tromped over on his way to the King's Palace. Fu-kai and five guards accompanied him.

Fu-kai tugged on a shoulder strap of his armored tunic, adjusting the fit, then asked, "Brother, why aren't you in armor?"

The coastal breeze whipped Kuang's silken robe. He had waited for that question since leaving his compound. "What message do you want to send?"

"Another lesson, Brother?"

"Of course, finishing your preparation is my duty, remember?" Kuang smiled.

"I think you take pleasure in pointing out how much I don't know."

"That too, Fu-kai," Kuang chuckled. "What message would I send by dressing in armor?"

"That you're always ready for battle, I guess," Fu-kai replied, hoping he was right this time. "It also reminds people of our victory. That's good, isn't it?"

"We're in the capital, going to the King's Court. Who should I prepare to battle? King Liao?"

Fu-kai laughed at the notion. "No, of course not, although I wouldn't mind seeing you clobber Kai-yü."

Kuang understood Fu-kai's predilection. Kai-yü was another cousin and King Liao's brother, the second of three in the family. He had a propensity to alienate and often targeted Fu-kai with bombastic petulance. Kai-yü enjoyed irritating Fu-kai, throwing barbs to test the younger cousin's mettle.

"Presence matters, always. Who will feel threatened by you? Who will be at ease? Which perception do you want to create? Be mindful of those questions at all times, Fu-kai."

"Yes, Brother, I understand."

At the foot of the steps to the Palace, Kuang stopped to caution Fu-kai. "Since we arrived home, we have received much praise and recognition for our victory. Don't expect that to continue at Court. When you find yourself in mixed circumstances, like those we will encounter inside, it's best to observe everything, but carefully target your words." Kuang turned to their escort, then instructed, "Wait for us here. I don't know how long this will take."

From state to state, region to region, a nobleman's need for personal protection remained constant, and even though there was less of a reason inside Meili, Kuang, like the other noblemen of Wu, was always accompanied by a security detail, sufficient to keep at bay a band of those who might want to relieve him of his pouch. But King Liao did not allow any guards, other than his own, to enter the building. That standing order reflected an insecurity held over from the machinations that allowed him to gain the sovereignty, and the constant fear of losing it.

Kuang charged up the brick steps to the Palace, which lay on a rise, head high from the street. Three buildings made up the complex. The center part, a long rectangle with the width facing the street, rose two stories. But the bottom floor was half-again taller than the top. The sun reflected brightly off the tannished, fired brick façade, which stood in contrast to the bluish-grey tiles of the two-tiered roof. The second story, smaller but balanced to the main floor, separated the rooflines, the corners of which turned upward, smiling at the Heavens. The lower roof's grin trained the eye to Palace Guards, who stood watch on each side of a balcony that wrapped around the top floor, running beneath overhanging eaves. And single story wings, set back from the primary building, on both sides, provided symmetry to the complex.

Three arching, double doors, all popping red against the lighter hues, allowed entrance into the Palace. They were alike, adorned with lattice work, but the middle doors reached higher, spanning three-quarters of the façade's height. Guards were posted on either side and in between. One opened the center entryway for Kuang, who stepped across the threshold, Fu-kai trailing, where King Liao's aide greeted him.

"Welcome back, Prince Kuang. Congratulations on your impressive victory," the aide said, then bowed.

Kuang stopped to acknowledge the compliment. "Thank you. It's good to be back."

"Prince Fu-kai, welcome to you as well," the aide said. He turned back to Kuang. "King Liao rescheduled Court for now, so that you would have a chance to refresh. He and the other noblemen are expecting you."

Kuang and Fu-kai stepped into the center corridor that divided the building. Ornamental columns lined the way to the Court. Carved beams, which supported purlins, were fixed to each column, and all were connected by tenons and mortises. The rafters, painted in the same red tint as the entryway doors, accentuated the room's height. Candles lit their way, where sunlight from open lattice shutters was insufficient. They passed an intersecting passageway, which led to the wings, then came to the end of the cloister and to another crossing hallway. To the left in the corner room, armored men gathered around the Chief Guard, listening to instructions. In the other direction, a narrow staircase, protected by two Palace Guards who stood ready to repel any threat to the King, separated a wall that was decorated by an expansive silk-screen drawing, celebrating the King's story as he wanted it told. The stairwell led to a vestibule, where other guards kept watch, then on to King Liao's second-story office.

Everywhere, King Liao's fear of losing control was obvious. His ascension to the Wu throne was not new, but he showed the palpable signs of fallible authority. The power structure within Wu relied on the troop strength of individual noblemen and their ability to use them effectively. Both Liao and Kuang claimed lineage back to King Taibo of the Zhou Royal Family. All of the noblemen did. But King Liao's rise to the throne had usurped Kuang's succession, the seed of which Kuang's father, King Zhufan, had sewn many years prior. The result haunted Kuang.

King Zhufan had three brothers: Yuzhai, Yimo and Zha. The youngest brother, Zha, possessed great ambition for the throne, and Zhufan had feared that thirst would pose a continuous threat to him and his two sons. He dealt with Zha, though, not by ending the peril's life, but by giving him, and his other brothers, a turn on the throne. Zhufan named each brother successor in order of birth. That decree solidified Yuzhai's and Yimo's loyalty to him and removed Kuang, and the much younger Fu-kai, as obstacles for Zha to realize his aspiration. It also eliminated Kuang's presumed birthright to the kingdom.

Zhufan lasted twelve years before meeting an odd death. It was claimed to have been a great fall during a hunting trip, but Kuang never trusted the explanation. Yuzhai followed and reigned for a few years more than his older brother, but Yimo only lived into his third year on the throne. He, too, met a bizarre death, which was marked by fits, raising suspicions that Zha would wait no longer and had plotted Yimo's death. But fate, through mounting mistrust, played a twisted game on Zha. He lost the needed support for his turn and, calculating his demise, orchestrated his son Liao's ascension in his stead. Openly, he claimed waning health prevented him from exercising his rightful duties as King, then left Wu for Jin shortly after Liao had taken the throne.

The transition to Liao created a momentary void that Kuang had tried to fill. He garnered support, arguing that Zha's decision to not take the mantel of power meant that succession could no longer follow the path decreed by his father and, therefore, should resort to the natural order of sons, which meant him. Liao, on the other hand, agreed that an oldest son should inherit the throne, but claimed his right as the oldest son of the brother who did not have his turn. Zha, though, had struck deals and made pacts prior to his announcement, solidifying Liao's placement. War was Kuang's only avenue for taking his birthright. And Wu moved to the brink of internal ruin.

King Liao ultimately achieved power; and his ability to keep it to this point turned on the single fact that his alliance was the strongest, albeit by a thin margin. The numbers had favored Liao but only after a timely assassination of Nobleman Tong, who had backed Kuang. King Liao, though, had never proven himself Kuang's equal on the battlefield. But once the balance clearly tipped toward Liao, Kuang chose to recognize his cousin's ascension, rather than subject Wu to an internal war that would leave it weakened against future attacks by Chu. He had opted for the lesser evil. For King Liao's part, he recognized Kuang's usefulness against the western juggernaut, but feared him, just as he feared everyone who had opposed him.

The main corridor ended across the intersecting hallway where Palace Guards stood on either side of a tall, double door that opened to the Court. They looked Kuang up and down. Kuang ignored their inspection. Great columns, bordering the doorway, bore the carved likenesses of the creatures marked on each prior King, except for Zhufan's. It was chiseled off shortly after Liao had assumed power. Another of King Liao's aides stood by the left column, blocking Kuang's view of the insult. "A marvelous victory, Prince Kuang, for Wu and for you." The aide bowed, moved to the side and opened the door.

Kuang nodded, then stepped into the room. Fu-kai followed.

King Liao stood at a table, looking over a drawing on a silk cloth that spanned the four corners of the long, wooden plank. Liao was at least ten years younger than Kuang and showed a stark physical contrast. He had the soft body of idleness, and his moon face bore none of the rugged lines of war or age. But his sunken eyes hinted at a deceitful mind.

The Chief Architect stood behind Liao. He was an older man, whose face revealed a happiness unburdened by the struggles of life. Noblemen, representing each family of Royalty, were usual to the Court and lined the near side. All turned, acknowledging Kuang's entrance, then bowed, except for King Liao and Kai-yü.

Kai-yü was one man who openly showed his distaste for Prince Kuang, contrary to the welcoming smiles at Court, and refused to recognize Kuang's victory as anything but ordinary. Whether strolling through the bustling markets or attending his brother's Court, he saw excitement, heard pleasant chatter and experienced the uplift people felt over Kuang's success. He was a sour man. It didn't take much to raise his ire, and the attention his cousin enjoyed disgusted him.

Kai-yü was slightly hunched at the shoulders and blamed his shortness on that slump. Of the three brothers, Kai-yü was the only one who didn't look like he belonged to the family, and that led to a wanting feeling that lurked below the surface of his anger. The fact that Chu-yung, his younger brother, so closely resembled King Liao remained a constant irritant and only served to heighten Kai-yü's need for recognition.

Chu-yung was next to Kai-yü. He was in awe of his older brother, King Liao, but often went along with Kai-yü's schemes. Kai-yü knew exactly how to maneuver him.

"Kuang. Good. You're here," King Liao acknowledged him with a brief nod. "What a great victory. I want to hear all about it. Everyone in Wu is talking about our success." He motioned for Kai-yü to make room at the table.

"Thank you, My King." Kuang abbreviated his genuflection. He stepped into the opening, next to Kai-yü, who was sure to be annoyed by having to breathe the same air as him. Fu-kai gathered to Kuang's right.

"Cousin, our strategy was cunning, and now the King of Chu must be convinced of our superior skill," Liao said, taking credit for the battle plan. The fact that Kuang had designed and executed it didn't matter. Liao would not recognize Kuang's role, other than as the Field Marshal who implemented the tactics, for which obvious credit was due. He would not turn his Court into a venue of appreciation for Kuang and steered the subject in a different direction. "Fu-kai, I understand you led the final sprint to close the trap. Well done." King Liao turned to Kuang, ignoring Fu-kai's bow, and asked, "What do you think Chu will do to retaliate?"

Kuang spoke without emotion. "Chu will try to take back Chou-lai and Chi-fu because the Gap is now exposed. We should watch for an attack somewhere along the Huai."

"Our peasants are back working the fields and will soon be fishing the rivers. The same must be true in Chu, so it doesn't appear to be an opportune time for them, does it?" King Liao postulated. "Wouldn't it be better for them to wait until their peasants are back in their winter huts, with idle hands and nothing better to do than go to war?"

Kuang clasped his hands behind his back. "I've heard of no reports of Chu moving troops, but I wouldn't be surprised if they attack before their summer harvest. Don't discount the possibility that they'll want to disrupt ours."

Liao considered the answer. "Or try to take it afterward. We must keep our spies well motivated."

Kuang nodded.

"Tell me, after Chu fled, what was the reaction of the Chi-fu and Chou-lai Overlords? I doubt they resisted."

"No, they behaved predictably," Kuang said, studying Liao's sunken eyes. "They ceded without trouble, but both were guarded. I think they're concerned the area will become a wasteland from future battles."

"So, their allegiance is fleeting. That's to be expected right now."

"Yes, but the benefits of being part of Wu are clear to them. It showed on their faces when I told them the levies you require. Chu took far more from them, so they view our victory as a positive development." Kuang opened his hands in front of him, embracing the point. "Their fortunes don't turn just on the fruits of their labor, either. They're also hopeful for other improvements to their lives."

"Yes, I wouldn't want to live under that King Ping or Chu's Prime Minister," King Liao acknowledged.

"Chou-lai's Overlord relaxed, after a while, and told me some of the stories. They were consistent with what we've heard," Kuang said. "Their lives will be improved under Wu, and they recognize it. They welcome the change, but they aren't convinced we can hold the territory."

"What should we do to make sure we keep it?"

"I left a complement of ships," Kuang replied evenly. "That sent the proper message, both to the region and to Chu. We'll protect the territory. And it gave the Overlords at least some sense of security, for now."

"Good, but what about the Overlords you didn't talk to? Chou-lai is farther in to Chu than the silk hills along our border. If those Overlords remain loyal to Chu, that will cause a problem for us."

"Word will spread fast enough, so I didn't stop at each town and village," Kuang said with confidence. "We can send our demands through envoys, and if any resist, we can dispatch warriors then."

Liao nodded. "I agree. Mobilizing for battle is costly. Better to do it only when needed. The growing season is ahead of us. The timing is perfect. I'll send envoys and have the Director of Market make sure he incorporates their yields. The silk and grain will be a great addition."

Liao's decision to send Kuang to attack Chu was a major deviation from his previous reactionary propensity, and the result was positive. Although Liao outwardly showed his happiness over the outcome, Kuang wasn't so sure that his cousin believed the news was all good. Kuang's stature had grown as a result of the victory, and King Liao would not like that, but it remained a subject to avoid.

"And their dialect is close enough to ours to be manageable," Kuang pointed out.

"Trying to communicate over the years must have given Chu fits. I doubt the locals learned to speak the Chu language. They probably didn't even try, and I can't imagine that the arrogance within Chu would have encouraged officials to learn their tongue." King Liao bent to the table, then rubbed his hand across the silk drawing, smoothing wrinkles.

"Are those the plans for Ku-su?" Kuang gestured to the map.

"Yes, I want to talk about the new capital today. Let's skip to it." Because of the ongoing conflict with Chu, King Liao planned to move Wu's capital from Meili to ground more easily defended. He called the new city, Ku-su.

"I had the Chief Architect draw them while you were gone. Chief, explain the layout." Liao looked up at Kuang. "And I want you to think about the city's defenses."

Kuang glanced at the drawing. It showed roads and waterways, markets and neighborhoods, as well as the Palace and administrative buildings, all of the structures needed for a capital.

"Prince Kuang," the Chief Architect began, "let me start with a brief description. We will build Ku-su near the eastern shore of Taihu Lake." He used a bamboo slat to tap the plat at the heart of the city's design. "Canals will ring the city," he said, tracing the perimeter markings. "And small waterways will run inside for people to travel. This main canal eventually will connect the city to the Yangtze River." He moved the pointer to show the route, starting at the southern border end and running north, all the way to the river. "Two other waterways will intersect the main canal." He pointed to lines that began at the lake's jagged shoreline. "They will run east, from the lake all the way to the other side of the city. We will enlarge this one . . ." he held the slat in place to designate the specific line, "into a canal, beginning at the city's eastern edge, then extend it to the sea."

Kuang took another look. "Good, encircling Ku-su with canals adds an effective barrier Meili doesn't have."

"And all of them will intersect these smaller waterways." The Chief Architect hurried the slat across those markings. "People can move around on water or over land."

Kuang leaned onto the table, then traced the markings that surrounded the city. "How wide are these canals?"

"They're wide enough for five fishing boats to travel side-by-side. Large wings can navigate the main canal, and the one to the sea, in single file. But we have to use these basins to turn them around." The Chief Architect pointed to four small dots placed on both sides of each basin. "Ropes secured at these stations will do that work."

Kuang studied the details. The defensible advantage Ku-su provided was obvious, but he realized that more could be done. "I like the plan. The narrow width of the canals may be inconvenient, but it's easier to defend against attack."

"Certainly, Prince Kuang. What more do we need?"

Kuang moved his finger along the lines that ran north to the Yangtze. "This main canal starts at the southernmost east-west canal."

"Yes, sir."

"I want you to extend it farther south – to here." Kuang tapped on the specific position. "So that it runs from the Yangtze to this southern bay. That gives us three different access points to the sea."

King Liao nodded agreement. "That makes sense."

"Wait," Kai-yü blurted. "That won't work. It cuts through my land."

"Why does that bother you?" King Liao interjected, maintaining a calm, inquisitive voice.

"Look at the path. It splits my land," Kai-yü knifed his hand across the cloth. "And there won't be any bridges. That means I have to ferry much of the harvest across the canal. And supplies!" His voice grew. "And materials!" Kai-yü shook his head and rubbed his fingers across his scalp. "I have to load and offload every damn thing!"

"It's not bad for you," King Liao said dismissively. "Traveling up and down the canal will be easier and save time getting to Ku-su."

"What do you mean, Brother! Uh, My King," Kai-yü sputtered, hoping Liao would ignore the offense of his informal reference during Court. To avoid a pause that his brother would feel the need to fill, he quickly continued, "Travel doesn't concern me. That's what peasants and oxen are for."

"They're also the ones carrying the load, Brother. It's not like you will be out there doing the work. Is it?" King Liao quipped.

Laughter erupted at the thought of Kai-yü doing anything more than barking orders. Fu-kai's bellow was the loudest, while Kuang limited his amusement to only a smirk.

Kai-yü's face flushed red at his brother's insult.

King Liao turned to Kuang, "Your idea is sound. It will help Ku-su function, and it will be good for me. Do you see anything else we should change?"

Kuang tapped the map and asked the Chief Architect, "Are these markings garrisons?"

"Yes. There is one at each corner of the city," the Chief Architect answered.

"Good. Build them with stone, so flaming arrows will be of no use, and add one at the midpoint of each perimeter canal." Kuang pointed to specific areas.

The Chief Architect glanced at King Liao, who nodded, then responded, "Yes, Prince Kuang."

"One more thing," Kuang gestured, circling his finger along the perimeter waterways. "Right now, your plan has the city ringed by canals. Inside, build a wall tall enough so that ship-mounted towers can't see over it. And set it back from the canals. We don't want ladders from ships to reach across to the wall. That way, when the enemy attacks, they'll have to offload first, then deal with the wall. Make it of stone, like the garrisons."

"I like that idea, too," King Liao seconded. "This is good."

"This will add construction time, but I'll include it," the Chief Architect said hesitantly.

King Liao tapped the drawing. "How long will it take to build?"

"I originally thought five years, just for Ku-su, but I was counting on all those convicts that are now free. Since they're no longer available, and with the additional work, I think six, maybe seven years. Plus a few more years to extend the canal from the southern bay all the way to the Yangtze River."

"Do it in five. I know the canal extensions will take longer, but Chu will continue to be a problem. They won't likely wait for us to improve our defenses. Keep the prisons empty if you need to, but get it done in five," King Liao ordered.

"Yes sir. That's an aggressive schedule, but I understand the importance."

"When will you start construction?" Kuang asked.

"We've staked the canals and roads. We'll start digging soon," the Chief Architect responded.

"You've done a splendid job," Kuang said with genuine praise.

"Lay the other drawing on the table," King Liao instructed.

A servant, who stood behind the Chief Architect, moved to the table, then unrolled another silk cloth.

"This is a more detailed view of the buildings that will exist in Ku-su. I suppose you are curious about where your families will live. You'll find your names marked on the specific compounds. Today's Court is now over. I'll leave you to review the diagram." Liao's eyes swept the noblemen. "The Chief Architect will answer any questions you may have." He turned and moved toward a back entrance to his office.

Once he had disappeared behind the closed door, Kai-yü leaned into the table, tapped on the location of Kuang's compound. "Well, Cousin, it looks like a victory over an enemy that flees from battle isn't great enough for our King to award you the best compound. How hard can it be to defeat leaderless cowards, anyway? Their General was dead before the fight began, right?" Kai-yü chided.

Kuang ignored the jab, for Kai-yü's stooped shoulders,

combined with a pitted face and a perpetually hoarse voice that made a funny croak when he spoke, worked to make the barb a pathetic attempt for attention.

"It looks like you have been reduced." Kai-yü bowed his chest. "Mine is the best compound. The garden gets good light, but there are more rooms in it that don't take direct sun. It'll be cooler during the hot months."

Kuang located the quarters assigned to him and with a stone face, said to Fu-kai, "Let's go."

"Fu-kai," Kai-yü shouted. "Why do you wear your battle tunic? Don't you know you're safe from Chu soldiers?" Kai-yü hoped for a laugh among the crowd, but no one joined him. Even Chu-yung remained silent.

"I do, Cousin. I simply don't know what you'll hurl at me when my back is turned." Fu-kai gazed down on the shorter Kai-yü. He knew that forcing Kai-yü to stare upward would grate on him.

"There is no reason for me to wait until your back is turned."

"Kai-yü, during your life, no one has found any endearing quality endowed to you by birth or achievement." Fu-kai spun on his heal, then followed Kuang through the door.

Kuang picked up his pace once in the hallway. Fu-kai hurried to draw to his side. They had passed the passageway leading to the wings when Fu-kai whispered, "Brother, Kai-yü's arrogance is maddening. He gave you no credit for defeating Chu. And Liao acted like the plan was his. And what about the new compound? Why is it of lesser rank?"

"Not here." Kaung threw Fu-kai a cautionary look, pushed open the door, then exited the Palace. They went down the steps to Kuang's awaiting escort.

Fu-kai could wait no longer. "Brother, Liao won't add father's creature to the column in the new Court, will he?"

Kuang stopped, then turned to Fu-kai, but the whistling

sound of an arrow, piercing the air, startled him. And at that moment, when his mind put an image to the sound, the impact spun his body, sending him to the ground.

9

TURMOIL IN WU

Fu-kai dropped to Kuang's aid. The bodyguards darted to their leader's position, forming a protective wall around him. Archers turned toward the direction of the arrow, looking for the assailant, bows ready to return fire. Their eyes peered through each break between nearby buildings, into each open shutter, and down the street, searching for any movement. No sign revealed the hidden assassin.

"Brother, are you all right?" Fu-kai shouted.

Kuang didn't respond but rolled onto his back. The arrow had pierced his abdomen, on the right side, and as he struggled to prop himself upright, the shaft moved with the jostle. Fu-kai steadied his brother, at the shoulder, and looked to his back. The green-copper head had blown through flesh and muscle, more at the side of the torso than through his back, and dripped blood.

"Brother, how badly are you hurt?" Fu-kai stared at him in disbelief. "What do we do?"

Kuang winced, then clutched the arrow and his robe together. His timely break from stride, when he had turned toward Fu-kai, kept him from walking fully into the arrow's path. He rolled onto his knees. Fu-kai grabbed Kuang's elbow and shoulder for support, then Kuang arose to his feet. His bodyguards gathered closer, shielding him, while their eyes searched outwardly.

"Back into the Palace," Kuang ordered. He held the arrow steady, trying to limit the spiking pain of its rub.

They crashed past Palace Guards, then through the doors. "This way," Kuang directed. He avoided the main corridor, opting instead for a passageway normally used by staff and others of lesser rank. Kuang shortened his stride, when stepping with his right leg, but it didn't lessen the pain. He grabbed the shoulder of the closest guard for balance. His escort adjusted, reducing the pace to match the gait of Kuang's limp.

The route met an intersecting hall that led to a side exit through an adjoining wing. At the juncture, the Chief Architect's servant stood, frozen in place, horrified by the armed men, who were not Palace Guards, rushing toward him.

"Turn here," Kaung instructed. "We leave through there." He pointed down the hall. Kuang stopped shy of the end, once they reached the doors. "Don't stop until we reach my compound."

Three of Kuang's bodyguards led the way, exiting the Palace first. Two trailed Kuang, but once outside, the escort formed a protective wedge. They all turned south, onto the main street that ran the length of the entire city. From the Palace, residential compounds of the noblemen lined the street, and Kuang's was second in line. The city was designed to provide the noblemen easy access to the Palace. It also signified their importance to the King and followed tradition. Many occupied the same compounds their families had lived in. Indeed, since reaching adulthood, Kuang had never known a different home.

With each step, he felt a sting in his side. His every movement worked the arrow in the wound, but by now, Kuang realized that the scraping pain would be much worse if the injury threatened his life. They charged through the gate to his compound, then through the courtyard, up the front steps and into his residence. Once safely inside, he turned to Fu-kai. "Go to the barracks. Return with four squads of men you trust. We don't know what kind of night we're in for. Bring the most skilled warriors."

"Yes, Brother," Fu-kai replied, but remained in place, too worried to move.

Kuang talked to the men in his escort. "Post warriors at each entrance to the house, at every gate and in the courtyards. Man the hallways, too."

His elderly Chamberlain stepped around the corner, responding to the sounds of distress, and upon seeing Kuang, pierced by an arrow, he commanded the House Servant, who trailed him, "Get clean water and honey. And bring a hand axe. Quickly!" He looked at the guard whose shoulder Kuang used to steady himself, and said, "Help Prince Kuang to his bed chamber,"

Kuang tapped Fu-kai's shoulder. "They'll tend to my wound. Hurry to the barracks."

Fu-kai glanced down at the arrow, then back to Kuang.

"The Chamberlain knows what to do," Kuang assured, easing his young brother's concern.

Fu-kai nodded. "Okay. I'll leave now."

Kuang limped toward the stairway. The initial jolt of adrenalin that propelled him away from danger had also masked the pain. Now, in the safety of his compound, the analgesic affect waned. He braced against the tiled wall, traversing each step up to the second-story landing. The guard helped from behind, maneuvering Kuang into his chamber.

The Chamberlain went first. He cleared rolls of bamboo slats and ink from a writing table that was pushed against the far wall. "Prince Kuang, sit here." He tapped on the corner. "I must tear your robe."

Kaung nodded. "How is it you always end up with the task of mending me?" he said to ease the tension.

"The Heavens have blessed me, I suppose," the Chamberlain replied in jest. He ripped the tear further with his hands, then used a knife to cut a wider swath and expose the wound. Next, he opened the robe, maneuvered the cloth around the arrow, careful not to move the shaft, then worked Kuang's elbow through the sleeve. He let the robe droop down below Kuang's waist.

The House Servant entered the room, brushing past the guard, then placed two bowls – one of water, the other containing honey – on a side table. He laid next to them clean cloths and a change of fresh robe. Kuang reached for the hand axe.

"Bring two cut logs from the wood pile," the Chamberlain ordered his subordinate.

"They'll be here momentarily," the House Servant responded. He stepped to the door and disappeared.

The Chamberlain swabbed around the entry wound, then looked at where the head had exited. "Good news, Prince Kuang, this is not nearly as bad as when your face stopped your enemy's blade." The Chamberlain wiggled his finger in the air, outlining Kuang's scar.

Kuang's memory flashed to when the Chamberlain struggled to manage his obstinacy, while at the same time, tending to the snaking cut. "Are you reminding me not to be so stubborn this time?"

"I would not presume to tell you how to act, My Prince." He revealed a simpering smile.

"Since when?" Pain spiked, as the arrow moved with Kuang's chuckle. He recoiled and said, "Your wit always makes me laugh."

"I'm honored you have found use for me over the years." The Chamberlain dipped a fresh cloth in the water, then daubed the wound to wipe away the blood. "The tip pierced between ribs. You're lucky your body was not turned more toward the direction of the arrow's flight. Infection will be your greatest risk." He motioned the guard to step forward. "But first, we need to break the shaft so I can remove the arrow."

"The logs are here," the House Servant said. He took them from an aide and made the delivery to the guard, who placed them on the table, behind Kuang.

"Prince Kuang, we need to place the arrowhead on one log and rest the shaft on the other. Because of the angle, we need you to stand, instead of sit." The Chamberlain motioned for the guard to steady Kuang's movement. "I must push the arrow farther through to extend the shaft out the back." He grabbed the nock, stopped, then held his hand open. "May I have the axe, Prince Kuang?"

"Are you afraid I may use it on you, Chamberlain?" The two chuckled.

"Only by reflex, My Prince." He took the axe, then pushed on the arrow.

Kuang squeezed the corner of the table, held his breath and clamped his jaw shut. He refused to let anyone hear his pain.

The Chamberlain steadied the arrowhead on one log. Once the arrow was secured between the two wooden chunks, the Chamberlain raised the axe, but before he completed the motion, Kuang stopped his arm.

"Don't miss and chop his hand," Kuang chortled. "We may need his sword tonight."

"Yes, My Prince. This is no more difficult than cutting off a duck's head." The Chamberlain drove the blade through the shaft and into the log.

Kuang exhaled through gritted teeth.

"I need to check for splinters. We don't want to leave any inside of you when I pull on the shaft." The Chamberlain spun the arrow between fingers. Fast or slow, it didn't matter. Both were sure to bring pain.

Kuang recoiled, his jaw still clenched.

"Ah, here," the Chamberlain said. He turned to the guard, "hand me your knife." He pinned the arrow's shaft against the log, then whittled at the tip. He spun the arrow again and said, "Prince Kuang," but before he finished speaking, he jerked the arrow out by the feathered end.

Kuang gasped, tightened his grip on the table, then caught his breath. "You could have warned me."

"My Prince, do you want me to put it back and do it over?"

"Funny." Kuang eyed the Chamberlain, hinting at a chuckle.

"We need to make sure the skin doesn't turn red and grow puss." The Chamberlain dabbed a wet cloth, wiping away the blood. He looked for signs of dirt in the entry hole, then did the same at the point of exit. "Bring me the honey bowl," he instructed the House Servant.

Once convinced the wounds were clean, he soaked two pieces of cloth in the honey, then used them to plug the holes. The Chamberlain added honey-drenched patches to the outside of the holes, holding them in place by wrapping cloth around Kuang's abdomen. "I'll redress the wound before you turn in tonight, then again in the morning."

"Thank you." Kuang reached out and squeezed the Chamberlain's wrist. "Hopefully, this will be the last occasion you need to apply your skill to me."

"Not likely, Prince Kuang." He retrieved the robe from the table. "Would you like assistance in changing?"

"Yes, but only with getting my arm through the sleeve." Now that the immediate danger was over, Kuang turned to his greater problem. *Who is behind this?* he wondered. He changed clothes, going through the motions, not paying attention to his movements. *Damn it! Who?*

The House Servant gathered the torn and bloodied robe, folded it, then placed the arrow's pieces on top. "This has been a troublesome day for you. Is there anything else I can do? Help you into your bed or something to drink, perhaps?"

"No. Wait, yes!" Kuang's curiosity stopped him. "Hand me the arrow."

Kuang took both pieces, then sat, resting an elbow on the table. He rotated the shaft between his fingers, studying it from the feathers down to the severed end. He picked up the green-copper tip, flipped it, then stared at the point. Nothing about it was revealing.

Kuang recalled the fight for rule, and the alliance that had allowed Liao's rise to power. In his run for the sovereignty, Kuang's support from Nobleman Tong was pivotal to his chances, and Tong's untimely death came from an arrow of a hidden assassin. Kuang was never able to determine who was responsible, but King Liao benefited the most. And the similarities here were too great to trust to chance.

It made perfect sense for Liao, along with his father, Zha, to have orchestrated Tong's death, making his involvement then appear evident. *But it doesn't make sense for Liao to do this. What does he gain?* The list of people to suspect had to include Liao's brothers, Kai-yü and Chu-yung. *Who else? What about the noblemen? Ho-Kwai, perhaps? He's always been aligned with Liao,* Kuang observed. *What does he have to gain? What does anyone have to gain?*

He remained in his chamber, racking his memory for any hints that would reveal who was behind the attempt, but a growing commotion outside of the compound drew his attention. He went to the front of the residence to investigate. The Chamberlain stood in the doorway, greeting Fu-kai.

"You're back sooner than I expected. Is there more trouble?" Kuang opened the door farther, then stepped past the

Chamberlain. He had instructed his brother to return with twenty men to guard the compound, but what Kuang saw was much different.

"Brother, I did not make it to the barracks. News of the attempt on your life spread quickly, and these men intercepted me. They wish to assist you."

Kuang looked in to the courtyard and saw many of the warriors who fought with him at Chi-fu. All were dressed in battle tunics and were armed with an assortment of swords, bows and spears. And the strength of their support was not limited to the courtyard. Kuang glanced left, then right. His warriors spilled out into the street and disappeared around both corners.

Fu-kai gestured in all directions. "We have encircled the compound, three times, and filled each outer courtyard. No one will make good on their designs tonight, Brother."

"No." Kuang raised his voice over the crowd and hailed, "No one will dare test your skill!" The warriors pumped their weapons overhead and gave a collective hoot. Kuang bowed in gratitude, resisting the temptation to grab his side at the pain that shot through him. *Don't show weakness.*

He did not bother to ask how the warriors had gained access to the armory, leaving that for another time. "The men will need food and drink," he said to the Chamberlain. "Make sure they have what they require." Kuang withdrew inside and left the details to the people who were accustomed to handling them.

The next morning, after the Chamberlain applied a fresh bandage, Kuang donned his battle tunic, preparing for King Liao's Court. It was unusual for King Liao to hold Court on back-to-back days, but the assassination attempt made it necessary. The initial shock and fright had waned, and Kuang awoke from a restless sleep with a boiling anger, although he did not show it. He wanted retribution. *Who?* That was the question he had to answer.

Kuang looked through a second-story window of his bed-chamber. During the evening, the number of warriors had grown, spilling farther into the street. A man carrying a small rectangular cage under an arm worked toward the corner of the compound en route to the kitchen. Squawking chickens fluttered inside the coop. On the outer edges of the crowd, another man maneuvered a cart in the same direction. Inside, the carcass of a butchered pig bounced as a wheel dipped in a rut worn into the crusted street. Various other merchants, each carrying an assortment of food and drink, worked their way among the crowd, and a few others on their way to the market stopped to peddle their wares. The combination made traveling difficult for anyone who desired to pass.

Kuang heard a shout from down the street. It was Kai-yü, and by his side was Chu-yung. "Out of the way! You're keeping us from the King's Court!" Kai-yü yelled. "Move it!" The two brothers pushed their way forward into the crowd, accompanied by a modest escort. The barrier of armed men thickened the deeper the two brothers penetrated, which reduced their stride to a child's pace.

Kuang felt a moment of light humor when Kai-yü attempted to strong-arm his way through and was met with contempt by the warriors. They were there for one specific purpose – to protect Kuang.

Kai-yü again shouted, "Move! Move or you'll be slopping pigs by the afternoon!" Kai-yü's bombast grew along with his anger. "Push through!" he yelled to his escort.

One of his guards bumped hard into the side of a warrior. The protector returned the shove, which drew the attention of his fellow warriors, who then closed around the two brothers and their escort.

"Move!" Kai-yü blustered. "Kill anyone in our way," he instructed his escort.

Kuang knew the threat was hollow. Everyone did.

"We take orders only from Prince Kuang!" a defiant

warrior called out, knowing there was little risk of retribution for challenging Kai-yü under these circumstances. It was rare that a member of the lesser class got away with such overt defiance toward the highborn.

Kuang laughed. This time, his warrior would. Kuang left his bedchamber and made his way to the front of the house. He stepped into the doorway and stopped.

Fu-kai joined him. "Are you in pain, Brother?"

"Never show pain unless you want your enemy to think you're vulnerable." Kuang drew a slow breath, so as not expand the rib cage too quickly. He looked over the crowd and yelled, "Warriors, a new day is here!" His men presented him with a bow. Kuang returned their respect, walked to the edge of the porch that overlooked the courtyard, then exclaimed, "Thanks to you, last night, I slept like a baby with a full belly." His words were answered with an echoing hoot. "Thanks to you, the assassin, who can't shoot straight, slept with one eye open." This time, laughter followed an even louder shout. "I'm going to the King's Palace. Would anyone like to join me?" Kuang opened his arms, inviting them all.

"I will!" the warriors bellowed as one.

The warriors parted, making an unobstructed path to the courtyard gate. Kuang felt pride in their loyalty. He drew from their strength. They fell in alongside him and Fu-kai, row-by-row, making an impenetrable barrier with Kuang in the center. Through the gate and turning down the street, his warriors moved in step, which pushed Kai-yü and Chu-yung across the street and against the wall of the opposing compound. A handful of merchants and other travelers, headed for the market, gathered next to them, but unlike Kuang's cousins, the others didn't mind the inconvenience.

Once at King Liao's Palace, the phalanx stopped and Kuang left all but his usual escort at the foot of the steps. The escort completed the trip with Kuang, but only as far as the main door. Yesterday's dash through the building was a deviation from the King's policy, which Kuang calculated would be ignored, but today was different.

Before Kuang disappeared inside, he looked back at his warriors. Their mass blocked not only the street, but entrance to the Palace as well. At the rear, he picked out Kai-yü's face. *He is sure to be red with temper.* The thought pleased Kuang.

Kuang and Fu-kai joined Liao's Court. Kai-yü and Chu-yung were late to arrive. Kuang glared at both to see if either cousin would meet his eyes. They stood by themselves, talking to one another, only casually greeting others who passed by. Neither Kai-yü nor Chu-yung met Kuang's gaze. Kuang searched the other faces around the room for any clue among their expressions. All showed only looks of concern.

Bells, summoning the noblemen to form a line facing the door King Liao would enter through, interrupted Kuang's study. He was near the center. Fu-kai was to his left. Kai-yü and Chu-yung stood at the far right, buffered by noblemen. The crowd went silent when King Liao entered.

Liao strolled to a large chair that sat elevated on a platform. His creature's likeness dressed the tall, arching back. He eased onto a red cushioned seat, then sighed, letting his sullen mood hang over the room. "Kuang, the attempt on your life yesterday is troubling. I'm glad you survived, and the source of this attack concerns me." King Liao took a deep breath. "Last night, I sent the Chief Guard to investigate, but he was stopped by those defending your compound. I've asked him to join us today and dismissed the usual participants, except for the other nobles. I want to address this matter. Tell me what happened."

Kuang nodded acknowledgment and began, "I left the Palace after your Court and was talking with Fu-kai. We had not reached the bottom of the steps when an arrow pierced the right side of my robe."

"One arrow alone Prince Kuang?" the Chief Guard asked.

"Yes, just one."

"That is correct," Fu-kai interrupted. He broke from merely observing to participating, charged by the death his older brother nearly suffered. "I saw only one as well."

"We are most fortunate that the assassin was no more accurate," King Liao declared. "Has he been found?"

"No," Kuang bristled. "I don't know who he is, and no one has come forward with information."

King Liao turned to the Chief Guard and instructed, "I want you personally involved in this. Find out who is responsible." The Chief acknowledged with bow. King Liao looked backed to Kuang. "Do you suspect Chu?"

"I should not ignore any possibility," Kuang replied.

"Your success at Chi-fu is bound to have inflamed tempers inside Ying. An attempt on your life makes sense, doesn't it?"

Kuang looked doubtful. "I don't know who is behind this, but Chu's retribution is more likely to be directed at all of Wu, not just one Prince."

"But you were responsible for Chu's defeat," King Liao countered. "Certainly, they must have special plans for you."

"If Chu is behind this effort, the assassin would've had help inside Wu. He could not have lived openly among our people. And I, then, should not be the only one here dressed for battle."

"Yes, we should all increase our escorts, at least until this matter has been solved," King Liao concurred. "We also need our spies along the Yangtze and Huai rivers to listen for talk about this."

"Speaking of a large escort," Kai-yü interjected, addressing Kuang, "your warriors are completely disrupting the street. I couldn't get through until after you left your home. How long do you intend to keep them there?"

"Once I know the effort was not directed from within Wu, I'll relax." Kuang stared at Kai-yü trying to bait a response.

"You think someone here is responsible?" King Liao asked, raising a curious eyebrow.

"It's possible." Kuang looked around the room, searching the faces in the crowd. No one showed discomfort, but no one met his stare.

"Who would do such a thing?" Liao said incredulously.

"I don't know, but until I do, I'll remain cautious." Kuang knew Kai-yü and Chu-yung were obvious choices, and their friendship with Ho-Kwai put him on Kuang's list as well. He didn't know about King Liao, only because he couldn't see Liao's gain from it. But Kuang knew not to trust Liao's sincerity. He looked into Liao's sunken eyes. *Does he really know nothing? Or is he better at hiding his thoughts these days?*

"I understand. The Chief Guard will assist you. His office is at your service," Liao offered. "It's obvious we have much to learn about this, and hopefully it will be brought to an end soon. In the meantime, do what you think is necessary for your personal safety, but try to allow people to flow up and down the street, at least as near usual as possible. For now, I leave you with that discretion."

Kuang nodded.

"Chief," King Liao said, "this matter is extremely important. I'm adjourning Court so that you can get started, and remember, report back to me daily on your progress." Liao exited through the back entrance.

Kuang watched Kai-yü, Chu-yung and the other noblemen leave the hall. No one had shown any sign of guilt or a hint of participation. Not Kai-yü, not Chu-yung, and not King Liao. Not any of the noblemen. No one had displayed even minor discomfort in his presence. Finding out who was behind this attempt on his life was going to be difficult. With the Chief Guard answering only to King Liao, Kuang believed that he would have to find the answer on his own.

10

KING LIAO'S NEW BURDEN

Shortly after King Liao dismissed Court, he summoned Kai-yü and Chu-yung. King Liao stood, his back to the door, staring out the window.

"Brother, you want to see us?" Kai-yü raced into the room. Chu-yung followed. "Good. I also want to talk to you. You must reconsider extending the canal all the way to the southern bay." Kai-yü demanded. "Kuang talked you into taking my land! Damn it! My land! Why did you agree to that?"

King Liao made no effort to turn around. Instead, he stood stiffly, his hands together behind his back. "Tell me you had nothing to do with trying to kill Kuang."

"Of course not, Brother," Kai-yü assured the King. He pulled a chair toward him.

"Don't bother to sit." King Liao barked.

"But Kuang behaves like he's King and not you." Kai-yü tried to focus Liao on his desires. "He didn't impose any special burden on himself, did he? You need to take control, Brother."

"You are not here to talk about the canal. That is done," Liao turned and cut his sunken eyes to Kai-yü. "You are here because I sense your hand in this assassination attempt. It was sloppy."

"You're obviously unhappy, Brother, but I assure you, I

126

did not arrange for anyone to kill Kuang. I would never do anything like that – and especially without discussing it first with you."

"Come here," Liao said with irritation.

Kai-yü walked over to the window, next to Liao.

"What do you see out there?"

Kai-yu surveyed the landscape and replied, "I see Kuang's mob, swarming about his compound, thick as summer mosquitoes. He must be scared, keeping so many men on guard."

"I see warriors. A lot of good, capable, motivated men, willing to put their lives on the line for one man. That man!" King Liao pointed toward Kuang's compound. "You know what I've heard?" King Liao didn't wait for an answer. "Kuang only asked for four squads, just twenty men. Look at them. They all came on their own, simply because he's in need. Are the peasants you call warriors willing to do that for you?" King Liao snapped.

Kai-yü remained silent.

Liao motioned for Chu-yung to approach. "What about you, Chu-yung? Are your peasants that loyal?" He poked the air, toward Kuang's compound, emphasizing his point.

Chu-yung said nothing.

"What about the noblemen who support me? Do you think they notice the significance of this? Yesterday's attempt, and failure, to kill Kuang has made him even more powerful." King Liao's jaw locked, seething with disdain for an internal problem he did not invite.

"It sounds like you wish the arrow had flown true, Brother," Kai-yü observed.

"Kuang is extremely useful against Chu. He's cunning, and his battlefield strategy and tactics are exceptional. But here at home, I now have this to worry about." King Liao waved toward Kuang's warriors. "Before yesterday, I didn't!" King Liao stared sharply at Kai-yü.

"Tell me, Brother, what would you think if the assassin had succeeded?" Kai-yü raised an eyebrow.

"The reverse of what I just said. I'd miss him in the fight against Chu, but here at home, I would not have to look over my shoulder."

"It sounds like you need your true friends to prove their battlefield skills. Then you would not need Kuang so much," Kai-yü offered.

Chu-yung chimed in, "It would be good to remind Kuang of our combined strength. It's not us who must enlist convicts to do our fighting. And it'll be good for the other nobles to see us succeed as well."

"You're a fool." King Liao turned to the window, then clasped his hands behind his back. His arms tightened, as one hand squeezed shut around the other. "Leave me."

Kai-yü bowed, unobserved by Liao, backed away, then left. Chu-yung followed.

Kuang is now an immediate threat. King Liao reasoned. *Will he try to take my throne?*

PART 3

THE STATE OF CHU'S DISCORD

11

PRIME MINISTER NANG WA'S VILLAINY

*I*n the Chu capital of Ying, built on the northern bank of the Yangtze River, over 1,700 *li* upstream from Wu (a distance that takes more than one month to travel), Prime Minister Nang Wa's angst grew. It was only a matter of time before news of the Chu army's defeat sent King Ping into a tirade, an eventuality postponed only by his heavenly duties as Intermediary to the Gods. The moon had changed almost two cycles since the battle, but Commander Wei Yue and the army had just recently returned to Ying, during the time when King Ping was preparing for the annual Sacrifice to the God of the Soil.

The King's mind had to remain clear of unpure thoughts, just as his body had to abstain from familial pleasures. That overarching need for purity, Nang Wa believed, would require King Ping to temper his screed until after the feast that followed the sacrifice earlier in the day. Nang Wa had enjoyed the delay, for it was he who was sure to receive the brunt of the King's harangue. But by the end of the evening, there would be nothing to keep King Ping from exacting punishment. And the loss of territory would fuel an outburst that was certain to be incendiary.

Nang Wa was a thinly boned man, who looked swallowed by his ornately fringed silk robe. His hair was thin, groomed to his shoulders in the Chu custom, and combed back, so that his receding hairline formed a point in the middle of his crown. When he bowed, the wedge aimed between his dark eyes that were fixed in narrow sockets. And the long strands of a mustache, which only developed on the corners of his lip, drooped below his chin, accentuating his lack of physical stature. There was nothing physically intimidating about him, but what he lacked in brawn, he made up for with cunning insight and dexterity in maneuvering through the political landscape. He needed that talent to survive the coming deluge.

King Ping's sacrificial duties, and this evening's feast, though, provided Nang Wa time to scheme. It also worked to his disadvantage by drawing attention away from more worrisome problems. He, as Prime Minister, carried a burden that encompassed more than any single military campaign, failed or successful, and the ongoing threat from the Northern Alliance was greater than any risk Wu posed. Ten States, all located north of the Huai River, made up the pact. They had formed it many years earlier for the sole purpose of convincing Chu to look elsewhere to satisfy its thirst for conquest. Their combined strength had worked, and even though the Northern Alliance and Chu were not now overtly hostile to one another, they were still enemies, under the surface of diplomatic exchanges. The State of Cheng, a coalition member, had sent its Emissary to pay diplomatic respect to King Ping, using the celebration's occasion as the official reason. But Nang Wa wanted to learn if there was a hidden motive for the visit, and the King's increased scrutiny of him was a distraction.

Nang Wa stepped into a corridor of the Palace, where Zuchan, Cheng's diplomat, awaited him. "Emissary Zuchan, my apologies for not meeting with you before now," he said, then exchanged bows with the envoy. "There was an unexpected matter that required my immediate attention."

"I understand. Think nothing of it. Your accommodations are splendid, and I've been well taken care of," Emissary Zuchan offered, acknowledging the attention he had received from the Palace Servants who accompanied him. Cheng's legate was a proper man, refined in speech and manner. His hair, pulled tightly into a top knot, accented a notable contrast between peoples of the two regions.

"Please, Emissary Zuchan, join me. The ceremony is about to start." Nang Wa waved his hand to the side, motioning toward a door at the end of the corridor.

"This is my first time in Ying since the new Palace was finished, and I must say, it is remarkable," Emissary Zuchan said with sincerity. "Truly impressive. You've created something special, Prime Minister."

"Thank you. King Ping finds it acceptable." The two men crossed the threshold into a courtyard. Servants hurried ahead to open the next set of doors.

"By now, the Hall of Feasts will be filled, except for the King and Grand Taishi. Because it's been some time since we had a chance to visit, I arranged for you to join me at my table. I trust that is acceptable to you." Nang Wa gestured the way.

"Quite so, Prime Minister. I very much enjoyed my last visit and of course, our conversation. We have much to catch up on."

Nang Wa stopped at an entrance to the rectangular Hall of Feasts. The ceiling spanned three stories, peaking at a joint in the center that ran the length of the room. King Ping's table was positioned at one end, forming the head of the arrangement. Rows of long tables filled the expansive room, separated down the middle by a walkway reaching ten paces. Chairs lined only one side of each table, facing the King, for no one dared insult him by turning his back. There were two fewer tables in the row to the left of the center walkway, creating a gap filled by musicians. Nang Wa's table was opposite from them, the closest to the King's, and two of Chu's most influential ministers were already seated there. The Chief Military Minister, General Po Chou-li, had spent the day with his grandson, Officer Po Pi, and Commander Wei Yue, going over the details of Chu's defeat. General Po, like Nang Wa, also felt uneasy about the coming torrent from King Ping. He sat at the end, nearest the outer aisle, and the Chief Civil Administrator was next to him. Behind Nang Wa's table were noblemen of Chu's various subservient states and spiritual advisors, followed by other Chu officials in descending rank.

Queen Ma and her attendants customarily occupied the first table, across the inner lane. Protocol required her front and center for everyone to see, and the table next to the musicians helped frame that focus. The Heir Apparent, the Queen and King Ping's first male born, usually sat behind her, but neither was there this night. Tables for the King's eleven other wives followed in successive order, joined by their children and attendants. The remaining tables were reserved for invited guests and visiting dignitaries of lesser importance.

Servants hurried about, tending to their assigned duties. One appeared from around an adjoining corridor holding a hand bell. "Prime Minister, King Ping has finished praying to his ancestors and has left the temple. We are ready to begin the ceremony," he said.

"Make the announcements," Nang Wa instructed.

The Servant entered the Hall of Feasts, and with a sweeping move of his arm, rang the bell. On the fourth ring, musicians pressed to their lips purple bamboo, end-blown flutes, sounding the signal for the crowd to rise. Nang Wa entered. Emissary Zuchan followed, and both walked to their assigned table. Nang Wa positioned himself in between Emissary Zuchan and the Chief Civil Administrator. He wanted the Emissary's attention for himself.

The crowd then turned toward tall, double doors, in the wall directly behind the King's table, and on the third strike of a gong, the doors opened. The Director of Ceremonies appeared first. He stepped to the side, then banged the end of his staff. The King's Grand Taishi, a slightly built, docile man stepped through the doorway. He wore a silk robe, adorned with stars sprinkled across a red and black background. Below the stars, a river meandered through a deep gorge before emptying into a broad lake. And from the lake, a dragon's head peeked out of the water, exhaling puffs of clouds that floated skyward. The Grand Taishi walked to the head table, stopping short of the chair to the right of center. Silence hung in the hall as everyone waited for the next knock of the staff.

After three more bangs, the Director of Ceremonies bellowed, "Our virtuous King, blessed by his ancestors and given the Mandate from Heaven, joins us for this splendid occasion."

King Ping appeared in the doorway, then waited for the next announcement.

"The King has arrived. Pay your humble respects." The Director of Ceremonies placed a jade tablet to his mouth, so as not to breathe a foul odor toward the King, then bowed, as King Ping crossed his path.

The King's blue winter robe, made of finely woven silk, draped over his body and flowed to the floor, hiding his fur-lined silken slippers. He was a wide man and waddled his frame to the table. The long robe trailed, waving with the wiggles of his movement. He walked with folded arms, which allowed only the head of an embroidered beastie creature to peek over his sleeve toward the ceremony guests. King Ping slowed to a stop, then drummed the handle of the ceremonial sword that was strapped to his waist, relishing his subjects' subservience. The King took a deep breath, making sure all eyes were on

him. Nang Wa had watched him do so many times, but when
the King spotted his favorite wife, Princess Mei, sitting at the
first table, he almost broke into an uncharacteristic smile.
Almost. King Ping nudged into his chair, then the Director of
Ceremonies' heavy rap of the staff drove everyone else to their
proper seats.

The musicians struck a tune, beginning the entertainment
for the evening's festivities. The music also signaled the servants to begin serving food and drink, and those tending to
King Ping did not allow the second chord to sound before
moving into service. They placed two large plates, one containing grilled fish and the other roasted chicken, at both ends
of the table. The tableware glistened a lacquered finish, and
each dish matched the food it carried. The first adorned a
detailed fish-scale design and the second was decorated with
beastie birds, bearing long, hooked beaks. Next came a large,
gold cauldron, resting on dragon legs. It held steaming rice,
which the servant then scooped into smaller bowls, also made
of gold, for the King to use. And off to the side, near both
ends of the table, servants waited to refill the King's goblet
with rice wine. They held tall pitchers, edged with patterns of
a phoenix feeding a snake to a creature having a dragon's head
and a tiger's body. And behind King Ping, out of sight, knelt
additional servants ready to satisfy his every desire.

Emissary Zuchan was slow to partake. He drank from
a goblet, then rotated it, studying the design. Inlaid on the
inside were figures carved into a scene of archers hunting deer.
He cocked his head toward carvings on the nearest column,
then the next one, absorbing the details. He marveled at the
furnishings, Nang Wa was certain. Emissary Zuchan then
fixed on the pole drum, played by a musician. It rested on
a green-copper base, cast in an interlacing hydra design that
balled into a mound.

Will he give Chu its due or assign credit for all this

magnificence elsewhere? Nang Wa wondered. An air of supe-riority was the way of Northern People. Nang Wa knew that. *He probably thinks it all came from Jin.*

Emissary Zuchan continued his gaze around the room. The structure was no less impressive. Tall columns held up the high ceiling that was ringed in gold. Gems and stones of various colors were inlaid inside the borders and arranged to resemble the celestial heavens. The spiking rays of a gold sun peeked over the horizon, toward one side of the hall, and a crescent moon tipped forward, spilling drops of rain, deco-rated the other. In between were stars of the Eastern Sky and a chariot, drawn by four steed dragons, carrying King Ping's likeness toward the Eastern God.

Nang Wa finished gnawing on the bone of a chicken, filling his cheeks full before throwing it over his shoulder. No sooner had the refuse hit the floor than a servant scurried to retrieve it, wiping the floor clean at the same time.

Emissary Zuchan pushed away the food, waving off a ser-vant who attempted to replenish the ware. He leaned back, stretched, then pulled the goblet close to him, holding it in both hands. He sat quietly, staring toward the musicians, un-consciously rotating the goblet in his hand.

He's bothered by something. No, he looks puzzled. But it probably has nothing to do with what I want from him, Nang Wa surmised.

Nang Wa looked forward to each of Emissary Zuchan's vis-its. It gave him an opportunity to learn more about the current political climate within the Northern Alliance, and a chance to test the latest rumors that filtered into Chu. The members' attitudes toward each other were only marginally warmer than their views of Chu. They struggled constantly against one another, either attempting to expand into or fight off the will of other States. And when the opportunity arose, Nang Wa was not against taking advantage of their internal strife. This night, the recent struggles between Emissary Zuchan's State of Cheng and its neighbor, Sung, sparked his curiosity.

"Emissary Zuchan, I heard you're having difficulties with Sung. You're wearing a troubled look tonight," Nang Wa observed. "If that's the reason for it, I hope you can put the worry aside, at least long enough to enjoy your stay here in Ying."

"Oh, I'm quite sure, Prime Minister. The Hua clan is rising in Sung and causing problems that sometimes spill over into Cheng. The stories you've heard were merely cross-border skirmishes, nothing more substantial. Sung aren't like the barbarians that you face," the Emissary responded, drawing an obvious parallel to Chu's recent loss of Chou-lai and Chi-fu and reminding Nang Wa that his attention should remain on Wu. "They respect protocol and proper battlefield decorum. It must be quite disturbing to face those who have no respect for convention, or for maintaining proper order. I mean, attacking when they did. It's unthinkable, not only on a day of such bad omen, but not even giving your men a chance to move into battle formation." Emissary Zuchan's subtle manner was cordial. It always was.

"Yes, well, since the Emperor lost Heaven's Mandate, all has not been well or according to convention, even within the Northern Alliance," Nang Wa asserted, doing damage control. "Just look at the constant struggles among your members."

"I didn't know the Emperor lost his Mandate," Emissary Zuchan fired back. "I just thought some among the Royalty have been too ambitious. The fact that the Northern Alliance exists is a result of that ambition from decades past."

The subtle jab was not lost on Nang Wa. "Chu expanded in the past because Heaven transferred the Mandate, Emissary Zuchan, not because of ambition."

"The Emperor will adamantly dispute that, I'm sure," Emissary Zuchan countered.

"Yes, well, he can ignore reality if he chooses, but if he were truthful, he would recognize that King Ping now possesses the

Mandate." Nang Wa tired of the direction the conversation had taken and changed the subject. "Tell me, is the Duke of Sung's power still intact? Sung's envoy has not been here for some time, so I don't have many details. I've heard that the House of Hua is the source of trouble for Sung."

"They've had their moments over the years, as I'm sure you know. This time, though, it appears the Duke has his work cut out for him. It'll be interesting to see if he can survive."

"It sounds like there may be an opportunity for Cheng?"

"I'm certain we'll make sure their conflict doesn't spill onto our soil, but my Duke is not opportunistic."

"Perhaps he isn't," Nang Wa replied, not believing the Emissary. He sipped from a goblet, then asked, "You haven't told me the reason for your solemn look? Is it the food that causes you distress?"

"No, no Prime Minister," Emissary Zuchan said with a placating smile. "The meal and drink were splendid."

"Is the air too damp?" Nang Wa submitted. "Our climate is a little different than yours."

Emissary Zuchan shook his head. "I feel fine. Really. I'm sorry I've given that impression, but nothing is amiss with me. You know, I can't get over the magnificence of this Palace. The furnishings are truly worthy of someone with the King's virtue, and the layout makes serving him and the Queen truly efficient. Every conceivable convenience is here." Emissary Zuchan's expression changed. It was the look of a nagging thought that had just appeared. He leaned closer to Nang Wa, so as not to be heard. "Prime Minister, I fear that I may have offended King Ping."

"I know of no such offense," Nang Wa assured him, surprised by Emissary Zuchan's concern. "How so?"

"The Queen is not at her table. Instead, Princess Mei is there. And her son sits behind her, not the King's Heir Apparent. I didn't realize something had happened to them and did not bring proper offerings of condolence."

"Oh, that," Nang Wa said calmly. "There's nothing to worry about. The Queen is in good health, but not necessarily in the King's good favor. That's something we don't talk about."

"Certainly, the King is a virtuous man, and I'm sure the matter is just." Although his voice held true to the words, the lines on the Emissary's brow showed disapproval of such an affront to protocol by excluding Queen Ma and the Heir Apparent.

He may think we're backward people, but he won't speak it, Nang Wa thought. Northern People viewed Chu as lesser, unsophisticated people, who behaved more like barbarians than dignified and virtuous men. Even the riches that Chu's success on the battlefield and its expansion over the century had brought, did not alter that opinion. In fact, the more opulent King Ping's effort, the more magnificent his possessions, and the more Chu attempted to emulate cultural life in the Northern Alliance, the more Chu failed to convince others of the status Nang Wa believed it deserved. Nang Wa was sure the Emissary's silent opinion was an example of that always present arrogance, and as a counter, Nang Wa never allowed a guest from the North to address him informally. But regardless of what characterization Chu deserved, its military prowess commanded respect. The Northern Alliance's very existence was proof of that, and Emissary Zuchan would not cross the boundaries of protocol.

"And Chien is also in good health?" Emissary Zuchan inquired.

"Yes, the Heir Apparent is fine, but I doubt he's in good spirits. King Ping banished him to Chengfu."

"Oh?"

"It's a soft banishment, though," Nang Wa explained. "He still enjoys his station in life, just not in Ying."

Nang Wa noticed the King's silent, stern summons, delivered merely with a sharp look. *He must be leaving. Why does he want my presence now?* Nang Wa could no longer avoid King Ping's mood, and an ill feeling returned to his gut. "Emissary Zuchan, I see that Princess Mei is joining King Ping." Nang Wa rose to his feet, "This evening is growing late, and because King Ping intends to hold Court in the morning, he will want my counsel before turning in, so I must excuse myself as well. Hopefully, we will have a chance to visit more tomorrow." Internally panicked, he gave no hint that his power was in jeopardy.

"Yes, thank you, Prime Minister. As always, you have been a most gracious host. I hope to visit with you tomorrow, too," the Emissary agreed.

⇢

In the hallway, leading to his Residential Palace, King Ping walked in front of Princess Mei, and without breaking stride, he motioned her to his side. She sauntered forward. Her quilted, black, silk robe flowed over her shoulders and tall, thin frame, down to her ankles. Underneath the robe, an undergarment clothed her legs and concealed her feet, which she shuffled in quick, short strides with balanced poise to keep pace.

Nang Wa followed, believing that King Ping's tirade was soon to come. It was unprecedented for the King to summon him on a walk intended to end at the King's bedchamber; such procession left for the wife he chose for the particular evening and his complement of servants and Palace Guards. Nang Wa was certain his presence could only mean something unpleasant for him. *Is it better to get it over tonight? Or tomorrow in front of a full Court?*

King Ping didn't talk, which made for a quiet walk because those in his entourage didn't speak either. The delights at the feast failed to assuage his mood, and no one, certainly not Nang Wa, risked drawing attention by breaking the silence. The hush remained heavy until they entered the Residential Palace and reached the hallway leading to King Ping's bed-chamber.

"You look out of spirit," King Ping slurred from too much rice wine. He turned to Princess Mei. "Why? Did the music and food not please you?"

"They were fine." The words floated from her lips with gentle ease. "It's nothing so important that you need be bothered," Princess Mei assured him.

"If you aren't happy, I will be bothered, especially if your mood does not change before the servants fold our robes." He flipped the back of his hand and staggered into the wall.

Princess Mei took his arm to steady his walk. She gave a gentle squeeze, inviting him. "That has never happened, has it my husband?"

Even when his mood is foul, he permits her to break protocol, Nang Wa observed. Royal conventions dictated that all address King Ping by his Heavenly appointed position of King. By referring to him with the familiarity of "husband", Princess Mei had broken from decorum. *She is bold, and he allows her that indiscretion, even in the presence of others. There are advantages to being the King's favorite wife.*

"No, I can't think of even a single time," King Ping acknowledged. "But still, whatever the problem, I can provide the solution. I do have some influence in this land, remember?" He laughed, breaking his sour mood.

Perhaps she can hold his attention the rest of the night? Nang Wa hoped.

Princess Mei tossed King Ping an inviting glance. She was less than half his age and stunningly beautiful. Her hair shone, like silk, spun by the High God's Weaver Girl. Her eyes danced, and her smile did more to lift his spirit than all the opulence in the Palace. Usually.

Palace Guards were stationed on either side of the door to the King's bed-chamber. Eunuch Kuo, who ran the Residential Palace, stood just beyond them in the center of the hallway, and a swarm of servants waited behind him, ready to satisfy the Royal whims. Once King Ping was within normal speaking distance, Eunuch Kuo lowered his head, bowed at the waist and raised a jade tablet to his mouth, all of which signaled the Guards and other servants to follow his lead.

Nang Wa felt relief sweep over him when King Ping turned toward the doorway without addressing him. A few more steps for the King and the night would be over without incident for Nang Wa. Only servants participated in preparing the Royals for the night. *He's saving his wrath for tomorrow. Only Princess Mei is on his mind now.*

King Ping stopped in the entryway and attempted to turn, but the doorway was too narrow and prevented his rounded paunch from rotating. His intake of drink, during the feast, didn't help. "You're not leaving now, Nang Wa," he shouted over his shoulder. "Come inside."

King Ping tottered to the foot of the bed and once Princess Mei reached her usual spot, directly opposite and facing him, the swarm of attendants and servants hurried to assume their stations, still in bent pose. Eunuch Kuo faced the bed, offset but between the King and Mei, within arm's reach of both and holding two wardrobe boxes, stacked one on top of the other.

He, like all other male servants who worked in the Residential Palace, underwent the cutting chair. Some in his family thought it good that his change in life came during childhood, others thought it cruel. To avoid temptations, each male, whose duties placed him in close proximity to the King's wives and daughters, was required to undergo castration. The practice eliminated all desire for him to receive tender pleasures, and ended his ability to deliver any that might be solicited from him. More importantly, under all circumstances, it prevented him from impregnating and tarnishing the royal bloodline.

The only female servants in the room, the First Chambermaid and the Second Chambermaid, scampered to their stations, behind Princess Mei, riddled with the nightly dilemma of waiting for orders and being as inconspicuous as possible in the interim. And on the other side of the room, aback of King Ping, was the First Attendant. Nang Wa remained near the door, out of the way, wanting the night to be over, while the Second Attendant scurried past him to place a pitcher of rice wine and a couple of goblets on the nightstand by the bed.

Once the Second Attendant assumed his usual place behind the First Attendant, King Ping commanded: "Begin."

Eunuch Kuo then nodded to Mei's servants.

What does he intend for me? Nang Wa wondered, looking over King Ping's shoulder to where his line of sight, when he dared to glimpse, drew directly on Princess Mei. Her eyes darted back and forth, uncertain, searching for something. It was an odd thing to see this reaction from her. Mei was known for an abundance of confidence, not the insecurity her hesitation indicated.

"My husband, I know your Heir Apparent's life does not include the pleasures of Ying. Chien has been without them for a long time," Princess Mei said sympathetically.

Nang Wa fixed on her elegance. Her robe folded across her body and high on the neck, preserving modesty. The quilted silk popped with a yellow-tuft fringe, and the sleeves were so long they covered beyond her reach, which completed the proper manner of dress that showed her skin only from the neck up.

"Why does that bother you?" King Ping stretched his arm to the side, almost touching Eunuch Kuo. The Second Attendant darted underneath, untied the belt, then removed the ceremonial sword."

"Do you think he resents me for it?" she whispered. Princess Mei raised her arms to the side, shoulder level.

Her two servants began their bustling work. In well-choreographed steps, repeated every night and reversed each morning, the Second Chambermaid maneuvered to Mei's front and unfastened the three buttons on the robe, at all times careful not to raise her head high enough to obstruct King Ping's view of his favorite wife. The First Chambermaid loosened the yellow, silk, rolled belt that wrapped high around the midriff. Once unbound, the robe fell open, partially baring Princess Mei to the cool night air. Chill bumps rippled across her body. She then lowered her arms, giving the First Chambermaid time to place the belt in the hands of the Second, then to prepare for the next task.

"He has his lands to administer. That's enough to occupy his time, and for pleasure, his concubines should be sufficient, if his wife isn't. Or, he can take a second wife – more if he prefers. So he may not spend his thoughts on the past." King Ping yawned, then continued, "But these days, I'm not sure what Chien is thinking. Why?"

The Second Attendant removed a silk belt, wrapped twice around King Ping, and when the robe freed from the tight stretch across the barreling paunch, it sprang loose, falling to a draping rest, down the sides of the King's rounded pot. The cold night air did not appear to have the same effect on King Ping as it had on Princess Mei.

The First Chambermaid took Mei's robe by the collar and gently raised it. And on that signal, Princess Mei pulled her arms back to allow the robe to effortlessly slide, first off her shoulders, then limbs.

"Well, he is your Heir Apparent," she emphasized. "What will happen once he takes the throne?"

The First Chambermaid handed the robe to the Second, who carefully folded it to avoid wrinkles, then placed it in the top wardrobe box Eunuch Kuo held open.

She knows how to maneuver King Ping and demonstrates her power over him in front of us, Nang Wa thought, impressed with her talent. He adjusted, so as not to be seen staring at Princess Mei, for his peep would surely bring additional attention from King Ping, a worry he did not need.

"He won't become King, until I'm gone. And even then, he's not certain to replace me," King Ping assured her. Surely, some will follow Chien, simply because I designated him my Heir Apparent, but ultimately, he will have to put together the strongest alliance. That has always been the way of our land, and it always will be. Why are you concerned about it?"

She's worried about her son's future, Nang Wa speculated. He slipped his hands inside the sleeves of his robe.

"I'm not concerned about me, my husband. My place will always be with you, even as you cross into the next life. And if it weren't, I would cut my ear in a vow of love and devotion to only you. But what will be our son's fate? Chen is so young, what will become of him?" she asked pleadingly. "Will Chien take out his resentment of me on him?"

"He will have to muster alliances himself, to survive. There are some things I can do to help, but it will be up to his wit." King Ping cocked his head and barked over his shoulder, "Nang Wa, do you know why you're here?"

"No, My King." The question jolted Nang Wa. His hands, hidden from sight, pinched the skin on his forearms, but outwardly, he did not reveal any concern. "Is there something particular about Court tomorrow you want to discuss?"

King Ping stepped out of his robe, and when the First Attendant reached to hand the wrap to the Second Attendant, King Ping snapped, "No, give it to Nang Wa." The order rolled off his tongue as easily as breathing. "Tend to my clothes, Nang Wa." For a long, awkward moment, the First Attendant froze. He dared not ignore the King, but handing a robe to the Prime Minister to fold was worse than breaking protocol, lethal if not managed delicately.

Nang Wa bowed, deeper than usual. The purpose wasn't

to show respect, demanded by the King, although it had that pretense. Rather, Nang Wa lowered his head to conceal the color that rushed across his face. *Now is not the time to reveal my true thoughts.* Everyone recognized the insult King Ping had just delivered. Nang Wa also understood the message it carried. *My power is tenuous.* But he could say nothing. He could only bury the dishonor. Had it come from any other source, Nang Wa could deliver a punishing response. But it hadn't. It came from the ultimate supremacy, the only authority that mattered. Such was the nature of power. He snatched the robe and gripped it tightly, struggling to show neither the anger nor humiliation that percolated inside him.

Nang Wa stared at the floor, unsure whether the weight of the silence or the focus of everyone's eyes was worse to bear. *What is next?*

Princess Mei broke the moment. "Our son is a long way away from wearing a Man's Cap. How will he survive?" she whispered. She ran her thumbs along the inside of her undergarment, beneath the belly button, then gently pulled the cloth away from her skin, inviting King Ping's attention. *She saved me,* Nang Wa relished the brief reprieve. King Ping was known for dispensing embarrassing moments. He enjoyed it, and once he started a harangue, it generally lasted until the King was satisfied.

The First Chambermaid reached across Mei and untied the underpants, which fell to a gathered jumble at Mei's ankles.

"Remember, I knelt before the Jade Disk at an even younger age than our boy is now. Although Heaven's Mandate passed to me then, I did not gain the throne immediately. My brother wrestled it away, even though he was put to the same test and knelt in the wrong place. Another thing he has in common with me is that I, too, was not born to my father's Queen. If our son chooses right, and kneels before the buried Disk, others will follow him no matter what his age or the fact that

Queen Ma is not his mother." King Ping watched Mei step out of the garb, then continued, "His struggle for power, though, will be difficult. Especially at first, because that's when he'll be most vulnerable. He must survive as I did," King Ping explained. "But eventually I took my rightful place, and so might he."

Princess Mei drew closer and placed her head against his shoulder. "Don't leave us, my husband, until he's thoroughly prepared." She released a long, sultry sigh.

Her skin felt warm. He pulled her closer. "I'm old, but I have no plans to go to the next life any time soon."

The Second Attendant knelt at the King's side, as did Mei's Second Chambermaid, but next to the bed, opposite from her counterpart. Both Seconds gently held the toe and heel of their masters' nearest silk slipper, mindful to not make physical contact with either body. Together, the King and Mei stepped one foot out of their slippers, then waited for the two aides to rotate left to assist with the other shoe.

King Ping's interest shifted. He grunted, "Everyone . . . leave."

Nang Wa was first into the hallway, and once across the threshold, his humiliation sank to the depth of roiling anger. He took several deep breaths, while the servants bailed out of the bedchamber. Eunuch Kuo, who was last to leave, closed the door. Nang Wa wadded the King's robe, then threw it, smacking the Second Attendant in the face. Nang Wa forced the stirring mix of emotions down into his gut. He fought to keep the volatility from erupting into a screech that would echo throughout the Palace. He let go another breath, then muffled the biting words, "If any of this night leaves that chamber . . ." he paused but only long enough to emphasize his words with an angry wag of a finger, then continued, "you'll lose your noses, and I'll give all of you to the pleasures of the nearest barbarians."

He didn't wait for a response and turned to leave. Nang Wa stepped not more than a couple of paces, then stopped. *Princess Mei could have drawn the King's attention back to her at any time, but her timing spared me. Why?* The question seized Nang Wa. *That was on purpose,* he thought, puzzled by Mei's decision. *What favor does she want from me?* And then another thought caught him – *a mother's protective nature. Princess Mei won't give King Ping any rest until she secures her son's future. How can I use this?"*

❧

The next morning, King Ping held Court. "The Cock announced morning too damn early," King Ping groaned, leaning back to finish a yawn. The room was a smaller version of the Hall of Feasts, absent the floating sky. The end, opposite from the main entrance, was raised by ten shallow steps, ensuring that King Ping would look down on all others at all times. He swayed, nestling into a comfortable slump on a grand throne, inlaid with gold and dotted with colored stones depicting the Eastern Sky. He took a steaming cup of tea from a Palace Servant, instructing, "Make sure this doesn't draw empty." King Ping tipped it to his lips, held the soothing brew in his mouth, then let the fluid flow gently down his throat. He closed his eyes for a moment, letting his brow relax from a throbbing pain left over from the previous night's feast.

"Yes, My King," the Palace Servant said. He scooted backwards, away from the King's ill temperament.

King Ping looked at Nang Wa. "Let's get started," he barked.

Nang Wa stood in his usual spot and nodded. He presided over all affairs of state, military and civil, and used the Court to influence matters in ways designed as much for his benefit as for King Ping's. Also in attendance were General Po, with Commnader Wei Yue at his side, along with the Chief Civil Administrator, and other lesser officials, who Nang Wa wanted present. They stood obediently waiting for the King's orders. Nang Wa began, "Before we address the first matter, Emissary Zuchan from Cheng would like to pay his respects to you."

"If Emissary Zuchan is first, then he *is* the first matter, isn't he Nang Wa?" King Ping said with annoyance.

"Yes, My King, thank you for correcting me." Nang Wa bowed lower than usual. "The Cock must have come early for me, too. Emissary Zuchan attended the festival last night and was most gracious in his praise."

"Make it quick. I want to get to this matter about Wu." King Ping flicked his hand. "I'm interested in your explanation, Nang Wa, and the more I wait for one, the more anxious I become."

Nang Wa turned to a servant, who was standing near the entrance, then motioned for the envoy to be escorted forward.

The Emissary entered the room, trained down the center aisle on a direct path toward King Ping. He stopped short of the King's platform, gave a short bow, and waited for Nang Wa to introduce him.

"Emissary Zuchan from Cheng, My King, brings respect and admiration from all of Cheng," Nang Wa announced.

"That's not all he brought," the King interrupted, pointing toward the two chests placed behind the Emissary. "Let's see just how much Cheng respects and admires me." The lacquered, wooden chests showed a dark glossy finish. Both displayed a phoenix design. Rows and columns of the bird, with wings outstretched and touching wingtips above, below, and to each side, decorated the lids. Each chest required two men to carry. Palace Servants, who, with jade tablets raised and eyes lowered, approached in succession, placed the chests at the King's feet, then removed the lids.

"King Ping, your kingdom is vast and beautiful. The gifts my State has to offer can in no way match what the artisans of Chu can create, but on behalf of the Duke of Cheng, I hope they will bring you pleasure." Emissary Zuchan gave no sign of his airy self-worth. He lowered his eyes to King Ping, which helped him conceal his true nature. Such was an envoy's role.

"Yes, yes. I'm sure they will." King Ping dismissed the comment with a backhanded wave. "I trust you enjoyed the festival last night?"

"I most certainly did," Emissary Zuchan continued the charade. "Your palace is magnificent. Even the Emperor doesn't possess such magnificence."

"I agree. He should witness my virtue firsthand, transfer the Nine Cauldrons to me, and recognize my Mandate from Heaven over all lands and all peoples, don't you think?" King Ping said pointedly.

"Your virtue is unmistakable, and my status is not worthy of engaging in such a discussion," Emissary Zuchan replied, continuing to observe the required obsequiousness.

The States within the Northern Alliance, although controlled by the nobility, still recognized the Emperor as the supreme power, even though the Emperor relied on the strength of the feudal lords for military backing. Countries outside the Alliance did not. Instead, they, like Chu, anointed a king, within their own lands, as their supreme ruler.

"Thank you, Emissary Zuchan. You've been gracious in your gestures," Nang Wa interrupted, attempting to manage both King Ping and the foreign dignitary.

The Emissary took the cue, bowed to King Ping, then exited before his grip on humility slipped.

King Ping ignored the envoy's departure. He handed his cup to the Palace Servant, dipped his hand into the first chest and sifted through the offerings. There were the usual tributes: embroidered silk, green-copper vessels and lacquered stag carvings. But it was the shape of an antler's tip, peeking out from underneath a silken cloth, that teased his curiosity. He tugged on it and pulled out an antlered bird. The curio was heavier than he expected. It had a long neck, on top of which a tuft accented the novelty's height. King Ping rotated the cast, examining the exquisite feathered details, and thought, *Mei will like this*. He held it out for the Palace Servant and ordered, "Take this to my chambers."

Nang Wa didn't wait for direction. "Next, King Ping, I have the grain inventories on the agenda."

"No, Nang Wa." King Ping pulled away from the chest, and leaned forward, his elbows on the knees. He continued curtly, "Dismiss everyone, except General Po and Commander Wei Yue. The rest of you, be ready in the morning to provide the details you intended to give today." He didn't wait for their departure. "Nang Wa, let me go over the role of Prime Minister, in case you've forgotten. You are the person who oversees all matters, civil and military, inside and outside of Chu. When things run smoothly, I stay out of your decisions. But when things are in disarray, you invite my daily input." King Ping sat back into his chair, then held his hand open for the Palace Servant to return his cup. "Now, let's go over what happened to us at Chi-fu. For years we planned and prepared to attack Wu, only to be surprised by them invading Chu. And even though we greatly outnumbered them, Wu routed us. *Your* military turned and ran back to Ying. Nang Wa, why should I not consider *your* military in disarray?"

Silence followed, while Nang Wa drew a breath. General Po stood stiffly, with eyes lowered, not wanting to be targeted. King Ping's bombast sent a chill down Commander Wei Yue's spine. He was slightly bent at the waist, keeping his head below General Po's even though he was the taller man.

"My King, there are two important reasons for this minor setback," Nang Wa said, hoping to downplay the defeat.

"Minor, Nang Wa? Minor?" King Ping slung the cup across the room, and with a violent wave of his arm, he bellowed,

"They took my land, damn it! My land! My . . . land!" Two Palace Servants hurried into motion. One replaced the King's drink, while the other wiped up the spilled mess from the floor. Both then darted out of sight before King Ping had reason to notice them.

Nang Wa lowered his head in deference. "First, General Yang Gai took fever along the way and died. That was most unfortunate."

"Did you have only one capable leader in the field, Nang Wa? You could have sent General Po, as well."

"No, My King. Commander Wei Yue assumed command. He was handpicked by General Yang Gai and has in the past proven to be a capable tactician." Nang Wa avoided King Ping's reference about General Po.

"If he's so damn capable, why did he lose?" King Ping spat.

"Certainly, he's not Yang Gai or General Po. But I think the second reason provides the proper insight."

Commander Wei Yue bristled at the verbal slap and fumed at not being allowed to defend himself, for he knew better than to speak before given the order.

"I don't want insight. I want the reason for your failure."

"Yes, My King. In the face of Wu's attack, Duke Chao turned and ran. Without Commander Wei Yue's order, he and his forces fled." Nang Wa let the King absorb the implication, then added, "The Dukes of T'ang and Sui saw Chao's forces pull away and followed. Again, without Commander Wei Yue ordering the retreat."

King Ping took a sip. His brow furrowed.

Nang Wa continued, "Retreating without orders was not the only problem. It led to a greater one."

"And what was that?"

"They retreated directly into Chu's main forces, preventing our regiments from entering the fray. Certainly, with our superior forces, we would have been victorious had our soldiers been able to engage the enemy, but the disobedient retreat prevented success."

"So, what are you telling me, Nang Wa?" King Ping scoffed. "Wu defeated us because three States ran?"

"Their retreat prevented us from deploying our greater numbers and best fighters. Commander Wei Yue was astute. He reacted quickly, saving our main force for another day."

King Ping turned to Commander Wei Yue and asked flippantly, "Is that true?

Commander Wei Yue dipped his head, then answered, "Yes, My King. I . . ."

"Shut up, Wei Yue," King Ping cut him off. He had no desire for Wei Yue, a lowly Commander, to actually respond. "You're a disgusting failure," he spewed. "Get out of here. Now!" He pointed toward Shen Pao, the unflappable Chief Guard who stood near the King's private entrance. "He will let you know if your head will still be on your shoulders the next time I see you."

Commander Wei Yue shuffled backward five steps, pivoted and scurried through the doors.

King Ping looked up at the ceiling. "Nang Wa, was it a mistake to send only one general into battle?"

Nang Wa dug deep and brought forth a great tone of capitulation. "Yes, My King," he said softly, barely above a whisper.

King Ping bit hard, then swallowed, and after exhaling a deep breath, he challenged Nang Wa. "Why did the States run?"

"I don't know. Whether it was cowardice or by design, I just don't know."

"By *design*?" the King said with emphasis. "You think such treachery exists within my kingdom? I'm not convinced, Nang Wa. Why would these Dukes risk their lands, their wealth, and their lives in order to side with lowly barbarians like Wu? Certainly they know what will happen to them."

"I'm not saying treachery was involved," Nang Wa back-pedaled. "But why did they retreat directly into our main force, making it impossible for our best soldiers to fight, instead of moving out of the way? That is the crucial question, and until we know their true motives, we should consider all possibilities."

King Ping's voice relaxed into a contemplative tone. "Nang Wa, the cost to mobilize our forces was high."

"Yes, it was."

"You understand the significance, don't you?"

"Yes, My King."

"Find out the truth, Nang Wa. I'm not convinced you understand what happened." King Ping leaned forward, then scowled at Nang Wa. "Duke Chao's behavior is damned curious, but I think Wei Yue's battlefield incompetence is the real reason. Whichever it is, get it right. The goal, remember, is to extend Chu all the way to the sea. I want Wu's fertile soil. I want Tin Hill and Metal Mount. I want their rivers." King Ping pounded his fist into the chair's arm with each demand. "That's what we spent years preparing for. Instead, we ran home in defeat and lost the Middle Huai in the process. Now our belly is exposed for Wu to strike."

King Ping paused to let his message sink in. "Unacceptable! Unacceptable!" He looked off, thinking, then continued, "But this notion of betrayal, this disloyalty . . . " King Ping's face tightened, straining to hold his anger, "is bothersome." He drummed his fingers. "Truly bothersome."

King Ping motioned to a servant. "Empty these chests. Let's see if those crickets from Cheng have tributed anything worth keeping. The rest of you, leave me."

The Court participants wasted no time scurrying out of sight, all relieved they each hadn't fielded the brunt of the King's bad mood. That is, all but Nang Wa. The junior officials didn't wait to see if he would then roll the King's wrath down the hierarchical line. Only General Po remained in Nang Wa's company.

They walked down the hallway, and when almost to his office, Nang Wa demanded, "General Po, send Commander Wei Yue to me, right away."

General Po nodded. "He's probably hovering near my office. I'm sure he'll seek my help in keeping his head."

Nang Wa turned into his office. A servant greeted him, "Is there anything you require, Prime Minister?"

"Yes, tell Fei Wu Chi that I want to see him, now."

"Yes, Prime Minister." The servant bowed, backed to the doorway, then exited Nang Wa's office.

Nang Wa sat behind his desk, gathering his thoughts. It wasn't long before Commander Wei Yue appeared at the door.

"General Po said that you wanted to see me, Prime Minister," Wei Yue said, sober to the reaming he expected.

"Sit down, Wei Yue." Nang Wa pointed to a chair across from him. "I want to talk about your failure at Chi-fu." Nang Wa matched his stern look with an equal tone.

"But Prime Minister, they didn't follow my orders," Wei Yue was quick to defend.

"Shut up and listen, Wei Yue." Nang Wa's narrow set eyes delivered an untrusting gaze. "We've gone over the details enough, and I want to be very clear." Nang Wa displayed no temperament for debate or discussion.

"Yes, sir."

"I saved your ass today. It would have been very easy to dump all the blame for this failure on your shoulders, Wei Yue, but I saved you." He poked his chest, underscoring the favor he had bestowed.

"And I thank you, Prime Minister," Wei Yue said, bowing his head.

"There are only two reasons that King Ping would notice someone of your rank – extraordinary accomplishment or extreme failure. He walked into Court, expecting to hear of a tremendous collapse in leadership. Yours, Wei Yue." Nang Wa wanted this experience to be unpleasant for Wei Yue.

It was. Wei Yue fidgeted in the seat, averting his eyes.

"Luckily for you, I maneuvered the King's attention away, but I can turn him back around. Do you understand that?"

"Yes, sir."

"Now," Nang Wa said with an icy stare. "I'm going to steer you through this, and if you're going to survive, you will do exactly what I tell you along the way. Do you understand?"

"Yes, sir."

"Now leave," Nang Wa ordered. *The beating was too short,* Nang Wa thought.

The look Wei Yue wore suggested that he felt otherwise. He tugged on his robe, bowed, then quickly left, brushing against another man, who stood silently outside.

Nang Wa noticed him. He let a moment pass, then called out, "Fei, get in here."

"Prime Minister, you sent for me?" Fei Wu Chi stopped in the doorway, not wanting to suffer any leftover tension. Fei was a low official who worked on the Chief Civil Administrator's staff. Soft features showed his aversion to direct confrontation, but a nose, which turned upward (his equals referred to it as a snout, when he wasn't present), hinted at a man who was unburdened by virtuous conventions, something Nang Wa had found useful in the past.

"Sit, Fei." Nang Wa expected Fei to be nervous. He intended for the minion to overhear his conversation with Wei Yue, just for that purpose. It was something Nang Wa enjoyed. "Have you been waiting out there long?"

"No, sir. I just arrived." Fei lied, afraid of the consequences for eavesdropping. "But I came as soon as I learned you wanted to see me. Can I help you with something?"

"Go to T'ang and Ts'ai and find out what the talk is about.

Make sure our spies are doing their jobs. Pay attention to what you hear in their markets, too. I want to know if anyone from the Northern Alliance has recently visited either State, and what the noblemen are up to."

"Certainly, Prime Minister. Is there something specific that you're looking for?"

"I want to know what is said about Wu and what the noblemen are planning, if anything." Nang Wa stared at Fei to strike an uncomfortable moment for the lackey, then directed, "Listen for anything that indicates the Northern Alliance's interference in Chu's affairs." He glanced away. *What is Emissary Zuchan's visit really about?*

Generations before, when Chu marched north across the Huai River conquering deep into the plains, it eventually annexed the State of Ts'ai, which borders the Northern Alliance State of Cheng. Nang Wa was always suspicious of Ts'ai's relationship with pact members because of that proximity. And the regional uncertainty Chu's defeat at Chi-fu brought now presented an opportunity for Chu's enemies to influence the Middle Huai.

"Is there anything else?"

"Yes. Don't waste time like you normally do. It's a long trip, so get started," Nang Wa snapped. "I want a quick answer. Now, get out of here."

Nang Wa didn't respond to Fei's bow. Fei was merely a tool in a plan, which was not yet developed. *King Ping wants an answer. What story can I weave? How can I gain?*

12

A PLAN BEGINS

*T*he moon had turned two cycles by the time Fei Wu Chi returned to Ying from his trip to Ts'ai and T'ang. He was immediately summoned by Nang Wa to the Administrative Palace.

"Tell me," Nang Wa said with barely concealed excitement. "You went to Ts'ai to find out what's going on with Duke Chao. What did you learn?"

"I spent a lot of time in the markets talking to the merchants and market officials. I also met with some of the local officials," Fei Wu Chi boasted.

"Get to the substance, Fei. Did you learn anything?"

Fei Wu Chi shrugged. "Nothing useful I'm afraid."

"Nothing?" Nang Wa shot him a skeptical glance.

"There was absolutely nothing. No travels down the Huai River or to the Northern Alliance."

"None?"

"None," Fei Wu Chi insisted. "Duke Chao didn't leave Ts'ai. His most recent travel was to Chi-fu and the battle. Even his brothers haven't left Ts'ai. He went hunting, but that didn't take him out of his territory."

"All right, so there's nothing direct. But people don't stay in power without maneuvering." Nang Wa snaked his hand through the air. "There must be something I can use to explain the Duke's behavior at Chi-fu. What was the talk of the battle?"

"All fingers pointed to Commander Wei Yue. Every person, who voiced an opinion, suggested that Wei Yue bungled the plan," Fei Wu Chi said with assurance.

"Did you talk to anyone who would know?" Nang Wa pressed for a different conclusion.

Fei Wu Chi nodded. "Quite a few of our spies – and they were from different stations in the city."

"The opinions were that united? No differing view?" Nang Wa prodded.

"No, none that I heard."

"Interesting." Nang Wa stroked one side of his mustache, beginning at the corner of his lip. "What was said about Duke Chao's retreat during the battle?"

"They think he acted wisely. He avoided the slaughter of their fathers, their sons and their brothers."

"Hmm . . ." Nang Wa twisted the thin strands of hair, until the tug on his lip awoke him to his contemplative habit.

"They truly believe that Wei Yue was inept," Fei Wu Chi asserted. "In fact, they question whether Chu can defend them, now that Wu has tasted victory."

"What!" Nang Wa scoffed. "That's ludicrous."

"They're so worried about it they all met when I was there."

"Who met?" Nang Wa sat up straighter.

"Duke Chao invited the Duke of T'ang. Apparently, there is much concern in the area over protecting against invasion through the Gap. By the way, Chien and Yuan were also there."

Nang Wa leaned forward, disbelieving what he had just heard. "Chien, the Heir Apparent, was there?"

"Yes, sir. Of course, I didn't make my presence known to him," Fei Wu Chi assured Nang Wa. "You know our history."

Nang Wa ran his fingers along the curve of his receding

hairline, from the point. "I know it well, and his hatred for you probably hasn't changed." Nang Wa paused to consider the news. A servant stepped forward to fill a cup that sat on Nang Wa's table, then held the pot toward Fei and offered him a refreshment as well.

"Yes, bring Fei a cup," Nang Wa ordered. "He's going to be here awhile." He stroked his moustache, reminiscing. *I planned for years to remove Prince Chien from my path to power. The first step required convincing King Ping that his son was a threat. But the King only banished Chien. Now there is an opportunity to persuade King Ping to finish the task. But like last time, he must believe he reached that conclusion on his own, and I'll use Fei to do it. He's expendable.*

Nang Wa mentally prepared for the opportunity to finish what he had started years earlier; to rid himself of a political enemy and solidify his power.

The day for Nang Wa ended only after he had considered every angle and rechecked them. He started the next day prepping Fei, and once satisfied with the details, he ventured to King Ping with Fei in tow.

"Now, remember, Fei, stick to what we discussed." Nang Wa stood in a back chamber of King Ping's Residential Palace, waiting for the King's arrival. Fei remained behind him.

King Ping opened the door, then waddled across the threshold. His scowl foretold his usual demeanor. "Nang Wa, I'm busy. What's so important that you had to interrupt me?"

Nang Wa disguised his excitement. "My King, something has come to my attention. Important news you should have immediately."

"Get on with it." King Ping flicked his hand.

"You charged me with determining what happened at Chi-fu, and I have information that suggests a scheme among the Dukes of Ts'ai and T'ang."

"Oh?" The King raised an eyebrow.

"Fei Wu Chi has just returned from Ts'ai." Nang Wa motioned to his minion. "Come forward and tell our King what you have learned."

"My King," Fei lowered his head, careful not to make eye contact, "Duke Chao has pledged Ts'ai's forces in an alliance that runs counter to Chu, and the Duke of T'ang has joined him. I went to Ts'ai to ascertain the negative impact on grain and silk yields that the loss of territory would have on us this year. While I was there, I also confirmed why the production numbers from Ts'ai dropped off so much this past year."

"You're just now getting to this past year's problem?" King Ping snapped.

Fei cringed, then quickly recovered. "It became obvious that the answer was connected to what I learned about their scheme."

"Fei, it takes you forever to get to the point," King Ping rebuked, shifting his robe over his rounded belly. "What makes you think they have designs against me?"

"They met while I was there."

"And what's wrong with that?" King Ping asked, tiring of Fei.

"It's that they met to discuss combining their efforts and forces to gain strength in the Upper Huai."

"How do you know that?" King Ping demanded.

"It was openly discussed in the markets. That's where I first learned of it."

"You mean only the fact the meeting took place was openly discussed," King Ping corrected Fei.

"Not just that." Fei shook his head. "The purpose was talked about as well."

"Really? Defying me was openly discussed in the market place?" King Ping challenged.

"Well, not in those terms, King Ping."

"What terms then, Fei?"

"They believe that if they don't support Chu, it can't defend its territories, which provides them with an opportunity."

"You think those two states, even combined, can defeat Chu?"

"No, not at all, and I don't think they do either."

"That doesn't make sense, Fei, which is not unusual for you," King Ping said, displeased. "If not autonomy, then why do this?"

Fei showed no reaction to the rebuff. "I don't know that, My King. I only know that the meeting took place and that they discussed combining their forces."

"Perhaps they gathered because of Wu," King Ping suggested. "Wu is a greater threat to them now."

Nang Wa had also grown impatient with Fei's inability to get to the point. "My King, if I may add, the proper protocol was not followed. If they were concerned about Wu, they would have sent for help with their fortifications. They would have sought assistance from Ying, perhaps requesting additional troop strength. Or at least they would have asked that someone from Ying attend to contribute in some way. After all, Chu's combined resources are considerable, and yet, they did none of that. It at least begs the question, *why?*"

"It's curious. I grant you that," King Ping replied, pondering the matter.

"Go on, Fei. Tell the King all of it," Nang Wa commanded.

Fei avoided the King's piercing look. "My King, I learned of additional stores of grain hidden from us. They hid the grain and failed to submit their levy. There were enough piculs to get them through a protracted siege or replenish crops that are destroyed in the field."

"That doesn't mean anything except they cheated on their allotment, and you're supposed to police that. I see now that you've failed," King Ping growled.

"Get to it, Fei," Nang Wa admonished. His narrow eyes turned a harsh look at Fei.

"Also in attendance, uh, were Yuan and your Heir Apparent." Fei's head moved slightly, as if to duck.

"What, Fei? Are you saying that Chien, too, is conspiring against me?" King Ping raged. "My son!"

That's the reaction I wanted! Nang Wa rejoiced silently.

"No, My King," Fei replied. "I don't mean to imply sinister motives, especially given the Heir Apparent's continued resentment over being sent to Chengfu and the sensitivities involved with him. I'm simply reporting the facts."

"Sensitivities?" King Ping's eyes went wide. "You mean my decision to take Princess Mei for my wife, don't you?"

"Yes, My King."

"It's been, what, nine years? Refresh my memory, Fei. Wasn't it you, while serving Chien as Junior Mentor, who went to Jin to select a wife for him?" King Ping said snidely.

"Yes."

"Wasn't it you who selected Princess Mei for Chien?"

Fei nodded. "Yes."

"Wasn't it you who brought her beauty to my attention?"

Fei started to answer but was cut off.

King Ping blurted, "Wasn't it you who suggested that I take her for myself?"

"Yes, My King."

"Wasn't it you who whispered day and night about Chien's displeasure with my decision?"

Fei didn't voice a reply; just gave a nod of his head.

"Then I must not be the only one Chien resents."

"That's why I'm sensitive not to raise improper inferences regarding the Heir Apparent," Fei offered.

King Ping threw down his hands. "I've heard enough, Nang Wa. Dispatch Shen Pao to bring Sheh here. I want to hear what Chien's Grand Mentor has to say about this."

"Yes, My King," Nang Wa said nonchalantly. But secretly he worried his grand scheme might backfire.

King Ping turned to the servant who stood quietly behind him and commanded, "Tell the Director of Lands to plan a hunt. I want to kill something."

Good. His temper has a new direction. Nang Wa enjoyed a moment's relief.

Fei followed Nang Wa into the corridor, and once out of earshot of the King, he quipped, "That went well, don't you think?"

"What was this nonsense about hoarding grain?" Nang Wa fired sharply. "You haven't been at this as long as I have, nor are you better at it. Defy me again, and you'll become a gate keeper in the far reaches of western Chu. Is that clear?"

"Yes, Prime Minister. I was just trying to be helpful." Fei understood the message. Isolation as a gate keeper in a remote area was a fate far worse than what Chien endured in Chengfu, and an experience a soft-bodied person like Fei would not suffer well. He shuttered at the thought of losing his snout to the punishing mutilation that would accompany such a sentence.

"It was unsophisticated," Nang Wa railed. "You risked credibility on a fact that can be disproved."

"But Prime Minister, that won't happen. There are abandoned storage pits in Ts'ai that I can have filled if the need arises," Fei offered, hoping to placate the Prime Minister.

"You may think you can maneuver through it before your credibility suffers, but it wasn't helpful. In the future, do as I say, or your station in life will abruptly change." Nang Wa glared at Fei. "Understand?"

"Yes, Prime Minister."

"Leave me." Nang Wa dismissed him with a contemptuous wave. "I need to prepare the King's summons of Sheh." *And I must carefully choose the words I want the King to issue.*

13

A DRIBBLE OF MISERY

*I*n the Northwestern outskirts of Chu, far from the capital city of Ying, was the desolate outpost of Chengfu. It was a place of deep sadness for Yuan, and the remoteness underscored his sorrow. He sat alone, his elbows leaning on a table in Chien's compound, waiting for the Heir Apparent and others to join him. He stared into the sun-dried brick wall, his distant gaze lost in the pitted crevices time had worn.

"Brother . . ." Shang strolled into the room, taking the seat across from Yuan. "Why are you so sullen? I leave tomorrow to arrange your marriage. You should be happy."

The table rocked on the uneven floor as Yuan pulled away, settling back into the chair. "I am pleased, about that," he answered, although the memory of his late wife tugged when he thought of marrying again.

"Then what's wrong?"

"I visited with Ga's family this morning. His death at Chi-fu still hits them hard."

"Again? You are a virtuous man, Brother, to take on that burden. Lesser men would simply move on with their lives."

Yuan looked at Shang, acknowledging the compliment, then said, "The days aren't getting any easier for them. His

166

brother's crippled leg keeps him from working the fields, like Ga did. The father's body is worn out, and the two sisters are trying to make up the difference."

"It's very sad," Shang concurred. "You don't blame yourself, do you?"

"No. I do recognize, though, that much has gone wrong surrounding our family, and people continue to suffer for it. We aren't the blame, but I must do something to help them, at least."

"Yes, we should. But remember, all is not bad in our lives." Shang offered a wide smile to enliven Yuan's mood. "The Shinyin family has been pleasant to deal with, and you will take a wife soon."

"Yes, Shang," Chien interrupted. He entered the room, followed by Yuan's father, Sheh. "That is good news. I'm happy for you, Yuan, although I wish we were all back in Ying, about to enjoy this moment with you." He sat next to Shang, and Sheh took the seat on the opposite side, beside Yuan.

For Chien, banishment to Chengfu meant isolation from his rightful place, as Heir Apparent to the Chu throne, and a life without the comfort and pleasure that Ying had to offer. Chien did not fully understand the reasons for his banishment. Although the official story was punishment, everyone grasped that more was involved. Chien was there because those who thirst for power wanted him out of the way, which also meant that those who served and protected Chien, like the others in the room, were sent to Chengfu with him, equally marginalized.

Sheh was a stately man, a demeanor expected of the Heir Apparent's Grand Mentor, and he was Chien's most important advisor. The lines on his face and the streaks of grey, running through his thin hair, revealed a man of wisdom. Yuan's older brother, Shang, was Junior Mentor. Both were important to Chien and were like family to him.

Yuan did not serve on Chien's staff, but was Commander of Chengfu when he wasn't called to the Chu army. Since his return from the battle, Yuan replayed the events that had led to Chu's defeat. He went into the battle fully expecting to restore his family's honor and change his future's course, which made the thrashing hard to take, especially without ever getting into the fight. Ga's death made it worse.

Fen Yang whisked into the room, carrying a folded silken cloth, which he gestured toward Yuan. "Here are the drawings for the city's new gate," he offered, then sat down next to Yuan.

"Thanks," Yuan said, taking the plans. He spread the cloth on the table for everyone to see the details, then ran his hand across it, smoothing out the crimps. "Fen Yang and I have worked on an idea about fortifying the city's gate." He tapped his finger on the sketch. "This is the current structure. It has only a single opening."

Others around the table hunched forward to gain a better view. Chien planted his elbows on the table, clasped his hands, then laid his chin on his knuckles.

Yuan slid the top layer off, exposing another design. Fen Yang grabbed the first illustration, then folded it along the creases and set it to the side. Yuan pointed to the second diagram and said, "We'll create a double gate structure, so that no force can enter this city without going through a contorted squeeze. The idea is to add an outer loop to the wall, starting here." Yuan tapped his finger where two lines met. "The new wall will curve around the current gate and attach over here." He moved his finger down the existing wall, past the main gate to the point where the current and new walls met.

"Yuan, the gate in the new outer wall is small compared to what we have now. Why?" Chien asked.

"It's narrow so that the enemy can't overwhelm the opening with numbers."

Fen Yang leaned forward and knifed his hand on the drawing, connecting the two gates. "Since they don't line up, the area in between will cause congestion and help keep our main gate from being overrun." He circled the inner space, punctuating his thought by rapping his knuckle into the center.

"Sound reasoning," Sheh said, offering his studied view. "This is well thought out. When will you start construction?"

"We are making bricks now," Yuan answered. "And once we have enough to keep ahead of the work, we will prepare the ground." Yuan looked at his brother and Chien. "Any questions?"

Both shook their heads.

Yuan folded the cloth. "Let me tell you about the trip Chien and I took to Ts'ai." He settled into the bench and propped his forearm on the table. "You know that Duke Chao invited Chien and the Duke of T'ang to hunt with him. I accompanied Chien and had a chance to visit with the Dukes about the battle and the threat of Wu."

"Good," Sheh said, anxious to hear about their perspectives. He tilted his head and gave it a little shake. "But first, go back to the battle. I'm struggling to understand something. Did Wei Yue start with a sound strategy?"

"Other than retreat?" Chien chortled.

The events were still too fresh and the result too grave for Yuan to find any humor in Chien's banter. He shook his head, then answered, "I don't think so. Wei Yue was content to only hold the line, engaging in a battle of attrition. Duke Chao saw that. And he watched Kuang completely outsmart Wei Yue." Yuan's jaw tightened, angry at the mere thought of Wei Yue bungling the opportunity. "Chao had no faith in Wei Yue's leadership going into the battle and what he witnessed only confirmed his belief. He was not going to allow his men to be decimated like Hu, Shu and Chen. He turned Ts'ai from battle, T'ang followed, then Wei Yue sounded the general retreat."

Yuan turned to Fen Yang, and said, "You know I agree with Duke Chao's assessment, but how do you remember it?"

Fen Yang slid his fingers underneath the tunic's collar, along the scar, and hung his arm. "The same. Wei Yue didn't even order Officer Po Pi's column, which was along the river, forward to fill the gap immediately after the three States chased Wu's retreat. He waited."

"That Kuang must be clever," Chien had to agree.

Yuan thought for a moment, remembering the details. "Wei Yue completely underestimated Kuang, then froze."

"I wouldn't want to be Wei Yue right now," Chien snorted. "Can you imagine what Nang Wa has in store for him? He's the first Field Marshal to have lost Chu territory, at least in memory. Someone has to take the blame, because you know Nang Wa won't."

Sheh asked, "How did Chao react toward Wei Yue after the battle?"

Yuan shrugged. "I had no opportunity to talk to them until our recent visit. After the retreat, they didn't regroup with the rest of us. Duke Chao headed directly to Ts'ai. He was not going to be convinced to re-engage the fight until someone more capable than Wei Yue led the effort." He shook his head and turned to Chien. "Your uncle spoke freely with us."

Chien jostled, bounced on his seat and nodded. Duke Chao was Queen Ma's brother, and Chien had grown close to him since the banishment. Chao often provided the Queen reports of Chien's life. They were welcomed communiques, albeit furtive, so as not to raise King Ping's ire.

Yuan glanced at a crevice in the wall. "But Duke Chao sees greater difficulty for himself in the future," he spouted.

"How so?" Sheh asked, sensing a grave danger he had not realized existed.

Yuan leaned onto the table, contemplating the answer. "Duke Chao welcomed us to discuss how best to defend the

Upper Huai River against Wu, but he is also worried that Wu's victory at Chi-fu signals a weakness within Chu, something the Northern Alliance will try to exploit. He doesn't know how that will happen but fears once it does, Ts'ai will become a battlefield wasteland in a fight over the plains within Chu that lie north of the Huai River. The Duke of T'ang shared the same concern."

Fen Yang mused, "How will King Ping reassert the power of Chu?"

Silence followed. Chien fidgeted, restless with pent-up energy. "Yuan, Father needs all of us back in Ying, not out here. He has the wrong people advising him." He turned to Sheh and lamented, "Grand Mentor, will we ever get back to Ying? It's been years since Father sent me here, not once allowing me back into the Palace. I still don't understand it. What exactly did I do to deserve this?"

He and Yuan were about the same age, but they were very different. To Yuan, Chien wasn't comfortable in his own skin, often dwelling on what he could not control, rather than taking charge of the circumstances he could. Yuan liked Chien, for he was an amiable man and fair, unlike many among Royalty. But he was a bit naïve and too trusting for a man of his position. That would have to change if Chien were to ever overcome the designs against him and succeed to the Chu throne.

Sheh also considered Chien's reminiscing to be a futile exercise, demonstrating an inability to allow his circumstances to ignite him into action. He corrected Chien, "We've been over this many times. You did nothing. You were used by others in a scheme to advance their own positions." Sheh's manner was always stately.

"But, Father must see that by now." Chien shook his head in bewilderment. "Surely he recognizes the truth. Why does he keep me here, where life is so austere? We've been here for so long, I don't know that we'll ever return. At least not until he dies, and I succeed him."

"Don't focus on the past, Chien," Sheh counseled. "Rather, concentrate on today and tomorrow. Look for opportunities to improve your situation. The truth about those who plotted against you, and manipulated your father for their own benefit, won't be enough to change your fortunes."

"Why? They're only administrators. At least most of them are."

Sheh nodded. "True, Fei Wu Chi is just a minor official. He's easily replaced, but Nang Wa has far more influence."

"But I'm Father's blood," Chien countered. "And what about Princess Mei? Would revealing her motives sway things my way?"

"You know that's a losing cause. Never underestimate a man's thirst for tender pleasures," Sheh said astutely. "Even if you demonstrate the truth, what does your father gain from it?"

Chien wiped his hand across his mouth. "He has eleven other wives, and even more concubines to satisfy his desires, so what hold could she possibly have over him?"

Sheh shook his head. "Even though a man may have numerous women tending to his wants, one will be his favorite, and for whatever reason, Princess Mei is King Ping's. Get used to it, because given her youth, she'll probably maintain that status until his death."

"She is beautiful, isn't she?" Chien put his chin on his hand and propped his elbow on the table. "Silky hair, skin so smooth, it's as though she has never seen a harsh winter. And she's pleasantly curvy, too, not squatty. For her to be in such good grace with Father, she must be quite skilled in giving pleasure." He shook his head. "Damn! She should have been mine."

"Chien!" Sheh admonished.

"I know. I know. To be king, I must first act like one. I

must be stately," Chien responded before Sheh had the opportunity to make the point.

"Which means that you must not talk of that, especially in public." Sheh sternly corrected. "Besides, if that kind of talk gets back to King Ping, you will have justified his decision to send you here. And may give him reason to . . ." Footsteps near the doorway interrupted his thought.

"Excuse me," Shen Pao blurted. He stepped into the room, wearing an expression as stiff as his rigid personality. "A House Servant told me I could find you here, Sheh."

"Come in." Sheh gestured, puzzled by the Chief Guard's presence. "What brings you to Chengfu?"

"King Ping wants to see you." Shen Pao delivered the message in the same manner he would order a meal at a chophouse. His demeanor never swayed. He handed to Sheh a roll of bamboo slats, then bowed.

Sheh read the message aloud: "Sheh, I request your immediate appearance. Shen Pao will provide safe passage for you from Chengfu to Ying." The roll contained King Ping's seal.

Of course, Sheh knew it wasn't just an invitation. It was an order, but the details were innocuous, devoid of any ominous implication.

Chien bounced to his feet, turned to Sheh and said excitedly, "Maybe this is what we've been waiting for."

"My men are waiting outside for us," Shen Pao prompted. "You should gather the things you will need for the trip now, so that we can leave today."

Yuan arose. "I'll go with you, Father."

"So will I," Shang piped up.

"No," Sheh shook his head firmly. "Yuan, you are Chengfu's Commander, and you must oversee the construction of the town's double gate." He turned to Shang. "And you're scheduled to meet with the Shinyin family as Yuan's

Intermediary. Arranging Yuan's marriage is too important to postpone."

"Lan and I will go with you," Fen Yang offered. "We'll make sure your trip home is safe."

"That works," Sheh agreed.

Shang waved his hand. "And I'll be back from my trip by the time you return. We will all have much to talk about then."

Yuan nodded.

Chien nudged Shang. "Maybe then you'll be able to tell Yuan that his future wife's looks are worthy. And let's hope Father doesn't fancy her for himself before the wheel rolls the third turn." They laughed.

Yuan was not amused and ignored the implications, but what Chien had said earlier about blame for the loss at Chi-fu triggered a thought. *Father will learn exactly how King Ping reacted to Chu's defeat and what he intends to do.*

14

THE TEMPEST GROWS

*T*he storm Nang Wa created was not known beyond the Palace halls and certainly not in Chengfu, when Shen Pao delivered King Ping's order to Sheh that one breezy afternoon. Of course, the King's summons was made innocently curious by its lack of detail, which was Nang Wa's design. He hadn't wanted Sheh to suspect any hostility.

Sheh had left with the Shen Pao the next day, accompanied by Fen Yang and Lan. But upon arrival in Ying, he was hustled immediately to Court, where King Ping awaited him. Sheh stood front and center, near the base of the King's platform, with Fen Yang slightly behind him and to the side. Lan chose to gather provisions at the market for the journey home, deciding that neither his duty nor desire required his presence at Court.

Sheh presented a calm, Grand Mentor's resolve. He did not have the anxiety of someone who expected the King's wrath. Nang Wa stood at his usual perch, with Fei behind him. A full Court filled the room. King Ping preferred a large audience when demonstrating his sovereignty.

Queen Ma was also in attendance. Her presence was unusual, and she stood near a side entrance, out of the way. King Ping wanted her there, to toy with her. He knew she would crave a chance to learn of Chien's spirit and status, and Sheh presented such an opportunity. Perhaps she would ask Sheh to return a message. King Ping wanted her to see that pleasure within her reach, only for him to snatch it from her.

"Sheh," King Ping began in a voice heavy with breath, "I sent for you because I want an explanation. Do you know what troubles me?"

"The subject, My King, remains a mystery," Sheh said evenly with a short bow. "Certainly, I'm always happy to serve."

"I appointed you Chien's Grand Mentor to school him in the ways and knowledge needed of a future king."

"I am honored to serve the Heir Apparent."

"As Grand Mentor, I expect you to teach him how to administer the lands and people."

"It is my great honor." Sheh gestured to himself.

"Tell me, Sheh, does Chien have drive?"

"Yes, My King. He has drive but not ambition."

"No ambition?"

"No, My King, none," Sheh replied, wondering where this was going.

"Why then does he plot and scheme to circumvent my interests?" King Ping sneered.

"He does not," Sheh answered, surprised by the question. He looked toward Nang Wa, seeking a reason for it, but got no response or reaction.

"I'm told that Chien met with Duke Chao recently," King Ping said accusingly. "Is that true?"

"Yes. The Duke of Ts'ai invited him. The whole region is concerned about the threat of Wu."

"Do they question my ability to protect *my* territories?" King Ping scowled.

Sheh was now acutely aware someone was poisoning the King's mind . . . but who? "No, My King. It's purely inward looking. A question of what can be done locally to defend the lands and people."

"If they are so worried about security, why wasn't someone from Ying invited? Nang Wa would have sent an emissary to address your concerns."

"Chien merely received an invitation," Sheh assured him, now knowing who the orchestrator was. "He did not organize the meeting, and I don't know why Duke Chao omitted Ying, if he so failed?"

"Are you suggesting that I'm making this up?" King Ping raised his voice.

"I'm just saying that I don't know if the Duke invited Ying, and I'm not willing to trust some who advised you." Sheh turned his head toward Nang Wa.

"My King, I protest this insolence toward you," Nang Wa jumped in.

Sheh addressed the King, "My observation is not directed toward you. I simply don't know what Nang Wa is spinning. Perhaps he will enlighten me." He raised his eyes to meet Nang Wa's charge.

"Silence!" King Ping barked. "Are you aware that they met to join forces against Chu?"

"No, My King, no!" Sheh said forcefully. "There is no such alliance. Who is the source of these lies? Let me confront him directly."

"Very well." King Ping motioned for Fei to step forward. "Tell Sheh what you learned on your trip to Ts'ai."

"Yes, My King." Fei walked around Nang Wa, and began. "I was in the markets of Ts'ai recently. The talk was loud and frequent about the meeting, where they discussed an alliance of forces . . ."

"And may I emphasize," Nang Wa interrupted, "that indeed no one in Ying was invited."

"You fear Chien's future power, don't you Fei?" Sheh

looked accusingly from one to the other. "You too, Nang Wa. Once Chien becomes king, you know that you'll pay for your past conniving. That's why you've concocted this nonsense, isn't it Fei? And Nang Wa, your mark is all over this. Fei has only the brain of a carp and is not capable of concocting such a scheme himself."

"Enough!" King Ping snapped. "Is that the real reason for this, Sheh? Chien becoming king? Does he think he can overthrow me?"

"No, My King!" Sheh raised his voice for emphasis. "There is no scheme. And there is no evidence of a conspiracy. I merely referred to the inevitable future, the same future you drew when you named him your Heir Apparent."

"No evidence, Sheh?" King Ping scoffed. "Why is it that all of Ts'ai understands the nature of the meeting, but you, the man charged with guiding Chien, didn't know?"

Sheh now clearly understood the machinations. "The only words Fei heard were from Nang Wa."

"I heard it all over the market place," Fei protested.

"Chien doesn't have it within him," Sheh objected. "The only scheme that exists was created within the minds of lesser men." He shot an accusatory glance at Nang Wa. "Men who attempt to divert your attention away from their own failures and their own ambition."

"Sheh, you've always been loyal to me and to Chien, but how do you explain the purpose of the meeting?" King Ping took a long breath to calm his temper and ponder the quandary before him. Sheh was convinced that there was no plot against him. Nang Wa was equally convinced the other way.

"It was simply a meeting to discuss the threat of Wu," Sheh's tone turned to a plea.

"Yet Ying received no invitation. You weren't there either, were you? So how would you actually know what took place?" King Ping challenged.

Sheh threw up his hands. "Chien simply doesn't have it within him, My King."

King Ping paused, then drummed his fingers on the chair. "Does Chien resent me for his current life in Chengfu?"

"He doesn't understand why you believe the word of minor officials over his. He has never betrayed you and has always remained a devoted son and loyal subject, My King."

King Ping deliberated for a moment, then looked at Fen Yang and asked, "Who are you?"

"I am Fen Yang, My King," he replied, bowing.

"You look uncomfortable," King Ping observed. "Why are you here?"

At the outset, the discussion had turned remarkably different than the subject Fen Yang and Sheh had expected. The muscles around Fen Yang's lips tightened, and the lump in his throat bobbled when he swallowed hard. "My King, I accompanied Sheh to provide safe escort."

"That doesn't explain the pained look on your face. What do you have to add?"

Fen Yang played dumb. "I have no information to participate in this discussion."

"Oh, you don't?" King Ping eyed him suspiciously. "Well, I'm sure Shen Pao has an opinion." He motioned for his Chief Guard to step forward. "Shen Pao, does Chien resent me?"

"Yes, My King," Shen Pao spoke boldly. "Prime Minister Nang Wa sent me to Chengfu with your order to bring Sheh to Court. When I walked into the room where Sheh and Chien were meeting with Sheh's sons and Fen Yang, I heard only the end of their conversation. I don't know what was said in its entirety, but Chien said that Princess Mei should have been his wife." Shen Pao appeared uncaring to the affect his words would have, and the fact that their importance would be exaggerated was of no concern.

Fen Yang tilted forward, just short of taking a step, anxious to speak. He didn't let a moment pass before interjecting, "My King, it is true that I was present, and Shen Pao didn't hear the full conversation. Chien was merely . . ."

King Ping slammed his fist onto the arm of his chair, stopping the explanation. "Shen Pao heard enough, Fen Yang. Chien's words spoke clearly of his mind." He rose from the chair. "Is that the sign of a loyal son, Sheh?" He didn't wait for an answer, but turned to Fen Yang and asked, "Who is Chengfu's Commander?"

"Yuan," Fen Yang answered with a grimace.

"Is that his son?" King Ping fixed on Sheh.

Fen Yang shifted his weight from one leg to another. "Yes, My King."

Sheh sunk. It was over. King Ping had a reason to believe that his own flesh and blood would betray him. It was that same belief that had convinced King Ping to send Chien away from Ying in the first place, and it drove his decision now. Of course, as King, he needed no justification for any decision. But having one allowed him to retain the self-image of a virtuous man.

King Ping shouted to Queen Ma. "Get over here." He pointed to the step even to Nang Wa's perch, but on the opposite side of the platform. "Sit there, on the floor."

Queen Ma shuffled to the spot. She was a proud Ts'ai woman, proper in all respects. She kept her head lowered, agonizing over what was next to come, then sat on the step, under the gaze of all eyes in the Court. She clutched her silken robe near her heart and buried her head.

The angst she wore pleased King Ping, and he returned his attention to Fen Yang. "Yuan is no longer Chengfu's Commander. You are now, Fen Yang. You will go to Chengfu and execute Chien. Shen Pao will accompany you, and if you refuse to carry out my order . . ." the King said through gritted teeth, "he will remove *your* head." King Ping looked at Queen Ma.

She tried to hide her emotions, diverting them by tightening her grip. Silence in the room made the moment stand still for her, except for the scream building within. Tears percolated from the corners of her eyes, then rolled down her cheeks. She slumped, leaning on the next higher step.

King Ping waited for the sound of her first sob. And then it came, almost like a whimpering cough at first. King Ping turned to Fen Yang. "Return here once it is done. Bring me his head as proof."

He leererd at Queen Ma. Her reeling was an emotional ride he had started years before. He remembered how she had reacted to the news of Chien's banishment. She had remained silent, seeking instead the use of others to convince him to change his mind. Those pleas were easy to dismiss, but rejecting them was not satisfying. King Ping wanted to reject her. He wanted to see her misery. He wanted to be the cause of even more.

He started her on that journey when he took Princess Mei as another wife. Before then, he was merely uncaring and indifferent to Queen Ma. Now she stood in the way of elevating Princess Mei to Queen.

It was the Queen's role to assist him in his celestial duties, and he hated that his beloved Mei wasn't there beside him. Queen Ma was, and he punished her for it. Although he had substituted Princess Mei for her in the formal role during festivals and palace ceremonies, he could not so easily replace the Queen in exercising Sacrificial Rites. To do so would greatly displease the ancestors and gods, something that would disrupt the natural world. And it was his ability to please the Heavens that kept all things in balance and his Mandate from Heaven intact. Crops grew sufficiently to feed the people, men and women followed their proper roles, and his empire remained strong. Upsetting the natural order would cause crops to fail and his subjects to deviate, all of which would leave

Chu vulnerable. Chaos would follow, and King Ping would not let that happen. That gave Queen Ma some power over him, albeit tenuous, and he hated her for it.

When he had directed his temper and wrath toward Chien, he enjoyed the effect it'd had on her. Now that the stakes for Chien were extreme, Queen Ma could not use surrogates to plead her desires. She would have to do it herself. King Ping enjoyed the feeling her submission gave him, and he didn't try to hide it. *Let her misery build.*

She lifted her head and rubbed her eyes. They welted red. Queen Ma drew a breath, then another, and said, "My husband . . ."

"You will address me formally, woman," King Ping scolded.

"Yes, My King." She wiped the tears, then straightened her back. "I feel I've done something to deserve your scorn, but I don't know what it is. When you stopped seeking my company at night, I did not complain. When you replaced me at Palace functions with a wife of a lesser tier, I said nothing. When you banished Chien from Ying, denying me the pleasure of my son's company, I remained silent. But now that you have ordered his death, I must plead on his behalf."

"There is nothing to be said." King Ping dismissed her, waving a backhand. She had plugged the leak of her emotions, but he wanted more.

"I have endured humiliation from you; I have borne the isolation you imposed on me, but please, please My King, don't make me suffer the death of my son, our son!"

King Ping tottered to her, hovering in guiltless pleasure. "What kind of son is he? He has plotted against me. Would a true son do that to his father?"

"It is not so," she pleaded. "He has done nothing against you."

"Why then has he gone behind me to form alliances?

It's because he still resents me for Princess Mei, and that resentment has turned to hatred. His venom is now joined by ambition."

Queen Ma shook her head. "I've heard the allegations, and at worst all he has done is make his life in Chengfu a little more secure. There's no threat to you. There's no plot against you. I'm from Ts'ai, remember? Duke Chao is my brother. All of my brothers are in Ts'ai. Once you rejected Chien, is it not reasonable that he would seek solace and support from my family?"

"A little more secure? You're naïve or blind." King Ping basked in her pain. "The combination of those forces when joined by the Northern Alliance or Wu could cause me to lose all of the Huai. I won't let that happen. I'm lucky to have learned of their secret plans in time to prevent this devastation."

Queen Ma cried out again, "My King, please. Please don't do this. Who has the most to gain from Chien's death? Have you asked yourself that question?"

Her tears invigorated him. "I didn't expect you to react any other way. That's why you are here now. I wanted to be present when you learned your son will be dead soon."

"*Our* son, My King." She clasped her hands and buried her face in them.

"He is the result of a wasted night with you," King Ping spat. "That's all."

Queen Ma spasmed a breath, then mustered a thinly veiled threat. "I'm sure that Chien's death will affect my ability to prepare the Sacrificial Meals. It's good that the Sacrifice to the Devine Intermediary is over, and the next Rite is a ways off. I need time to somehow overcome the burden you have placed on me."

King Ping wobbled back to his throne, then said, "If you want to join Chien in his Mound, I'll grant him a burial befitting of my son. Perhaps you can do a better job of guiding him in the next life than his Grand Mentor did in this one."

"Killing Chien will take away the only pleasure I have. Will that please you? Do my tears energize you? Why do you do this to me?" Queen Ma sprawled on the floor.

"Seeing you helpless to my power pleases me," he answered. He had punished her. He had humiliated her. He had broken her spirit. She would accept his offer to join Chien in the next life. He was certain of it. *I can elevate Princess Mei to Queen without offending the Heavens and disrupting the balance.* "Send a servant to Nang Wa in the morning with your answer. We need not speak to each other again."

King Ping turned to Fen Yang. "If she chooses to join Chien in the next life, execute him, leaving his body intact. But if she doesn't, cut off his head and bring it alone back. See Nang Wa tomorrow. He will let you know Ma's choice and the manner in which I want Chien returned to Ying." He turned to Sheh and said, "I will wait to decide your fate until after you have thought about your failure in mentoring Chien. Take him away." King Ping left the Court, pausing momentarily next to Queen Ma, revelling in her misery.

Palace guards surrounded Sheh. He cut a sharp look at Nang Wa, who avoided eye contact but showed the hint of a smile. Sheh said, "Whatever your plan is, Nang Wa, it's working. But for how long?"

15

FEN YANG'S BURDEN

*I*n Chengfu, Yuan lay asleep in his bedroom caught in the fuzzy world between sleep and awake, suffering his usual haunt. The baby would not birth. That's how the nightmare always began. His wife's screams of agony, replacing panting breaths, followed. Her back arched, as pains of the failed childbirth spiked through her body. Her face tightened with the convulsion. Every muscle did, from head to toe, but the wrinkles on her brow showed more than her anguish. They revealed fear.

Yuan knelt beside her, not knowing what to do for his wife and unborn child. Nothing he did eased her suffering. Yuan had lost track of how many days and nights had passed since her water had broken. *Was it two or three? Was it more?* Whatever the answer, it had been too long. That is what her worry had shown.

She lay unbundled on a pallet of furry hides. Her silken robe, soiled and tattered from the journey from Ying, parted at the middle, exposing her pregnant belly. The delicate lace had torn from the fringe and was entangled with her fingers. She flicked her wrist to free her hand, then tugged at the furry cape that gathered at her hip and covered the rest of her from the waist down. Yuan pulled the cape over her shoulders. The cold wind kicked up sparks from the fire that crackled in a small pit next to her. He looked into the night sky, in the direction of the wind, and saw not a single star. The arid, northern Chu was no place for his wife, especially while pregnant. In the dim glow of the fire's light, Yuan watched another spasm lift her again off the pallet. The bedding offered little comfort from the hard ground, and the fire did little to protect her against the bone-chilling freeze that filled the night air. But those discomforts were minor compared to the fatal agony of laboring with a baby who would not be born.

Each convulsion sapped her reservoir of strength, and the last one had taken just about all she had left. Once the spasm ended, her body rested listlessly. Her long, silky hair, disheveled compared to the finely combed mane she was accustomed to, matted over her flushed, swollen cheeks. Beads of feverish sweat that belied the plunging temperature rolled off her forehead. She laid her head on the bedding and moaned. Yuan moved to wipe her brow, but as he stretched for her, she shouted his name in a panicked gasp, threw off the furry cape, rolled to her side, cradling her pregnant belly in the crook of one arm and extended the other to grab his hand. She cried for him to help, and at the moment his fingers wrapped around hers, a gust of wind swirled around him. Yuan squinted and blinked as dust blew into his eyes, then he heard a voice that was out of place, one not part of the usual haunt, calling his name.

"Yuan?" a man whispered.

The image of his wife faded into a funnel of dirt that drifted skyward. Just as quickly as his wife's image disappeared into the breeze, so, too, did the nightly image of a man standing over him appear. He knew the voice. It belonged to Lan.

"Yuan, you must wake up," Lan insisted.

Yuan had gone to sleep, unaware of his father's plight or King Ping's order for Fen Yang to execute Chien. No one in

Chengfu knew of those plans. Yuan rubbed his eyes, his vision still blurred. The room was too dark to see, even when alert.

"Yuan," Lan repeated. "I'm sorry to wake you this way, but I couldn't risk other people knowing I'm here. King Ping has ordered Chien's execution. You must come with me."

"What?" Yuan saw Lan standing over him, his bow was strung, but no arrow was nocked. Yuan sat up and swung his feet off the bed. "What is this?" He raised his voice, not believing what he had heard.

"Please lower your voice. No one must know I'm here. We don't have much time because the sun will be up soon. Come with me. I'll explain on the way." He turned for the door, prompting Yuan to hurry.

"Where are Fen Yang and Father?" Yuan asked with grave concern.

Lan froze. He had been so worried about not waking anyone, except Yuan, and with helping Chien, that he forgot the obvious question. He tucked his eyes, searching for words. "I'm sorry Yuan, Sheh is in prison. King Ping ordered it."

Yuan recoiled. "Why?"

"Something happened during King Ping's Court. It's terrible. Nang Wa is behind it."

Yuan didn't like surprises. He was adept at thinking on his feet, but he preferred a planned approach to things, and this news took him out of that comfort. He dressed, secured his short sword to his belt and followed Lan.

Lan gave a cryptic sketch of what took place in Ying and King Ping's orders to Fen Yang that resulted. They stopped at the back gate to Yuan's home and looked around to confirm they were alone, then proceeded to Chien's compound.

Yuan held his scabbard to silence the clanging noise. At that hour, no one was out to notice, except for the guards stationed at the front of the building. For a King's son, it wasn't much of a home, resembling more of a lesser official's residence in

Ying. The guards were relaxed, unaware of any concern. Yuan and Lan proceeded down the street, hugging the edge. They walked a wide arc to Chien's place, then approached from the kitchen's side entrance. The structure was separate from the main building but joined in the back by an enclosed courtyard. The outer wall of the compound was made of sun-dried brick, plastered over with a mud and straw mixture. Weathering over time had caused the wall to pit, forming convenient footholds. They stopped to make sure no one was watching. Yuan placed one foot in a pitted hold, then pulled himself up and over, landing softly next to the kitchen. Lan plopped down beside him. Yuan led the way into the main building, careful to plant each foot to not make noise that would rouse the staff. They paused at an intersecting hallway. To the right was the first of a series of inner apartments, occupied by Chien's wife and two concubines. Chien's bedchamber was to the left. Moonlight filtered through a window at the end of the hall, illuminating their way, at least well enough so they didn't bump into each other. Yuan slid his hand down the wall, just to make sure the shadows didn't deceive him.

The sounds of snoring reverberated through the halls. Usually, an obnoxious chorus, but this night, it confirmed that they had remained undetected. They reached Chien's door, and Yuan pushed, but before it opened wide enough for him to enter, it creaked. He waited for the snoring inside to continue, then timed the squeaks with Chien's nasally respire. The room was black, so dark that Yuan could barely make out where the windows were located, but Chien's nighttime bellowing gave his location away.

Lan maneuvered around Yuan, hugging the wall until he reached the first window. He opened a shutter. The clap of wood jolted Chien awake. He sat up, startled by the dark figures of two men hovering over him.

Yuan leapt to the bed, covered Chien's mouth, then forced

him back to prone. "Forgive me, Chien. It's Yuan and Lan. You must not call out because your life is in danger."

In the same sleepy puzzlement to which Yuan had awakened, Chien nodded. Yuan relaxed his grip.

"What is this?" Chien protested. "Why are you here?"

Yuan backed away. "I know that this is a surprise, but it's important that you not draw anyone's attention," Yuan cautioned. "We've come to warn you."

Chien rubbed his face, trying to wipe away his drowsiness. "Warn me? About what?"

Yuan jumped to the crux. "King Ping has ordered your execution and sent Fen Yang to carry it out."

"What?" Chien shook his head in disbelief. "This can't be! It doesn't make sense."

"It is true, Chien." Yuan said with certainty. "Fen Yang will be here soon after sunup. You must leave Chengfu now."

"Why? What's this all about? Father would never order my death."

Lan checked for sounds on the street, then turned to Chien and answered, "Apparently, he believes that you and Duke Chao are conspiring against him. But we don't have time to sort it out now. I don't want to take part in your execution, Prince Chien, but if you are here when Fen Yang arrives, there is nothing that can be done. Please, you must leave now."

"Leave? Where will I go?" Chien stepped toward a table, lit a lantern and turned to gather his clothing.

"For now, the tree line north of town will provide the best cover," Yuan reasoned. "I will bring your wife and son to you in a couple of days." Yuan turned to Lan, but stopped short of speaking his thought.

Lan knew Yuan's mind and volunteered, "I'll go with him."

Yuan looked at him searchingly. "Are you sure? You know what this means, don't you?"

Lan nodded. "I thought about this during the entire trip

from Ying. My decision to warn Chien sealed my fate. I will be blamed. Fen Yang will be under suspicion. But you and Shang won't be implicated."

Chien put on his robe and tightened the silk sash to hold it in place. "Surely Father will see his mistake and change his mind."

"No," Lan insisted. "You must not expect that he will. He gave the order fully cognizant of what he was doing, and he sent Shen Pao along to make sure Fen Yang carries it out. If Fen Yang refuses, Shen Pao must execute him." Lan swallowed, repulsed by the circumstances, then said with absolute assurance, "You will die if you stay in Chu."

"Lan is right, Chien," Yuan agreed. "You have to leave."

"And go where?"

Yuan thought for a moment. "First, we must get you out of Chengfu and safe; then we can decide where you should go. I'll have a plan for you when we meet up in a couple of days. But let's get you out of here. Now. We came in through the kitchen courtyard. We'll head for the North Wall that way." Yuan addressed Lan. "Do you see anyone on the street?" He wanted no one else to know who was involved in helping Chien escape King Ping's order.

Lan glanced through the shutter. "No. It's clear."

"It should be. Everyone is asleep." Chien's attempt at sarcasm fell short of humor, and no one in the room laughed, for they were still grasping the latest turn life had taken. He finished dressing, took a lantern from the table and left the bedroom.

Yuan was relieved that Chien had decided to spend the night alone. Having to manage both him and a wife or concubine would have been too difficult.

They turned the first corner expecting the lantern to shine on an empty hallway. Instead, a House Servant appeared, startled by their presence. "I heard voices, Prince Chien. Is something wrong?"

"No," Chien replied, equally surprised.

"Is there something you need?" The House Servant looked to see who stood behind Chien, but the darkness revealed only the outline of two men.

"No, you may return to your quarters. I can't sleep and a walk may help." Chien shrugged, unable to think of a better reason to be up at such late hour. It didn't matter. The servant obeyed, as was expected.

The trio stopped at the kitchen to gather supplies to last Chien for a couple of days, then went on, not speaking until they reached the outer wall. The silence gave Yuan time to think. It was obvious that Chien struggled to believe it all. He had trouble grasping it as well. *Is it true? Am I doing the right thing? Is running the only way?*

"Chien, I know you're taking my advice on faith. We just don't know many of the details," Yuan whispered. "But there is no harm to leaving, even if the order to execute you turns out to be false. The same is not true if you stay, and Fen Yang arrives prepared to carry out that order."

Chien nodded.

They stopped at the wall, away from the North Gate. "Cross over here," Yuan said. "The guards won't see you. The sun will be up in a couple of hours, and you need to be out of sight by then. Once you make it over the wall, don't stop until you're safely away from Chengfu." He placed a hand on Lan's shoulder. "You won't be able to return, my friend."

Lan nodded.

"Let me hold your bow while you climb the wall." They looked at one another, both understanding the change their lives had just taken. Lan scaled the wall, then paused once on top. Yuan handed him the bow. "I'll see you in two days. Be safe!"

The soldiers who guarded the gates looked outward away from town. They didn't police inside the perimeter walls. That made the trek to the wall and the climb over it easy, but once they were on the outside, Chien and Lan were exposed to the numerous eyes trained over the open areas, looking for movement.

From the wall to the nearest cluster of trees, they had to traverse more than a short sprint could take them. "Wait for the moon to disappear behind clouds," Lan whispered to Chien. Once a wave of darkness reached them, Lan motioned, then dashed into the nighttime shadows. Chien stayed close behind. The moon reappeared, and Lan stopped Chien. They stooped down to the ground, waiting for the next opportunity. They worked toward the cluster of trees, ducking here and there, and once in the thicket, they were out of possible sight.

⤞

Yuan walked back to his home. He wanted details, but they would have to wait for Fen Yang's arrival. The possibilities were too numerous, and his thoughts drifted to the greater implications. *King Ping wants Chien dead. Lan is now doomed as well. What about Chien's House Servant? He saw us. And if he does not remain silent and details of the Heir Apparent's escape gets back to King Ping, I'll be executed.* Yuan entered the house, closed the door behind him and stopped dead in his tracks, contemplating his doom. *The servant must understand before Fen Yang arrives that no one is safe, not even a witness who talks. I must emphasize that his life is at stake, too.* He walked to his office, took a seat at his desk, then leaned back, stretching his legs out in front of him, and stared at the ceiling. Chien was safe, at least for the moment. *But what about Father?* And now he too was ensnared in whatever was going on.

After sunup, Yuan had a frank talk with the House Servant, setting the appropriate expectations, he believed, then walked to the Main Gate, pretending to inspect the construction of the outer wall. But he was really there to catch an early glimpse of the number of soldiers from Ying that accompanied Fen

Yang. Yuan spotted a low dust cloud hovering in the distance. *Probably a platoon,* he surmised.

Fen Yang and Shen Pao arrived early in the afternoon. Both men were on the same chariot, leading the show of the platoon's force. Shen Pao maneuvered the horses around stacks of sun-dried bricks to be used for the new wall, then entered through the Main Gate and didn't stop until they reached Chien's compound.

Fen Yang dismounted first. He alone carried the burden of having to execute Chien, and his walk through the compound's courtyard to the front door was difficult. Each step seemed heavier and slower. Shen Pao trailed closely, and two squads of five soldiers each followed behind him. Fen Yang raised his knuckles to rap on the door, then paused. *Did Lan arrive in time? Is Chien still inside? I don't want to do this!* He knocked hard, then waited for what seemed to be an unusually long time. A House Servant finally opened the door. Fen Yang noticed his furrowed brow and wondered, *Does the expression on my face look as disturbed as his?*

The House Servant bowed and said somberly, "Fen Yang, welcome back to Chengfu. How can I help you?"

Fen Yang exhaled heavily. "Chief Guard Shen Pao and I must see Chien. Immediately."

"I'm sorry, Chien is not here," the House Servant announced, still in a bow.

"Where is he?" Fen Yang strained not to show his relief.

The House Servant shook his head worryingly. "No one knows."

"That doesn't make sense," Fen Yang said in feigned protest.

"I'm afraid it's true," the House Servant insisted. "But Yuan and Shang are inside talking with members of the staff. Maybe they have more information. Do you want to join them?"

Shen Pao bumped Fen Yang to the side, then spun the House Servant around by the arm. "Take us to them. Now!"

Yuan and Shang were in a small anteroom. Four House Servants huddled with them. Shang was animated and flustered. Yuan hadn't told him about the events of last night and his concern was genuine.

"Fen Yang, you're back. Good," Shang said, expecting a friendly response. "Chief Guard Shen Pao, this is a surprise to see you, but perhaps you can help."

"Shang, you and Yuan need to listen to me," Fen Yang said, avoiding all pleasantries as he stepped into the room. He tugged on his tunic's collar, cupping his fingers underneath. His voice turned doleful when he said, "King Ping has ordered me to execute Chien and return with his body." Nang Wa had told him the day he departed Ying that Chien was to be given a Royal Burial. Queen Ma had ceded to King Ping's wishes. She had abandoned all hope for her son and, for herself, the desire to live. She had chosen to sacrifice herself to ensure Chien's body would be returned whole.

"What?" Shang shouted. "I don't believe this!"

Fen Yang raised his hand to halt Shang. "There's more. King Ping put your father in prison."

"Why?" Shang blurted incredulously.

Shen Pao stepped even with Fen Yang and interrupted, "Enough about Sheh. I want to know where Prince Chien is."

Yuan glanced at the House Servant, who was now standing opposite him, and shot him a quick warning look. *I hope he doesn't crack under pressure.* He turned back to Shen Pao and, to focus the Chief Guard's attention on him, said evenly, "We don't know."

Shen Pao scratched his cheek, not sure what to make of Chien's absence. "How long has he been missing?" he asked.

Yuan answered without emotion, "Prince Chien retired for the night as usual, but this morning when the House Staff awoke, he was gone."

The House Servant nodded. "That's right. I was the first into Prince Chien's room, but he wasn't there."

Shen Pao demanded, "Where have you looked?"

"Everywhere in the compound," the House Servant attested. "We were thorough."

"What about the rest of Chengfu?"

"No, Shen Pao, Shang and I just learned he was gone shortly before you arrived," Yuan piped in to minimize the House Servant's opportunity to let the truth slip.

Shen Pao turned to a squad leader, standing nearby, and instructed, "Divide the platoon. Search the civil buildings, the market, houses, everywhere. Probe the whole town, then report back to me. Go now!" This was a circumstance he had not considered on the way to Chengfu. He poked Fen Yang on the chest and grumbled, "This is not good for us!" He cocked an eye and emphasized, "You or me!" He started to leave the room, but stopped in the doorway and turned back to the others. "I'm going to talk to the guards who stood watch last night. All of you stay inside this compound. Do not interfere."

They watched Shen Pao disappear around the corner. Silence hung over the room until he was well outside. Yuan addressed the House Servant, "I think it's best the staff return to their usual duties." He wanted to talk with Fen Yang and Shang but away from others who could listen to the details. The servants bowed and left. Yuan turned to Fen Yang, anticipating his question. "Chien is out of the town." He was careful not to better define Chien's location. "Lan is with him."

"Good," Fen Yang replied, then tugged at the collar of his tunic. "We must get him out of the country."

"Wait, what?" Shang spoke up, surprised the other two knew something he didn't. "You know where he is?"

"No, I don't," Yuan told Shang. "I just know that he is not in Chengfu."

"How do you know this?"

Yuan cautioned his brother. "There will be time after Shen Pao leaves, but we must be silent until then." He turned to Fen Yang to brainstorm. "Yes. Chien must leave Chu. He can seek help from his uncles in Ts'ai."

Fen Yang nodded. "But Ts'ai can't protect him from Chu long term. His uncles will only be able to supply his journey. They won't want to risk the King's ire."

"Then it has to be somewhere in the Northern Alliance," Yuan said decisively. "Hopefully, one of the States will give him sanctuary and keep his presence there a secret. I expect King Ping will put a hefty bounty on his head."

"Yes," Fen Yang agreed. "And there are too many people who will abandon scruples for the right reward." Cheng was the Northern Alliance member closest in proximity. The southern tip of that country bordered Ts'ai, making it an obvious choice. "I learned in Ying that Cheng's Emissary Zuchan had been there recently. I'm worried about his relationship with Nang Wa."

Yuan nodded. "I understand. He may not want to offend King Ping by helping Chien. What about Sung? It's the next closest choice among the Northern Alliance." But they knew that to reach Sung required a longer journey across Chu territory, traveling to Ts'ai, then through Chu's subservient State, Chen.

"I also heard of trouble in Sung. The Hua family is stirring," Fen Yang recalled. "I don't think there's a revolt yet, but one could break out." He tilted his head curiously, then mused, "Chen lost its Duke at Chi-fu. Do you think Chen people will take out their anger on Chien? Crossing that State to get to Sung could be treacherous."

"No," Yuan shook his head, "not from what I learned while in Ts'ai. They're more likely to let Chien pass, benignly poking at King Ping. The relationship of Cheng's Emissary with Nang Wa is a greater risk, so let's choose Sung. Chien should go there first. If it's not hospitable, he should take the safest path out," Yuan concluded. All nodded agreement.

Yuan tapped Fen Yang on the shoulder. "Now tell us what happened."

"Yes, and what about Father?" Shang interrupted, unable to wait any longer. Chien was safe for the time being, but Sheh was not, and that was what worried him most.

"I fear I'm partly responsible for all of this," Fen Yang said in a solemn voice. "Their fate remains in the balance because of me." Fen Yang tucked his head.

"Give us details," Yuan said, keeping his tone neutral.

"We were at Court. King Ping grilled Sheh about Chien striking an alliance with Duke Chao. King Ping claimed that there is a pact against him."

"Where did he hear that?" Yuan asked.

"Fei Wu Chi said he heard it while you and Chien were in Ts'ai."

Yuan rolled his eyes. He knew there was more at play. "But why do you think this is your fault?"

"Do you remember the day Shen Pao arrived for Sheh?" Yuan nodded.

"He walked into the room just as Chien said Princess Mei should be his wife. He repeated that to King Ping. I protested that Shen Pao didn't hear the full conversation and didn't know the context, but King Ping was already angry and wouldn't allow an explanation. He removed you as Commander of Chengfu and named me instead, then ordered me to execute Chien. And if I refuse, Shen Pao is supposed to kill me. The only way I saw out of this was for Chien not to be here when we arrived, so Lan and I decided he would sneak away last night and get Chien out of Chengfu. Shen Pao knows that Lan wasn't in camp this morning and will connect him to Chien's disappearance. But he doesn't know my involvement."

"And he won't learn of it," Yuan assured him.

Fen Yang held his head in disgust. "At the end of Court, Palace Guards took Sheh to prison. Sheh's power comes from being Grand Mentor. And he is a risk to people only if Chien remains capable of vying for the throne. If I had carried out the King's order, Sheh, alive, would no longer be a threat. King Ping might let him go." Fen Yang rubbed his brow and said regretfully, "I'm sorry. I just couldn't go through with killing Chien."

"You're not at fault," Yuan put a soothing hand on Fen Yang's shoulder. "I'm sure Nang Wa fed the King's desire, and King Ping heard only what he wanted to."

Fen Yang's eyes lit up. "That's what Sheh said."

"Yuan is right. Don't blame yourself," Shang agreed. "Now, what do we do about Father?"

"I'm afraid I sealed his fate," Fen Yang said, saddened by his role in this quagmire.

"I'm not sure there's anything we can do, except wait and see," Yuan replied. He turned to Fen Yang, "But you had nothing to do with it. Whether or not Chien lives or dies, Nang Wa's scheme has already worked against Father."

"How can we do nothing!" Shang protested loudly. "We should go to Ying and argue for his release. We owe that to Father."

Yuan held up his hand to calm Shang down. "We must set Father free, if we can, but going to Ying won't accomplish that."

"But we must try, Yuan. We must try something!" Shang pleaded.

"Trying something that is bound to fail isn't really trying," Yuan counseled. "We need to see how King Ping reacts to the news of Chien's escape, then decide what to do."

"His reaction will be to execute Father in Chien's place," Shang said, shaking his fist.

"I'll go to Ying," Fen Yang offered. "I'll tell King Ping that Chien escaped. If the King's temper moves him to look elsewhere to vent his anger, then let him turn to me."

"Why do you think Shen Pao won't execute you here for violating the King's order?" Yuan shook his head, then quickly vowed, "I will not let that happen!"

Fen Yang wagged a finger in the air. "King Ping ordered Shen Pao to execute me *if I refused* to kill Chien. I have not declined. Chien just wasn't here. And I will explain that had I taken part in warning Chien, I would have run with him. Lan's absence helps me make that point. Shen Pao will blame only Lan and give my story credit. King Ping might as well."

"I do not like this, Fen Yang," Yuan frowned. "Shen Pao will believe you were involved, and King Ping will not care. You will die simply because Chien escaped, and the King will take it out on you. We can't ask you to take that risk."

"You're not asking me to, Yuan. King Ping gave me the order. I disobeyed it when I sent Lan ahead to warn Chien. The King should focus his anger on me, not Sheh. I will return to Ying." Fen Yang smiled, then said, "Besides, I'm now the Commander of Chengfu, and I out rank you." He slapped Yuan on the shoulder and chuckled. "And now I must convince Shen Pao to take me back with him."

16

THE TOLL EXPANDS

*P*rime Minister Nang Wa scowled, holding back his anger while Shen Pao gave him the news of Chien's early morning escape.

"We searched all of Chengfu, Prime Minister, but Chien was gone. Somehow, he must have learned of the King's order," Shen Pao said, not sure what reaction to expect from Nang Wa.

Nang Wa had failed to anticipate that the King's order would be circumvented, and it was that failure that angered him most. "Shen Pao, who do you think warned Chien? Fen Yang?"

Shen Pao cocked his head and grimaced. "I don't think so. Commander Yuan's archer, Lan, accompanied our return to Chengfu, and he slipped away after we retired to our tents the night before we entered the town. Chien was nowhere to be found, once we reached Chengfu, and Lan was gone, too."

Nang Wa drummed his fingers on the table and nodded. "Where do you think Chien is?"

"My guess is that he's somewhere in the Northern Alliance."

"What makes you think that?"

"I sent out teams to search for his trail. We didn't find

one, but I think he'll seek refuge out of Chu, and the Northern Alliance offers the closest safe haven."

"Did you follow?"

Shen Pao shook his head. "No. I sent a squad north to see if I'm right but warned them to keep away from the Northern Alliance. They are to return to Ying once they know where Chien is hiding."

"Dead, I hope." Nang Wa said.

"Those orders are clear." Shen Pao was fully committed to the King's wishes.

"Good." Nang Wa cracked a wily smile.

"When will I present this matter to King Ping?" Shen Pao asked.

"You won't."

Shen Pao shot Nang Wa a curious glance. "Prime Minister, there was much concern in Chengfu for Sheh. What will become of him?"

"I'll handle it from here." Nang Wa abruptly dismissed him.

"Shall I tell Fen Yang to stay in Ying in case King Ping has any questions?"

Nang Wa nodded, but thought, *No. Don't let Fen Yang muddy what I can do with Chien's escape.* Ridding himself of Chien was only part of his plan. "That is a good idea, for a few days. I'll report this matter to the King, and if something more is needed from you or Fen Yang, I'll let you know." *I'll let him stay but only for as long as my pretense requires.*

Nang Wa dismissed his servant, who stood in his usual spot near a corner. The news, although not exactly what Nang Wa wanted, was not all bad for him. Chien was out of Chu, out of the King's favor, and out of hope for a future spot on the throne. *Or is he?* Nang Wa questioned. If Chien outlives King Ping, he could garner support from the Northern Alliance and return. To reduce that possibility, the hunt for Chien had to continue, even if not officially, and Chien's support from within Chu had to be eliminated. *But who exactly does that include?* For now, the answers would have to wait.

Nang Wa walked down the main corridor of the Administrative Palace, toward the Court. King Ping was in his office attached to the back of the room. He often secreted himself inside when he did not want to be disturbed. Only his personal servants and Nang Wa could interrupt him there, and the servants did so cautiously. Nang Wa, however, had the King's ear, even though openly, King Ping treated him with disdain. Their history together spanned most of their adulthood and during that time, King Ping had become increasingly reliant on Nang Wa's abilities in overseeing all civil and military affairs. During his tenure as Prime Minister, King Ping's empire and treasury had expanded and prospered. And with each success, King Ping relinquished more and more authority to Nang Wa, concentrating instead on his duty as the people's Intermediary to the Gods. The more time King Ping spent on Heavenly matters, his knowledge of the details surrounding the country's business dwindled to the point that no one's importance to the daily administration of Chu matched Nang Wa's.

Nang Wa kept his power intact by dividing all functions below him and making sure that he was the only one who knew the details of each. That also directed to him the flow of all information necessary to successfully scheme.

Nang Wa approached King Ping's office. A servant appeared from the room, closing the door behind him.

Nang Wa detained him. "Is King Ping in?"

"Yes, Prime Minister," the servant replied. "I'll announce you."

"No. That's not necessary." Nang Wa brushed past him, knocked on the door, then opened it. "My King, may I interrupt?"

"Come in, Nang Wa," the King said. "I'm wrapping up some last-minute details. This is the first good day I've had in a while, but I suppose you're bringing me bad news."

"It's not exactly what you expect."

"Oh?" The King sat back, then leaned to one side. "You have my attention."

"By the time Fen Yang returned to Chengfu, Chien was gone."

King Ping's lips tightened, holding back an outburst. "Where to?"

Nang Wa filled in the details he'd learned from Shen Pao.

"Damn," King Ping scowled. "I chose Fen Yang to execute Chien to divide loyalties inside Chengfu and thought the presence of Shen Pao and a platoon of soldiers would ensure success. But even when faced with execution, some people can't keep their mouths shut!"

Nang Wa watched King Ping deliberate the news.

"Find out what you can." King Ping made a frown. "We may never know who's responsible." He drummed his fingers on the table. The rhythm was slow, at first, then quickly cascaded, ending with a sharp rap of his knuckles. King Ping looked at Nang Wa and asked, "Who do you think is really behind this scheme against me? Chien doesn't have the ability to organize it."

"So much information is missing. It's sketchy. Duke Chao may be behind it," Nang Wa said with conviction. "Sheh could be as well."

"Chao, I believe. You know he's the Queen's brother. It makes perfect sense for a member of her family to use my son against me. But Sheh? He's never been a man to pursue a course that is without virtue. He's a teacher, a very wise man, but not one accustomed to such risk." *All the same, he's in the way to rid myself of Queen Ma. I must remove him.*

"What do you intend to do with Sheh?" Nang Wa inquired, testing whether or not the King needed prodding.

King Ping stared past Nang Wa for a long moment, then growled, "Execute him. Yes, kill him. If he's not involved in the scheme, he failed to guide my Heir Apparent down the proper path." He paused and stared at the ceiling for a moment, gritted his teeth, then said "And send Feng Yang to the executioner as well."

Nang Wa saw the opportunity to eliminate one more obstacle, but he didn't want to be hasty. "Before I have your order carried out, may I suggest we persuade Sheh to send for his two sons? They may know something about this scheme and about Chien's flight. They were both in Chengfu when Fen Yang arrived, and Yuan went with Chien to Ts'ai."

"Good idea. I want both of them brought to my Court."

Nang Wa saw another opening. "Perhaps Sheh can help us prevent his sons from following Chien."

King Ping took the bait. "How so?"

"Let Sheh think he'll be released if his sons appear at your Court and tell you everything they know about Chien's escape and the plot against you. Maybe he will ask them to come here."

"It's worth a try. Have General Po join you. Sheh despises you, but he has always held General Po in high regard. And dispatch Shen Pao to fetch Sheh's sons." King Ping interrupted his thought with a long pause. He looked past Nang Wa, then gave his head a slight nod. "Hold off on executing Fen Yang. Send him with Shen Pao. Let's hope his presence will lessen concern that Sheh's two sons may have about following my orders."

"I see your wisdom, My King. They will think that if you suspected foul play, you would have ordered Fen Yang's death."

King Ping chortled, then said, "Tell Shen Pao that he'll have to eat dust to and from Chengfu once again. He isn't going to be too thrilled about another trip, but he is who I trust to carry out this order. His sense of duty guarantees the job will be done right."

"I'll get to it. Thank you for your time." Nang Wa bowed, then exited King Ping's office.

※

He proceeded to General Po's office and summoned Sheh from prison. Sheh appeared undernourished and in need of fresh clothing. He knelt on the floor before Nang Wa and General Po. Guards stood over him, ensuring that he remained submissive. It was for Nang Wa's pleasure. He enjoyed dominating, especially a man who loathed him. Nang Wa twisted the tip of his mustache, looking over Sheh; a hint of a smile behind his wrinkled face. Sheh, though, maintained his stately manner, despite the worn appearance and subservient pose. That annoyed Nang Wa.

"Step outside," General Po ordered the guards. "I'll call you when we're done." He nodded to a servant, and pointed to a tray on a nearby table. "Give Sheh something soothing to drink."

The servant handed Sheh a cup of tea. It had been many weeks since Sheh's imprisonment, but he showed less strain than expected.

Sheh sipped the brew. He welcomed the simple pleasure, but he detested the circumstances. "You don't look well, Nang Wa."

Nang Wa ignored the jab. "Sheh, against my advice, King Ping decided to spare you from the executioner's block. But he placed a condition on his generosity." Nang Wa knew Sheh would not trust anything he said, so he made promises only in the King's name.

"You have certainly peaked my interest, Nang Wa, but having done nothing to deserve this treatment, I'm not sure there is anything that can be done now, except for you to confess your plot."

"Sheh, that doesn't help," General Po interrupted. "Your

troubles disturb me, but I think there's a way you can avoid execution. Take advantage of it."

"What do you want, Nang Wa?" Sheh said contemptuously.

"Nothing. I prefer that you go straight to the executioner's block, but King Ping has decided otherwise. He wants to fully understand what scheme is at play against him. Now that Chien fled, avoiding his death, the information you have is valuable."

"Use it to bargain, Sheh," General Po urged.

"What?" Sheh reacted, surprised. "What's this about Chien?"

"I'm sorry, of course, isolation doesn't allow access to that kind of news," Nang Wa mocked Sheh. "By the time Fen Yang arrived in Chengfu, Chien had fled. Somehow, he learned of the King's orders, and that is what provides you with an opportunity to save yourself."

Sheh simply smiled. "How is this an opportunity for me?"

"Yuan and Shang were in Chengfu when Yang arrived," Nang Wa explained. "They may have information that will help uncover what is really going on. Talking to Yuan is even more important, because he accompanied Chien to Ts'ai. If your sons come to Ying and tell King Ping what they know, he will spare you. That is the King's mandate."

Sheh stared into Nang Wa's narrow eyes. "You're manipulating." He turned to General Po. "My old friend, don't you recognize that? Nang Wa is the one King Ping should watch."

"Sheh, don't let your hatred drive you. This is a chance to avoid the executioner. Just send for your sons," General Po pleaded.

"No it's not," Sheh argued. "Nang Wa is offering a chance to include my sons in my fate. I won't do that. I won't be the cause of their deaths." Sheh raised the cup to his lips and sipped. "You've watched Nang Wa connive for power throughout his life. Why don't you recognize what he's doing?"

"Whether you send for your sons or not doesn't matter," Nang Wa scoffed. "I'll make them the same offer, but I'll tell King Ping that you didn't cooperate. Your sons will come. After all, what son could resist the ultimatum: Appear in Ying, and your father will be spared. Fail to show, and he'll be executed?" Nang Wa wagged his finger at Sheh. "But if you don't ask them to come, you won't get the benefit of their effort. Personally, I prefer that outcome," Nang Wa finished with a grin.

"That won't work," Sheh replied. "At least not completely."

"Why not?"

"Shang will come because he'll feel it's his duty. Yuan will not. He'll see the trap. But someday he'll fulfill his duty to me by avenging my death."

Nang Wa laughed. "How could he possibly do anything about it? King Ping will turn all of Chu against him."

"Sheh, be practical," General Po counseled. "What can one man do against all of Chu?"

"Yuan is tough minded and can endure whatever hardships fate throws his way," Sheh said with pride. "Eventually, he will overcome them, and you will feel his sword, Nang Wa."

"You're not realistic. Not even the Northern Alliance could take Ying, and that's what it will require to get to me," Nang Wa scoffed. "One man can't possibly do it."

General Po saw Sheh's chance to help himself slip away and cautioned, "Are you seeking comfort by believing in something that can never happen?"

"Perhaps, General. Perhaps. But I will not invite my sons to their deaths." Sheh handed the cup to the servant, then turned back to General Po. "What about you?"

General Po returned a confused glance. "What do you mean?"

"Sooner or later Nang Wa will view you as a threat. What will become of you and your family?"

"I keep my enemies outside of Chu, and I haven't and won't do anything against King Ping, Nang Wa or Chu that will cause me to join your fate."

Sheh gestured around him. "I did nothing wrong, yet here I am. Nang Wa can view you as a threat for any reason, even one that does not exist. It doesn't have to be justified. And what will happen to your grandson? Do you want this fate for Commander Po Pi?"

Nang Wa let out a jeer.

General Po sighed. "This is not about me, Sheh. It's about you. I feel for you. You have served Chu well, and I don't want your end to come this way. Please reconsider, for your own sake."

Sheh shook his head.

"What do I tell King Ping?" Nang Wa smirked.

"Tell him that killing me will seal the same fate for himself."

Nang Wa laughed, then called to the guards, "Take this prisoner away."

17

YUAN'S DILEMMA

*T*he news of Sheh's imprisonment cast a pall over Chengfu. Yuan and Shang knew the general nature of their father's circumstances, but the details weren't current. The two brothers occupied their time, waiting on news, with distractions. This day, they were outside the town's gate.

Yuan worked to develop his skill with a bow; he nocked an arrow, placed its shaft on the shelf, then drew the string to his cheek. His eye fixed on a bundle of straw wrapped in solid cloth that hung from a makeshift tripod, made of three crooked branches. Yuan took a deep breath, exhaled to comfort, held steady, then loosed the arrow.

"Missed again," Shang chuckled. His laugh was more forced than natural, struggling to find some respite. "You're not as good as Lan, are you?" he quipped.

Yuan ignored Shang's strained attempt at humor. His mood held no place for even a modicum of joy. "Would you care to show me how?" He grabbed another arrow from the quiver.

"No. At least you've hit the target a few times. I couldn't land even one arrow. Seriously, Yuan, how can you be so skilled with a sword, yet so ineffective with a bow?"

Yuan tapped the hilt of his sword that was sheathed and strapped to his waist. "The blade feels natural, like an extension of my arm. But the arrow seems to have a mind of its own." He looked away and paused for a moment, then gave a faint smile. "Lan makes this look so easy." He shook his head. "I once saw him pluck dinner out of the sky. Whatever he wants to hit, the arrow finds that mark."

"I will miss him, too," Shang consoled. "Do you think we'll ever see him and Chien again?"

"I don't know. I used to believe that I controlled my future. Now, I'm not sure what to think."

Shang changed the subject, his voice softening in sadness. "When do you think we'll have news of Father? Shouldn't we have heard by now? This is damned frustrating."

"I know," Yuan responded, "but there is nothing to do until Fen Yang returns or sends word." He wouldn't show the gloom he felt. He picked up his quiver and said, "Come on. Help me retrieve the arrows, then let's go in."

The chore took longer than expected. The search for the arrows that flew wide of the target proved challenging. Shang removed two from the dangling bag, unhooked it and tossed the bundle over his shoulder, holding firmly to the tether. "Give it up. You'll never find them in the tall grass," Shang said.

"Yeah, you're right," Yuan groaned. "Time to go in." He slung the quiver over his shoulder, hung the bow on the other, then started toward the town's gate.

"Aren't you going to unstring the bow?" Shang asked. "Lan always does. He said it is good to relax the limbs of the bow."

"I will later. It's easier to carry this way."

The two ambled through town and to Yuan's residence. Before they reached the front door, a House Servant met them in the courtyard. "Ah, Shang. There you are. I thought you'd be with Yuan. A messenger from Ying sent this to you."

Shang reached for the long, slender pouch. "Thank you." He hurried to remove the bamboo slips.

"Has there been any word of Sheh?" the House Servant asked.

"No, none," Shang replied. "Maybe this is about Father," he said, waving the slips.

Shang grimaced as he read silently. "It's not about Father. Not directly, at least. It's from the Shenyin family. Let's go inside." He held the door open for Yuan, then entered the house, while the House Servant closed the door behind him. Shang took a couple of steps, then came to an abrupt stop, looked away from the message and sighed. "They've called off the marriage because of Father's circumstances. They think it reflects badly on our family and believe that offering their daughter as your wife no longer benefits them." Shang balled his fist around the slats. "Oh Yuan! This is painful. Are we going to drown in this drip of fate? We used to be a family of importance, one that had influence even in the Royal House. Our stature has fallen little by little since we left Ying, and now, Father is in prison, and our name is no longer worthy, not even of marriage."

Yuan said nothing. He remained stoic and continued down a short corridor. Since Sheh's imprisonment, Yuan had not thought about his future marriage. Although the loss at Chi-fu had not tarnished him, it certainly had done nothing to elevate his status. "We can't blame them." He shook his head. "The totality of our circumstances is more than the Shinyin family is willing to risk. I understand that." The hollow pit he felt whenever he thought about his first wife rumbled in his stomach. He beat the images back and stepped into his office.

It was a small room furnished without grandeur. A simple four-legged table served as his desk. He hung the bow and quiver on pegs in the back wall next to a pair of sheathed knives that he often strapped to his arms, concealing the blades under the sleeves of his robe. He removed his sword, then placed it on the table. A modest three-legged cauldron, which sat on a table in the corner adjacent to the door, provided the only decoration.

Shang followed him into the office, taking a seat away from the door. He slumped in the chair and said, "We should have gone with Fen Yang."

"What could we accomplish doing that?" Yuan challenged. "Do you have special influence over Nang Wa?"

"No," Shang lamented.

"King Ping?" Yuan raised his voice.

Shang lowered his head and mumbled, "No."

"Then what could we do? You yourself said that we've lost our influence in Ying."

Shang shrugged and spoke somberly. "I don't know, I just want to do something."

"Shang. Yuan," a voice called from the hallway.

The two brothers looked up to see Fen Yang, accompanied by Chu Palace Guards, enter the room. Yuan recognized their leader, Shen Pao, who stepped through the doorway right after Fen Yang. Four guards hovered near the door.

"Fen Yang!" Shang exclaimed. He bounced to his feet. "Where is Father? What news do you bring?"

"It's not good." Fen Yang said soberly.

Shen Pao burst past him, then blasted, "Shang, Yuan, King Ping has ordered your presence before his Court."

"What is this?" Yuan demanded. He used the table to push himself upright.

When Shen Pao first appeared unannounced in Chengfu, Sheh landed in prison. Yuan wondered, *What will this surprise bring?*

Fen Yang cut a puzzled stare to Shen Pao. "I didn't know this. What's going on? You said nothing of this during our travel here."

"I was ordered not to discuss this with you, but to let you believe I had other reasons to be in this region," Shen Pao answered coldly. "Because of Chien's escape, you are no longer trusted." He turned to Yuan and said, "King Ping has ordered that if the two of you return with me and answer questions before his Court, he will spare Sheh's life."

Shang stepped toward Shen Pao. "Certainly, we'll go."

"No, we won't," Yuan spoke up.

Shang turned to Yuan, astonished by his defiance. "What do you mean? You heard him. We can save Father's life."

"No, we can't, Shang," Yuan replied coldly. "All three of us will die once we arrive in Ying."

"You don't know that!" Shang objected.

"Father has done nothing to justify his execution, yet King Ping has ordered it," Yuan pointed out. "The King believes that Chien was scheming against him and ordered *his* death, yet we know that no such designs exist."

"That's right!" Shang pleaded. "That's why we must go. We must tell King Ping the allegations are false."

"What makes you think he doesn't already know that?" Yuan let the question sink in, then calmly added, "The truth doesn't matter to him."

"What do you mean?" Shang was too focused on the opportunity to free Sheh to catch the import.

Yuan remained unflappable. "For whatever reason, King Ping ordered Chien's execution. We, along with Father, are tied directly to Chien and his fate. And so long as his fate is death, so will be ours."

"Refusing is not a choice, Yuan," Shen Pao stated.

"I'm not going Shen Pao," Yuan crossed his arms in defiance.

"Brother, if we don't go, Father will die. What honor is there in that?" Shang argued.

"There is no honor in traveling a path we know will fail. It's better to live and avenge Father's death."

"And if we fail, our family name will be disgraced, and our names will be a scorned for all times." Shang waved a dismissive hand at Yuan. "You're wrong, Brother. I'm going to Ying to do what I can to save Father. If you are right and Father and I are executed, then . . ." Shang paused; his face grew tight; he locked eyes with Yuan, "avenge us both."

Shen Pao stepped toward Yuan and barked angrily, "There is no choice. You're both going or you will die here." He reached for his dagger-sword.

Yuan spun around, grabbed his bow off the wall and an arrow from the quiver, nocking it to the string before completing the full turn. He drew and took aim at Shen Pao who stopped, not quite within the sword's reach. Yuan had the advantage.

Two Palace Guards who accompanied Shen Pao stepped into the room, drawing their weapons. Fen Yang, though, was quicker. He shoved the tip of his blade to the throat of the closest threat, nicking the skin.

"Easy now," Fen Yang cautioned. "You don't want things to get out of hand."

The sound of men, running outside the room and getting closer, turned the other guards' attention away. Chengfu men hurried to Yuan's aid.

"I will not go," Yuan challenged Shen Pao. The bow creaked from his pull. His chest pounded from adrenalin. He didn't want to kill Shen Pao, but he was certain that returning to Ying would end in death. Not only his death, but Sheh's and Shang's as well. Silence followed. Yuan felt the string tug at his fingers, but he remained fixed on Shen Pao, waiting for his enemy to blink.

Shen Pao snorted, "You're sealing your fate, Yuan. And maybe Sheh's as well."

"Ping has already done that," Yuan scowled.

"You dare speak about the King in this way! No one dares such insolence! No one! You will die for this."

"At least now there's a reason for King Ping to execute me."

Shen Pao pulled his blade back, choosing to capitulate to Yuan's upper hand, but not with words. "Yuan, your arrogance is foolish."

"It's not arrogance. It's anger. Extreme, hostile anger!" Yuan wanted to let the arrow fly. He needed to lash out. He yearned to strike at the Chu beast for all that had gone wrong for his family.

Shang stepped to Shen Pao's side. "Put down the weapons." He softened his tone. "I'll return to Ying with you." He placed his hand on the hilt of Shen Pao's sword, then pressed it down. "Let us leave now."

The tension in Shen Pao's face eased. He returned his weapon to its scabbard, but Yuan kept the arrow trained on him. Shen Pao's soldiers disappeared from around the corner first, and Shen Pao followed. Yuan eased the bowstring's tension and watched his brother follow Shen Pao out of the room, but Shang paused outside the doorway. Yuan sensed that this would be their last moment together, but he did not see that awareness in Shang's eye. Neither spoke. Yuan offered a sorrowful smile, thinking, *Rest peacefully with the ancestors, Brother.* They bowed to each other, then Yuan looked up to see Shang walk away.

Yuan and Fen Yang stood frozen, staring at one another. *It's not safe here,* Yuan knew for certain. *Nowhere in Chu is safe.*

18

A SON'S DUTY

hang's trip was dispiriting. He spent much of the travel time thinking about what he would say to King Ping and rehearsing the details. And when he didn't focus on that, he thought of Sheh and Yuan.

But on his arrival in Ying, Shen Pao delivered Shang straight to prison, not to King Ping's Court. And it was there Shang joined his father in a four-foot square, bamboo cage shoved into the corner of a large room. Side-by-side, similar cells lined the walls of the cavern-like prison. Darkness, interrupted only by the flickering light of torches, blanketed the windowless keep. And that was a good thing; it allowed Shang's mind to drift to a place far removed. The dim light, though, did nothing to stop the pungent, invasive, acrid reality of the bodily smells.

Shang fidgeted, bouncing from standing to sitting, then back upright again. He leaned forward into the cage. His hands clasped together outside the coop while he braced his elbows on the frame. He was relieved, when he arrived earlier in the day, to see his father was still alive, but their reunion was quickly dampened by the realities of prison. *This is not how I expected to be treated.* He let out a capitulating sigh.

Sheh watched patiently. "This is your first day in here. You will learn to tolerate it," he counseled Shang.

Shang rubbed his nose, then asked Sheh, "Do you think Yuan left Chengfu? Is he with Chien by now?" It seemed to help pass the time by talking of matters beyond the restraining walls.

Sheh sat upright and cross-legged, stately even in hardship. The confine allowed him that much room. He removed a wooden shoe, lifted it above his head, then delivered a swift blow to a cricket that ventured across the floor. Sheh picked it up, checking to make sure it was dead. He dropped it into a bowl of gruel, then swatted at another crawler. He instructed his son, "If you don't add *meat* to the bowl, you won't be able to keep your strength or your health."

Shang didn't openly show his opinion of the nauseating advice. "I suppose I haven't been here long enough, Father. When did you start eating them?"

"Not long after they jailed me. The gruel is simply not enough food. Here, try it. Mixed together, you can't tell the difference." Sheh held the bowl out for Shang to take.

Shang waved off the gesture. "That's because it all tastes bad. It's not even cooked." He turned away, drawn to the faint outline of a smaller cell, stacked on top of another. Inside, a docile man lay tucked in a fetal position. At first glance, Shang thought he was dead, but a slight movement of the man's foot proved there was still life – very little of it left – Shang believed. "Father, since we've done nothing to deserve this, why do you suppose he is here?" Shang pointed across the room. The poor lighting couldn't obscure the bony man's weakened body. A state, Shang knew, brought about solely by imprisonment.

Each cell was designed to break a man's will and cause him to submit to the designs of those who imprisoned him. Every moment of every day, prisoners spent their time in the cages eating, sleeping and answering the call of nature. Life in the smaller, more restrictive cages was especially bad, and the prisoners in the bottom chambers experienced greater misery because of the drip from above. Food rations were reduced below that required for a person to maintain sustenance, and after malnutrition took hold, disease followed, all of which brought the man to the fetal position.

"It's not saying much about our life when we look at others and are glad just to have a cage tall enough to stand up in. Is it, Father?" Shang turned dejectedly to Sheh.

"No, it's not, but don't get too comfortable," Sheh cautioned. "We'll probably end up in one of those before this is over." He nodded toward their listless companion.

"Thanks for giving me hope," Shang scoffed.

Footsteps caught their attention. "Sheh, Shang, you're coming with us," a Prison Guard commanded.

The Prison Guard was accompanied by six others, bent on maintaining control and power over their prisoners, just in case one had enough gumption and energy to try an escape. The guard unlocked the cell door. Both Shang and Sheh stepped out, and were surrounded by the other guards. They were escorted in tandem to a man dressed in a fine robe. Torchlight cast brightly enough for Shang to recognize him. It was Fei Wu Chi. *Finally,* Shang thought when his eyes fixed on Fei, *this is my only chance to put things right.*

"Bring them," Fei ordered pompously. With no more conversation and no explanation, the group made a steady-paced march out of the prison wing. Once in the main corridor, Fei turned left.

When Fei reached the door to the outside, he stopped and waited for a Prison Guard to open it. Shang crossed the threshold, stepping into the bright sunlight. He ducked his head into the crook of his arm. His eyes, unaccustomed to the brightness, squinted to make out what was in his path. The front entrance to the prison faced the main road leading between

the Eastern Market and the Administrative Palace. In front of
the building, for all to see, was the executioner's block. Next
to it, stood a man of sturdy build, holding a heavy axe. A
crowd of onlookers was forming. Some had gathered earlier,
noticing the activity. Others continued to arrive, all driven by
curiosity.

"What's this!" Shang cried out. He heard laughter from
various spectators.

"Silence!" Fei snapped at Shang, invigorated by the power.
Fei unfurled a bamboo slip and read, "Sheh, you have been
sentenced to the executioner's block for your treachery against
King Ping. Confess your crimes now, so that your ancestors
will accept you in the next life." He lowered the slip and raised
his nose, awaiting Sheh's reply.

"Wait!" Shang shouted. "The King ordered my presence
in Ying to speak to him. I can absolve my father! Fei, look at
me!" Two Prison Guards closed around Shang, grabbing his
arms to maintain control. He yanked against their clutches.
"King Ping promised to spare my father's life if I came to Ying.
I demand you take me to the King's Court immediately!"

"I'll get to you next," Fei said, dismissing Shang out of
hand.

Sheh, though, had bearing. Pleading was useless. "I've
done nothing to confess," he said with composure.

Sheh's poise angered Fei, leaving him unsatisfied. "Very
well then." He motioned for the guards to bring Sheh forward.

One took hold of Sheh's arm, then nudged him toward the
block. Once the grip tightened, though, Sheh turned to the
Prison Guard, made certain their eyes met, and said, "That
won't be necessary." He nodded to the man's hold of his arm.
Sheh straightened his back and walked without assistance, his
head raised in defiance, not giving Fei the satisfaction of seeing
him submit his will.

Sheh pulled his robe to the side, tightened the flap, then

knelt. He started to lower his body to the block, but stopped short, jerked up, and gave Fei a piercing glare. "I lived my life serving Chu. I did so with honesty, dignity and virtue. When I arrive in the next world, I'll make a special point to visit your ancestors."

Sheh placed his neck on the block. Wear from years of use held his chin firmly in position, forcing his head into the proper alignment.

Sheh had realized much earlier than Shang that nothing they could say or do would prevent this fate. Shang now knew it, too. That dawn wore heavy on him. He struggled for words, but all he could muster was, "Father!" The axe came down. The mob groaned first, then cheered. Shang recoiled, turning away.

"Display the head," Fei ordered, then turned to his next victim. He looked down at the bamboo slip and read: "Shang, you have been sentenced to the executioner's block for your treachery against King Ping. Confess your crimes now, so that your ancestors will accept you in the next life."

Shang lurched against the two guards, who shuffled him forward. A fog of frantic thoughts raced in his mind. Sheh's fate, Yuan's warnings, and disbelief that this was his end, all jumbled together, obstructing the clarity of the moment. He searched through the crowd, looking for a friendly face, hoping for some reason to believe that he would be spared.

"Traitor!" yelled an old woman, who shook a hateful fist. She spat, accenting her contempt. Next to her was a young boy pointing at him and laughing.

This is entertainment for them. That, as much, was clear to Shang. The weight on his shoulders sank into his stomach, like a great boulder fixing him in place. *How can they find pleasure in this?* His eyes skimmed other faces but found no comfort. He was alone. There was no support in his last moment.

Strong arms forced his body to the block. He was numb from the swift turn of his expectations to the reality of life's end. His sense of time vanished. He wiggled his neck into position, heard the executioner step closer, but before the axe fell, he whispered, "Yuan, avenge us."

"Post the head. I'm going to feed my belly," Fei said contently, then walked off, his chore for the day now finished.

PART 4

THE NORTHERN ALLIANCE

19

CHAOS IN SUNG

*Y*uan and Fen Yang made it north of the Huai River. And after a brief stop in Ts'ai to learn from Duke Chao of Chien's destination, they arrived in the State of Sung, where they joined the others from Chengfu. It hadn't been difficult to find them, for an entourage from Chu, traveling with a woman and child, stood out. People in every village and town where they stopped remembered them, making their trail easy to follow. Lan and five foot-soldiers, who normally served in Yuan's chariot complement, had fled with Chien.

Yuan saw directly the trouble brewing in Sung at the hands of the Hua clan. In open defiance of the Duke of Sung's power, the Hua clan had burned a small village that was under the control of a noble who remained loyal to the Duke. The news Fen Yang had heard in Ying about the unrest was true, something Duke Chao had also confirmed. And although the turmoil had not yet erupted into civil war, the locals braced for it.

They stopped in a town within the Hua clan's influence to eat, brush off the travel dust and assess things. Chien's wife and son needed rest the most. Neither were used to the long days of walking, and their bodies felt the wear. The building was a modest structure, rectangular in shape, set adjacent to the cartwheel-worn road through town. The kitchen was separate, attached by a breezeway. Tables and benches spanned the room, arranged in two columns and separated by an aisle down the middle. They had chosen a spot to sit near the back and away from the locals, although the size of the place made privacy an illusion. The five soldiers took the table between the others and the main door, providing a buffer.

"I should not have left Chengfu," Chien uttered. He stared out of the open shutter, not intending his remarks for anyone in particular.

"No good would have come from you staying," Yuan responded in a lowered voice, barely above a whisper. He hoped Chien would notice the caution and adjust his volume. "Your death would not have changed our circumstances." He sat on the bench near the middle of the table and across from Chien.

Fen Yang was beside Yuan, at the aisle's end, shaking his head. He unfastened his belt, removed his sheathed sword, then laid it along the edge. "Truth doesn't matter to the likes of Nang Wa. He maneuvered King Ping and would not have stopped with your death. You are a threat to him, certainly, but those who support you are, as well. That puts us at risk, too." Fen Yang waved his hand in a circle, indicating everyone in their group.

"Then you shouldn't support me." Chien's shoulders slumped.

"We are here because we chose to be here," Yuan reassured him. "It is right. Even if we had decided differently, Nang Wa would not have relented."

Chien rubbed his face with both hands, then laid his elbows on the table, leaned forward and asked, "What do we do?"

"We will seek refuge inside the Northern Alliance." The cloud of chaos hung over all of Sung, drawing the Duke's attentions to problems important to him, Yuan feared. And he thought that the Duke's hospitality would either run its course or be forced to end. "The State of Cheng is the closest Northern Alliance member. We'll go there."

"Yes," Fen Yang concurred. "But getting there has challenges, too." The journey required them to travel across Sung through the Hua stronghold.

"There is no perfect answer, but let's leave Sung and go to Cheng," Yuan suggested.

Chien nodded, glad for Yuan to take the lead.

A waiter approached the table and plopped down two large serving pots of ground wheat, boiled into a porridge. A tall boy stood in wait, balancing three bowls of food on his outstretched arm. A cloth bundle dangled from his fingers, and he held a stack of empty, smaller bowls in the other hand. The waiter took the latter, passed them to the table, then reached out his hand. The boy gave him the bowl of chicken first, then the one containing pork, followed by the heaping serving of dumplings.

The waiter placed each one near the center of the table, then handed the bundle to Yuan. "Here are the dates you wanted."

Yuan nodded. He dipped his fingers into a leather pouch that was hidden inside his robe, then removed a handful of green-copper coins. He plopped seven into a small wooden cup that was near the center of the table. The eatery was busy with patrons, and the staff wasted no time taking the payment, then moving on to the next table.

Chien's wife was beside him, and their son, Sheng, was next to her, wiggling from youthful discontent. She poured the thick gruel from the serving vessel into a bowl, slid it to Sheng, then began to fill another with meat.

Sheng was a young child of harmless age, about eight. Yuan had watched the boy grow through the years; the isolation of

Chengfu had allowed for it. It was a rare pleasure during a time that had been mired in so much misery. Sheng raised the bowl to his lips with one hand and used chopsticks in the other to scoop the food into his mouth. Porridge had no sooner hit his tongue than he dropped the bowl and clenched his teeth, struggling to keep from spitting. His brow wrinkled, eyes squinted and lips pursed. He swallowed hard. "That's bad!" he said, wiping his mouth on his sleeve.

"Shhh," his mother admonished. She moved a cup of tea closer to him, and commanded, "Drink this and don't complain."

Sheng washed the taste away, then pinched with the chopsticks a lump of meat in the closest pot.

Yuan chuckled. "You know, Sheng, your name and my brother's name, Shang, are almost the same. And he doesn't like gruel either."

Sheng smiled.

"Would you like a date?" Yuan pulled one from the bundle.

Sheng's mother turned to her boy. "You cannot travel on dates," she said tersely. "Eat meat and dumplings if the gruel does not please you."

Yuan sat the fruit on top of the bundle. He knew her rebuke was meant for him, even though her gaze was directed at her son. "Your mother is right," he said to Sheng. "I should not have offered before you finished the meal. Perhaps, it will be appropriate later."

Sheng's mother nodded.

Yuan filled a small bowl with pork, raised it to his lips, then shoveled chunks of the meat into his mouth.

Sheng ate until he'd had his fill. He spun on the bench, then leaned his back against the table. The boy tugged on his mother's arm and asked, "Why don't we wear top knots like them?"

"Shhh. Don't point. You'll draw attention. Turn back around," his mother reprimanded him.

The boy's question prompted Yuan's thoughts to drift. *We certainly stick out here and in all of Sung.* That realization hung with him for a moment. He rotely picked up the date from the bundle, then tossed it up into the air.

Sheng giggled, watching it arc into Yuan's mouth.

Yuan chortled with him, until he saw Sheng's mother's glare. "I think I'm a bad influence on you, Sheng."

Lan, who sat across the table from the boy, laughed. "He's a bad influence on me, too. And just look at Yuan's effect on Fen Yang." He wiggled his finger across his neck and mimicked a scraping sound with his mouth to highlight Fen Yang's scar.

Sheng chuckled, then became distracted by another patron. He leaned into his mother and asked, "Why do people keep looking at us?"

Yuan heard the question and glanced over the boy's shoulder to the next table. He saw a man at the far end of the room meeting his gaze. The look wasn't particularly worrisome, nor was it friendly. The man made no attempt to hide it. Others' faces didn't either, Yuan noticed, when he searched the room. Yuan and the boy weren't the only ones to notice.

Lan leaned toward Yuan. "Look to the door." Ten battle-ready men entered the room. At the lead was a tall, broad-shouldered man, whose top knot accentuated his height, just as the collar plates of his armored tunic did for his breadth. His face wore disapproval, which didn't change while he walked toward them.

Movement outside the open shutter caught Yuan's attention, too. An equal number of men huddled at the edge of the road. Yuan's soldiers bolted from their table and formed a barrier in the aisle, their hands at the ready to draw swords. The hum of chatter that had filled the air fell hush.

"They fly the Hua banner," Lan whispered.

Yuan remained steady. The placard, held by a Hua clansman near the road, whipped around its staff.

The big leader closed the distance from the door, his men spread two abreast into the aisle behind him. His voice was gruff and demanding. "What are you doing in Hua territory? We do not tolerate spies."

Yuan rose from the bench, then moved to meet the Hua clansman. He eased through the gap between two of his soldiers, stopping face to face with the Hua leader. "We are travelers. That's all," he said, hoping to placate the leader.

"If you are not spies, what is your business in our land?" the Hua clansman challenged.

Chien rushed to stand, but tripped while stepping away from the table. He caught his balance, then tugged on his robe, straightening it. "I am Chien, Heir Apparent to the King of Chu. We are not spies," he nervously assured the clansman.

Yuan hoped that word of King Ping's orders for Chien's death had not traveled to Sung. He also wanted their presence to be anonymous, especially with such a small escort. "We're on the way to Cheng."

The leader glared at Chien. "I think you're too clumsy to be a King's son. Besides, that doesn't explain why you're in Sung."

Laughter from the clansmen erupted. Chien winced in embarrassment.

Yuan took charge. "We came here not knowing the Hua had reasons to quarrel with the Duke of Sung. We are headed for Cheng, so that we don't get caught up in your grievances."

"Why Cheng?" the Hua clansman demanded. "Why not return to Chu?"

"We mean to visit both Sung and Cheng. Cheng's Emissary to Chu is on friendly terms, and we intend to pay our respects," Yuan offered, reasoning that a fulsome explanation would only complicate things.

"The Duke of Cheng is expecting you?" the Hua clansman challenged.

"He may be surprised by the timing, but he'll understand once he learns of the circumstances here." Yuan kept his hand away from his sword to appear non-threatening.

The Hua clansman cut a sharp look toward Chien, who was the only man among the group from Chu not dressed in a battle tunic. "The Hua's disagreement with the Duke of Sung is well known. We expect him to seek help from outside the State. And here you are, Chu's Heir Apparent. I don't believe in coincidences." His eyes darted to Chien's wife and Sheng, then back to Chien. "You travel with a woman and child. That is a clever way to disguise your true intentions. But I suspect you're in Sung to exchange messages between your King and the Duke of Sung." His arm jerked the hilt of his weapon.

The quickness of his decision to draw gave no time to argue. Yuan grabbed the hilt, stopping the weapon's removal, simultaneously lifting a knife sheathed to his arm, slipping it upward between armored plates, then ramming it into the Hua clansman's chest cavity. The big man gasped. Yuan circled the tip of the blade into the heart, planted his shoulder into the man's chest, sending the Hua leader collapsing into the next clansman in line. He pulled on the hilt of the leader's dagger-sword, finished drawing it, then blocked the oncoming blade thrust toward his neck from another clansman. He stepped forward, shoved his knife into the man's outstretched arm, then swung the sword into the enemy's throat.

The foe stepped backwards, cupping his hands over the deep cut, while blood spurted between his fingers, spraying the nearby table. He gurgled, trying both to breathe and speak, but no air filled his voicebox. Screams, though, from the nearby table, and the sound of benches overturned by patrons scurrying out of the way, would have drowned any command he could have given. The frightful yells rang beyond the walls of the building.

An arrow flew from behind Yuan and thwacked into a clansman near the end of the line. *That's Lan.* A guttural cry followed the arrow's impact. Yuan heard a thud on the table beside him and glanced that way. One of his soldiers jumped on top, then to another table, before crossing in front of him to engage the next Hua man. Another soldier did likewise on the other side.

The remaining patrons scrambled away from the clash. Some rushed toward the door, while others jumped out of windows, all yelling or screaming in harried confusion. The other three men from Yuan's complement advanced a wider span in the room, taking on Hua's two-by-two threat. Yuan looked over his shoulder and saw Fen Yang ready to repel any attack on Chien and his family. Sheng clung to his mother, sandwiched in between her and Chien.

"Lan!" Yuan shouted. "Take out anyone who comes through the door."

Lan jumped on a table, then adjusted his aim. He waited for the last patron to barrel out of the eatery, then loosed an arrow. The impact took out the first Hua enemy to step into the doorway. Lan nocked another arrow, then waited for the next target.

Yuan took a quick survey of the room. Twelve of the Hua enemy were dead. The patrons had fled, but the staff huddled near the breezeway to the kitchen. *Start moving. Don't let them regroup.*

"There are more outside," Lan shouted. "We'll get picked off going through the door."

Yuan looked to the ceiling, then to Lan, "Can you get to the roof?"

Lan's glance followed the nearest column up the structure. "I can punch through the tiles."

"Do it," Yuan ordered.

Lan handed his quiver and bow to Yuan, pulled a table next to the column, then climbed onto the tabletop.

Yuan said to the others, "When we hear Lan's first arrow fly, we'll leave out of those windows." He pointed to the ones near where they had eaten, then tapped the two soldiers who were closest to him on the shoulders. "Protect Chien and his family." He turned to the other three soldiers and ordered, "You will be with me, leading the way." Yuan looked back at Lan, then commanded, "Go!"

Lan grabbed a support beam and pulled himself up. He made sure his feet were secure on a strut, then pulled on a slat, which supported the roof, using his weight to pry it away. He repeated the chore four more times, pushed his fist through overlapping tiles to make a hole, then pulled at another, crashing it on the table. Shards scattered in all directions. Two more tiles shattered beside his foot. Sheng ducked behind his mother to avoid the fallout. Lan climbed into the hole, then reached his hand back through.

Yuan stepped onto the table, then handed the quiver and bow to Lan, who soon after disappeared onto the roof.

They tracked his progress by the sound of his footsteps until he stopped, near the ridge. Yuan froze, taking in every noise. Nothing indicated an arrow flying off the string until the thud of an impact and following yelp made it clear.

Yuan jumped out of the window, accompanied by the three soldiers he appointed. Fen Yang and the others followed. Three Hua men, with a trailing fourth, met them at the building's corner. Lan's arrow took out the straggler, and with the numbers having turned against them, the Hua men stopped abruptly, looked at each other, then turned and ran away, joined by the remaining laggards of the Hua band.

Lan climbed off the rooftop, onto a column, then scaled to the ground. He trotted to the others, and said, "By my count six got away. Does this change our plans?"

Yuan shook his head. "No. There is danger either way, but Cheng is safer once we get there." The simple act of eating a meal had turned into deadly mayhem. And soon, the Hua clan would hunt down and try to kill all of them. Chien's wife and son were sure to slow their pace. They could waste no time. "I don't know how much of a head start we have, but we need to go." He stepped toward Sheng, who still clutched his mother, knelt and told him, "Hop on my back. I'll give you a ride."

From the eatery, they headed west toward the State of Cheng. They traveled for many days, and the closer they got to the border, the less worried they became. The mood of the local peasants also relaxed their concerns. But their journey had also taken a toll on Chien's wife and son. They had crossed the border into Cheng and stopped to break from the rigors of forced travel. Yuan reached into a pouch, retrieved a wine-soaked date. He left the last village with a small bundle of them, and now, the supply was almost gone. Yuan showed the fruit to Sheng's mother, motioning to the boy, who leaned wearily against her.

She nodded her approval.

"Sheng, do you want a date?" Yuan asked.

Sheng looked to his mother for permission.

She smiled, and stroked the crown of his head.

He held out his hand, and Yuan placed the date in the boy's palm. Sheng immediately tried to duplicate Yuan's toss to the mouth. He watched the date fly above his head and arc – his mouth open and ready. But the date bounced off his nose and dropped to the ground. Yuan laughed as Sheng hurried to pick it up. No sooner had he retrieved the fruit, than the boy's mother grabbed it from him. She brushed it off, then returned it to Sheng's outstretched hand. The boy didn't mess with the toss this time. Instead, he plopped it between his teeth and bit down.

"Yuan?" Sheng asked with a puzzled inflection.

"Yes, Sheng."

"How do you do that trick?"

"It takes practice," Yuan smiled.

"And a big mouth," Lan added. "Let's hope your's doesn't grow wide like Yuan's."

They laughed. Even Fen Yang couldn't resist bursting with a chuckle. It was one of the few moments of respite they had enjoyed since leaving Chengfu. Perhaps they were finding comfort with their circumstances, or just relieved that they were not in immediate danger.

"Yuan?" Sheng smacked on the fruit.

"Yes?"

"Why does this date taste funny?"

"It's soaked in wine," Yuan replied. "Is it funny good or funny bad?"

"Good," the boy answered. He sighed, sat down on a grassy patch beside the road, rested his elbows on his knees and his head in his hands, and withdrew to the simple pleasure of the snack.

The villages along the way made obtaining food easy, although their meals had not come as frequently or were as filling as Sheng was accustomed to, and traveling this way had more than wore thin.

Yuan was anxious to leave Sung far behind. Mountains rose above the plain in the distant horizon. They were the eastern-most extension of a range that reached west to the Yellow River, and the nearest edge fanned into webbed toes as it descended toward them. *Can the boy make it?* Yuan worried. "Sheng," he said, getting the boy's attention. "Do you see those mountains?" Yuan pointed westward.

Shen nodded.

Yuan knelt beside him. "The front of that mountain looks like a dragon's claw. Do you see that?"

Sheng perked up, squinted, then answered, "Yes."

"The city we're going to lies around the corner to the north. There are two ways to get there. One is a shortcut through a mountain pass, but it's a hard climb. The other way is an easier walk on this road." He waved his arm back and forth, showing the direction. "It goes around the mountian, but it's longer." He didn't know how to better quantify the choice for the boy. "Which way do you want to go?"

Sheng looked at his mother, then at the mountain. "The road," he said with confidence

"Thanks, Sheng," Lan happily piped in with a chuckle.

"Yes. You saved us all from having to climb that mountain." Yuan smiled. "Come on, I'll give you a ride." He picked up Sheng and whirled him around, landing the boy on his back. "One more push, and we'll be in Zheng, the capital of Cheng. Are you ready?"

"Yes!" Sheng let loose a wide smile.

Their travels took another two days but once around the mountain's fanned edge, the road peeled off from the plateau to Zheng's East Gate. Guards stopped them there, outside the tower, which was attached to a sun-dried brick wall that was half as tall. The massive gate was raised, allowing a free flow of traffic into and out of the city.

Yuan approached four Cheng Guards stationed outside of the city's walls. "I am Yuan, and we escort Prince Chien, the Heir Apparent to the State of Chu. Can you direct us to Emissary Zuchan?"

A Guard looked over them, then asked, "Who do you wish to see?"

"Emissary Zuchan," Yuan repeated. *Should I have kept Chien's identity a secret?*

"That would be Chief Minister Zuchan," the Guard impassively corrected Yuan. "You aren't Cheng people and must have permission to enter the city. I'll send a messenger to see if the Chief Minister will grant you access, but don't count on it. The fact that you thought he was still an Emissary suggests you don't know him well. He may not care to see you." The

Guard motioned to a boy, who sat near the door to the gate house, then ordered Yuan, "Wait here."

Chien knew Zuchan, when he was the Emissary, but it had been a long time since their last meeting, and Zuchan's rise in rank, Yuan reasoned, would prove helpful. He joined the others to wait for the messenger's return, hoping the Guard's doubts were wrong.

They were huddled against the wall, away from the bustling traffic. It was late in the afternoon, but the markets were still open, and merchants wheeled past them, pushing carts with their products. One in particular caught Sheng's attention. A skinned carcass lay in the cart, its rear end still showing a pig's tail. Caged chickens, squawking as if they knew the butcher's cleaver was near, were next in line, all of which whet Sheng's appetite. His stomach let out a growl. Everyone heard it. He was not the only one who felt hunger pains.

Yuan patted the boy's belly and said, "It was a long walk on not enough food, wasn't it Sheng? You'll taste meat again soon. But we don't know how long our wait will be, so let's sit." Yuan plopped down, then leaned against the wall. He felt relief take over his body, but aches soon cascaded down his spine. *It's almost over.*

The others followed. Sheng curled next to his mother and laid his head in her lap.

Yuan lost track of time, but eventually he saw the messenger boy weave through the crowd. An older Guard and a handful of lesser rank Guards accompanied him. The boy messenger pointed to Yuan. The older Guard approached first. Yuan rose to meet him.

"I am Captain of the Guards. Who did you say you are?" The Captain looked over the group as if he didn't believe the boy messenger.

Yuan brushed himself off. "I am Yuan, and we accompany

Chien, Chu's Heir Apparent. We seek an audience with Chief Minister Zuchan. Is he available?"

"You look squalid and desolate. I would expect a different mode of travel for a King's son." The Captain grunted, then said, "Follow me. We will take you to the Chief Minister's home."

They followed the Captain through the gate and into the city, past shops and boarding houses, then beyond the East Market to the main road leading north. The buildings were thinly spaced, with gaps between them large enough for only one cart to pass at a time. They continued to the other side of the North Market and to Chief Minister Zuchan's compound.

A servant greeted them at the front gate. The compound was surrounded by a wall taller than a man, about half again. A series of interconnected courtyards wrapped the structure.

"Please follow me," the servant said. He led them inside the house and down a short hallway. The aroma of roasted meat teased them through an open doorway. "Help yourselves," he said, pointing to heaping plates of pork and chicken displayed on a table that was set against the back wall. He turned to Chien's wife and instructed, "Eat, then I will take you to accommodations that will better serve you and your son." And more appropriate for their status was the unspoken reason. Sheng bounded for the food.

Another servant entered the room and placed cups on the table. He filled them with tea and handed one to Chien. The pork and chicken was the first meat they had eaten in a while, having traveled mainly on boiled bread and dates, and they did not hesitate to accept the gratuity.

Chief Minister Zuchan entered, curious to see them looking so fatigued, their clothes dirty and tattered. "Prince Chien, it's been many years," the Chief Minister remarked. "This is a pleasant surprise."

Chien bowed, and said wearily, "Yes, Chief Minister Zuchan. It's good to see you again."

"What brings you here?"

Chien was hit with both relief in the hope of having found a safe haven and the gloom of his circumstances. "I had to flee Chu."

"There have been rumors, but I didn't believe them," the Chief Minister said. "I sensed not all was right when I was in Chu for the Sacrifice to the Gods, but I couldn't get a straight answer from Nang Wa. You know how he is."

"Yes, unfortunately. I do not know why, but it appears my father believes that I was plotting against him, which is far from the truth. He has ordered my execution." Chien paused, swallowing hard, then added, "Obviously, I can't return to Chu."

Chief Minister Zuchan nodded his understanding. "I'm sorry to hear about your misfortune."

"Chief Minister, this is Yuan." Chien extended an open hand toward his companion. He then did the same in turn, introducing Lan and Fen Yang. Chien didn't introduce the rest of the men. It wasn't expected. "We are grateful for your hospitality," Chien said. "These men helped me escape to Sung, but that country appears to be on the verge of revolt. So, we came here."

Chief Minister Zuchan exchanged bows with each of them.

"Yuan's father, Sheh, is my Grand Mentor," Chien explained.

"I see. I'm sorry, Yuan. I never met your father, but I knew him by reputation. He was a fine man, and I'm sure your brother was as well. Their end was tragic, and I extend my sympathy."

"What?" Yuan blurted. He straightened his frame and cocked his head.

Chief Minister Zuchan paused, taken aback by Yuan's reaction, then shook his head. "I thought you knew."

"Knew what?" Yuan raised his voice, alarmed by the implication.

Chief Minister Zuchan spoke softly. "Both Sheh and Shang were executed. I'm very sorry, Yuan." There was no need to recount the gruesome details.

Yuan fought back a surge of emotions. He stepped away, as if facing a different direction would somehow change reality. He leaned one hand against the wall and folded the other across his abdomen. He had believed King Ping's summons meant death. He'd told his brother as much, but Shang's sense of duty convinced him to go to Ying and plead for Sheh's safe return. Now, though, his brother's and father's ends were real, and the hope of being wrong and Shang right had to give way to truth.

Lan placed a sympathetic hand on Yuan's shoulder. "There was nothing that could be done." His voice cracked before he finished the sentence.

Yuan nodded and took a deep breath.

Fen Yang pulled on his collar, then lowered his head. He squeezed his eyes shut, then recovered. "Yuan, they died as they lived, honorably. I'm sure of it. That's the men they were."

Yuan's jaw clinched, and his lips tightened. He fought against the images of Sheh and Shang bowing to the executioner's block, then blinked back tears. *Avenge us both*, he remembered the last thing Shang said to him – a tall task given his circumstances.

An awkward hush fell over the room, and the discomfort urged Chief Minister Zuchan to fill the space with words. But he had none that could bring solace, so he changed the subject. "There's plenty of time for us to visit about why this situation exists, but for now, how can I help you?"

Chien lifted his head from his hands. He wiped away

tears. "I didn't know who to turn to. We need asylum, and I didn't think I could seek an audience with your Duke Ting directly. I'm embarrassed to ask, but would you do so on our behalf?"

"Please, Chien. There is no need to be embarrassed. I would be honored to speak for you. Of course, I can't decide for Duke Ting, but I'm sure you'll be welcome here in Cheng. And you'll be my guests until I can formalize things." The Chief Minister turned to a House Servant, then instructed, "Make the necessary arrangements for all of them, and be sure their accommodations are worthy of their positions. Chien, please take advantage of the comfort my hospitality can provide."

"Thank you, Chief Minister. You are most gracious. We left Chengfu and Sung so abruptly, we weren't prepared to make this trip. It was most difficult for my wife and son, and we are grateful for your generosity."

They exchanged bows, then the Chief Minister excused himself.

⇜

Days had passed since their visit with the Chief Minister. Chien's anxiety had abated, but Yuan remained distant and withdrawn. The living quarters Duke Ting had provided were a two-story compound, looped on the outside by a continuous courtyard. It was on the other side of the market from where Chief Minister Zuchan resided, which allowed them to come and go without a feeling of Royal eyes prying. The structure was made of four buildings fitted together so as to wrap around a center quad. Though small in comparison to the Chief Minister's palatial residence, the compound was still more spacious and the furnishings better suited to their stations in life than Chengfu had provided. Food was always available. Rice wine flowed, and silken robes, refreshed each day, felt luxurious on the skin. The smooth silk was a nice change from the battle tunic Yuan had worn since leaving Chengfu.

They had grown accustomed to congregating in a parlor that overlooked the front courtyard. This day, though, only Yuan and Chien were present. A silk screen stood head-high near an interior corner, hiding a serving table and servant entryway. Chien stepped out from behind the screen, sipping a cup of tea. A House Servant had just finished opening shutters to windows that lined the wall across the room, then stepped past Chien and disappeared through the servant's door.

Chien glanced into the yard, and once certain he and Yuan were alone, he turned and signaled with a nod to get Yuan's attention. But Yuan didn't react. He, instead, stared at a blank spot on the wall next to the main door, lost deep in thought. "Yuan," Chien called. He didn't wait for Yuan to acknowledge him and continued, "There is no man I respected more than Sheh. He was more to me than Grand Mentor, and I will miss him and his calm guidance." Chien looked down, reflecting solemnly on Sheh's fate, then finished, "I could always rely on his counsel. And I am certain that Shang would have become the same man as Sheh. But now, I need your advice. What should I do?"

Yuan moved closer to Chien. "So long as we stay in the Northern Alliance, we will be safe from your father's orders."

"Do you think Duke Ting will be suspicious of me?" Chien asked.

To harbor Chien would certainly raise the ire of King Ping, which meant risk for Duke Ting, but it would also provide an opportunity to gain further insight into King Ping's intentions, desires and plans, and most importantly, to win the trust and friendship of the person who could one day legitimately claim the throne of Chu.

"The Duke will be curious," Yuan answered. He sat down on a wide chair, its back adorned with the spread wings of a crane carved into the center. A small round table separated him and Chien.

Chien placed a cup onto the table and leaned forward. "But how will I live? I have no lands, no subjects of my own." The words came out timidly.

"It's not unusual for someone in your station to be granted lands somewhere. But it is too early to address that." Yuan paused, interrupted by a voice from the doorway. Chief Minister Zuchan walked into the room wearing a welcoming smile.

"Prince Chien, I have good news. Duke Ting is happy to extend the hospitality of Cheng to you for as long as you need." Chief Minister Zuchan hesitated for a moment, then his demeanor turned serious. "There is something the Duke asks of you, but he wants it understood that his help in your time of need is in no way contingent upon this favor."

"Certainly." Chien felt immediate relief. "Tell us what we can do for him."

"Your recent trip to Sung gives you a unique perspective as to what's going on there. We hope that their problem stays in Sung and doesn't spill over into Cheng."

"Oh, I don't see that happening. The problem is internal. I didn't see anything to worry you," Chien offered.

"Yes, of course, but Duke Ting would prefer that you consult with him directly on it."

"We would be happy to." Chien gushed with eagerness to be helpful.

"And then travel to Jin to inform them as well." Chief Minister Zuchan explained, "We're all a part of the Northern Alliance, and we each try to keep abreast of unusual circumstances such as yours. We're like siblings that way. There is no hurry, though. You'll have plenty of time to recover from your recent journey."

"Of course. We will be happy to do so," Chien reassured him. The news of Duke Ting's offer uplifted him, and he was eager to cooperate. "How long do you expect the trip to take?"

"That depends on how long you stay in Jin and enjoy their generosity. There are many pleasures there. Of course your wife and son are welcome to remain here as my guests."

"Thank you, Chief Minister. When does Duke Ting want to visit with us?" Chien asked.

"This afternoon."

"I will be happy to meet with him as he wishes."

"Good, I'll be back shortly to accompany you."

Yuan remained quiet, choosing instead to observe. Chien, though, enlivened by the positive turn, straightened his back and released a smile, the first in a long time.

20

SECRET MESSAGES

C hien's meeting with Duke Ting had enlivened him. At last he was treated like royalty, and with newfound optimism, he left for Jin.

Upon arrival, he wasted no time seeking an audience with Duke Ching and Prime Minister Zhou. Lan and Fen Yang, along with the Chengfu foot-soldiers, had escorted him to Jin. News of Chien's circumstances and King Ping's reward to anyone who demonstrated proof of Chien's death had arrived in Cheng before Chien, and the same was probably true for Jin, so the escort stayed close at hand. Yuan, though, needed time alone to mourn the deaths of his father and brother, so he remained in Cheng.

Chien had already delivered the bound message from Duke Ting and was in Jin's Palace, waiting for a personal meeting. Lan and Fen Yang accompanied him safely to the Palace, then waited outside as protocol demanded. Chien stepped into a sitting room and was immediately struck by the splendor. The room reminded him of better days in Ying. An embroidered silk-screen spanned a long wall. Chien stared at the details, remembering the days when he enjoyed the finer things being Heir Apparent had allowed. He'd been too caught up in staying alive over the past months to think about the pleasant, lighter things in life. But now that he was in Jin, a place known for cultural splendor, he took notice of why the Jin artisans held their reputation.

In the background of the screen, a mountainous splendor rose into the clouds, while at the fore, a waterfall's flow cascaded downstream through a chain of lakes, finally easing into a still pool. A majestic garden cupped the near edge. Twelve courtesans, whose robes were adorned with a single, spectacular bird, frolicked in the garden scene. Chien marveled at the artistry. The robe of the first courtesan sported a crane, wings spreading as it took flight. Fibers of each feather were meticulously present. Chien ran his fingers across a wing. *Painstaking work,* he thought. A magnificent chariot occupied the path to the mountain, upstream from the garden. So intricate was the work, the wheels showed eighteen spokes. He yearned for his old life. *Will I ever return to Chu?*

It was a nice break from the things that weighed heavily on his mind. The initial shock of his father ordering his death, the turmoil in Sung, and the news of Sheh and Shang's executions, all continued to burden him. The trip to Jin, though, had provided Chien time to think. The first opportunity to calmly digest all that had happened and consider what faced him now. And what he had to do to salvage his future occupied most of his waking thoughts.

It's not unusual for someone in my station to be granted land, he remembered Yuan telling him. *But how do I get it? I suppose Jin is better able to provide it than Cheng. Should I focus here? How much land is too much to seek? I don't want to be unappreciative, but how do I get the most? How do I ask for it? Or do I? Should I be subtle or blunt?* Chien took a deep breath, fretting over the questions. *Sheh always said that to be King, I must act like one. A King always gets what he wants, so I should just ask for it.* He shook his head at the quandary. *I wish Yuan was here. I need his guidance. I should not have come to Jin without him.*

"Excuse me," a Palace Servant interrupted. "Duke Ching and Prime Minister Zhou will see you now. Follow me."

Chien trailed the servant into a large room where two men stood, one with a welcoming smile. Jin's Prime Minister Zhou stepped forward. He was a tall man with a dignified manner, bordering on fatherly. He reminded Chien of Sheh, except for the bushy eyebrows.

The Prime Minister greeted Chien, and then introduced Duke Ching. The Duke was about the same age as the Prime Minister but wore no expression.

"Thank you both for taking time to meet with me," Chien said, after straightening from a bow.

"Prince Chien, please, think nothing of it. We are glad to help where we can," Prime Minister Zhou reassured him. "Have you been offered refreshments?" He pointed to a servant, who stood quietly near a table where rice wine and tea were ready for him to serve.

"Oh yes. Thank you. Your staff has taken good care of me." The small talk didn't ease the nervousness Chien felt.

"And your accommodations here, are they adequate? Have you had an opportunity to enjoy the splendor of life in Jin?" The Prime Minister hoped to keep Jin's qualities at the front of Chien's mind.

Yes, quite so. You've been most gracious."

"Good." The Prime Minister's tone had changed. He sat down at a square table, joined by Duke Ching, then motioned to the empty place to his left for Chien to sit. "We've looked at your situation and know that this is a troublesome time for you. You have our sympathies."

"Thank you, Prime Minister." Chien matched the serious tone. "You are right. These are difficult times for me."

"Have you given much thought to what you'll do, now that you can't return to Chu?"

"I haven't thought much about anything else." Chien tried to make eye contact but couldn't hold it.

Prime Minister Zhou turned his chair, so that he faced Chien, then leaned his right elbow on the corner of the table. "Tell us, what have you decided?"

Chien cleared his throat, "Well, I'd like a parcel of land, Prime Minister, just enough so that I can maintain my station in life, of course." *That was clumsy,* Chien thought.

"Of course," the Prime Minister said. For only a blink of an eye, he showed a partial smile. "What land are you thinking about?"

Chien lowered his head in embarrassment. "I don't know. That detail is part of my troubles."

"I see." Prime Minister Zhou looked over at Duke Ching, and after receiving a confirming nod, asked, "You were in Sung recently, weren't you?"

"Yes. When I left Chengfu, I traveled to Sung, seeking from them the hospitality you've been so gracious to extend."

"We're very curious about what is going on there. What can you tell us?" The Prime Minister fixed a steady gaze on Chien.

"I'm afraid I don't know much. The Hua clan looms, bent on righting some wrong, and I suppose taking control of the country. We didn't stay long enough to learn the details, and having seen the Hua clan's disposition firsthand, I think we didn't leave soon enough." Chien chuckled, hoping to ease his nerves.

The other two men remained silent, keeping a serious demeanor. "These times are tumultuous, not only for you," the Prime Minister concluded.

Chien cleared his throat, then awkwardly returned to a serious demeanor. "Yes, they are."

"Prince Chien, Duke Ching and I have been on this world much longer than you, and chaotic times are normal. There will always be trouble somewhere." The Prime Minister struck a tutorial air. "Someone will always want what you have. That is the way of man and therefore, the way of States."

Chien rocked on the cushioned seat. "Yes. I've learned that lesson."

"You certainly have. No one, though, has been able to do to our Duke Ching what has happened to you. Tell me, do you know why that is?"

Chien struggled for an answer, shrugged, then replied, "No. I don't."

Prime Minister Zhou leaned back. "It's because we understand, and have for many years, that the only way to survive is to forge long-lasting friendships."

"Yes, I see the wisdom," Chien nodded, attempting to appear worthy of their interest.

"Duke Ching and I like you and want to help. Tell me, what is your greatest threat?"

Chien looked past the Prime Minister. "It's my father. So long as his order stands, I'm not safe."

"So, you must either overturn the order or the man."

"Yes. But how?" Chien was anxious for that direction.

The Prime Minister's eyebrows lifted, one slightly more than the other, into his wrinkled forehead. "You have friends here in Jin. I do mean that, and I hope you'll come to accept our friendship."

Chien shook his head. "Oh, I do Prime Minister. You are most kind." He glanced at Duke Ching and thought it unusual the man hadn't spoken.

The Prime Minister removed bamboo slips from a leather pouch, then lifted it in plain sight. "Prince Chien, do you know what was in the message you brought to us from Duke Ting?"

"Not the details. I was told it was about Sung, and there was something in it describing my situation."

"What I'm about to tell you, I do so in confidence. Can I count on you not to reveal my words?" Prime Minister Zhou provided emphasis by locking his gaze on Chien for an uncomfortably long pause.

"Certainly, Prime Minister," Chien said eagerly.

"Duke Ting recommends a surprise attack against Chu. He wants you to gain access for us to the Middle Huai through Ts'ai and solicit your uncle's help to get it. Once that route is secured, he suggests that Jin and Cheng jointly attack. His plan is to lure Chu into believing that Wu is attacking farther up the Huai River, cause it to mobilize against that threat, then strike from two sides. He seeks 500 chariots from Jin to join 200 from Cheng. He expects you to accompany Cheng's forces. If we're successful, you'll succeed your father, and your future will be restored."

Chien rolled his shoulders back, feeling a sudden jolt of enthusiasm. "If we're successful, it solves my problem."

"Don't get too enthusiastic," the Prime Minister cautioned.

"You don't think the strategy is sound?" Chien said, confused by the Prime Minister's wariness.

"We happen to know that Duke Ting is attempting to deceive us, and he's using you to do it."

Chien slumped. The excitement dissipated as quickly as the surprise had swept through him. "What do you mean?"

"We've known for some time of the relationship between the Hua clan and Duke Ting. He is secretly helping them take over Sung. You see, Duke Ting has a long-running hatred for the Duke of Sung, and he's using the Hua clan to seek revenge and gain an ally on his border."

"I don't understand," Chien said, baffled by the news.

"Once the Hua clan takes control, they'll owe him for his help, and payment of that debt will be to combine Sung's forces with Cheng against us." The Prime Minister waggled his finger. "But Jin is the real goal. In order to succeed, he needs Jin's army occupied elsewhere. Your predicament has provided him with a timely ruse, so he's trying to coax us into attacking Chu, dividing our army and leaving Jin exposed. He has no intention of actually sending 200 chariots farther than is necessary to maintain that deception." He looked off, drumming his fingers on the table. The muscles around his lips tightened. "I am certain he has made plans for Chu to learn of our invasion well in advance, which will only ensure that Chu and Jin will weaken each other," he speculated. "I can only guess that he plans to turn you over to your father. That way, he'll deny being a part of the attack on Chu and gain favor with King Ping. While all that is happening, Cheng's chariots and soldiers will be redirected to attack our southern border. He will also invade us from the east, with help from Sung."

Chien's lift from the thought of returning to Ying to capture his rightful place quickly disappeared, and the emotional fall came as quickly as the uplift. "This is incredible!"

"As I said earlier, we have survived, remained stable and prospered because we know how to choose friends." Prime Minister Zhou motioned to a servant, who brought Chien a drink, and after sipping from his own cup, he continued, "You, we believe, are worthy of our friendship. We're looking to the next generation and believe that you can be a trusted ally of Jin for many years. Will you be?"

Chien sat frozen. He balanced the cup, as if ready to lift it to his lips, but his arm stopped before completing the movement. "Of course. Forgive me, but I am still stunned by all of this. I have been in Chengfu too long, because all I saw was a strong Northern Alliance. I didn't know about your internal struggles."

"That's to be expected. This must be a surprise for you." The Prime Minister took another sip. "You are right that the

Northern Alliance is strong and will remain committed against the threat Chu presents. But when your father is not occupying our attention, less virtuous members within the pact look to better their positions."

"I'm not sure what to do," Chien said in confusion.

"We've watched this materialize for some time, but we weren't sure what Duke Ting's true goal was until he used you and your situation. Now it's obvious. He wants Jin vulnerable because he intends to attacks us."

"So what do you do about it?" Chien patted his chest and asked, "What do I do?"

"We have three choices. We could have done and said nothing, simply choosing to reject the proposal. But that would leave you subject to Duke Ting's whims and exempt him from any consequences for attempting this scheme." The Prime Minister cocked his head, then continued, "Or we can let Duke Ting know that we're aware of his plans and cause him some discomfort in some punitive way. That, though, would leave him in place to plot against us again. The other option is to send him to his ancestors."

Chien's nervousness turned to anger at the thought of being used. He had suffered enough from events in Chu, and now Duke Ting's designs insulted him. "What is it you said earlier about my father? 'I must overturn his order or the man.' Better to send both to their ancestors, I think. That's the only result guaranteed to last."

Duke Ching broke his silence and interjected, "We are all hardened by personal experiences, and those of us who survive chaotic times learn from those experiences. I'm convinced that you are a survivor. Your presence here has proven that much. Chu will become yours one day, I'm certain of it, and we can help you."

Chien smiled. "What do I do? I can't go back to Cheng with Duke Ting's devious intentions toward me."

"But you should go back," the Prime Minister insisted. "In fact, we have an idea that, I believe, will make up for the troubles you've suffered. As we speak, we are mobilizing forces sufficient to defeat Cheng. They are being moved to various places along the border. They will strike Cheng the morning after the next full moon. Duke Ting will be dead by then."

"Dead? How?" The revelation overwhelmed Chien.

"We want to protect you, so you should not learn those details. The only thing you need to do is introduce a man to Duke Ting, and then stay out of the way. He'll do the rest."

"A man?" Chien replied, startled. "Who?"

Prime Minister Zhou ignored Chien's question. "Once Duke Ting is out of the way, Cheng will quickly fall, and all of it will be yours to rule, until we are able to help you return to Chu. We don't want Cheng. We care only about maintaining the safety and security of Jin. And friendly neighbors are an important part of it. I am now convinced that Duke Ting is not who we want on our border, but you will be, won't you?"

Chien shared smiles with his new allies. "This is all so much to consider . . ." Thoughts raced through his mind. All of Cheng to rule in the interim and help later in taking the throne of Chu was more than he had hoped for. The answers he wanted were before him, and to achieve it, he only had to make an introduction. He sat the cup on the table and asked, "What if Duke Ting doesn't grant me an audience with him?"

The Prime Minister folded his arms across his chest and mused, "He will want to know if we sent a response to his message. Our message will say that the information is too sensitive to commit to writing. It will tell him that the man, who accompanies you, possesses the details. Duke Ting will summon both of you to find out those details. You will introduce this man, whose name is Chuan Chu, to the Duke, then excuse yourself." Prime Minister Zhou raised his hand and in a softened voice said, "This is very important. Leave the building immediately. Make sure you depart by yourself and return to your guest quarters, as if nothing is wrong."

"But if he accompanies me, they'll accuse me of participating," Chien pointed out.

"True, there is some risk for you," the Prime Minister acknowledged. "But remember, they didn't involve you in the details of their scheme against us. They won't automatically assume that we did. You simply delivered messages between two Dukes who have shown you generosity in your time of need. Is that risk acceptable?"

"You survived the entire might of Chu," Duke Ching cajoled, "so this won't even get your blood raging."

Chien wondered if his smile looked strained. It didn't feel natural, like the Prime Minister's.

Duke Ching offered friendly encouragement. "Your rule of Cheng will be a great thing for that State and the Northern Alliance. I'm convinced. Wouldn't you like to see the expression worn by your father when he hears how you turned your fortunes around?" He cackled. "Of course, ruling Cheng means you're a part of the Northern Alliance, and with our backing, eventually you'll take your rightful place on Chu's throne. In the meantime, your father won't be able to carry out his plans for your death without invading. And if he does, the Northern Alliance will share that burden with you. Your immediate problem is solved, but your return to Chu, though, will take more time and planning."

Prime Minister Zhou motioned to a servant, who handed a box to Chien. It was wooden, inlaid with colored stones and supported at the corners with green-copper serpent figures. "I'm sure there are some things that you and your people will need to get you through this period. In that box you'll find five hundred gold pieces to help."

"Prime Minister!" Chien exclaimed.

"Prince Chien, please take it," Duke Ching insisted. "I

know your predicament, and it's a small matter for us to help someone who will become a great friend."

"Thank you, again, you are most gracious," Chien said tentatively.

Prime Minister Zhou pressed, "Chien, no doubt this is very serious. Are you willing to help us? Are you willing to help yourself?"

Act like a King, he thought. "Yes, Prime Minister. I expect our friendship will be life long."

21

TURMOIL IN ZHENG

*C*hien stood with his back against the wall near an outside corner of the parlor. He had returned to Cheng and was in the guest compound Duke Ting had provided. He wanted to feel at home in it, but didn't. Whether his mood was driven by ambition or anxiety, he didn't know, but whichever the answer, he was far from comfortable.

His attention vacillated from the window to the wooden box given to him when he was in Jin. It was on the table beside him. He played with the lid, lifting it, then putting it back in place without looking inside. Four times he went through the motion, and in-between each one, he gazed into the courtyard.

Yuan had noticed this nervous change in him since Chien's trip to Jin. Chien remained agitated and distant. *What's he edgy about?* Yuan wondered. The days had been tranquil and a peaceful spirit should have ruled his demeanor.

He had inquired about Chien's mood before, searching for the source of the angst, but to no avail. This day, though, he was committed to finding answers. He walked over to Chien but the sound of footsteps in the hallway interrupted him.

"Excuse me," a House Servant said at the doorway to the room. "Prince Chien, I have word from Duke Ting. He will see you and Jin's envoy in the morning."

Chien picked up the lid again, stopped, then replied, "I'll tell the envoy."

"Is there anything you desire now, Prince Chien?" the House Servant asked.

"Leave us," Chien snapped. He slammed the lid shut.

The House Servant bowed, then exited.

Yuan eyed Chien warily. "What's bothering you? This should be a pleasant day."

Chien stepped away, breathing heavier. His look turned from irritation to almost giddy, and once the servant's footsteps faded out of range, he said, "Tomorrow, our fortunes turn."

"How so?" Yuan asked, puzzled at such a bold declaration.

"But there may be trouble, so we should spend the day here in the compound, except for the brief time I'm with Duke Ting." Chien worked to keep from bursting with excitement. He looked exhilarated, but his secretiveness was most unusual. He had not told Yuan of Jin's plan, and holding it in didn't come natural to him.

"What do you mean? What's going on?" Yuan persisted.

Chien paced to the other side of the room, then answered, "I can't say. I promised Jin's Prime Minister."

"Tell me what's going on." Yuan squared his shoulders, not liking what he heard.

Chien looked away, toward the window. "I can't."

Yuan threw out his chest and blurted, "What do you mean, you can't?"

Chien remained guarded. "All I can tell you is that change is coming, and trouble may follow."

Yuan huffed. "Before you left for Jin, you said that you needed my counsel. Now is the time to seek it," he urged, his frustration growing. "This has something to do with the man who returned with you, doesn't it?" Yuan thought the man's burly stature was odd for a Jin envoy. He had a physical prowess inconsistent with the Jin nobility. They led too easy a life to develop such a hardened body.

Chien went silent, his eyes darting one way then another.

"The man from Jin is no envoy, is he?" Yuan proposed.

Chien shook his head and muttered, "No he's not."

Yuan stepped closer and lowered his voice. "Chien, you must tell me!"

Chien let out a sigh. "Duke Ting was just using me to lure Jin's forces away so that Cheng can attack Jin."

Yuan cocked his head, puzzled by the news. "I don't believe it."

"I didn't either at first. But Duke Ting asked Jin to join Cheng in attacking Father," Chien explained. "His plan was for Jin to send 500 chariots and for Cheng to commit 200. He plans to turn before the battle with Chu, while Jin's forces are split, and rush to attack inside Jin. His chariots will strike from the south, and the remainder of Cheng's forces, combined with the Hua clan and the rest of Sung's army, will attack from the east."

"Sung?" Yuan scoffed. "How are they involved?"

"Duke Ting is secretly supporting the Hua revolt. Once they gain control of Sung, they'll repay Duke Ting by joining the fight against Jin."

Yuan ran his hand along the side of his forehead and down the back of his neck. "So what does Jin have planned for Duke Ting?"

"He'll die. Tomorrow."

Yuan shook his head in disbelief. "How could you get involved in this?"

"Yuan, you of all people should understand. After what happened to Sheh and Shang, don't you want to be on the side that delivers the end instead of the one that receives it?" Chien reached out and tugged on Yuan's arm. "I'll never be burdened again by such designs – not from Nang Wa or Fei – not even from Father."

Yuan raised a halting hand. "Are you sure Jin's not the one manipulating you? Are you being Jin's fool?"

"No. Of course not," Chien sneered, incredulous at the thought.

Yuan stepped closer and asked in a somber voice. "Did you test them?"

Chien pulled back. "What do you mean?"

Yuan paused to wipe his brow. "Tell me how you learned of Duke Ting's plan?"

Chien shrugged, then paced back toward the table. "Duke Ting wrote it in the message he gave me to deliver to Duke Ching."

"Did you read it?"

Chien dismissed the implication. "Well, no, but the Prime Minister gave me the details."

Yuan took a deep breath, then sighed. "You didn't see it?"

Chien straightened his back. "No. Why does that matter?"

"You simply believed what they told you?" Yuan's brow furrowed, dejected by Chien's decision. *You weren't being naïve. You were being stupid!* He continued to press, "And how do you know Duke Ting is involved in Sung?"

"Jin's Prime Minister explained it to me. Duke Ting was going to turn me over to Father," Chien insisted. "Fortunately, the Prime Minister brought this to my attention and has offered me a way out of the scheme. Tomorrow is the day I repay Duke Ting for his plan. And it is the first step toward gaining my kingdom."

"Oh Chien, you've read this badly." Yuan's brow furrowed. He looked away for a moment, then turned back to Chien. "What exactly do they want you to do?"

"I only have to introduce Chuan Chu to Duke Ting. Shortly afterward, the conniving Duke Ting will be with his ancestors, and I'll be out from under his designs. He deserves this fate for using me."

Yuan shook his head in disagreement. "I'm not convinced he's the one using you, Chien."

"You weren't there. I was, and the Prime Minister was very convincing."

"I'm sure he was," Yuan nodded. "Nang Wa is convincing, too. How do you think he reached his station in life? But do you believe anything he says?"

"No." Chien squirmed with his answer.

"Then why do you trust Jin's Prime Minister?"

"Because he seeks my friendship and an alliance with me."

"If Jin is scheming, wouldn't they want you to believe your friendship is what they desire?" Yuan didn't wait for Chien to reply, but pushed for more answers. "What are you supposed to do immediately after Duke Ting suffers this fate?"

"I'm supposed to make the introduction, then leave. And be visible on the street, outside the Palace before it's done."

"Why would this assassin want to give you time to get away?"

"It's part of Prime Minister Zhou's plan," Chien said, still hanging on to his righteous belief.

"Chien, I'm dumbfounded." Yuan heaved a groan, then rubbed his brow. But it did nothing to wipe away the worry lines. "Then what?" His tenor turned to disgust.

"Stay out of the way, as Jin invades. After they defeat Cheng, I'll rule it. You said I might be granted land some-where, remember? Well, this is my chance," Chien implored. "It's so much more than I expected. It's the whole State of Cheng, until it's time to take Chu from Father. And then I will have the Northern Alliance backing me," Chien leaned into his words, accenting the opportunity.

"How do you expect to rule people who are loyal to others? You have no troops here, but the nobles do. You won't survive four sunsets. None of us will." Yuan read Chien's face. The so-ber questions brought a haze of confusion to the naïve Prince.

Chien paced across the room, farther away from Yuan.

Yuan glanced at the wooden box, curious as to why Chien had been distracted by it. He opened the lid and saw a leather pouch nestled inside. "What's this?" Yuan turned it over and dumped the contents. Gold pieces tumbled out. Yuan groaned. "Look at it this way. You don't know which side is telling the truth."

Chien threw up his hands. "You're right."

"Chien, I know you feel isolated, probably even helpless, but we have no base of support and no true allies yet. Sooner or later, we may have to take sides, but this is not the time. For now, get out of this mess between Cheng and Jin. Go now to Chief Minister Zuchan, and tell him that you've just discovered what Jin is attempting to do. Tell him Jin plans to use you and your meeting with Duke Ting for its own gain. Let him know you're not a part of it."

Chien lowered his head and mumbled, "I'll have to add Jin to the list of places hostile to me. Chu's out. Jin's out. How am I going to survive?"

Yuan put his hand on Chien's shoulder, "I'll go with you." If Jin is playing you, Chief Minister Zuchan will not be pleased. But we don't want him to think that you repaid his hospitality with treachery. You must avoid that perception."

Chien released a heavy sigh. "Walk with me, but I think I should visit with him on my own." *It's what a King would do.*

The two left the guest quarters for the Chief Minister's compound, located on the other side of the market, along the main street that led to the Palace.

They passed through the market. It was busy with vendors, artisans, craftsmen and shoppers. Once on the other side and a short distance from the Chief Minister's compound, Yuan stopped. "Let me go with you."

"No, I'll see you back at the house," Chien replied, not looking forward to the chore that lay ahead.

"I'll leave you here, then," Yuan agreed, against his better judgment. "I know these are difficult times for you, and it's easy to cling to the people who offer your dreams, but considering what we don't know, this is the safest choice. Right now, we should not take chances, because if we're wrong, we'll pay for it with our lives."

Chien nodded his agreement. "I'll see you back at our quarters," he said, then sauntered away.

Yuan watched until Chien disappeared through the gate of the Chief Minister's compound, then he walked back to the market. His hand rested casually on his sword's hilt while he strolled among the crowd, making his way to the other end. Yuan stopped at an eatery for an afternoon meal, and in a spot out of the way from most of the traffic, he settled down. People came and went, and soon his thoughts drifted. He stared across the market at all of the men, young and old, going about their daily lives. One artisan sat tucked near the back of his shop, carving a wooden figure. His young apprentice, probably a son Yuan guessed, tended to customers while the old man paid close attention to every detail. His attentiveness was not of interest to Yuan, but the way the senior artisan worked his tongue from side to side provided a light moment.

Yuan enjoyed the pleasant diversion during the hours that passed. He had not intended for so much time to slip by, but it had, and the sun neared the horizon. Shopkeepers began to close and lock up, and looking around, he noticed that he was the only customer in the eatery. How long he had been alone, he wasn't sure, but it was time to return to the guest house. *I hope Chien was able to make amends. The Chief Minister will be angry, but if he believes the notion that Chien just learned of Jin's plans and was not a participant, his temper will ease,* Yuan surmised. Chien was gullible, his judgment showed as much, and any information he had to provide unrehearsed worried Yuan. *Better go back. Chien must have returned by now.* He pulled a pouch from an inside pocket sewn into his robe, removed a green-copper coin, then flipped it to the center of the table.

The orange glow of dusk lit his walk back, and the nightly curfew was soon to commence. Yuan entered the courtyard, then stopped near a Servant Gardener, who gathered tools under his arms, bringing an end to his day's work. "Have you seen Prince Chien?"

"No," the man replied.

Yuan entered the house and saw Lan and Fen Yang at the other end of the hallway. Lan was animated, and the expressions both men wore revealed that something was very wrong.

"What's happened?" Yuan asked.

"Chien is dead!" Lan blurted out.

"What?" Yuan couldn't believe the news.

Yuan's five foot-soldiers huddled beside Lan. "Some of the men and I were north of the market when I saw several men dragging Chien's body down the street, feet first. One of the House Servants from our guest quarters was with them."

"Damn! Someone must have heard us." Yuan pressed his hands over his crown, then down the back of his neck. *Chief Minister Zuchan helped Chien in a time of need, and Chien repaid the favor with a plot against his country. That's all the Chief Minister heard.* "I should have been there."

"Look! Guards. A lot of them," Fen Yang shouted, pointing toward the courtyard.

Yuan looked through the open door and saw a threatening horde running toward them. "Go!" he shouted.

They scurried away from the oncoming Cheng Guards. Yuan was near the rear. Lan, leading the way, turned toward the inner apartments.

"No, Lan. The other way," Yuan pointed, "toward the back apartments."

"But our battle tunics are in our rooms," Lan rushed to say.

"There's no time!" Yuan took the lead, turning down the hallway, then busted through an inner courtyard. Three sides of it were bordered by apartments. They hurried through the closest door, where Chien's wife stood clutching Sheng. Yuan slowed when she reached for him.

Tears streamed from her eyes. "Please Yuan! Please! Take my son. Save Sheng for me. Please!" she begged.

He snatched the boy from her and placed him on his hip. Yuan spun her by the arm, then shouted, "Come this way." There was no time to weigh the choices. They both would make escaping more difficult, an obvious reality Yuan ignored.

"No!" She cried. "You have a better chance without me. I'll just slow you down." She waved them off, then hunched forward, wailing. She cupped her mouth with one hand, and clutched her stomach with the other.

Yuan felt Sheng tug on his collar, while the child reached for his mother's arms. Goodbyes were a luxury they could not afford. They had to keep moving. The hallway ended at an intersection with a corridor, and after Yuan turned the corner, he heard the sound of Cheng Guards stop where he had left the woman.

"Please! Please don't!" Yuan heard her beg, followed by her shriek, then a clamor, rumbling toward him.

Yuan ducked into an unused bedchamber and put Sheng down. Lan, Fen Yang and the foot-soldiers followed. The last one through the door closed it. Another wedged a small table against it in an effort to slow the pursuers.

Yuan knelt in front of Sheng, took the boy's head between his hands and whispered, "You must trust me. You heard your mother ask me to save you, didn't you?"

Sheng, stunned, responded with only a slight nod of the head.

"Be very quiet, and do as I say. We have a difficult journey ahead of us. Do you understand?" Circumstances didn't allow for a soft touch.

Again, the boy nodded, then wiped tears from his eyes.

"We must get out of the city, and out of Cheng!" Yuan opened the shutters to a window that led to an outer courtyard. He looked left, then right, and saw no Cheng Guards. Night had almost fallen, and the glow from lanterns, positioned along the wall, provided visibility. *Good. We have a chance,* he thought. The window was just large enough to squeeze through, one at a time. Lan and Fen Yang went first. Yuan followed with Sheng, while the others leaned against the door, holding back the Cheng Guards' charge. With each thrust, the door cracked, then closed with the soldiers' counter.

Yuan made it one step into the courtyard, then heard frantic shouts from around the corner of the house.

"Over here. There, by the wall!" barked a Cheng Guard.

Lan scurried to the top of the wall. Yuan grabbed Sheng, then lifted the boy over his head, while Lan pulled from above. Yuan followed, as did Fen Yang.

"Hurry!" Yuan yelled to his men.

The last soldier jumped out of the window, hit the ground, then shouted, "Go on!"

Waves of two and three Cheng Guards ran toward the soldiers. They seemed endless. Yuan watched long enough to see two of his soldiers advance side-by-side to meet the charge. The soldier on the left, wielding a short sword, ducked below the swing of a Cheng Guard's blade, then countered with a slashing blow across the back of his enemy's calf. The guard's leg collapsed, causing him to fall onto his side. He grabbed at the wound, not seeing the final strike. Yuan's soldier slipped his weapon in between two plates of the man's armor, then drove the point hard into the chest.

Yuan hopped off the wall to the other side before the

piercing squall ended. Lan lowered Sheng to him, then followed. "The West Gate is the closest way out. We'll go that way," Yuan said. Fen Yang leapt from the wall. Yuan paused to see if his other men were next, but the clash of swords and shrieks of pain from inside the courtyard informed otherwise. Yuan put Sheng on his back and took off.

They sprinted to a point where Yuan felt the need to see who followed. He turned toward the courtyard wall and saw that one of his soldiers had crossed over, hobbling near the center of the road. Two others joined him. Behind them, Cheng Guards scaled over the wall in pursuit. The outline of one, the Captain of the Guards, Yuan believed, stood atop the wall shouting orders. The only chance for them to escape was to get lost in the night, outside of the city. Their hobbling companion was in no shape to join them, Yuan realized.

Lan drew his sword, turned to Yuan, then said, "Take Sheng and get out of here! We'll buy you as much time as we can."

"No, we must go with them," Fen Yang insisted. "They can't get past the gate alone."

"Fen Yang is right," Yuan agreed. "All of us need to get out of the city." He looked at his soldiers near the wall. Only three of the five had made it over. The one who hobbled waved him on. Yuan paused. They were too far away to meet the eye of each one. He bowed, grateful for their sacrifice. Yuan adjusted Sheng on his back, then darted off, hugging the street's edge.

Twelve blocks down and a couple over, near the West Gate, Yuan stopped, put Sheng down, then stepped in between two shops to examine their situation. The sun was behind the horizon. They knelt in the darkness counting the Gate Guards. The crew stood watch on the ground, plus the Gatekeeper, who manned the heavy timber door from the tower. "Too many to fight," Yuan whispered.

Yuan saw torches up the street, approaching from where

they had come. The Cheng Guards' numbers had grown. "We'll have to cross over the wall somewhere away from the gate," he whispered. That presented a different problem. The wall was more than twice a man's height. They couldn't scale it like the compound wall. Instead, they would have to find something to use as a ladder, all the while keeping out of sight of the pursuing guards. But the sudden sound of gongs and drums that rang from a nearby signal tower forced him to reconsider. Yuan didn't know the details, but he was sure it relayed news of their escape. Now the entire city knew.

"We're running out of time." Lan pointed to the pursuing mob.

A Cheng Guard stood in the middle of the street, about two buildings ahead of the horde. He bent down, then moved a torch back and forth, like a tracker inspecting a pool of blood left by his wounded prey. A shadowy figure emerged from between the buildings. Yuan couldn't make out in the darkness which foot-soldier it was. He only noticed that his brave man struggled with an awkward limp that revealed tremendous pain.

The soldier moved within arm's reach of the hunched guard. Surprisingly close, Yuan recognized. The guard spun, startled by the menace who stood over him. He swung his sword but was too late. The soldier blocked the wide swing, then countered with a blade to the Cheng Guard's head. The guard fell backward, then rolled to a stop, face down. Yuan's soldier pushed the tip of his weapon into his enemy's back. He stepped onto the man's ribcage, then worked his blade loose from the flailing body. He paid no attention to the man's shrill, even though he knew that his own end was soon. He picked up the torch, and waved it overhead.

Yuan pulled Sheng close, lying low to avoid being seen. *He's drawing their attention.* Gate Guards shouted, pointed up the street, then dashed toward the torch, ready to trap the soldier, while more Cheng Guards closed from the other end of the street. Only four guards and the Gatekeeper stayed behind at the gate.

Yuan spoke quietly. "Follow me." He pulled Sheng along with him, stepping quietly out from between the buildings.

They moved along the edge of the street until they reached the last shop. Yuan, Sheng by his side, kept his hands away from the sheathed sword, hoping to present a disarming sight. They walked divertingly toward the gate, Sheng in full view. Lan and Fen Yang trailed, until four Gate Guards, all abreast, met them. One was across from each of them. Sheng stood in a stunned haze.

"This is as far as you go until I receive further orders," the Gate Guard, standing directly opposite Yuan, barked. "You know it's past curfew and did you not hear the signal?"

Yuan forced an unworried smile. "How long will that take?" He crossed his arms in front, his hands hidden inside the sleeves, then bowed. *I'll have to kill him and the one across from Sheng,* he calculated.

"Not long, here they come," the Gate Guard said, pointing to the returning band.

Yuan bowed a second time, removed a knife concealed under his sleeve, then jerked up and grabbed the guard by the back of the head. With a quick burst, he shoved the thin blade into the man's throat. Yuan pushed the guard backwards, turned and caught the next Gate Guard's elbow, blocking the enemy from swinging his sword. Yuan countered with a crossing fist to the guard's jaw, then jabbed the knife underneath the foe's arm and into the heart.

Screams to the left and right followed. Lan and Fen Yang had finished off the other two Gate Guards, then the heavy timber gate closed with a crashing thud. Yuan looked up to the second level of the tower, at the Gatekeeper and heavy wheel, then back at the approaching mob.

"Hurry!" the Gatekeeper yelled, signaling to the Cheng Guards that were up the street.

"Let's get the gate," Lan yelled. Fen Yang was already heading toward the staircase entrance before Lan had finished the thought.

The Gatekeeper was a strongly built man, conditioned by the heavy work required of his job. His face, missing a nose, showed the punishment for a crime that did not justify beheading. Those who were lucky enough to receive something less than death for their offences often received disfigurement as punishment. Afterward, they were routinely given jobs that allowed for isolation, so they would not have to bare constant public ridicule. The Gatekeeper's work, in a secluded tower, was one such job.

The second level of the tower platform was crowded by the heavy gear and turn wheel that maneuvered the gate. Fen Yang made his way near the top of the narrow stairs where the Gatekeeper was ready, armed with a heavy axe that was always present in case he needed to quickly sever the horsehair rope wound tightly around the massive wheel. The purpose was to keep people out.

The Gatekeeper raised his weapon and swung downward. Fen Yang dodged to the side, barely avoiding the blow. The axe blade lodged in the step. Fen Yang lunged past it, thrust his sword into the Gatekeeper's unprotected stomach, and drove the stocky man back, grunting through his clinched teeth.

The Gatekeeper grabbed Fen Yang's elbows, then stumbled over the side, Fen Yang with him. They flipped in midair, then landed on the ground with Fen Yang on bottom. Bones cracked on impact.

Yuan cupped Sheng's head and pulled him to his side. The boy buried his eyes into Yuan's hip, seeking shelter from both sight and sound.

"I'll raise the gate," Lan yelled. "Get out of here!" He

pulled on the spokes of the massive wheel until the brake tumbled into place, then grabbed the next spoke and repeated the motion.

The gate lifted in steps, and once it was high enough off the ground, Yuan pushed Sheng underneath, then rolled under it himself. "We're out!" Yuan yelled. He couldn't see Lan, except for the obscure motion visible through a small window in the tower. Lan struck at something with the gatekeeper's axe. *He's cutting the rope! He's not coming!* "Lan, don't! Get out! he yelled.

The gate slammed again. *He severed the rope!* Yuan heard the screams of men, dying by blade and braun. None sounded like Lan, then there was a thud, and the clash of metal stopped. Yuan wanted to thank Lan and the others but couldn't. He wanted to grieve for them, but didn't dare. There was no time.

Yuan and Sheng now had a head start, though barely. The immediate task was to lose the pursuing Cheng Guards. Yuan returned the dagger to the sheath strapped to his arm, tugged on the hilt of his sword, making sure the weapon was secure, then looked north to the corner of the city's wall. Torch light illuminated the sky. *Can't go that way!* He turned south and saw the same. *West!* Yuan put Sheng on his back and darted away from Zheng.

Yuan avoided the main road, opting instead for a lesser worn path into the darkness. He slowed the pace, once they were out of sight of the city, and alternated between carrying the boy and having him walk, resting when the moon disappeared behind clouds and continuing their flight when the radiance allowed.

Well into the night, the adrenalin subsided, and fatigue hit Sheng. Yuan felt him slump and his grip loosen. Sheng began to slide off Yuan's back.

"Are you tired?" Yuan asked.

Sheng nodded.

"I am too." Yuan stepped off the trail for a rest.

The seasonal change brought a cool night. The two of them lay down on hard terrain, trying to find some soft spot to settle on. Sheng curled next to Yuan, took a couple of deep breaths, then soon fell asleep. Yuan's thoughts flittered. Everyone who had accompanied him from Chengfu save Sheng was now dead. *They were all good men.* Both Lan and Fen Yang had been with him during good times and bad, difficult battles and friendly banter, and they gave their lives for him and the boy. And as the thought of their deaths came forth, a wave of guilt smacked him. *Is this all my fault? If I had left Chien to play out Jin's scheme would they all be alive?* He looked at the boy. *And would Sheng now be with his mother? What if I had gone with Chien to visit Chief Minister Zuchan? Could I have secured a better result? Or did Chien's collusion with Jin seal all of our fates anyway?* Yuan raised his hands to his face, pressed them against his forehead, then ran his fingers down to his jaw. But the painful introspection continued. *What would have happened had the assassin succeeded? Could Chien have avoided immediate scrutiny or would he have been killed soon after Duke Ting?* His train of thought stopped abruptly, remembering what Lan had told him while they were gathered in the hallway, shortly after he returned from the chophouse: '*A House Servant from our guest compound was with the men who dragged Chien's body down the street.*' *Someone knew – probably the House Servant. That servant must have overheard Chien describe Jin's plan when we were in the parlor. He made haste to the Chief Minister.* Yuan shook is head in disgust. *In no way was Chien capable of maneuvering through that turn of events. I should have ignored his position and protocol and gone with him anyway. There was too much at stake to let him go alone!* It didn't matter now, though. It was done. Danger still lay ahead, and he needed to focus on the present.

It would be sunup before the Cheng Guards could search for their trail, which gave him a few hours to rest. *Better take advantage of it,* he thought. He closed his eyes, then eventually drifted off, but it was not a restful sleep. Every noise woke him, and every rock, pebble and dirt clod underneath him added to the hardship, until just before daybreak when a chorus of chirping birds drove him to give up the effort.

He rubbed his eyes and sat up, but decided to let Sheng sleep a few minutes longer while he collected his thoughts. *Where do we go?* The State of Jin was no longer an option, and Sung's turmoil eliminated it as well. *No place inside the Northern Alliance is safe,* he surmised. And, of course, they couldn't return to Chu. That was definitely out of the question. Yuan had only one choice: *The State of Wu.* He stroked his brow, realizing that their troubles would not end at Wu's border. *I will not live long after we cross that line. Chu has caused too much misery for Wu, and I've killed too many of its warriors. But King Liao will recognize the value of helping an heir to Chu's throne, especially one King Ping wants dead.* Yuan nodded resolutely. *Wu offers the best place for Sheng to stay alive. And making that happen at all costs is now my mission.*

He stretched his back, then looked around. *Damn! We're on the wrong side of Zheng. We spent the night moving west, exactly opposite from the way we need to travel.* To get to Wu, they now had to turn south, into the mountains, then east through the pass back into Sung. The road that brought them into Cheng, he assumed, would be patrolled by now. From Sung, they would then have to work their way to a tributary, following it downstream to the Huai River. And once at the river, they would be back in Chu territory, facing the danger King Ping presented until they reached Wu. *What happens if Wu doesn't see the wisdom of helping Sheng?* Yuan considered. *Leave that worry for a later day. I have enough to concern me right now.*

He turned to Sheng, reached out to nudge the boy but paused. *What would my son have been like had fate not cheated him?* He had no idea what to do with the boy in these circumstances, especially one so young. *What expression will I see on his face when he awakens?* Sheng's last image of his mother was of her clutching her stomach and cupping her mouth. *Will that be his first thought?* He poked the boy's shoulder. "Sheng, the sun is up. We must get moving. Cheng Guards are out looking for us."

Sheng rolled over, yawned, stretched his arms over his head, then dropped his hands to his lap. He murmured something unintelligible, his voice bereft of energy.

"We need to get going." Yuan guarded his emotions, but emphasized the urgency. "Those guards who chased us last night won't stop until they find us, or until we're out of Cheng territory."

"Yuan?" the boy asked timidly.

"Yes."

Sheng sat up, stared at the ground, then asked, "Is Mother dead?" He spoke softly, dreading the answer, then sniffled, fighting back tears.

"I don't know," Yuan answered simply to get past the moment. Every instinct told him that she had died in the hallway, soon after they had departed, but he thought it best to change the subject. "Come. We have a long journey ahead of us." He pushed away the branches of a bush, opening a path to the game trail they'd followed during the night.

Sheng moved alongside him, rubbed his eyes. "Is Father dead?"

"Well . . ." Yuan didn't want to answer. He eased Sheng along, pressing the boy forward with a hand to the back.

"When I was with Mother, we heard a House Servant say that he was dead. Is he?" Tears rolled down Sheng's cheeks.

Yuan looked down at him. The little eyes, puffy and red,

showed despair beyond Yuan's knowledge of how to deal with the boy's anguish. "Yes. I'm sorry Sheng. I really liked your father." Somehow the words were easier to say, knowing that he was not the first to have told the boy. Yuan patted Sheng on the shoulder, wanting to provide comfort. But it felt awkward, and he was sure it hadn't done Sheng any good.

Yuan turned them south and didn't look at the boy. While they walked, neither spoke.

Sheng was silent to keep his emotions from erupting, but once he felt under control, he wiped away sniffles. "Yuan?"

"Yes, Sheng."

"Are all your friends dead?" He twisted and looked up at Yuan.

The questions weren't getting any easier. Yuan replied, "I don't know."

Sheng lowered his head. "I thought we were going to die last night. Yuan?"

"You're full of questions this morning," Yuan said, trying to relax the mood.

"Are we going to die?"

Sheng's fear struck Yuan like a punch. He stopped, then knelt to the boy's level. "No," Yuan said to keep the boy from giving up hope, when in fact he had no idea what lay ahead. "We must keep moving fast, and go as far as we can." He stepped down the path, nodding at Sheng to follow.

"Yuan?"

Yuan wanted to roll his eyes at the boy's stamina. "What?"

Sheng grabbed Yuan's hand, squeezing tightly around two fingers. "Why did they kill Father?"

How do I answer this? It was much too complicated for the boy, and he did not want to leave Sheng thinking about Chien's missteps. "Your father was caught up in a scheme by powerful people. He didn't deserve any of this." Yuan gently tugged Sheng's hand. "Your father was a good and virtuous man." Yuan stepped over a fallen branch, then pulled Sheng on top of it.

Sheng hopped off. "Yuan, what's a scheme?"

"Well, let's just say bad people did bad things to good people like your father. Do you understand?"

"Yes. Yuan?"

Yuan lifted him up and over a prickly bush that obstructed their path. "What is it?"

"I'm hungry. When will we eat?"

Yuan pushed past the brush. A twig hooked his robe, then snapped. *I'm leaving a trail,* he rued. "I don't know. Try to think about something other than food and last night."

"Yuan?"

Yuan looked down at Sheng. "How is it someone so small has so many questions?"

"I'm thirsty," he said forlornly.

"Hopefully, we'll find a stream to get a drink. Don't think about it. That just makes it worse."

Sheng held steady. "Yuan?"

Yuan rubbed his forehead, fighting impatience. "Yes."

"Will I see Mother again?"

He's not ready for the truth, but I shouldn't lie. Don't answer, Yuan decided. "Here. Climb on." Yuan picked up Sheng, then put him on his back. "Now, rest awhile, and see if you can take your mind off of things."

"I don't think I will see her. I think she's dead," Sheng said. Tears gushed. He laid his head on Yuan's shoulder.

Yuan felt the tears drip onto his neck, and in that moment, he thought about the son he almost had. He would have been about the same age as Sheng. Maybe that was why he'd taken on the additional burden. Lan and Fen Yang certainly thought Sheng was worth saving. *They sacrificed their lives for him.*

22

FLIGHT INTO TREACHEROUS MOUNTAINS

"Sheng. I need you to walk for a while." Yuan knelt down and eased the boy to the ground. He had carried Sheng for hours, and the extra weight was draining. He stretched, arching his back and lifting his chin skyward.

The trail was beaten to a width that required them to walk in single file. Yuan led the way.

"Yuan?" Sheng asked as if seeking permission to speak.

"Yes." *Here come the questions,* Yuan lamented, thinking of the interchange they'd had earlier that morning. He held a branch away from the path so that it wouldn't spring into the boy, then turned to Sheng.

"I'm still hungry." Sheng slipped past the branch.

Yuan let the limb snap back in place. "We have nothing to eat, so try not to think about it." He looked down at Sheng. *I have no clue what to do for you, except save your life.*

"But when will we eat?" Sheng patted his stomach.

Yuan stopped, took the boy by the shoulders, and spoke softly, "We fled the city to escape people who want to kill us. There was no time to gather food or any comforts that we're used to. Do you understand that?"

The boy lowered his eyes dejectedly, then nodded.

"I have no bow, no quiver of arrows and no means to hunt. We don't have time to stop and look for food either, because if we do, those Cheng Guards will catch us and finish what they had planned for us last night. Do you know what that means for us?"

Sheng nodded, understanding the import.

"Did you hear the drums earlier?" Yuan didn't wait for a response. "I think they found our trail. We don't have much time to get out of Cheng. And the more you think about food, the worse it gets. Concentrate on something else, something pleasing. Now let's keep moving, and when you talk, whisper."

Take it easy with him. He's too young for this. Yuan felt completely unprepared to manage a young child and, at the same time, guilty for adding to the boy's misery.

The cool air brought a refreshing breather to their trudge, which had led them into the pass from the plain through the foothills, then into the mountains. And the higher and deeper they hiked into the pass, the more difficult the altitude made their going. Yuan wasn't used to the thin air. It sapped his energy. He took his own advice and thought about something pleasing and diverted his attention toward their next step. *How do we get past the Guards garrisoned at the other end of the pass?* The post was there more to police traffic into Cheng than to protect against invasion, but too many Garrison Guards lived there.

Yuan had heard signal towers beat the alarm of their escape during the nighttime flight from the city. Throughout the city, platforms were placed at intervals. When necessary, City Guards would drum messages that rang throughout the city and beyond. Although Yuan did not understand the actual message, he was certain that it applied to them and that the Garrison Guards were on alert. To think otherwise was reckless.

They had evaded the Cheng Guards thus far, but they had to survive the mountains, as well. The pass meandered up and down, over and about, sometimes bordered by towering walls; other times, opened on one side to a dramatic gorge. Trees and brush thinned, providing less cover with the rise in elevation. If they made good time, they would reach the garrison tomorrow, Yuan surmised, but before that, they could very well meet a patrol sent from the post, or be caught from the rear by those who gave chase.

"Yuan?" The boy furrowed his brow and grumbled, "I'm thirsty."

"I am, too." Yuan stopped to survey the area, his eyes canvassing the landscape. "Look for a depression that might hold water."

"What's a depression?"

"It's like a shallow hole or a little dip in the ground." Yuan cupped his hands together to demonstrate. He looked up at the rock formation to one side.

"Would a depression be up there?" Sheng asked in desperation.

"No. It'll be on the ground. I'm looking for watermarks coming off the mountain. You see, rain falls on top of these mountains then gets funneled down certain paths. If we can find those paths, we may be able to find a depression that's been carved out of the rock. See there?" He pointed at a sharp face across the gorge. "You see those streaks?"

"Yes." Sheng's eyes widened.

"Water made them. If there's a place where the water regularly hits, over the years it will eventually wash out some of the rock and leave a depression. There may be water from recent rains in there. That's what we're looking for, except on this side of the gorge."

"I see."

The trail did not allow for a fast pace, but Yuan believed

that if they could make it to nightfall, the Guards, both in front and behind, would think it too treacherous to pursue until daylight. That would give them time to rest and plan.

They reached a slight dip in the narrow path where the mountain rose, towering above them on both sides. "What's that?" Sheng asked pointing to a fissure in the rock wall.

Yuan pulled back the bramble that shielded the entrance. The fissure was wide enough for a man to walk upright, but only a few steps before the gap began to close. "Look here, Sheng." Yuan stepped aside, letting the boy slip in front. "You've found water. Go ahead. Step up in there and take a drink."

The boy squeezed between the bushes, working his way toward a shallow pool of water that had gathered near the two sides that narrowed to his shoulders. He bent down onto his knees beneath where the fissure closed above, leaned forward and cupped the water with his hands. He let the first puddle run through his fingers. The next one he lifted to his lips and slurped a mouthful. "This water tastes bad," Sheng said, wrinkling his face.

"It's been sitting there, so that's not unusual. Take all you can because we don't know when we'll get another drink." Yuan heard Sheng slurp the water. The sound made him acutely aware of his own thirst. The inside of his mouth was parched and his tongue felt thick.

Sheng finished, crawled backwards, then returned to the opening. He wiped his mouth with a sleeve and showed a smile when he ducked past Yuan. "Your turn."

Yuan maneuvered deeper inside the fissure. The mountain squeezed him from both sides. He knelt down, then crawled closer, but the gap closed to his shoulders, preventing him from reaching the water. He stretched onto his belly, then crawled as far as the tight squeeze would allow, but the water still remained out of reach. It was just beyond his outstretched hand. The smell and sight teased his senses. He licked his lips, feeling the dry paste of thirst.

"Let me do it," Sheng said.

Yuan backed out, and again Sheng entered the fissure. Yuan looked for something he could use as a cup.

"Here," Sheng said. Yuan turned back to the boy and saw him on his knees, his body twisted at the hips, holding out cupped hands. "Take a drink."

Yuan welcomed the first sip, although the boy was right. The water was acrid. It didn't matter though; he believed what he had told Sheng. They did not know when their next drink would come.

Once Yuan finished, he crawled out. Sheng followed, and they continued on their way. For much of the day, their search for water had occupied their minds, but now, the jagged peaks of the mountains caused intermittent patches of night-like darkness along the path. The towering wall across the gorge from the fissure abruptly disappeared exposing them to a sheer drop. Sheng stepped behind Yuan and hugged the rock face. Yuan stopped after only a short distance from the waterhole, looking down in front of their feet. A crevice in the ground, left where the path had broken away was too wide for Sheng to make. Yuan straddled the crevice and leaned against the mountain for support. With one arm, he lifted Sheng across the divide.

They hiked around a bend, and once to the other side of the blind curve, the trail ahead rose to about shoulder level. Yuan bent to one knee and motioned for Sheng to do the same. He moved forward, keeping crouched, until he was able to see over the top of the rise.

"What is it?" Sheng asked.

Yuan held up his hand to quiet the boy. The mountain's shadows from the late afternoon sun played tricks with his sight. He squinted, studying the movement up ahead. It was what he expected, but sooner than he had thought. A patrol from the garrison was heading their way, closing quickly. They would have to backtrack.

Yuan lifted Sheng onto his back and took off down the trail moving faster than caution allowed. He turned the corner, leading to the crevice, and without breaking stride, leapt across the gap. Sheng's body trailed slightly in flight, and once the boy's body jolted back, the impact caused Yuan to stumble into the rock face. He bounced off the wall, regained balance, then darted into full stride.

Every second counted, and Yuan did not stop until reaching the waterhole, where he pulled back the bushes and set Sheng down, pushing him into the fissure. Yuan paused long enough to look down the path. The patrol had not turned the bend, but they would soon. Yuan looked the other way. There was no sign of the Cheng Guards, but he knew they had to be coming. He and Sheng were trapped.

Yuan stepped inside with Sheng. By no means did the brush hide the fissure or them, and if anyone in the patrol grew curious enough to look, they would be seen. *Where can we go?* Up was the only possibility. He studied the distance between the two sides of the crevice. It appeared to be about the same all the way to the top, but a shadow darkened his view at a point about twice his height. He paused to make sure he didn't miscalculate. He pressed his back against one side of the rockface and lifted a foot to the opposing wall, parallel to the ground. He wiggled it firmly in place, then raised the other foot to the same position and locked his knees. Yuan put his hands against the crevice wall at hip level, then pushed his back up the rockface. He stepped his feet into place, then locked his legs, preparing to repeat the climb.

Sheng watched, puzzled by how Yuan could suspend his body off the ground. "How do you do that?"

"Shh!" Yuan whispered. "We must not talk. They're

coming for us." Yuan pulled Sheng up and onto his lap. He lifted his back up the wall a little, then worked his feet to catch up.

Voices from the patrol startled him. He expected them, but not to be so close. He scaled one step after another, frantic to keep ahead of the patrol, but he could move up the fissure only inches at a time. He made it to the point where the dim sunlight from the day's end cast a shadow darkening the walls. They were almost to the halfway mark, just outside of the opening.

Two Garrison Guards from the patrol plopped down near the entrance. Yuan froze. He covered Sheng's mouth. The boy understood the message. Any sound and they would be discovered. Yuan looked down and saw one member of the patrol preparing a torch. He and the others in the patrol had no idea Yuan and Sheng were suspended above. Yuan was not sure how long he could remain there. He felt his thighs begin to strain and knew that holding stationary sapped strength he needed to finish the climb. He pushed his hands against the rockface, and lifted his back higher. One leg followed, then another.

Sheng clutched on to Yuan's robe, steadying himself for the ride. One misstep by Yuan and both of them would tumble down. Sheng buried his face into Yuan's chest.

Yuan continued to scale, concentrating his sight on the opposing wall and his mind on bodily mechanics. The muscles in his legs now burned. He paused to rest and assess how much more he had to climb. Yuan looked up, encouraged to see that the top of the wall was near. He took the next step, but the force against the wall broke off a sliver of chalky loess, causing his foot to slip and shards to fall. Fear jolted him. He slid downward and reflexes took over. He straightened his other leg, which sent pains of fatigue shooting through his thigh.

"What was that?" one of the Garrison Guards clamored excitedly.

Yuan looked down. The glow from torches illuminated the path and crept over the bramble at the opening. He saw a man push back the brush and peek into the fissure.

"Did you hear that?" the Guard said with serious concern.

"It's a mountain. Rocks fall all the time," another member of the patrol said sarcastically.

"Hand me a torch," the Guard called out.

The crevice wall blocked Yuan's view. He could only see a hand, holding a torch, extend into the opening.

The Guard took the torch, then leaned curiously into the fissure. "Look at this," he said excitedly, the flames illuminating the weathered opening. "I've never noticed this before. I'm going to see how far back it goes." He drew his sword.

"Watch out for wolves!" another Guard chuckled.

Yuan cupped Sheng's mouth again, and whispered, "Don't let them feel your eyes." He held his breath, while the Guard knelt where the fissure narrowed.

The guard held the torch deeper inside the fissure, leaned his head down and twisted slightly to the side to see farther back. "It stops here," he said.

"Of course it does." Another round of sarcasm was aimed at the Guard.

Yuan watched the Garrison Guard pull back the bramble and return to the others outside the fissure. He waited for them to become lost in conversation, hoping that their attention to each other would drown the noise coming from scaling the wall. And once they settled into a relaxed banter, he continued to work his way toward the top.

Yuan could see the rock walls open to the night sky. *Only a few more steps.* He adjusted for the next one. The rockface jutted inward. Yuan bent his knee, stepped, and then lifted with his hands, but granules of the wall gave way, causing his hands to slip. The back of his head slammed against the rock face, and his body stiffened, which lodged him awkwardly but stopped the slide toward a fatal fall. His feet remained where the last step began, but his shoulders were pressed against the wall at a point that was lower than his feet. Loess shards fell to the ground and bounced out of the fissure near the Guards.

Sheng clung tighter, then saw that escape over the top of the fissure was within reach. He grabbed a handhold near the top, stepped on Yuan's crotch and onto an outstretched leg, then shimmied out of the fissure. It was all Yuan could do to keep the jolts to his body from sending him tumbling to his death. He was relieved that Sheng's wiggly weight was gone.

"There's your wolf again," the sarcastic voice howled below. Laughter followed.

Yuan's legs trembled. He panted for breath. *Careful so they don't hear me.* He walked his feet down the slope until his back rested squarely against the rock wall, then resumed scaling upward. He worked his body until his head and shoulders popped above the surface. The clear night sky improved his field of vision and shined a dim light over the narrowing closure. Yuan stiffened his legs, pressing his back harder against the rockface, then studied his options to climb out. Below, where Yuan and Sheng had drank water from the puddle earlier in the day, the fissure was narrow, less in width than Yuan's shoulders. It was no different at the top and was within arm's reach to his left. Yuan grabbed the ledge with his left hand, then bounced his back off the rockface, twisted around and clutched the ledge with his other hand, then pulled himself up and over the top. He rolled, first to the side, then onto his back, safely above the pass and the Garrison Guards. He lay still, his chest pounding for air and his body aching.

Sheng crawled to him and whispered, "Yuan?"

"Yes," Yuan managed between labored breaths.

"What do we do now?"

"We sleep. I have no strength right now." Yuan answered, his chest panting rapidly.

Sheng crouched down beside him. Out of the protective fissure, the wind swept across the mountain's spine engulfing them with cold air.

"Yuan?" Sheng persisted.

"What," Yuan whispered.

Sheng's stomach grumbled. "We still didn't eat."

"No, we didn't." Yuan was too tired to think of anything other than recouping his energy.

Sheng nudged Yuan, then rubbed his arms. "I'm cold."

Yuan rubbed the back of his head, where it had slapped the rockface. "Lay down on the other side of me so that my body breaks the wind."

Sheng climbed over Yuan, then snuggled next to his only source of warmth and closed his eyes.

The numbing chill blew against Yuan's back, but the wave of exhaustion displaced the cold, and soon he fell asleep.

The orange glow of morning woke Yuan. He stretched, then stood to survey the surroundings. He rubbed his arms, still feeling the cold of the night, and looked around. They were near the top of the mountain with no idea of how to get down. That was the bad news. The Garrison Guards, who pursued them were down on the path – a substantial improvement. Yuan and Sheng could walk along the ridge without detection, but eventually Yuan would have to find a way down. He hoped that it wouldn't involve scaling another cleft.

Sheng began to stir, catching Yuan's attention. The boy rubbed his arms and yawned.

"Sheng?" Yuan whispered. He nudged the boy's shoulder.

The poke startled Sheng awake. He looked at Yuan, then wiped his eyes.

"Are you cold?" Yuan asked.

Sheng nodded but did not speak. His mind was numbed by the events of the previous days.

"Sheng," Yuan said louder, to get the boy's attention.

"Yes?" Sheng responded, still feeling confusion.

Yuan stood over him. "Are you hungry?"

"Yes."

Yuan knelt in front of Sheng. "Are you thirsty?" He knew the answer.

"Yes."

"Me too," Yuan said flatly. "To eat, we must get off this mountain. To drink, we must get off this mountain, and to break the cold, we must start walking. Are you ready?"

Sheng didn't answer. But he rolled onto his feet, then stood up, a little wobbly and dreary from the previous day's ordeal.

Yuan paused long enough to peek at the Garrison Guards below. One stoked a fire for the morning meal. The need to search wasn't so pressing that their patrol had to do so on empty bellies. They didn't suspect that their prey was now above them.

Yuan and Sheng followed along the mountain's boney ridge. Footing was tenuous at times and slowed their progress. Yuan walked to a vantage point to search for a landmark that he might recognize to judge their location. A mixture of small, loose rocks tumbled down the backside slope. Yuan was glad the rubble hadn't fallen on the pass side of the mountain. He looked outward, but saw nothing familiar from their earlier travels into Cheng.

They were approaching two days since their last meal, and yesterday's water break had been their only drink. Sheng struggled against the hunger, the thirst and the elements. His little body wasn't conditioned for such harshness, and he simply couldn't keep the pace that Yuan believed necessary.

"Here, Sheng. Climb on." Yuan knelt down on one knee,

and the boy took advantage of his protector's offer. Yuan knew he could not maintain the pace for very long either.

By now the patrol from the garrison and the Cheng Guards were well on their way to joining up and discovering that they had somehow missed their target. Once they did, they were sure to backtrack. Yuan had to get past the Garrison Guards stationed at the gateway before the strength of their pursuers beat them to the gate. The pace was still slow, even with Sheng on his back, but Yuan plugged along, alternating between carrying the boy and letting him walk. By afternoon they reached a point where the ridge began a pronounced descent. Yuan guessed they were on a knuckle of the dragon's claw he had seen when pointing out the Funui Shan to Sheng on the day they were in Sung, about to enter Cheng. Sheng had said he didn't want to take the pass, and would rather walk around the mountain. Had he chosen differently, Yuan would now know what lay ahead and how better to traverse the danger.

"Wait here," Yuan said, then walked the short distance to the edge, where he surveyed their challenge. The mountainous pass below funneled traffic past a Guard Station to a walled gateway. The path to Sung was through that passageway, but getting there undetected was the immediate worry. First, they had to traverse a series of slopes that stair-stepped down the mountain. Outcrops formed the riser of each step, and at the very bottom, barracks were built into the side of the mountain. From the barracks, there was an open sprint to the gate. There was no cover to hide their movements between each outcrop or from the barracks to the guard station.

Yuan returned to Sheng, who sat crossleggged with his elbows on his knees and his chin in his hands. "Can you walk a little more?"

He didn't want to, but acquiesced. "Yes."

Yuan summoned an encouraging tone. "Good. Let's find a way off this mountain."

From the ridge, Yuan and Sheng hiked down the slope to the first outcrop. The two squatted behind the rocky protrusion while Yuan assessed the length of the drop to the base of the outcrop. The distance was short and of no concern. Rather, it was the risk of being seen or heard that worried him.

Yuan lowered himself to the next level. All but his lower legs were blocked from the Garrison Guard's sight by a boulder. Yuan motioned to Sheng. The boy backed off the ledge, feet first, sliding on his belly until Yuan guided him safely into outstretched arms.

Now they were fully visible and could not dawdle. There were two ways to traverse the slope, Yuan noticed. They could dart from one outcrop to another resting behind each one. Their other choice was to crawl slowly. Yuan chose the latter. He lay on the ground and angled his body downhill. He felt gravity pull his weight to his chest. Sheng climbed onto his back. The green, silken robes, tattered and soiled, provided a stark contrast to the yellowish tint of the chalky dirt, which allowed for easy detection. Yuan lifted his body with his forearms and pushed forward with his feet, advancing only inches before repeating the effort. Sheng buried his head in Yuan's robe trying not to make any sudden moves.

They reached the cover of one outcrop and then the next. Yuan looked toward the station below and the Garrison Guards, who showed no awareness of their presence. One Guard went inside the station and another leaned against a tall, wooden column next to it. The tall post was one of a pair that formed the gate, and atop of each column was a carved dragon, their mouths snarling.

"Yuan?" Sheng said.

"Shhh, we must not talk. They'll hear us," Yuan whispered.

The boy wrinkled his brow and buried his head on Yuan's back.

Yuan returned his focus to the slope. *Could be worse. Could be suspended over a squad of curious guards with a torch lighting my ass!* He turned his head toward Sheng, then whispered, "Let's go." Yuan proceeded off the outcrop and onto his belly. There were no shadows to aid their concealment, and they were now just as exposed as they were last night in the fissure.

It seemed to take forever to span only a normal step. Sheng passed the time lost in thoughts of his mother and his last image of her. *Is she alive? Will I see her again?* He began to cry, but tried desperately to not make a sound. He breathed out of rhythm and held a short gasp, struggling to bury his thoughts while his mind searched for anything else on which to focus. He clutched tighter to Yuan's robe, but that didn't help either, and he began counting the ups and downs his body went through as they crept across the terrain.

They made it to the last outcrop and ducked behind knobby rocks. Yuan hunched down next to the boy and saw him fighting back tears. Yuan placed a reassuring hand on Sheng's shoulder, not knowing whether the tears were from fear, thoughts of the boy's mother and father, or the totality of the ordeal. He counted the Garrison Guards milling about, unwary of his and the boy's presence. *Most are out searching for us,* he surmised.

Shouts from up the pass startled Yuan. His first thought was that they had been seen, but his fright eased when he saw four Garrison Guards running toward the guard station and none paid any attention to where he and the boy were. He looked up the mountain trail to see if more were coming, but he saw none. "Stay down," Yuan whispered.

The two Garrison Guards at the Guard Station were the only people who responded to the commotion. *Damn it! There were only two, now there are six.* He watched them gather at the station. One pointed up the pass, but none turned toward him and Sheng. *Others must be close behind. We have to go now before more return.*

Yuan turned to Sheng. Tears had worn tracks down the boy's dirty little cheeks. He whispered gently and raised Sheng's head so that their eyes met. "Sheng, you've endured a great hardship and overcome a tremendous ordeal. What you've done is truly admirable, especially for someone so young. But now you must turn your feelings inside. You must reach deep within yourself to overcome the obstacles that lie ahead. Use your emotions to ignite that determination and not cripple you. You must feel the fire in your belly." Yuan poked the boy's stomach, managing to turn one corner of his mouth into a smile. "Feel the flame. We will survive this." He took Sheng by the shoulders, and assured him, "We will."

Sheng looked into Yuan's eyes and found strength, not so much in what was said, for the words he didn't fully understand, but in Yuan's expression. His eyes showed certainty, as if Yuan could see the future. From the guest compound's courtyard, to the fight at the city's gate, to scaling the fissure, Yuan had maintained the same look; a look of resolve, as if he would succeed no matter what life threw at him. And it was that confidence that brought a sense of calm faith to Sheng. He blinked back his emotions, swallowed hard, wiped the tears from his eyes, then nodded.

Off they crawled, lifting up, pushing forward and bumping their way toward the barracks. Yuan paused to determine which end of the building would conceal them best once off the slope. The structure was a series of rooms under one roof. The line of sight from the Guard Station created a blind spot on the right side of the barracks. Before he could crawl farther, two Garrison Guards broke away from the station and headed for the barracks. Any movement would certainly catch their attention, but lying there in the open might do so as well. Yuan buried his head in the dirt and whispered to Sheng, "Stay still."

The calm tone of the Guards' voices indicated they had not discovered Yuan and the boy. The two men continued in their direction, reaching a point near one of the fire pits that lined the front of the barracks. It was the only one with flames. The others showed only remnants of the morning meal, but the one that burned appeared to have a chicken roasting on a spit. The smell whetted Yuan's appetite.

Gurgling sounds of hunger began a chorus within Sheng, too. He held a deep breath, trying to hush his stomach, to no avail. He shut his eyes tightly, but that wasn't any help either.

Yuan heard the creaking of a door opening, then closing. *They're inside.* He rotated his head to peek past the barracks to the Guard Station. The other four Garrison Guards were still there. *This is the best chance we'll get.* Yuan crawled until he was almost to the edge of the outcrop, right above the back of the barracks. The roofline of the building trained Yuan's eye directly to the fire pit, then on to the Guard Station. Yuan heard the door open, then out walked one of the Guards toward the fire. He was a burly man who looked like he hadn't missed any meals. He need only look up, and he would see both Yuan and Shang.

Yuan froze.

Sheng closed his eyes, remembering what Yuan had told him the previous evening. *Don't let them feel your eyes.* He tried to picture Yuan's confidence, but the only image he could see was the Garrison Guard walking toward the spit.

From inside the barracks, the other Guard called out, but Yuan paid no attention, concentrating instead on what to do next. The brawny Guard turned away from the pit with the chicken in hand. He stepped toward the barracks, while separating a leg from the carcass.

Yuan peeked at him. He saw the man sink his teeth into the meaty leg. The smell of chicken grew stronger, and his mouth began to water. Yuan checked on the men down at the

Guard Station, and there was no change. Only the backs of two Garrison Guards, who stood in the doorway, were visible. Yuan reached back and tugged at Sheng to slide off. He then quietly eased off the ledge, landing with a soft thud next to the barracks. Sheng followed. They were now out of sight.

They stopped under the overhang of the mud and straw roof. There was a small, square window in the sun-dried brick next to where they were standing, and Yuan listened to the Guards' conversation. The smell of food, much stronger than before, caused Sheng's stomach to rumble again. Yuan cupped his hands around Sheng's ear, and whispered, "Walk inside the door, and ask for food. Go completely inside. Do not . . . do not look toward this window. Look only at the food."

Sheng's face tightened further from fright.

"Don't worry, you're not a threat to them," Yuan said confidently. "They won't hurt you. Understand?"

Sheng trembled, but nodded.

"Do not look this way. Just concentrate on getting something to eat. Now go." Yuan nudged Sheng with a soft hand to the back.

Sheng walked past the window – too short to be visible – then disappeared around the corner.

Yuan pulled his dagger from the sheath under his sleeve, placed it in his mouth, then adjusted his sword's scabbard. He crouched below the window, and peeked over a corner of the sill, waiting to hear Sheng's voice.

Sheng stepped into the doorway, but didn't speak. The two Guards sitting on benches across the table from one another, were startled by the presence of a small, quivering boy standing before them. The Guard facing the window stopped chewing. He sat there, dumbfounded, a tender morsel hanging from the corner of his mouth.

"Can I have some food?" Sheng asked timidly. His faint voice was barely audible. He looked at the chicken's breast lying on the table and licked his lips.

A shot of adrenalin jolted Yuan. He pulled himself up by the roof's timbers and launched himself through the window, feet first, into the room. The stocky Guard Yuan had seen by the fire pit was the closest and sat with his back to the window. Yuan took the dagger from his mouth, closed the distance of three steps, grabbed the Guard's top knot, then drove the blade into the side of the Guard's neck. He shoved the body aside, hopped onto the table and jumped behind the other Guard, who was too late to react. Yuan cupped the man's chin with his right hand, held the back of the Guard's head with his left, pulling his head backward. And with a quick twisting jerk, he snapped the man's neck.

In a matter of seconds, it was over. But there were four more Guards at the station. Yuan took a couple of deep breaths, checked on Sheng, who was standing against the wall next to the door. The boy's eyes were glazed over. Yuan took Sheng by the shoulders and sat the boy down at the table. "Don't think. Just eat." A hide flask lay on the table. Yuan took it in hand and bounced it a couple of times to feel how much water was in it. He then removed the plug and drank, gulping generously while he walked toward the door.

He returned the plug, placed the flask back on the table. "Sheng, drink as much as you want." Yuan tore off meat from the chicken's breast, then turned toward the Garrison Guard whose head rested contortedly. *Is there time to take his armor?* Since their flight had begun, Yuan had been handicapped, not only in numbers but by a lack of protective armor as well. And the green color of their robes was a giveaway. If he had time, the layers of lacquered leather would narrow his enemies' targets. He turned back toward the doorway. "Damn! Here they come!" he whispered. His adrenalin amped up. "Grab the food and the flask and stand over there," Yuan commanded, pointing toward the corner.

Sheng shoveled in another mouthful and picked up the chicken and flask, then moved to the corner. He didn't look at the fallen Guard near his feet and blocked the burbling sound that came from the man's severed windpipe.

Yuan looked back at the approaching Garrison Guards, glad to see that only two were heading toward him. *The others must be in the Guard Station.* He pushed the table into a corner of the back wall, then dragged the lighter Garrison Guard's body onto the tabletop. He propped the body against wall, letting the head droop unnaturally, then closed the shutters, which cut off most of the light. Yuan walked to Sheng and assured him, "You're going to be fine." He knelt to the burly Guard's body, retrieved his dagger, then stepped next to the door.

First one by surprise, Yuan thought. *The second one, hopefully before he can call for help.* He drew his short sword and gave Sheng a comforting nod. He then backed up against the wall to the side of the door. He didn't see the Guard near Sheng's feet reach over and grab hold of the boy's torn robe.

A gruff voice from outside drew closer, demanding: "Where's my chicken?"

His comrade laughed and squawked, "Their mouths must be full of your meal."

Yuan heard footsteps almost to the door. He raised the dagger and readied to strike, but the footsteps stopped.

Yuan mentally assigned the voices to the two men. The hoarse voice belonged to the tall, strongly built man, he guessed. *I hope he's first through the door.* He wanted the greatest challenge first and wasn't worried about the other scrawny Guard.

The raspy voice spoke. "It's dark. They must be sleeping off my food." He stepped into the threshold, then stopped to let his eyes adjust. He first saw the boy, standing in the corner, then his fallen comrade's posed body on the table. The corpse sat with slumped shoulders and a dangling head. He jerked at his sword.

Yuan closed the gap and grabbed the back of the Guard's

head, then thrust the dagger toward the throat. But the Guard raised his forearm to knock Yuan's arm off trajectory, causing the blade to pass over his head. Yuan was too fast, and his thrust too strong. The blade sliced across the Guard's arm and the altered line changed the strike from the Guard's throat to his head. Yuan drove the dagger into the man's eye. The bellowing scream of sharp, excruciating pain echoed. Yuan shoved the man out of the doorway and into the trailing Garrison Guard.

"Let's go!" Yuan called to Sheng.

The slightly built Guard hit the ground with his screaming mate on top, and by the time he rolled the man off, Yuan was there. Yuan slashed his sword across the Guard's exposed thigh, which was the quickest way for Yuan to end the fight. The screech rippled down the pass.

"Sheng, hurry!" Yuan called, looking back into the room, but Sheng didn't follow. Yuan darted back inside, and saw Sheng lost in a foggy haze.

The boy stood there, his mind having shut out the current world. He clutched on to the flask with one hand and the chicken with the other.

"Sheng!" Yuan snapped.

The boy blinked back to the present. He stepped toward Yuan, but the Garrison Guard, who lay next to him, held tightly to Sheng's robe and caused the boy's foot to miss the full stride, tripping him.

Yuan kicked the Guard's hand, freeing the robe from his grasp, picked up Sheng off the floor, then barked, "Let's go."

Yuan ran toward the gate. Sheng lagged behind. The remaining two of the six Garrison Guards sprinted toward them from the Guard Station. Yuan heard the sound of scrambling feet from up the pass, and turned to see five men rapidly approaching. *They heard the screams!* The Guards were still too far away to help the two from the Guard Station.

Yuan concentrated on the immediate threat. *Separate them. Make them fight one at a time.* He sheathed his dagger, took his short sword in one hand and its scabbard in the other. The two Garrison Guards approached side by side. The one on the left was young and his manner showed a lack of confidence. The other one, though, daringly pointed his sword at Yuan, taking measure, then leapt forward. Yuan waited until the last moment, then darted to the right, planting both feet so that his body offered only a partial target. He raised his scabbard along his forearm, blocking the Garrison Guard's swinging blade. Yuan countered with a plunge of his sword into the man's thigh and followed with a swift kick to the knee of the same leg. The Garrison Guard hit the ground, screamed in pain and grabbed at his wound.

Yuan now had his back to the gateway. He stepped toward the single Guard, but his youthful foe backed away several steps, reluctant to pursue the fight. *He only has to stall until the others join him.* The five from up the pass were running at full speed on a collision course with him. Yuan raised the tip of his weapon toward the young man's chin and said, "Don't let this be the day you die. Don't follow us."

Yuan backed away several steps, returned his sword and scabbard to their usual place, then picked up Sheng. He ran past the Guard Station, through the gateway, down the slope and onto the plain, heading east toward Sung.

23

CHENG GUARDS IN HOT PURSUIT

*Y*uan had come upon a trail, after fleeing the garrison, that led in an easterly direction. It was a path stamped out by wildlife that provided neither a direct route nor an easy trek that man would leave. He'd crossed the open distance from the mountain pass and had traveled deep into the woods, carrying Sheng on his back, when he found the trail. The sun had floated directly above them, once they had reached the path, but was now close to the horizon. Yuan didn't know how many Cheng Guards followed, but he knew they would continue the chase. That much was certain. And he and the boy were sure to lose if their flight depended on a foot race. They needed a break to have any chance of staying alive. Nightfall was his immediate wish, and fortunately it was near.

Yuan expected the Cheng Guards to halt pursuit for the evening, once darkness blanketed the wooded cover. And they did. But the night also made Yuan's task of navigating harder. The canopy blocked the moonlight, making it difficult to see the trail and impossible to plot a correct course. Yuan and

Sheng were barely visible to each other, and Yuan worried that they would end up wandering aimlessly in circles or maybe even back toward Cheng. The meandering trail's many twists and turns, he reasoned, might be useful to lead those who hunted them rambling for the first few hours of the morning, but that did not leave much time for rest, something both he and Sheng needed badly.

Yuan turned to Sheng and whispered, "We'll stop here for a few minutes. I want to see if they're still following us." He needed nothing more than those few words to convey his concern. He led Sheng fifteen paces away from the trail, counting each step.

Sheng plopped down among the soft bed of leaves, still clutching tightly to what was left of the chicken. His grip had minced the meat. Yuan peeled a small piece off the breastbone. Sheng laid his head down, giving in to the urge to sleep. The feel of cushioned ground was inviting and noticeably more pleasing than the hard rocky terrain of the mountain. Sheng listened to the sounds of the woodlands. Overhead, he heard the wind rustling through the trees, as well as the lively refrain of crickets. He also felt the difference in temperature. Although cool, the air was comfortable, and the wind was only a slight breeze.

"Drink from the flask, Sheng. You need the water. And eat. You need that too," Yuan instructed, then turned his attention to the woods, listening for any sound of the Guards. Twigs snapping underfoot, leaves crumbling under weight or voices chattering in the distance. Those were the things he waited to hear, but there were none. It was just as he'd hoped. *The patrol halted for the night.* Through the dense brush, quite some distance away, he thought he saw the flickering light of a campfire. But he also knew his eyes might be playing tricks. Whatever he saw, it wasn't too close, and he intended to get farther away.

Yuan nudged Sheng and whispered, "Let's go."

Sheng propped up on one arm, rubbed his face and complained, "I was almost asleep. Can we stay here?" He matched Yuan's low voice.

"No. We need to keep moving."

"But I can't see," Sheng whined.

"Grab hold of my scabbard, and don't let go."

They moved at a slow, deliberate pace down the path. Yuan held on to the hilt of his sword, making sure the drag of Sheng remained constant. He felt his way through each step to determine if he had strayed from the path. He came upon a bushy shrub that blocked his way. Yuan pulled back limbs to open the trail and saw that the woods gave way to a clearing only a short distance ahead. *This is a break!* he thought. He put Sheng on his back, then hurried to the tree line. Moonlight lit the field. He glanced over his shoulder, hoping once again the Guards stopped the search, then took a chance. He picked a tall tree at the farthest point across the open terrain, then walked quickly to it. It was more difficult to find another trail to follow into the woods once he reached the mark.

The trek returned to a painstaking slog until they reached another small break in the woods. The distance they put between them and their pursuers took much of the night, and after hurrying across another small moonlit gap, Yuan selected a cluster of trees in which to rest. He wanted the last of nightfall for at least some sleep and veered from the path a little ways to bed down. Sheng didn't need the chorus of the wilderness, tranquil as it was, to induce sleep, and neither did Yuan.

In the morning, Yuan awoke wondering how long he'd slept. Just as the canopy screened out the moonlight during the night, so did it prevent the full light of the morning sun from reaching through. He searched a short distance for an opening in the dense cover to peer skyward, and once he found it, his sense of urgency grew. *Damn! I didn't expect to sleep this long.* The sun was higher than the ambient light let on, and his pursuers, he was certain, had already resumed their search.

Yuan shook Sheng. "Let's go! We must hurry!"

He didn't wait for Sheng to emerge completely from his slumber. Yuan picked him up, placed the boy on his back, a routine that had become all too familiar, then marked the direction with a distant tree that towered over a clustered thicket. The morning sun hung above it. He dashed to the tall tree, found another landmark, then repeated the task until they were well away from their nighttime resting spot. Yuan put Sheng to the ground. He searched for the next feature, eventually settling on a tree that had a split trunk.

"You ready?" He asked, looking back at Sheng.

The boy adjusted his robe and walked toward him. Yuan started slowly, so that Sheng could keep up. Yuan spotted a clearing a little ways beyond the forked tree, but unlike during the night, he chose to skirt it, staying inside the woods to reduce the chances of being seen.

The morning trek had been quiet, both lost to their own thoughts. Sheng broke the silence, calling out softly, "Yuan?"

"Yes, Sheng."

"Where are we?"

"That's a good question," Yuan smiled. "It's hard to tell exactly. We may be close to Sung."

"Didn't we leave there because of trouble?" Sheng's youthfulness showed. He could not fully grasp the breadth of their plight.

"Yes, we did."

Sheng, perplexed, asked, "Why are we going back there?"

"We have to in order to get to Wu," Yuan replied. "Remember?"

"Oh, yeah. Will we be in trouble if the Hua clan sees us?" Sheng's question harkened back to the fear that had prompted them to leave Sung for Cheng.

"It won't be anything like what the Cheng Guards have in mind for us, but let's concentrate on not letting anyone catch us," Yuan said, trying to give a perspective that a young boy could comprehend. "Understand?"

"Okay," Sheng responded, placated for now.

Yuan stepped around a tree and held back the branches of a thorny bush. Sheng maneuvered through, trying not to get poked. The boy stepped onto a fallen trunk and hopped off. The decayed condition of the log caused it to crack under his weight. Yuan stopped to see if there was any movement behind them, looking for anyone who might have heard the snap. Once certain that no one was near, he pulled Sheng to the side, avoiding a thorn bush, then ducked under an overhanging branch.

They skirted the edge of another clearing, continuing through the woods on the course that was least obstructed. Each step took far more effort than was comfortable, and their pace was cumbersome. The men who pursued them would not waste time being quiet.

Yuan turned and knelt down to Sheng. "You see that tree? The one with the broken limb." He pointed toward a spiraling trunk from which a branch dangled precariously.

Sheng nodded, acknowledging Yuan's sense of urgency.

"Go hide behind it, and keep out of sight."

Yuan backtracked to a point near the previous clearing and hid behind a clump of long-leafed bushes. He peered through the draped foliage, down the trail. *There they are. Damn they're close!* His heart rate sped up. *Scouts! Three of them.*

The one in front, bent to a knee, was staring at the ground. A scrubby bush hid all but his forehead and top knot. Another hunched over his shoulder, concentrating on something on the ground Yuan couldn't see. Yuan recognized him as the young Garrison Guard from the Guard Station, and shook his head. *I told him he'd die if he followed us.* Yuan removed both his sword and dagger, careful not to make any noise. His view of the third scout was obscured by the first two.

The lead tracker stood up and said something while motioning with a wave of his hand, pointing to the trail. Yuan was too far away to hear the words. But fortunately, the scouts didn't know where the snaking path turned, leading directly to Yuan's hiding spot. He ducked behind the low thicket of brushwood, pressed against a cluster of saplings.

The trackers followed the traces left by Yuan and Sheng. Yuan watched the first man sidestep a prickly bush where the trail turned sharply. They approached a tree; shrubs to the left were clumped tightly against it; then they stopped abruptly. The soft soil revealed Sheng's heel mark. They progressed in single file, stepping between thorny bushes near the rotting tree trunk that had fallen across the route. The first scout stepped sideways and scooted through the scrub, pushing away a branch. He held it back for the young Garrison Guard to clear, then stepped over the trunk that blocked the path. The lead next bent under an overhanging branch. The bob caused his quiver to fall off his shoulder. He stepped askew, then stooped to pick it up.

"Look out!" The young Garrison Guard shouted, fear jolting him alert.

Yuan had sprung from behind the cover, leapt over a leafy bush toward the lead scout. He thrust his sword, barely missing the man, who had rolled clear of the blade. Yuan jabbed a second time, but the weapon's point glanced off the scout's armored collar as he spun again. Yuan closed the distance, jumped on his enemy's back, then drove his dagger into the side of the neck. The lead scout bellowed. Yuan twisted, then shoved his short sword, arcing upward underneath the Garrison Guard's jaw.

The young guard had frozen at Yuan's ambush and hadn't unsheathed his weapon. His eyes hinted at the memory of

Yuan's warning at the Guard Station, then rolled once the blade exited through the back of his head.

The young guard fell to his knees. Yuan kicked him in the chest to dislodge his blade, then turned to the third scout, who yowled with such force it sounded as if he channeled the miserable deaths of his two comrades. He sprinted off in the opposite direction.

Yuan snatched the bow off the ground and hurried to nock an arrow. He drew the string to his cheek, took aim and launched the arrow, missing wide. He watched the scout disappear in the brush, dashing to get help.

Yuan slung the bow on his shoulder, grabbed the quiver, then sprinted back to Sheng. He picked up the boy and ran frantically. The larger contingent of Guards would soon learn where they were. He jumped across felled bramble onto a game trail that headed easterly. Yuan pushed past a grassy patch, then broke through a thicket at a pace he could not sustain for long. And with each step, Sheng bounced on his back, on the verge of flying off.

Sheng's forehead knocked against the back of Yuan's head. "Ouch!" the boy cried. He crossed his arms around Yuan's neck. "I'm very thirsty." Sheng's voice reverberated on the bounce.

Yuan tugged at the boy's arm, easing the pressure against his windpipe. *We have much more to worry about,* he thought. "We can't stop to look for water." Yuan forced the words out in choppy breaths.

"Can we stop when we get to the river?" Sheng's voice hinted at a plea.

"Yes, but that's likely to be much later," Yuan said between pants.

"Why?" Sheng cried, pressing to get what he wanted.

"Sheng, I need . . . my breath, . . . to keep pace," Yuan answered, irritated by the questions and struggling from the winded sprint. "Talk later."

"Okay, but the sound of water is making me thirsty," Sheng said wistfully.

Yuan came to a dead stop. "What?" He huffed for a breath.

Sheng slid to the ground. "The water. It's making me thirsty."

Yuan bent over to catch his breath, his hands on his knees. His chest pounded and his thighs buzzed from the strain. The noise from crashing through brush had drowned out the faint sound of rippling water, but now the slosh against rocks was unmistakable. And the smell of water hinted at what he heard. But the scrubland had prevented Yuan from seeing it.

Footsteps trampling through the woods drew his attention back to their immediate danger. "Come on!" Yuan said anxiously. He pulled Sheng onto his back, then raced toward the water. He didn't bother trying to find the easiest path, barrelling through the brushwood on a direct line.

Yuan heard a Cheng Guard shout from behind, "There! There they are." Yuan busted through heavy underbrush, disappeared from his foes' view, then heard other shouts. "Hurry! Hurry!" There was something familiar about the gruff voice. *Is it the Captain of the Guards?* he wondered. Yuan stepped around a clump of bushes, and the woods opened to near waist-high grass through which a narrow river flowed.

Shouts from the Cheng Guards and noise of thrashing brush were getting closer. He looked around, searching for safety. Grass ran from the trees to the river, picked up again on the other side's bank, then eventually gave way to a forested ground. Upstream and down, the landscape was no different. He looked toward the river's flow at a nearby bend where the water rushed over the shallows before disappearing behind a thick cluster of trees.

Above the tree line, Yuan saw dark plumes of smoke, spiraling skyward. Wind, high above the tree line, mixed the columns into a single dark cloud, pushing it southeasterly. It was a distinguishing sign of warfare's cruelty – a sacked village.

Yuan and the others had left Sung because of the trouble that had been brewing, and apparently a rebellion had erupted during their absence. Now, remnants of the Hua clan revolt were within sight, which meant they or Sung soldiers might be nearby. *Lead the Cheng Guards into harm's way,* Yuan decided.

They reached the other side of the trees, which opened to a cultivated field. Remnants of a burnt village, set back from the river's floodplain, lay where the rows of a plowed field ended.

Shouts rang again from behind him. "Take your men over to the other side. Look downstream." It was indeed the Captain's voice. He sounded like a huntmaster, closing in on a prey he hadn't yet spotted. They were at the river. "Take yours across, and go upstream," he commanded someone else. "Fan out. They're probably in here, right underfoot."

Yuan ran toward the village with Sheng still on his back. It wouldn't be long before the Captain reached the same conclusion as Yuan and followed the smoke. Yuan slowed once he reached the village's perimeter. The stench of death wafted throughout the charred ruins. He put down Sheng. The boy promptly grabbed his nose and gagged.

A lone woman wailed over the crackle of burning debris. She crouched in front of the scorched remains of her hut, mindlessly working a grindstone, while holding a young girl's body. The child's tender head drooped, unsupported as the mother rhythmically worked the stone with one hand.

Yuan stepped into the village and around a heap of ash and timber from a smoldering hut. He took Sheng by the hand and walked cautiously toward the woman. Her shrill cries stopped, replaced by incoherent mumbling. The woman worked next to a cooking pit. A water bucket balanced precariously on the edge of the hearth. She was a curiosity, juxtaposed to the fiery wreckage all around. Hides, used for bedding, poked out from underneath the seared remains of her shanty. Nothing else was left of the shelter.

Yuan looked back, across the field and into the trees. He couldn't yet see the Cheng Guards. He quickly surveyed the village. Circular piles of rubble ringed the village. Every hut had been burned, and bodies were scattered among heaps. The woman apparently was the only survivor.

"Woman," Yuan said softly, trying to coax her attention. His voice was calm, but that was only a façade which masked his desperation.

"Grind the wheat and make the meal or we don't eat. Grind the wheat and make the meal or we don't eat," the woman said to herself. She rocked on her knees and worked the grindstone, the lifeless girl's body rolling with the rhythm.

"Are Sung soldiers nearby?" Yuan asked in a low voice. His sympathetic approach belied his anxiousness.

Her hair, singed on the ends, fell over her face. The woman gave no indication that she knew Yuan and Sheng were nearby. "Grind the wheat and make the meal or we don't eat." She arched her back, held her chin skyward, then let loose a piercing shriek. She pulled her child close, hugging the little girl; rocking her.

Yuan looked at Sheng and touched his temple, sending an unspoken message about the woman's state of mind.

The woman carried on, "Grind the wheat and make the meal or we don't eat."

Yuan could hear the Cheng Guards' voices. They were in the field. He pulled hides from her hut, then took the bucket of water and doused the exposed smoldering rubble. He picked up end poles that had once supported the roof, then propped them on a crumbled pile of sun-dried bricks. Next, he laid the hides over the sizzling ashes he'd just drenched, then held open two layers, and told Sheng, "Crawl in between. Hurry!"

Sheng dove inside. Yuan scurried about, covering Sheng, quickly tossing soot on top, then replacing the poles to make it look as it did when he arrived. He drew his sword, then crawled in between the layers. The hide felt warm where his hip pressed to the ground. Smoke whisked into his face, burning his eyes. He used his sleeve to wipe them, but froze when he heard the Captain of the Guard's voice saying, "Find them, and let's get out of Sung."

"Shut your eyes, and don't think about the guards," Yuan whispered to Sheng.

The woman's lament was a steady drone. "Grind the wheat and make the meal or we don't eat."

"Check over there!" the Head Guard shouted. "Woman! Have you seen a man and a boy come this way?"

Yuan heard footsteps grow closer, shuffling to a stop in between the woman and their hiding spot. Sheng twitched. Yuan grabbed the back of the boy's robe to constrict his movement. He didn't know that Sheng's foot had slipped out from under the cover.

The Head Guard churlishly asked, "Where are the rest of your people, woman?"

But she merely repeated her refrain.

Sheng let out a breath that was too loud for Yuan's comfort. Yuan tightened his grip and felt the boy tremble. Fear had taken hold, compounding the risk of giving away their presence.

The hide wasn't thick enough to protect them from the burning coals that lay underneath, and Yuan's next breath, filled with smoldering ash, tickled his throat. He wanted to cough and was sure that Sheng suffered likewise. His eyes continued to sting, and his hip felt hot, almost too hot for comfort.

Yuan was surprised Sheng had endured this long but was certain that the boy couldn't last much longer. His mind darted between trying to envision what the Cheng Guards were doing and calculating whether it was best to launch at them by surprise or to simply remain hidden.

"Check under the . . ." before the Captain could finish his command, an arrow swooshed across the village, striking his arm. The impact knocked him to the ground.

Yuan heard the thud, then the Captain's howl, followed by the trample of footsteps as Cheng Guards ran to assist their fallen leader.

"Fall back! Fall back!" the Captain yelled.

Yuan could hear the shuffle of feet. *The Captain's men helped him up.* He heard next the unmistakable whistle of another volley, then shouts from soldiers charging into the village from downstream. A crashing thump occurred next to them as the Captain stumbled on Sheng's foot, then tumbled to the ground.

Yuan held tightly to Sheng for fear of the boy's reaction. He kept a hand on his weapon's hilt, ready to spring.

"Hurry! Let's go," the Captain shouted.

No sooner had the sounds of feet sprinting away faded, than the clamor of others following in pursuit grew louder.

Sheng squirmed to bolt from the heap.

"Not yet," Yuan whispered. He put his hand on Sheng's shoulder, then pressed the boy to the ground.

"Grind the wheat and make the meal or we don't eat," the woman sang while soldiers, skirting the village, stampeded past.

Sheng brushed Yuan's hand off his shoulder, then burst out from the cover, slapping at his hip. "I'm on fire," Sheng cried, trying desperately to keep his voice down.

A thin stream of smoke puffed from the boy's robe. Yuan patted the cloth until there were no embers, then looked around to determine if they had been seen. He saw only the backs of men dressed in armored tunics, running across the field in pursuit of the Cheng Guards. He watched them all disappear into the tree line.

"Are we safe now?" Sheng asked. He was covered in soot

from head to toe. He buried his head into the side of Yuan's robe that had been spared the grime and wiped his eyes.

"No. Not completely, but we're a lot safer than we were when we woke up this morning."

"Will they come back?" Sheng asked.

"The Cheng Guards won't, but those other men are either Sung soldiers or the Hua clan. They will chase the Cheng Guards out of the country, then return. But they don't know we're here, so they won't be searching for us."

"Do they want to kill us, too?" Sheng fretted.

"I don't know, but let's not find out." Yuan felt confident they had caught a break.

Sheng took solace in Yuan's hope. He rubbed his nose and asked, "What do we do now?"

"Grind the wheat and make the meal or we don't eat." The woman's sobs drew Yuan's attention.

He looked over at her, then turned back to Sheng, patted him on the back. "Let's clean up at the river. Then we'll eat and stay nearby the rest of the day. We'll leave in the morning."

⇒⇒⇒

The next morning, Yuan was jarred awake. He sat up to see the morning sun rising over the woman's shoulder. He and Sheng had moved downstream of the village, choosing a location more pleasant to sleep than the smoldering village. Yuan was surprised to see her standing over him.

She shoved a partially charred basket into Yuan's chest. Dirt and soot still caked her face.

He looked inside and saw boiled bread, balled into clumps. The woman wore the look of a person whose mind, ravaged by extremes of war, had retreated from reality. She appeared no more coherent this morning.

"What is your name?" Yuan asked, but received no response. He glanced toward the village, wondering what she had done with the little girl's body. He was in a different land

and wasn't sure of the burial customs among her people. And in her condition, the woman couldn't dig a grave or build a pyre. "I am Yuan. Can I help you with your child? Do your people bury the dead?"

"You must leave. Boy too." Her tone had changed from a sorrowful wail to an even drone.

"What?" Yuan said, taken aback.

"You must leave. Boy too," she repeated, then walked over to a fire pit near the river.

Yuan didn't intend to stay but wondered why she was so insistent that they leave immediately.

Cold air, funneling off the mountains, swept across the flat terrain. It tickled the back of Yuan's neck. He turned toward the morning fire, stretched off the effects of sleep, then joined her.

She took a handful of twigs off a stack of firewood piled to the side of the pit, then tossed them into the morning flame.

"Why must we leave right now?" Yuan asked. "Is there some reason? Did you see soldiers this morning?"

The woman stoked the coals, gazing blankly into crackling fire, but said nothing. She walked to the water's edge, where a woven creel leaned partially on its side in the shallows. She grabbed the two handles that arched over the wicker top and removed a small, shallow-rimmed basket that covered the opening. She retrieved a fish from inside, then a knife. The woman laid the fish on a flat board, slit its belly, then tugged at the string of entrails, dumping them into the water. She cut away the remaining guts, then scraped at the scales. "You must leave," she said, dipping the fish in the river and swishing it around. She plopped it back onto the board, then rasped the other side.

"The boy is hard to rouse this morning," Yuan said. "His name is Sheng." He took a fish from the basket to assist. He noticed the catch was yesterday's, but he had gone without food long enough and didn't care. He pointed toward the boy and said, "This journey hasn't been easy for him. Better let him sleep." Yuan glanced upstream, toward her village, then said sadly, "Looks like it hasn't been easy for you, either."

"They won't just let us fish and tend to our fields," she said, offering the first intelligible response.

"Yes," Yuan agreed glumly. "These are difficult times, and you have been caught in the worst part." He sliced open another fish.

The woman raised her knife, then jammed the point into the board and blurted, "The noblemen can't agree who will rule, so we suffer for it." She dropped the prepared fish in the small basket, then walked over to the fire.

Her oddity intrigued Yuan and not solely because her remarks weren't always grounded. He watched her kneel by the flames, place the basket beside the pit, then stack rocks on the opposite sides of the makeshift hearth. Next, she tied together three thin sticks, each about arm's length, using a long thin strip of leather, finishing the task with a quick tug. She spread the opposite ends apart to make a tripod, and after setting it in place, behind the stack of rocks that formed the hearth's near edge, she constructed a similar tripod on the other side of the pit.

"Are you the only one from your village left alive?" Yuan asked but received no reply. He peeled bark off three sticks that lay next to the creel, dipping the shafts into the water, then joined her by the pit. "Winter is coming soon. What will you do?"

The woman ignored the question but took the sticks. She heard Sheng stir and said to him, "Eat." She turned back to the pit and skewered a fish.

This was the first waking moment in days where they were not hunted. No one was gaining on them, but the break was sure to be brief. They would use the limited time to relax by the warm fire, fill their bellies, and plot a direction. Simple things, like the smell of a cooked meal, brought a sense of ease. But the morning was still marked by an apprehension that hung over them. The relaxing moment would not last long because the journey had other dangers. *The river dumps into the Huai, but in Chu territory. We must be careful,* Yuan reminded himself.

The woman removed the fish from the spit, then held it toward Sheng. "Here," she said without expression.

Sheng joined them by the fire, drawn by the sizzle of food. "Thank you," he said, trying to be appreciative, then snatched it from her, giving in to hunger pains.

She placed another skewered fish over the fire. The flame singed the wet skin while coals crackled from a steady drip. When the meat was ready, she pinched off a clump, turned to Sheng, then plopped the morsel into her mouth. The women looked at Sheng but showed no emotion; held the gaze a few minutes, then rotated the fish, cooking both sides until done.

It did not take long for Sheng to pick the meat off the bones. He tossed the skeletal remains into the coals, then patted his stomach. "May I have some more?" he asked. She handed him another from the spit, remaining silent, then walked down to the riverbank. She knelt, splashed water on her hands, and retrieved a skin flask from a boat that listed at the water's edge. She drank from the flask, then returned to Yuan and Sheng.

"Drink." She spoke not so much a request, but an absolute, tossing Sheng the flask. She reached into the basket Yuan had placed near the kindling pile, then pulled out a dumpling. "Eat this," she directed the boy.

Sheng gulped a mouthful, swallowed, then bit into the dumpling. His lips smacked. He wiped his mouth with his sleeve, then offered the flask back to her.

"Keep it," she said plainly. "You must leave." Her eyes darted to her village, then in the opposite direction, downriver.

Yuan stepped to her side. "Yes, we have a long journey ahead, but tell me, you keep saying that like there's some urgency. I know about the Cheng Guards. I know about the turmoil in Sung. And the men who chased away those who hunted us will return, no doubt, but is there something you know that I don't? What else makes you tell us to leave quickly?"

A lone tear dripped from her eye, tracking its way through soot and down her cheek. The woman picked up the creel and tossed it hard to Yuan. "Go. Leave." She fell to her knees and began to weep.

Yuan motioned to Sheng. He gathered the bow and quiver he'd taken from the Cheng Guard, along with the creel and flask. "Is there something I can do for you? Do you want to come with us?" he asked, feeling her pain. "We can help you get to a village where you'll be safe."

"Go!" she shrieked.

Yuan nodded. "Let's go," he said to Sheng. Yuan loaded the creel and flask in the boat, then added the bow and quiver. Sheng hopped onto the shallow, flat-bottomed craft, but Yuan stopped short of climbing on board and turned back toward the woman. *I can't leave her. She was lucky to have survived the massacre, but she will die, soon probably, if she stays behind.* He stepped to her and said firmly, "You are coming with us." He took her by the shoulders, lifted the woman to her feet, and led her to the boat.

She didn't resist but staggered on the first step onto the hull. Yuan steadied her, helped her take a seat at the middle of the vessel, then moved to the rear. He pushed away from the bank with the long scull, turning downstream. Before Yuan had rowed a third rotation, she lurched to her feet and dove into the water. Her splash slapped Yuan in the face as he reached too late to grab her. He wiped his eyes and sat idly while she swam to shore, and once she climbed onto the bank, he turned his head downstream and moved the craft deeper into the current, leaving the woman to her misery.

"Why did she do that?" Sheng blurted in alarm. "Shouldn't we go back and get her?"

"No, she is resigned to her fate." Yuan glanced over his shoulder and saw the woman walking away from the bank. *She believes her doom is inevitable, and that her earlier escape from death was only temporary. She thinks we will be swept into her fate. That's why she was so insistent on us leaving. She couldn't save her daughter – she can't save herself – but she sees an opportunity to save us.*

Sheng looked back toward the village. "Yuan?"

"Yes, Sheng." Yuan had grown accustomed to the way the boy demanded his attention.

"She's not right is she?" Sheng said sadly.

Yuan replied thoughtfully, "No. Life can do that to some people."

"What will happen to her?"

"I don't know. She's in for a rough time, probably." Yuan kept to himself what he truly thought of her chances for survival. If the men who burned the village didn't return to kill her, scavengers and cutthroats would come and take the other boats from her and whatever else they wanted to plunder. Eventually, she would be unable to fend for herself.

Yuan looked at the woman. She was rocking on her knees next to a small mound that was covered with a charred hide. He could not see who or what was under the heap, but guessed it was the little girl the woman had clung to the previous day.

"Sheng, there's nothing we can do for her, especially since danger has not completely passed us by. It's a long way to Wu, and we must cross Chu territory to get there." Yuan sculled the craft into current, then aimed it downriver.

"Won't they kill us in Wu since we're Chu people?" Sheng asked.

"Wu and Chu are enemies. That's a fact. But I'm the one they will likely kill, not you." Yuan shook his head, realizing he hadn't offered reassurance. "You are Chu Royalty. The King of Wu will want to cultivate a relationship with you so that your line to the Chu throne can be an advantage for him."

"If they are going to kill you, please don't take us there," Sheng pleaded.

"Don't worry. They will want to learn from me Chu's plans against Wu. I'll be fine." Yuan knew better, though. *They'll kill me once I have no more information to give.* Yuan realized he had said too much and needed to comfort the boy, even if it took telling him a white lie, which he hated to do. But he could not risk Sheng doing something foolish, like refusing to cross the border, in order to protect Yuan.

Sheng rested his chin on a hand, elbow propped up on his knee. "How do we get there?"

"I think we're on a tributary of the Huai River. At least it flows in the right direction. We'll follow the course to where it empties, hopefully into the Huai, then take the river downstream until we're in Wu."

"Yuan?"

"Yes, Sheng."

"Do we have enough fish in the basket?"

"No. We'll have to catch more."

Sheng wrinkled his brow. "But how?"

"Well, I have a bow now. We may have to hunt, or if we come upon a shallow pool, maybe I can strike more fish. Let's just keep an eye out for the right chance, okay?"

"Okay, but you're not very good with it. I saw you miss

that Cheng Guard, and if you can't hit something that big, how are you going to get a fish?"

Yuan chuckled, glad for a happy moment among their journey. "You sound like my brother."

Sheng smiled, stretched his legs onto the hull, and shot Yuan an inquiring glance. "Why did the woman keep saying that stuff about grinding wheat?"

"Because she's not in her right mind," Yuan said with compassion.

Sheng's curiosity fixed on that which he was too young to grasp. "Why did she want us to leave now?"

"I don't know, Sheng," Yuan said sorrowfully. He didn't say what experience had taught him. The woman had lost everything: her friends, her way of life, her daughter. And she had given up the will to live. He understood that the men who chased away the Cheng Guards were likely the same men who destroyed the village. They must have seen they had missed one – the woman – and they would return to kill her and finish the job. The woman had accepted this as her fate but did not want the same for them, especially Sheng.

Sheng looked past Yuan. The village was no longer visible. He could see only the river and forested areas, broken intermittently by fields of bramble and grass. "I'm not scared now," he said, blanketed with relief.

"I'm not either," Yuan concurred. "But there are times when it's good to be afraid. That's your instincts telling you to do something. Don't ever ignore them." A warm sensation suddenly overcame him. It was one he had experienced only briefly before, long ago when his wife was late in her pregnancy. Like then, the feeling now was paternal, but this time binding him to Sheng. Fate had cheated both of them out of people who should have been in their lives – Yuan, a son, and Sheng, a father. *Maybe that's my purpose in life – to guide Sheng as a father would.*

Sheng turned to face downriver. The breeze felt cool on his face in contrast to the morning sun. He eased to the stem, laid his head on the edge, then dipped his hand in the cool water. The steady slosh of water against the hull brought a soothing calm. He pulled his hand out of the water, folded his arm under his head and soon after, closed his eyes.

Yuan plopped down at the stern. He leaned against the scull and watched Sheng drift into sleep. It didn't take long, which wasn't a surprise, considering the energy and flood of emotions spent getting to this point. The easy flow of the river was relaxing, and Yuan felt his body in need of the rest that traveling by boat would allow, though he wasn't ready to be lured completely by the peaceful surroundings. Sung remained tumultuous, and Chu territory lay ahead. He took quick inventory of the food the woman had given them. There was enough fish and dumplings to feed them for two days, maybe three if they stretched the meals, but they were on their own after that. *Do we dare stop at a village along the way? I can't pay for rations.*

⌒⌒⌒

Yuan and Sheng traveled by day and took a break from the water at night, making camp on a bank away from people. The moon during the previous night had been bright. Its tranquil light danced on the water. They passed by fishermen who worked the river, and villages that were sprinkled near the water along the way, choosing to engage in only casual contact with a wave and nod. Interest in them appeared to garner no more attention than what was to be expected from occasional onlookers who were simple villagers and not a threat. Yuan wasn't wearing a battle tunic and, aided by the boy's presence, posed no danger that would attract heightened attention from the villagers.

Yuan and Sheng had eaten the last of the dumplings the night before, and had finished off the fish a day before that. The tributary had not yet dumped into the Huai River, and now food was again a worry. *Damn! I may have to try and use the bow,* Yuan thought.

Sheng sat quietly at the stem. Yuan left him to his thoughts and looked over the boy's head to the banks downriver, searching one side, then the other, for any sign of danger. The water's scour through the land widened up ahead before turning to a sharp westerly bend. *What's around the corner? Hopefully, nothing that's a threat.* He'd asked and answered that question many times since taking to the water. It was late in the afternoon, and he would soon need to find a place to pitch for the night. He sculled the boat to the outer edge of the current and settled on a course.

They made the turn and saw no surprises, but another bend, snaking in the opposite direction, was before them. A haze blanketed the late afternoon sky, and rising above the tree line, Yuan saw smoke. The source was blocked by the river's serpentine course. It wasn't indicative of a sacked village, though, which eased Yuan's mind. Rather, it looked to be from normal cooking fires, and a lot of them. *It must be a big settlement,* Yuan surmised. He looked to see where the sun was in relation to the horizon, but trees obstructed his view. *Should I find a place to camp now, or wait until we pass the village? No food. Let's push forward.*

They made it past the next turn of the river and beyond another. The sun had almost set. Yuan noticed a large village set back from the inside bank. He saw people milling about, but they were too far away, and the daylight too dim, for them to notice anything unusual about a boat carrying a man and a boy. A fisherman waded in the water next to his partially banked craft, tying creels to the stern, then setting them each in the water.

Should I bank, wait for him to leave, then grab the fish? Yuan deliberated. The land protruded slightly into the water a short distance ahead. Yuan could hide the boat there and backtrack on land. He looked at Sheng, who was asleep and thought, *Better not chance it.*

The current quickened when they made it past the bank's jutting edge. Yuan worked the scull to keep the boat in the center of river, but the sun dipped below the horizon and darkness fell quickly, making navigation more difficult. He looked for a place to bank. The trees appeared to break away from the water's edge a short distance ahead, and Yuan steered toward that gap. The moon was not yet high enough in the sky to give any light, and once he made it to the edge of the trees, he looked landward. Fire pits glimmered in the distance. Yuan drew his gaze along a line leading from the firelight through the woods toward the settlement. *It's a big town. Get away from here!* He looked downriver and couldn't see well enough to traverse the course. *Wait for the moon to rise.* He sculled the boat toward land and saw a cove where runoff fed the river. Boats lined the bank, protected by the land's curve that naturally formed a cape. He sculled toward them, searching for shapes and movement that would give away a person's presence. *All clear!* Yuan eased the craft alongside the nearest boat.

Sheng awoke to the bump against the bank. "Where are we?" he asked groggily.

"Shhh," Yuan cautioned. "People are nearby." Yuan crawled to the front, then whispered to Sheng, "Stay here."

He stepped quietly onto the ground, grabbed the boat's stem, then pushed it into the water. He rotated the craft, working his hands along the boat's edge to the stern, then pulled the vessel back onto shore, making it easier to get away. Yuan turned to Sheng and dipped his hand to convey, *Lay down.* He walked down the line of boats, looking inside and in between each one, stopping about two-thirds of the way up the cove. He saw the rounded top of something that appeared anomalous to the water's calm surface. Two loop handles gave it structure. *A creel!* He eased into the water, careful not to make a splash,

then waded in between the boats. Yuan picked it up. It felt
fish-heavy. He removed the small, cupped, wicker plug, then
looked inside.

"Hey, what are you doing?" a voice called out.

Yuan turned to see a man walking toward him carrying
a torch. *Do I run or remain casual?* Yuan ignored the man's
question and started back toward Sheng, as if he hadn't heard
the man.

"Stop! That's my fish." The man hollered.

Yuan looked back. The man was running toward him.
Yuan darted down the line of boats, tossed the creel next
to Sheng, pushed the stern off the bank, then jumped in. He
worked the scull with furious strokes, moving them into what
he hoped was near the center of the river.

"Come back, thief!" the man yelled. His shout echoed over
the water.

Yuan concentrated on maneuvering the craft and didn't
look back. "What's he doing?" he asked Sheng, anxious to see
if the man gave chase.

Sheng looked toward the bank. "He's just standing there.
Do you think he'll come after us?"

Yuan paused the scull and turned to see for himself. Sheng
was right. The angry man stood where Yuan had launched,
one hand on a hip and watching them. "No," he said flatly. "A
basket of fish isn't worth the fight to him." Yuan took a deep
breath, returned his attention to the river, then worked the
scull with long easy strokes.

"Can we eat?" Sheng begged. "I'm hungry."

"I know you are. We haven't eaten all day, but we need
to get away from this town. We will eat tonight, but farther
downriver."

"Okay," Sheng sniffled. He crawled along the hull toward
the stem, curled up in ball, then laid his head down.

The moon was not yet high enough to help Yuan navigate.

The night had darkened, and Yuan figured clouds had blocked the stars. He couldn't see that the boat had drifted toward land, and the sudden sound of water lapping against the bank startled him. He sculled the craft away to where he thought the river's midpoint might be.

Yuan couldn't tell if the flow had quickened. He thought so, not because he could fix on a reference point to gauge the speed, rather he heard rushing water in the distance. *Is the river getting narrower or shallower?*

"Sheng," Yuan called out.

The boy didn't respond.

"Sheng!" Yuan spoke louder.

Sheng rubbed his face, turned and answered sleepily, "What?"

"Get to the center of the boat. We may be getting into rough water."

A swell slapped against the hull, rocking it. Sheng's head bumped hard against the bow's lip. He braced with one hand and checked the soreness on his cheekbone with the other, then crawled away from the edge to where Yuan had instructed. The water churned, propelling the craft faster. Yuan steadied the scull with both hands, while the river tugged at it one way. The stem rose quickly, fell just as fast, splashing on impact, then repeated the pound. *I can't see anything.* Options raced through his mind. *Get to land! But the current will roll the boat if I turn toward the bank.* He quickly assessed the river's strength and determined that even angling the craft landward would risk capsizing the boat. A swell sent the stem up, then quickly down, crashing into something Yuan couldn't make out. And on the smash, the front of the craft lodged into woody debris, the outline of which was barely discernible. The current pivoted the hull, and once the boat was almost perpendicular to the river's flow, the rushing water flipped it.

Sheng was the first to fall overboard. Yuan grabbed for

him, but the boy was just out of reach. Yuan took the plunge next, then surfaced, gasping for breath, while the torrents whisked him away from the overturned craft. He worked his arms to stay afloat. "Sheng!" he shouted. The boy was no-where in sight. "Sheng!" he called again.

He kicked in the water, continuing to tread, and when he stroked again, a snag under the surface caught his ankle. His foot stopped in place, while the water's rush pulled him under. Yuan jerked his leg, but the catch held firm. He tried to bend at the waist, toward his foot, but the rushing water was too strong. He grabbed the back of his thigh and pulled, then reached just below his kneecap and pulled again, working to bend his leg. He moved his hands down his shin, then to his ankle. His foot was trapped in the fork of a branch, and was so lodged in place, it didn't budge. Yuan held tightly to the branch, pushed his ankle, then slid his leg out from between the open prongs. No sooner had he freed his leg, than the water's gush swept him away.

Yuan popped his head above the surface, gasping for breath, while the surge slammed him into the spiked remains of a branch, broken off from a wedged log that protruded into the rapid's path. The point dug into his ribs. He grabbed on to the stalk, held himself up and shouted, "Sheng!" The current twirled him to the downstream side, turning his body so that he faced upriver. He swiveled to look the other way, searching for the boy.

The roiling water drowned much of the noise a child would make while struggling to swim. But then he heard coughing, like someone whose lungs had gulped water. He looked toward the sound, but saw only blackness. He made out the sound again, but this time, it was farther downstream. *He's still in the rapids!* he realized, frantic to save Sheng.

Yuan pushed off, rolled to his stomach and into the current. Clouds opened a small gap, letting through the moon's light just enough for Yuan to see what looked like a head bobbing in the water. *He's alive!* Yuan flattened his body on top of the water's surface, as best he could, then rolled, using backstrokes for buoyancy. He did it again, then paused to search for Sheng. *There!* He saw the boy's arms splashing in the water, trying to keep himself afloat.

The moon disappeared behind clouds again. Yuan came out of another roll, but before he completed the turn, he crashed headfirst into the dulled end of a tree limb, about the same diameter as his leg that rested just above the water's surface. Pain spiked down the back of his neck, then left a twinge as a reminder of the impact. Darkness, combined with the water's agitation, made it impossible to see the obstruction before his forehead, above the right eye, planted into the river's surprise. The rapid's churn twirled him around the obstacle. He grabbed for his head, a reaction in response to the pain, then quickly resumed treading. He didn't know if the drip running down his face was blood or water. There was not enough light to tell.

The river thrust Yuan toward Sheng, and once he was within reach, he snatched the boy. "Got you!" he said, making it doubtless by the strength of his grip.

Sheng grabbed Yuan tightly around the neck, then tried to work to a higher vantage. There was nowhere else to go, but that reality didn't resonate with the young mind. He went into a coughing spell, spitting up water.

"You're okay now," Yuan patted the boy.

Sheng clutched on to Yuan, not ready to accept that he was safe.

Yuan felt Sheng's little body tremble. The water was cold, which alone would account for the shimmers, but fear had everything to do with it now. "We'll survive this," Yuan encouraged the boy.

The river rushed them into a spot lit by the moon through a break in the clouds. Yuan saw that ahead of them the banks jutted inward, forming a neck. Water blasted through the shoot, which was about to discharge them. "Climb on my back," he told Sheng. "Hold on to the collar. Be strong. And get ready to hold your breath. We might go under."

The water's rush swooped them toward brush entangled in the river bottom. Yuan stroked with his arms to steer clear, but as they passed by, his sword snagged a branch hidden beneath the surface. The catch, combined with the current, jolted, then spun him. Sheng fell off his back, and Yuan swiftly latched on to him, pulling him to his side. The river's churn quickened and forced them into the restriction.

"Take a deep breath!" Yuan shouted. He fought against the undercurrent but to no avail. It dragged them down into a swirling roil, then squirted both to the other side. Yuan surfaced first, then jerked Sheng up.

"Are you okay?" He gasped and caught his breath.

Sheng wiped his face, coughed, then nodded.

The current changed, both in direction and speed, after spitting them through the swell. Yuan looked around, treading with one arm and holding Sheng with the other. They were in a broader body of water and floating slowly, easterly.

"We're at the Huai River, Sheng!" Yuan's excitement exceeded his fatigue. "Hold on to my collar again. I'll get us to land."

The river's drift pushed them to the far bank, but it made for an easy swim. Yuan reached land, then stepped onto the low incline. Sheng followed. A chilling wind slapped the clothes to his skin. Yuan hadn't noticed the cold while in the water. Clouds still blocked the moon's light. Yuan turned upstream, searching for signs of people, then down river. But they were alone.

Sheng folded his arms across his chest. His shoulders hunched and his teeth began to chatter. "What do we do now?" Sheng asked, bouncing on the balls of his feet.

"Let's get dry? Then we'll figure things out."

24

A PERILOUS SHORTCUT
TO WU

*Y*uan awoke under a blanket of fog that hovered shoulder high over the river valley. He took a couple of deep breaths. His lungs, tightened by the damp air, worked harder than usual. He and Sheng had slept in a depression against the base of a steep hill. The washout was large enough for only Sheng to lie completely underneath the overhang. Yuan faced the concavity, providing a screen to the cold blast for Sheng. The wind, while the two slept, funneled along the Dabie Shan, somehow finding its way into the crease between Yuan's exposed robe and the skin on his back, making an already miserable night in the elements even worse.

A sharp pang spiked from the base of his skull down his stiff neck, the result of when he'd smashed face first into a log while fighting the rapids. He sat up; his head pounded from temple to temple. He gently touched his hand to the gash above his eye. It felt puffy, but he did not press for the soreness. He checked his ribcage next. Nothing was broken, and the slash wasn't worrisome, but his ankle concerned him. It was swollen, and not only did the throb seize his attention, the joint felt weak.

Yuan rose to his feet to test his ankle. He leaned gingerly at first, then gradually added weight. *Not sound, but not too bad.* His sword was on the ground, next to where he had slept. He shook his head. *How did that stay with me in the river?* He picked it up, then worked it into the layers of his belt, wrapping an extra twist of the cloth around the scabbard. He felt for the sheath strapped to his arm, under his sleeve. *I still have my knife, too.*

He looked about. *Where are we?* Their journey had taken them to the Huai River, and now, to get to Wu they had to follow it downstream to where the Dabie Shan's southward bend met the undulating hills that fanned to the Yangtze River. There, they would have a choice – follow the river to Wu, which would take longer, or turn deeper into the hills and take the shortcut through Chao Pass. Either way, the risk of capture was high. He knew to stay away from villages and people.

Chu's subjugation of the region did not necessarily equate to political allegiance of all the local people, but not knowing who to trust was a problem. Certainly, the general ill feelings toward Chu were felt throughout the area. Yuan was well aware of that, but there were always people willing to better their position in life at the expense of others. Yuan and Sheng's predicament presented an occasion for such opportunists.

They had lost the boat and creel of fish, their only supply of food. The bow and quiver were gone, too, not that they were useful tools in Yuan's hands. Time was not on their side. He needed to bring an end to their journey. *Chao Pass it is.* The route was an eastern gateway to and from the hills, used to cut across the elbow of the Dabie Shan's foothills. Once through the pass, they had only to cross the Yangtze River to be in Wu.

The flapping wings of birds fleeing their evening roost brought the morning to Sheng. He rolled out of the washout, sat up and looked around for Yuan, but he saw only the mid-torso of a figure standing in the distance. He rubbed his eyes, startled by the eerie sight of the man's shoulders and head disappearing into the fog. He fought back the urge to scream.

Yuan heard the boy rustle and turned. His movement swirled the thick, moist air away, revealing his body fully.

Sheng let go a sigh, comforted at the sight of his protector.

Yuan knelt beside Sheng. "How do you feel? Does your body hurt?" Yuan asked, making sure that the morning hadn't brought new pain to the boy that had been missed last night.

"I'm fine," Sheng said wearily. It wasn't only his voice that was tired. He crossed his legs in front of him, then rested his elbows on the knees.

Yuan explained what they faced.

"I don't want to ride in another boat," Sheng proclaimed. "I thought I was going to drown last night. And I'm tired of walking. Walk. Walk. Run. Run. Splash! That's what we've done." He picked up a handful of dirt and tossed it.

"I know," Yuan nodded. "And a hungry belly doesn't help. We'll take a shortcut through Chao Pass. That will lessen the journey by days." He stood and held out his hand to Sheng. "We're both marching on empty bellies, so let's get going while we have the strength."

The boy grabbed hold, then pulled himself up. "Can we get something to eat at the pass?"

Yuan shook his head soberly. "If they find us, they will kill me. I'm not sure what will happen to you."

Sheng remained silent for a few minutes, considering what it meant to get caught. His brow wrinkled curiously. He had seen firsthand what the Cheng Guards had done, and more of it lay ahead. "Yuan, if they kill me, will they let me eat before?"

Yuan grunted, not knowing how to answer and not wanting to explain. The boy's questions, however, showed that he didn't have much strength left. "Let's move on."

"Which way?"

"This way to Wu," Yuan motioned with a nod. "We still want to avoid people, so keep your eyes on alert."

The morning turned into midday, and their trek was slowed by the precautions they took when sneaking by a small town that was nestled against the mountain. Yuan chose a shady spot to wait for a lag in the fishermen's comings and goings to slip past unnoticed. He snatched a flask from the hull of a boat, wishing there had been something to eat as well. The sun soon fell on the horizon, and they settled in for the evening in a clump of trees, away from the river's bank. Yuan leaned against a trunk, then pulled his knee to his chest and stroked his swollen ankle. He ringed his leg, rubbing the aching muscles with both hands. But relief came more from being off the foot than massaging the pained area.

There was no reprieve from the throb in his head. Yuan ran his fingers back and forth over his scalp, then down and across his forehead. Congested sinuses added to his troubles. He was acutely aware of every ache and pain, along with the agony each brought. He looked over at Sheng, who had slipped off to sleep without any complaint for having missed another meal. Yuan took a swig from the flask, then sprawled onto his side, hoping to drift into slumber himself.

They awoke the next morning much like the way they ended the previous day, hurting and hungry. Their slog followed the water's edge, and before the sun was directly above them, they came upon a path that led to where the Dabie Shan's foothills formed a series of peaks. The route to Chao Pass parted from the river, directing all traffic between twin hills, eventually leading to the gateway and the Yangtze River. Yuan patted Sheng on the back, then pointed down a well-beaten footpath. "This way." He stroked his head. The pain dulled the realization of having come to the last critical juncture.

They followed the trail up a rising trace to where the path

meandered under a canopy that began at the base of the two hills. The foliage filtered the daylight, blending shadows into a dark blanket, which made Yuan question what lurked behind each tree, bush and shrub. The dim ambient light created an eeriness. He stopped, studied the path, then up the sides of both hills. *Good. No movement.* Yuan maneuvered cautiously forward. There was not so much as a semblance of a breeze or any noise of nature, which hung a chill over the worn track. No leaves rustled. Birds didn't chirp. There wasn't even the hint of a cricket.

We've been lucky, Yuan admitted, for they had been the only people on the trail. The trek would have been tranquil, Yuan believed, had their lives not been at risk.

It was so peaceful that Sheng began murmuring out loud, forgetting the need for caution. "Yuan, I miss my mother." He spoke as if she was home and he need only return.

"Shhh," Yuan cautioned. He knelt to the boy's eye level and whispered, "I know you do, but we must not use our names. Remember, we are in Chu and there are bad men who want to do us harm."

Sheng nodded his understanding.

"Remember how quiet you were when we hung over the Cheng Guards on the mountain?"

Again, the boy nodded.

"You must be that quiet now, too. Understand?" Yuan took Sheng by the shoulders to accent the need for vigilance.

Once more, Sheng nodded solemnly.

Yuan patted him on the shoulder, then turned down the path. Sheng took up the rear position. They moved deeper into the foothill's cleave, which eventually led them to where the hill on the right broke into a deep crease.

Sheng tugged on Yuan's robe and whispered, "I'm tired."

Yuan, too, felt in need of rest. He pointed upslope from the trail. "You see that flat rock exposed through the brush up there? It looks like a shelf."

"Yes." Sheng heaved a sigh.

"Let's take a break up there."

Yuan went first, angling his body sideways to the slope. He planted the edge of his foot and dug it into the soil. Pain shot from his ankle. He turned around to position his other leg upslope, then sidestepped up the hill another stride. He unlooped his scabbard, then held it out for Sheng. "Take hold. I'll pull you up."

Sheng gripped tightly, then stepped onto the steep grade with his toes turned uphill. The soft soil under his foot dislodged as soon as he leaned on it, causing the boy's foot to slide out from under him. He tumbled to the ground. "It's baichi to climb up there," he spat.

The thought of Lan flashed in Yuan's mind, triggered by the boy's use of *baichi*. The word had always been Lan's pet saying when he didn't like what he saw or heard. Yuan quickly snapped to the present. His eyes darted up, then down the trail. *Still alone.* "Turn sideways, like me," he instructed softly.

Sheng tried it again, this time relying on the sheath to steady himself. They worked uphill to the rocky perch. The slope above the ledge levelled for a distance of about two steps before resuming the incline. Some animal or person had burrowed into the earth, leaving a slight depression behind the rock, which made for a good place to rest. Yuan pulled the flask off his shoulder, bounced it in the palm of his hand and said, "Here, have a drink. It feels light so there's not much left. Take what you need, just leave a little for me."

Layers of leaves provided a pleasant cushion against the hard ground. Sheng nestled into them, snatched the flask, then turned it up taking a big gulp.

"Whoa. Take regular sips," Yuan cautioned.

The boy held a mouthful, sat the flask on his lap, then swallowed.

Yuan unlooped his sword's sheath from his belt, reclined

against the curve of the hollow and put the scabbard beside him. He closed his eyes, but the respite wasn't relaxing. A wave of aches spread. Soreness penetrated his joints and muscles from his swollen ankle to the throb between his temples, spreading misery throughout his body. He touched his forehead, which felt hot despite the cool air. *Fever. Damn,* he rued. He tried massaging his brow, but it didn't bring relief.

The sound of men's voices startled Sheng, and he tugged on Yuan's robe, starting to point with the other hand. Yuan stopped the boy's arm. Although the low resting spot was hidden from the path below, it was too shallow to conceal them. And the travelers on the path would see Yuan first. He couldn't make out their conversation to know if they were soldiers, but he assumed as much to be prepared. He pulled himself closer to the wall of the impression, tunneled his left foot under the brush, then spread leaves over his leg, covering the limb from his knee down. He bent his right leg so that it was clearly visible, then reclined hoping that he and Sheng would be mistaken for harmless travelers – a crippled father and his son – resting from the rigors of walking the pass. "When they get closer, take small sips from the flask, but don't take your eyes off of them. Tap my hand if they make any move toward us." Yuan shielded his sword from view, then readied his hand on the hilt.

The voices grew louder with their approach. Sheng fidgeted, struggling to remain calm. There were only two men, and they were dressed in hempen tunics, not armor. They were peasants and didn't carry weapons. Sheng felt relief and glanced at Yuan, searching for confirmation, but Yuan's gaze was focused on the two men.

Unlike the top knots worn in Cheng, these men wore their hair long like Yuan and Sheng, an obvious sign that they were Chu. "Drink," Yuan said to Sheng. "Short sips." In Yuan's haste to make himself look harmless, he'd overlooked a critical flaw in his plan. *Why would a cripple climb the slope?* He raised his leg out from underneath the brush, giving up the charade. *My mind is tired! I'm glad they aren't Chu soldiers.*

Sheng pressed the flask against his lips. He didn't swallow before raising it for another swig. Water squirted from the corners of his mouth, then dribbled down his chin. Sheng reflexively pulled the flask away in a quick, sudden burst. He wiped his mouth on his sleeve, and when his eyes returned to the two peasants, they were standing still, staring directly at them. A feeling of unease overwhelmed the boy, and he jabbed at Yuan to get his attention.

Yuan squeezed Sheng's thigh. "Take another sip," he whispered through his teeth without moving his lips.

Sheng pressed the flask again to his lips. The peasants chuckled, then returned to their purpose. Yuan lifted his head barely enough to see down the path at the men who turned away. The encounter provided a clear reminder that the trail's tranquility was deceptive. He and Sheng had to keep moving, and couldn't stop until they were safely beyond the pass and in Wu.

"Let's hurry," Yuan exclaimed, leaping to his feet. He pushed off the ground, then sidestepped his way to the path. Sheng opted for a different way down. He remained seated, lifted his butt off the ground and pushed himself forward, dislodging loose soil and scooting downhill, ending up at Yuan's feet.

Yuan felt lucky to have survived the encounter without raising any suspicions. But he could not rely on remaining an anonymous traveler, uninteresting to the soldiers guarding the pass; his ailing condition called into question whether or not he could manage as he had done in Cheng. *Fighting against the odds is out. I don't have the strength. We must bypass them.* How he would accomplish that remained a mystery.

Positioned on Chu's side of its border with Wu, Chao Pass was heavily guarded, not too different than Cheng's mountain garrison, but the terrain was less formidable. Somewhere along the way they would have to forge a path across one of the lofty hills, avoiding the guarded gateway to the Yangtze.

They walked well beyond their stop at the rock shelf, still unsure of how much farther there was to go before reaching the post, when they came upon an easy sloping rise, presenting Yuan with a question. *Is anyone on the other side?* The path narrowed at the peak where the terrain fell abruptly away on the right and squeezed against an outcrop on the left, which allowed for only two people to walk abreast. Yuan slowed once they neared the crest, then stopped when he was first able to peek over the top. *No one!* He breathed a sigh of relief.

They stepped onto the ridge and Sheng yanked on Yuan's elbow to get his attention. "Yuan, can we . . ." But howling laughter interrupted him.

Yuan grabbed Sheng's shoulder to silence the boy, then bent to a knee. The trace dipped immediately once over the pitch. A squad of Chu soldiers sat on the side of the path, casually conversing among themselves and showing no particular urgency. Yuan couldn't see the trail's sharp drop until he peeked over the top of the rise.

The men were enjoying an entertaining moment, laughing at some story being told. Yuan froze, trying to decide what to do. He was certain they wouldn't let him and Sheng pass without scrutiny, and even a basic inquiry would lead to more questions, which was too risky. He chose to reverse directions and circle back uphill of the path to sneak around the soldiers.

Yuan nudged Sheng with an elbow, then motioned with a nod. He put Sheng on his back and made haste back to where the path's rise began. He grabbed a low-hanging tree limb and climbed upslope. His first step dislodged loose soil that slid onto the path. Pain shot from his swollen ankle. He moved his feet quickly to catch his balance, then sidestepped short strides, holding the hilt of his sword to quiet its clang.

He traversed the incline to a point he thought was even with the rock shelf, where they had rested earlier, then paused to catch his breath. The narrow leveling of the slope remained only a couple of steps wide and appeared to ring the hill. It ran in both directions roughly forming a tree-dotted lane. The gradient above it steepened abruptly, and the trees and brush were too thick for him to see how much farther there was to climb. Yuan saw no obvious trail that would lead them to higher ground. His eyes peered down the flattening passageway, which he hoped would allow them to pass by the soldiers unnoticed, but the forested growth screened his view and he couldn't be certain. He adjusted the boy on his back, then took a step. The snap of twigs breaking under his foot rang too loud, despite Yuan's caution. He stopped, then turned toward the path below, relieved that no one was there.

He looked down the hillside lane. The same leafy mixture covered the way. It was likely to be loud, traversing along this route. He used his foot to sweep aside the first layer of brush, exposing softer, pliable bedding. He nudged his toe into the divot, followed by the heel, then put weight on his foot, calmed that there was little sound. He took the next step, then repeated the effort, moving at a laborious pace.

Yuan continued the slow progress until he spotted the crest of the path's rise. A line of trees angled from where he stood down to the path below, blocking his view of the soldiers, but he heard their voices. He tapped Sheng's leg, indicating for the boy to slide off to the ground, and whispered, "Be very still and quiet." He crouched to peer through the brush. The tree line's thickness broke beyond the clump where he hid, and he saw that the passageway he was on followed the hill, like he'd hoped, but around a bend. Yuan had no idea what dangers lurked beyond where the hill curved. He looked downslope. The soldiers remained on the other side of the path's crest where the trace dipped. Once he and Sheng stepped beyond the tree line, they would be visible to the soldiers. Yuan pondered what to do.

One of the soldiers was particularly animated when he spoke. He was a pudgy man whose stories took on the same liveliness as his broad smile.

"Where is this place?" a young soldier asked the chunky orator, as if hoping to discover the exact location of a treasure trove.

"It's behind the Southern Market," the bard explained. "Once you get off the boat, it's the first square inside the city gate on the North Road. Go past the silk shops, and at the next street, turn right."

The oldest soldier, at least judging by his receding hairline, arose and fired at the new hand, "It's not surprising that the cub is asking for directions." He playfully poked the young soldier's arm, spurring the round of laughter that followed. "Perhaps directions to Madam Wong's aren't the only instructions you need. You sure you know what to do when you get there?"

The young soldier picked himself off the ground, not enjoying the others' fun at his expense. "Well, I heard that you . . . Oh, never mind," he scoffed. His ability to muster a clever retort failed, making the moment even more embarrassing.

Yuan watched for any sign that his and Sheng's presence was detected but saw only the humiliated soldier trot away while the others roared.

"Come on, we'd better join him. If he gets lost, we won't have anyone to laugh at," the pudgy storyteller chuckled. "Wait up!" he shouted to his green cohort, who scampered over the path's crest.

Yuan instantly felt relief that he had decided to circle back, otherwise he would now be face-to-face with the two men who broke off from the group. But they weren't well-concealed. The tree line shielded him and Sheng from the view of the soldiers who remained in the dip, but the other two need only turn their gaze up the hill to spot them. Yuan grabbed Sheng's shoulder to steady the boy.

Something caught the tubby storyteller's attention. He stopped, turned toward the slope and made eye contact with Yuan. But he didn't speak. He stood frozen for a moment, bewildered by Yuan and Sheng's presence. "You up there," he called out. "What are you doing? Come down here."

Yuan didn't respond. "Get on," he whispered to Sheng. He put the boy on his back, then sprinted off along the high lane, ignoring the shouts from below. All he could think about was getting around the bend and staying ahead of the soldiers.

Yuan made the corner and looked uphill, searching for the best route up. He saw the base of a steep rock face. But the tree-studded slope made a direct line to it impossible. Yuan grabbed a sapling, planted the edge of his foot, then angled uphill, ignoring the pain spiking from his ankle. He worked to the crag, then stopped to look up. Between him and the summit, the hill turned straight up. And the rock face was too steep to climb. The overhang extended left and right, as far as Yuan could see in both directions. Whether they proceeded in the direction of the gate or backtracked, he guessed, it didn't matter. Finding the easiest way up and over the cliff was simply a matter of luck. He chose to press forward.

Yuan heard louder voices down below, along with the sound of twigs snapping underfoot. Yuan adjusted Sheng on his back, then bent to duck under a bushy tree limb that hugged the crag. A twisted trunk jutted out from the base of the cliff, forcing him to step downhill to maneuver around it. His thighs burned when he squatted under a limb. He grabbed hold of a brittle branch, which snapped under his weight when he swung around to the other side of the tree.

"Over here!" Yuan heard a soldier shout. He couldn't see the man, but the voice was too close for comfort.

"Where are they?" another yelled.

"I don't know. I can't see them," came the answer.

Yuan pushed through tangled scrub and found the luck he needed. Part of the cliff had broken away over the centuries and provided their avenue to the top. Huge, jagged rocks created tall steps which lead up to a point that left a wall to scale of about twice Yuan's height. He let Sheng down, then lifted the boy onto the first rock step. Yuan followed. They continued, climbing to the next landing, then another.

Yuan put Sheng on his back again, then leaned against the rock face. "Hurry! Step up on my shoulders and lean against the cliff."

Sheng wiggled his right foot into place, then pushed on Yuan's head to lift himself up. He hesitated briefly, then gingerly tested Yuan's directions, leaning against the wall with one hand.

"That's it. Now, you see that rock sticking out?" Yuan pointed to the left of a fissure in the cliff that ran from the top down to where he stood.

"Yes," Sheng answered, but not sure what to do.

"Step there."

Sheng put his foot on a hold opposite the fracture from where Yuan had pointed.

"No, over here!" Yuan redirected the boy, slapping his hand against the rock as close to the foothold as his reach allowed. "Hurry, Sheng!"

Sheng grunted, then adjusted his step.

"Good. Now, you see that crack in the rock?" Yuan made no effort to protect against being heard.

"Yes?" Sheng's response rang more of a question. "But what do I do with it?"

"Slide your hand into it, just above your shoulder, and try to make a fist."

"What is inside?" Sheng asked hesitantly.

"Nothing. Just rock."

Sheng cautiously stuck his hand into the crevice.

"Good. Did you make a fist?"

"I can't. It's too small," Sheng cried.

"You don't have to close it all the way. Just enough so that your hand won't come out," Yuan assured him. "Understand?"

"I can't," Sheng whimpered. His eyes began to tear.

"Sheng look at me!" Yuan saw the boy's panicked expression, and relaxed his tone. "You can do it."

Sheng nodded, took a breath, then slid his hand back into the rift.

"Now, curl your fingers to your palm," Yuan calmly instructed, then asked, "Got it?"

Sheng sniffled, then replied, "Yes."

"Close your fist as much as you can."

"I'll try."

"See if you can pull your hand out. Can you?" *This is going too slow!* Yuan struggled to hide his distress.

Sheng tugged his arm. "No, I can't," he said, confused with Yuan's instructions.

"Good. That's what you want. Now, look down. You see that rock to the right, about knee high?"

Sheng didn't answer but looked down at a narrow protrusion, created when the boulder broke away from the cliff.

"Step onto it. Your fist will keep you steady."

Sheng apprehensively put his right foot on it, but no weight. "This one?" he asked, scared to trust his selection.

"Yes. Good. Now, you see that little rock sticking out above your head."

Sheng reached for a hold about eye level.

"No, the one a little higher. The one with a curved edge. Grab hold of it, and step up so that your weight is on your right foot."

Sheng stepped up, then pulled himself against the rock face, hugging it like his life depended on it.

"Good. Good job. Don't worry. Trust me," Yuan said. "I'm here to catch you." He stepped back to observe, and heard soldiers trampling up the wooded slope. He didn't see them, but worried, *If they have not heard my voice by now, they will soon. Hurry Sheng!* He wanted to bark, but refrained. "Just two more to go," he encouraged the boy. "Now, take your hand out of the crack."

"It's stuck!" Sheng cried. His voice showed fear.

"Relax your hand. I mean, straighten your fingers, then pull your hand out."

Sheng unballed his hand, then slid it out of the crevasse.

"Good. Look for something above you to grab, like another crack or a rock.

A scrawny bush grew out from a chink in the rock face. Sheng reached for a limb.

"No, no!" Yuan rushed to warn. "Not the bush. You can't trust it to hold." Yuan watched the boy reach for a rounded nub. His angst eased. "Yes. Good. That should do, but test it. Don't let go with your other hand until you're sure it's sound."

Sheng yanked on the hold and grunted, straining to remain steady.

"Now, there's a place to put your left foot, by your knee. See it?"

Sheng didn't wait for Yuan's next instruction. He stepped to it, groaning with the exertion while he climbed higher.

"You're almost there." Yuan couldn't begin his ascent until Sheng was safely on top. He glanced over his shoulder in the direction of the soldiers, then back at Sheng. "Look up."

Sheng's head cocked back, causing his body to pull away from the cliff.

"No, no. Don't lean back. Keep yourself close to the rock," Yuan cautioned.

The boy leaned into the crag.

"There. See how close you are? One more step, and you'll be able to reach the top."

Sheng puffed but didn't answer.

"There's a place to step next. It's above your left knee."

Sheng lifted his right foot, and looked down.

"No. The other knee. That's where you need to step but with your right foot. Understand? You have to twist your body."

Sheng stepped across his body and asked, "Like this?"

A snap of a branch startled Yuan. He looked toward the sound and saw no one. *I pray they do not catch me during my climb.* He turned back to Sheng and said, "Find a place for your right hand to grab."

Sheng reached for a jagged hold.

"That's it. Now, go up. Your head is almost as high as the top. You see that!"

Yuan heard bushes rustle behind him. Bramble blocked his view, and the soldier's line of sight to him. He snatched the dagger sheathed to his arm, then leapt down the rock landings toward the noise.

Yuan moved around the brush, coming face-to-face with the young soldier who had been the brunt of his squad member's joking, catching him unprepared for Yuan's sudden presence. The soldier's sword was still sheathed and his bow didn't have an arrow nocked to it. One step, then another, and Yuan was on top of his foe. He grabbed the soldier by the hair that hung down the back of his head, then shoved the knife's blade into his throat.

Brush rustled farther downslope. Yuan grabbed the bow, snatched an arrow from the quiver that was still draped over the fallen soldier's shoulder, then nocked it to the string. He spun into a squat, facing the sound of footsteps. He saw another soldier maneuver around a clump of drooping bramble.

Yuan drew the bow's string to his chin, then let the arrow loose. He uncoiled his body and watched the weapon's flight, the head driving into the trunk of a tree. *Missed. Damn!* he cursed himself, after hearing the thud. The soldier disappeared behind thick bushes growing in between saplings.

Yuan looked toward Sheng just as the boy pulled his last leg over the top of the ledge. He dashed back to the rock face, hopped up the three boulders, then dropped the bow into a opening where the rock had separated from the outcrop. He jumped up and grabbed a hold, stepped onto a jagged protrusion, then searched for the right width along the crevice. He inserted his hand, balled his fingers into a fist, then pulled up to the next step. The swishing sounds of arrows piercing the air, forced him to ignore caution. He jumped onto the bushy limb he'd warned Sheng to avoid, scurried up the cliff, then rolled over the ledge. An arrow pinged off the cliff face below him, while another whizzed past his ear.

"Let's go!" He picked up Sheng and surveyed the hilltop. Thinly spaced trees dotted the level surface, which ended in an abrupt drop on the Yangtze River side of the foothill. He dashed in between the trees, scrambled around tangled brush, then reached the precipice of the other side. The panoramic view of the Yangtze Valley revealed Yuan's sanctuary. He quickly plotted a path down to the river, using the boulders that had broken away from the towering outcrop. The trailing soldiers were close, but Yuan didn't look behind. Time was too critical.

Sheng slid to the ground. Yuan bent down, and leaning on one hand, plopped to a sitting position with his legs hanging over the edge. He rolled to his stomach, then turned onto his side and eased himself off the ledge, blindly searching by feel for a firm place to stand.

He brought Sheng down to his side. "Stand here." From where they stood, a boulder protruded outward from the hill and provided the next step. Yuan jumped over a narrow gap, landing on a ridge. He held out his hand to help Sheng along, then they climbed down to another large rock that had weathered partially away from the hill's sharp face.

Yuan hopped to the abutting shelf, landing awkwardly on his sore ankle. Pain shot up his leg. He placed the boy on his back for another ride. He leapt off the mantle, where the rocky terrain gave way to a grassy slope. His thighs burned, but the pain in his ankle was worse.

The slope required him to turn sideways but allowed a gait that trended to the gallop side of a hop. The strain on his muscles was different. With each step, his down-slope leg absorbed all of the weight, then after a few steps he turned to the other side, so that one leg didn't suffer the full brunt.

He aimed for a clusters of trees that dotted the lower hillside. The timber grew thicker toward the bottom where the valley flattened into the floodplain. Yuan sidestepped a bushy clump, and was startled by the sudden whistle of an arrow. He darted away from the sound, then heard two other arrows swooshing past. They landed with a vibrating thud in a tree behind him.

He reached the bottom but slowed as the terrain leveled. Yuan pulled a branch out of the way, ducked under another limb, then churned through waist-high brush. His lungs pounded. He sprinted through a clearing and continued along the easiest path that led deeper into the disputed area that both Chu and Wu claimed. Voices shouted from two directions. Those behind him, Yuan figured, were the soldiers who chased him over the hill. The others, though, came from the direction around the hill, upstream toward the mouth of Chao Pass. *They must be from the gateway's garrison.*

He broke free of tangled cover, adjusted Sheng on his back, then stepped onto the Yangtze River's floodplain. For the first time since their journey had begun that horrible night in Zheng, Wu and Sheng's safety was within reach. Yuan's legs quivered. He gasped a short breath, and looked across the river into undisputed Wu territory. "It's too far across to swim," he said, helping Sheng to the ground.

Now what? Yuan looked back to see how many soldiers were closing in, but brush and tree cover blocked his view. He could only hear them. A small boat drifted far away from the bank, but upstream from him. *Wrong direction! We need to get downstream.* Yuan judged the boat to be halfway between him and the gateway's soldiers. A fisherman fiddled in the hull.

Yuan waved and yelled, "Hey! Hey! Will you help us?"

The fisherman paid little attention to the bustle. He raised his head, on the crown of which casually rested a wide-brimmed, flat, round hat. The fisherman showed no sense of urgency. Yuan motioned again, but the man did not respond.

Both Yuan and the boy ran upstream, closer to him but also toward the danger. Yuan cupped his mouth and yelled, "Will . . . you . . . help . . . the boy!" Again, the man only stared back. Yuan heard the soldiers stomping through the woods. He glanced toward them.

The fisherman eased the nose of his boat toward Yuan and sculled the craft. His pace was the normal leisure of just another day on the water. Back and forth, he worked the oar with smooth steady strokes.

Sheng tugged on Yuan's arm. "Soldiers!" he shouted with alarm. "I see them!"

Yuan turned to assess the distance between them. They were within arrow range, but the cover blocked a clear shot.

The fisherman finally spoke. He shouted over the water, talking in a broken dialect, "Are you Chu?"

"Yes. But please help the boy!" Yuan pleaded. His voice carried over the water. "He is Prince Sheng, and those soldiers are trying to kill us!"

"Chu Royalty?" the fisherman asked, then cocked his head toward the soldiers.

Sheng pulled close to Yuan, as if to hide behind him. "There's something on the man's face. What is it, Yuan!" Sheng shouted, more frightened of the man's markings than the pursuing soldiers.

Yuan looked at the boy, puzzled by the comment, then back at the man. In the middle of his forehead, the fisherman wore a third eye, open and always alert. Below it, a creature's snout followed the lay of the man's nose but flared over the bridge onto both cheeks. The fisherman's mouth provided the general outline for the beast's maw, and scales drawn into the body gave the creature a menacing look.

"Don't worry, Sheng. It's not real. Wu people mark their faces," Yuan explained.

The boat's hull pulled within reach. Yuan stepped to the water's edge, then lifted Sheng onto the boat. The boy clung to Yuan, not taking his eyes off the figure imposed on the fisherman's face. Yuan pushed Sheng farther onto the bow and reassured him, "You'll be okay."

Empty creels were piled above the sides, from the front of the craft to the opening of a low-arching, woven roof that hung across the middle of the plank boat.

"Get over there," the fisherman said, pointing to the covered area.

Sheng crawled over, then around the creels, making his way underneath the roof.

"Lay down," the fisherman said.

Sheng did as told. He wasn't sure if it was the man or the creature who spoke. He knew Yuan had said the beast was not real, but Sheng wasn't convinced. It looked to be a part of the man.

An arrow whistled over Yuan's head. He dove into the water and came up on the other side of the boat. By that time, the fisherman had turned the craft away from land and was heading downstream. Yuan grabbed a rope attached to the bow, keeping the hull between him and the shore. Yuan peeked over the frame in time to see Chu soldiers running down the riverbank.

The fisherman stood at the stern, and moved the long scull from side to side. Yuan stayed in the water, holding onto the rope while the craft dragged him downstream. "What are they doing?" Yuan asked, keeping all but his head in the water. He was out of sight but heard one of the soldiers shout, "There! Look, under the roof!" They had seen Sheng.

"Stay down," Yuan told Sheng, who had popped his head above the creels.

The fisherman sculled faster, quickening the boat's pace. "They're drawing bows!" he yelled frantically.

Another arrow flew, arching past with too much lead. A third, launched immediately afterward, hit the side of the craft, near the fisherman. A fourth and fifth sailed high.

Yuan waited for the whistling sound of another, but it didn't come. The fisherman sculled a frenzied pace, maneuvering the boat into the full strength of the river's current. "What are they doing?" Yuan asked.

"They're just looking at us," the fisherman said. "We're out of range."

Yuan wrapped the rope around his arm to lessen the drain of his strength. The fisherman eased the oar into a smooth rhythm, and once they reached the river's bend, Yuan asked, "What do you see?"

The fisherman turned his head to look upstream. "No one," he answered. With quick bursts of the oar, the fisherman completed the bend, then veered toward the near bank. "They're gone! Hold on a little longer. Looks like we're out of trouble, but don't try to climb aboard until we reach the bank."

Yuan remained submerged in the water, holding on to the rope. His hands cramped from fatigue, and his grip began to slip.

"Almost there. You should be able to stand up now," the fisherman said calmly.

Yuan held tightly to the boat's rim, steadying himself, while he pushed to gain his feet. He lifted his leg out of the water, then stretched to hook his foot over the boat's edge but missed and splashed back into the water.

The fisherman hopped overboard. He propped Yuan up, while he pulled the boat and Yuan onto the bank. Once the hull settled in the soft mud, the fisherman bent Yuan across the rim and rolled him over the edge and onto the plank. Sheng moved a stack of creels, making room for Yuan. The fisherman pushed the nose of the boat downstream, then hopped back onto the stern.

Yuan sat upright, then looked upstream. He wished they were on the opposite bank, away from Chu but was relieved that there were no soldiers to give chase now. He then turned to Sheng, tapped him on the shoulder and smiled. "We made it to Wu!"

25

RACE TO THE BORDER

T he fisherman sculled the boat downriver. Yuan slumped onto the hull, suffering the combined effects of sickness and exhaustion. The boat jostled from port to starboard with each stroke of the oar, rocking Yuan's body and bringing every ache and pain to the fore. Chills cascaded over him, and his head throbbed, overwhelming his other pains. He wiped sweat from his brow.

Sheng rubbed his cold arms. "Yuan?"

Yuan stroked his forehead but didn't respond to the boy's call.

"I'm cold. You're sweating. Why are you hot?" Sheng worried.

"Boy, he does not appear well," the fisherman interjected. "We'll take him to my home. My Overlord can help." He steered the boat back into the current, sculling leisurely.

Yuan dipped his hand in the river, then splashed his face with water. "How far is it to your village?" he strained to ask, not bothering to make eye contact with the fisherman.

"Not too far," the fisherman shrugged.

The sun was well past the day's high mark. Yuan laid his head down and covered his eyes with the crook of his arm. When they neared the Yangtze River's sharp turn east toward the sea, the fisherman turned the boat landward. He steered the craft to a flat bank on the western side of the river. The terrain rose gently from the water toward a distant village, not close enough to make out any activity except for smoke rising into the sky. Afternoon shadows stretched onto the river's bank in line with boats that rested securely on the soft mud at the water's edge, which the fisherman used to guide his approach. He aimed the craft for the end of the line.

The boat's abrupt stop joggled Yuan. He managed to sit up and look around at the surroundings, making sure they were still safe. He was not ready to give in to thinking otherwise. The fisherman stepped off the boat and into muddy shallows, then helped Sheng to dry land. Yuan rolled over the boat's rim and into the water, splashing face first into the river. The fisherman darted to his aid.

"Wait!" Yuan shouted. He shoved the fisherman into the brink, then drew his sword.

The fisherman held up his hands. "What's wrong?"

"We didn't cross the river. We're still in Chu!" Yuan barked.

"No, we're not. It's okay," the fisherman begged to be believed. "This side of the river is Wu, too." He pointed to foothills visible to the west. "These are the Silk Hills, and up there," he stretched his arm for emphasis, "is my people's winter village."

Yuan looked to where the fisherman directed. His head pounded. He rubbed his forehead and thought, *Have I lost reason?*

The fisherman lowered his hands. "But across those two hills is another village, and they are Chu," he cautioned.

Yuan shot a questioning glance at him.

"Do I look Chu or Wu?" the fisherman asked, attempting to bring logic to Yuan's confusion.

Yuan nodded. "You cropped your hair and marked your face like Wu people."

"You and the boy are safe here. Believe me," the fisherman promised.

Yuan sheathed his sword, placing faith in the man's veracity, just as he'd done when they initially came into contact. *If he were Chu, he would have left us to the soldiers. He wouldn't have gotten involved.*

The fisherman took Yuan's arm and draped it over his shoulder, then helped him to wade through the mud and onto the grassy, high bank where Sheng stood.

"I'm sorry. I should not have doubted you," Yuan offered apologetically. "I'm not feeling well or thinking straight."

"Yes, I can see that. I'll take you to my home. My woman will feed you, while I fetch the Overlord."

"You've been a tremendous help," Yuan forced in a painful breath. "What do your people call you?"

"I'm Tan, and my village is Pei-liang."

Yuan leaned against him. Almost every part of his body hurt, even his teeth. "I'm grateful you came along when you did." Yuan removed the scabbard from his belt. "I have nothing of value to repay your kindness, except for my sword," he said gratefully. He stopped, stepped backward, then turned to face Tan and bowed. He held his weapon out, offering it to Tan. "It's worth 100 gold pieces. Please take it."

Tan chuckled. "Is your name Commander Yuan?" he asked, already knowing the answer.

Yuan nodded, surprised by Tan's reaction. "Yes."

"I thought so. You fit what I heard from some traders. King Ping has offered fifty thousand piculs of grain and the office of Jade Baton Holder to anyone who returns you or your body to Chu. Your sword doesn't compare, does it?" Tan grinned.

Yuan withdrew his outstretched arm in confusion. His instincts drove him to grip the hilt.

"The reward means nothing to me," Tan shook his head

decidedly. "I have no desire to help Chu. So, keep your weapon. Come now, I'll help you to my home."

Tan took Yuan's arm again and pulled it over his shoulder, then headed toward the village.

Sheng watched Yuan struggle. He moved to Yuan's other side. "I'll help."

Yuan gently put his hand on the boy's shoulder and patted him.

Their walk took them westerly, into the hills. Yuan was still uneasy, having spent so much of the journey with his mind fixed on stepping foot on the eastern bank of the Yangtze River before reaching safety. The cool air made the misery of his wet clothes worse, and by the time they reached the village, Yuan was shaking badly.

When they reached Tan's home, he opened the door and called to Mother Tan, "Prepare skins for bedding." He turned to Sheng, then directed, "Go on in."

Sheng walked through the doorway and into the one-room winter home. He stepped to the side, not sure what to do or say. Girl Tan sat near the front of the room, on the dirt floor next to the fire pit, where a large-mouthed pot of water sat over hot coals. She held a stick with silk wound tightly around it, a single thread lead to the pot and to a silkworm's cocoon floating in the water. Grandmother Tan sat next to her.

Mother Tan walked around the bedding that lined the back wall. "Hop up," she said to Boy Tan, who was tickling his baby brother, discharging the pent up energy that accompanied the cramped confines of winter life. Mother Tan took a layer of hides from the boys' bedding and made another pallet near the fire pit. Girl Tan put aside her task of winding the silk, then scooted to the front wall. "Bring the man here," Mother Tan said.

Tan helped Yuan to the bedding, where Mother Tan removed Yuan's wet clothing and wrapped him in a hempen cover. She and Tan eased Yuan to the pallet, who then rolled in between furry layers of hides. Yuan curled underneath the soft covers. The room was dry and warm, and more importantly, it was safe, at least for Sheng.

"Boy, fetch water from the well. We're low," Tan instructed his son. He turned to Mother Tan. "I'm going to let the Overlord know about them," he said, motioning toward Yuan and Sheng.

"You hungry?" Mother Tan asked Sheng.

Sheng nodded, still not sure what to do.

"Come sit by the fire," Girl Tan said to Sheng.

Mother Tan scooped rice into a small bowl from a large pot that sat on the edge of the fire pit, then handed the serving to Sheng. He quickly shoveled a heaping portion into his mouth.

Yuan looked over at him and saw the tension in the boy's shoulders disappear upon swallowing the first bite. Yuan smiled, then closed his eyes, letting his body relax, too. The chatter inside the room faded and was replaced by that fog between wake and sleep. A vision of his father and brother popped into his mind. Their likenesses, though, stood still, hovering over him in eerie silence. *"Avenge us both,"* Shang's final words reverberated in his head. *That's not possible, Brother.*

26

YUAN'S FATE

Yuan felt a nudge to his shoulder, then heard a voice. "Wake up." He rolled to the side and saw Tan standing over him, holding a flask and bowl of rice. A pair of chopsticks balanced on the lip of the bowl. The door to the hut was open, and from the light that penetrated the room, it appeared to be morning.

Two men, garbed in battle tunics, stood behind Tan. One pulled him to the side, then brushed past stepping toward the back wall. He snatched from the corner Yuan's sword, along with the knife Yuan normally kept concealed under his sleeve. Yuan glanced toward the door at the other man, while a third entered the room. *Wu warriors!* Their armor and unsheathed swords at the ready were dead giveaways they weren't here to welcome him.

The warrior who carried Yuan's weapons left the shelter. Yuan felt naked without them. He sat upright. The sudden movement made him dizzy. He leaned on one hand, paused to let the feeling subside and rubbed his face. "How long have I been out?"

"This is the fourth day. Your fever broke yesterday," Tan spoke up. "You need to eat. You have gone too many days without much food." He held out the bowl and flask for Yuan

352

to take, but the warrior behind Tan sprang forward, grabbing the chopsticks.

"We have been told you are a dangerous man even without your sword. Use your fingers," the warrior commanded. "I don't want these," he waved the sticks, "to become a weapon." The creature marked on his face was a raptor whose beak curled with the curvature of the man's eye socket. A wing, sprawled onto his cheek, fluttered when he spoke.

Yuan gazed at the creature, then nodded. He shoveled a lump of rice into his mouth. His stomach gurgled. He finished chewing, swallowed, then asked, "Where is Sheng?"

"He's outside waiting for you. He and Boy Tan have been inseparable these last couple of days. He's fine," Tan assured him.

An eerie hush filled the room. The warriors never took their eyes off Yuan, and once he'd finished the rice, the man holding the chopsticks ordered Tan, "Get him up. It's time."

Tan extended his hand.

Yuan tipped the flask to his lips, swished a mouthful of rice wine, then took Tan's hand. He stood wobbly, shuffled his feet to catch his balance, and grabbed Tan's shoulder to steady himself.

Tan made sure Yuan was stable on his own two feet, then leaned toward a table by the fire pit where Yuan's robe lay. It was still tattered, but Mother Tan had washed and neatly folded it.

Why did she bother? Yuan thought. The image of an executioner's axe flashed in his mind.

Tan retrieved the clothing, then passed them to Yuan.

He dressed, unconsciously going through the motions while his mind worked to brush away the leftover affects of his sickness. He would need his wits about him to successfully obtain a safe haven for Sheng.

Tan handed Yuan the sash used to belt the robe. "Take my shoulder. I'll help you walk."

Yuan nodded, then tied the sash around his waist. His eyes met the warrior's stare. *He's the Squad Leader,* Yuan surmised.

Their glower remained locked until the Squad Leader motioned to the other warrior and said, "Bind his hands and feet." He then pointed his sword at Yuan.

Yuan shot back, "I accept my fate." He straightened his back, lifted his chin, and extended his hands in front of him. *Their precaution is overkill. My body is too weak to give them much of a fight.*

The warrior, holding a horsehair rope in one hand, pulled Tan out of the way with the other and stepped toward Yuan. He wrapped a loop around Yuan's right wrist, tied it with a single knot, then did the same with Yuan's left hand, leaving a long lead that gathered on the floor. He cinched the wrists together, finishing with a hard yank to test the knot.

The tug jerked Yuan from his arms to the shoulders, but he did not take his eyes off the Squad Leader.

The warrior bent to a knee, then repeated the task at Yuan's ankles. He left enough slack so that Yuan could walk, but only in short steps. He picked up the lead, looped it around the ankle bindings, then pulled, drawing Yuan's hands downward, securing them. The warrior backed away until the lead was taut, then nodded to the Squad Leader.

Tan left the hut first. The warrior holding the rope's end was next. He yanked on the lead, forcing Yuan to follow. Yuan tripped on the first stride, caught his balance, then stagger-stepped to the doorway where he stopped. Five warriors stood in a semi-circle arcing from the hut to an oxen-drawn cart. Yuan looked at the man closest to the door. He glanced at the next guard in line, then to the third and fourth. Each warrior returned stone-cold stares.

Sheng was sitting on the back of the cart, his legs dangling off the edge. The boy's eyes were fixed on the menacing beast blotched on the face of the warrior nearest him. It was a dragon that snaked from the forehead down to the man's jaw. A scar severed the beast's body, which appeared to give added reason for the eye's ominous glare.

Beyond the head of the cart, by the lone harnessed ox, five more warriors, who were no more welcoming than their compatriots, waited silently. Each of them fixed their eyes on Yuan. The warrior with the rope whipped it, then heaved on it, pulling Yuan's feet out from under him. His head whipped against the hard ground. Two guards closed around him, lifted him by his arms, dragged him to the cart, then chucked him onto the plank flooring. Sheng rushed to his side. "You'll be fine," Yuan assured him, although he had no idea what lay ahead for either of them.

The Squad Leader gave the chopsticks to Boy Tan, who stood near the door waving a sad goodbye to Sheng, then took Yuan's weapons from the warrior who had retrieved them from the hovel. He called to Tan and ordered, "Let's go."

Tan stepped to the front of the cart. He took from a warrior the leather strap leading to a ring that pierced the ox's nostrils. Tan tugged on the rein, beginning their descent to the river.

The wheels jolted forward, racking Yuan against the side of the cart. He rolled to his side, then pushed his feet into the cart near the open end to steady his body. He looked beyond the Squad Leader, the guard who held his leash, and the other warriors who followed, to the Dabie Shan. Memories of the harsh journey cascaded through his mind. But the sacrifice of Lan and Fen Yang, along with the rest of his men, struck him most. Their selflessness and unwavering support warmed him as much as it fed the wave of guilt that swept over him. They had died so that he and Sheng could live. *But did they die in vain?*

The cart pulled over a sharp dip, jarring the frame and bouncing Sheng. He landed on his tailbone. "Baichi!" he blurted.

Yuan chuckled to himself. He was grateful to have a final moment of humor.

They made it down the slope to the bank of the Yangtze, where they transferred to a boat. It was a miniature version of the small wing warcraft Wu was so adept at using in battles on rivers. The boat had a deep hull, unlike Tan's flat-bottomed boat, and was manned by six men, two abreast, with a ramming beak in the shape of a menacing creature protruding from the bow. Four guards boarded first, then two more tossed Yuan onto the stern. He rolled to a stop at the feet of the closest guard, who grabbed him by the collar and dragged him to the bow. Sheng was escorted to his side. The warriors who flung Yuan onto the boat climbed aboard and took up oars with the other four guards. The other warriors climbed aboard one at a time, each man keeping his eyes trained on Yuan. The attendant guard who kept Yuan's leash sat down next to him. He pulled the rope taut, emphasizing his control.

Yuan looked back at Tan, who yanked on the strap to turn the ox. The Squad Leader grabbed Tan's shoulder and commanded, "Get in the boat. You're coming with us."

Tan looked puzzled but did as told.

"Sit at the back next to me," the Squad Leader instructed him.

Sheng tugged worrisomely on Yuan's robe. "Why is Tan sitting back there?"

Yuan shook his head. "I don't know." He chose not to speculate openly, although Tan appeared to be in trouble of some sort. *Is it because he saved us?* And from the perplexed look Tan wore, Yuan was sure he didn't know why either.

Sheng grimaced. "Will we go home with him?"

It was an obvious query that struck at the heart of their unknown fate. But Yuan didn't want the boy to worry. "I don't know, Sheng," he responded calmly.

Sheng folded his arms, guarding against the chilly breeze.

Yuan turned to the stem and looked out across the river. He knew little of what was waiting for him once they reached the eastern bank, other than he had no control over the result. And the warriors' hostile demeanor gave him no reason to be optimistic. He thought about who awaited them and what he would say to plead for Sheng's life. He focused on the value a member of Chu's Royalty could bring to Wu. Of course, his mind also drifted to his fate – questioning, torture and beheading dominated the imagery.

Sheng slumped below the rim of the vessel, out of the cold wind that blew over the open water. He stared at the long sword strapped to a warrior's belt, tapped Yuan's leg. "They only have swords. Don't they use bows, too?" he asked.

The question snapped Yuan back to the present. He mustered as much of a trouble-free glance as he could, under the circumstances, to give Sheng. "Yes, they do. But not these men."

Sheng studied the warrior's weapon and wrinkled his brow. "Maybe they are like you and are no good with a bow."

Yuan chuckled. *Thank you, Sheng, for giving me reason to laugh.* He turned toward the front and could see the boat on course for a landing with two small hills in the background. Three chariots, set upslope from the bank, were positioned abreast. A squad of warriors, armed with spears held to the side with tips upright, stood in between each chariot and on the outer edges. *For there to be so many of them, they must be protecting someone important. That's good. He'll be high-ranking. But they must also think I'm very dangerous. How do I cut through that worry to save Sheng?*

They reached land, and the warriors, who were not busy stowing oars, hopped overboard to pull the boat onto the bank. The vessel slid to an abrupt stop. Yuan arose, preparing to be lifted off, but a foot to his back sent him tumbling over the stem. He slammed onto the ramming beak, then hit the ground, first where his shoulder and neck meet. Pain spiked down his spine and into his right leg. He was lucky the muddy bank softened the impact.

The warriors roared with laughter. Two of them pulled him to his feet while Yuan's attendant guard picked up the boy by the robe's neckline, then lowered him to the ground. Afterward, Sheng leapt to Yuan's side. The Squad Leader, Yuan's weapons in hand, was next off the boat, followed by Tan.

The warriors who escorted them from the village formed two lines, creating a bordered lane to march Yuan and Sheng up the hill. It looked too much like a gauntlet for Yuan's comfort. The Squad Leader stood at the opposite end, observing Yuan's every move.

Yuan stiffened, his head facing the Squad Leader while his eyes looked upslope at the warriors. They were hardened men, each in their own right, who looked to neither take nor give favors. He scanned the chariots, trying to identify who was in command of this show of force. His eyes fixed on the center chariot. *Prince Kuang!* Yuan had only seen his Wu nemesis in battle, but he was certain that was him, the middle charioteer.

The Squad Leader raised Yuan's sheathed sword. "Separate them," he ordered.

Yuan bowed his chest. Four warriors surrounded him, while another pulled Sheng away from Yuan's side.

Sheng cried out, "No! Yuan?"

Yuan shot the look of certainty the boy had come to trust. "Sheng, they won't hurt you. Go with them." *I just hope they don't make you watch them kill me. You must not ever blame yourself for my death.*

The Squad Leader gave the order and began the short march toward Prince Kuang. Even though Yuan was neutralized, the warriors had their weapons at the ready, all the same.

Yuan felt a shove to his back, prompting him to stag-ger-step forward. He looked over at Sheng, whose head had slumped glumly. *At least he's walking on his own.* Yuan was relieved the boy was not being manhandled, until he glimpsed an expression of horror on Sheng's face. It pained Yuan. *What can I do?*

Tan hesitated until the Squad Leader motioned to him. He looked over his shoulder at Sheng, then Yuan. His escort was not as cautious as the men who guarded Yuan.

They had walked about half the distance to the chariots when Yuan saw a sturdy-built warrior, carrying a wooden block, step off fifteen paces in front of Prince Kuang. The warrior set the block down, then twisted it to a level, stable rest. Yuan swallowed hard, for it looked to have the height and breadth of an executioner's block. Even at this distance, he could detect the smell of dried blood on the wood.

The rugged man disappeared behind the back of the far right chariot and, after a moment, reappeared holding a wooden box. Ornate carvings adorned the chest, but that didn't catch Yuan's attention. The size did. *Will Kuang use it to deliver my head to King Liao?* The warrior placed it on the block, then stepped away.

The moment was eerily quiet. Yuan didn't hear so much as a bird chirp. The uncertainty over whether or not he had made the right decision for Sheng was taxing, even his legs grew heavy, each shortened step more laborious than the last. The angst was nothing like anything he had ever experienced. No skill with a weapon was great enough to shift control over his fate back to him, even if he were unbound and had his sword; no amount of fight within him could be summoned to overcome these odds, clearly the best of the best of Prince Kuang's warriors.

The Squad Leader stopped within a few paces of the box, halting their progression. Tan followed suit. He remained facing forward, then bowed to Prince Kuang, as did the warriors. Yuan, though, didn't budge.

Prince Kuang took note of Yuan's refusal to kowtow. His eyes briefly met Yuan's gaze, the first time the two enemies had fixed upon one another at such close proximity.

That's curious, Yuan thought. *He did not lock on to me. Kuang barely noticed my insult. He just dismissed me.*

Prince Kuang dismounted, then walked to the box.

And why should he react? My head will fill that box soon enough. Yuan watched Kuang say something to the executioner. The words were inaudible. 'Get the axe,' Yuan guessed. *Sheng is going to see me executed after all,* he lamented.

Kuang turned to Tan. "Come forward," he commanded. Fu-kai joined him but stood offset from Kuang's shoulder, holding a single arrow.

Yuan wondered who he was.

Tan was quick to respond, not out of excitement but from fear. His gait jerked a half step, then sped to a full stride, although he'd rather not have hurried into this unknown.

Prince Kuang looked directly into Tan's eyes and surprised him with the glimmer of a smile. "Tan, you have shown bravery. Unarmed, you defied Chu's King. Without the prospect of personal gain, you flouted Chu's soldiers. Without armor, you faced Chu's arrows." Kuang paused momentarily, then said in a raised voice, "Your valor benefits all of Wu!"

A synchronized boorish yelp issued from the warriors, followed by raising spears overhead in a quick, single pump.

Kuang waited for the echo to subside, then said to Tan, "Thank you for bringing to me the grandson of Chu's King."

The boy looked at the creature marked on Kuang's face. It glared back at him. Sheng bolted for Yuan, but a warrior instantly grabbed him by the collar and pulled the boy tight against his legs.

Prince Kuang motioned to the burly warrior, who picked up the box and presented it to Tan. "This is a token of my gratitude for your deeds."

Tan took the handles and was surprised by the weight, almost pulling his arms down to full extension. He bowed to Prince Kuang, pledged his ongoing allegiance, then moved back into the lane. He wanted to peek inside but didn't, for to do so would insult Prince Kuang's generosity.

Prince Kuang spoke directly to the Squad Leader. "Bring him to me."

The Squad Leader moved to behind Yuan, then commanded, "Move."

Yuan's body convulsed from another shove in the back. He stagger-stepped forward. They stopped near the spot where Tan had stood. Yuan was now closer to Kuang than he'd ever been at Chi-fu. *If Wei Yue had not been inept, you and I could have met on the battlefield. Which one of us would have lived?* Now standing face-to-face with such a formidable man, being measured, felt a bit surreal. *I never expected to die without a sword in my hand, fighting to the end.*

The creature on one side of Kuang's face was unlike the markings the other warriors bore. His appeared to be a living, breathing beast.

Kuang turned his head, a movement that, if Yuan hadn't known better, looked as if the creature contorted to gaze upon his next victim, snarling at him through jagged teeth. The beast, drawn from Kuang's hairline down past his jaw, eventually disappearing under the collar of Kuang's battle tunic, wore scaly armor that glistened in the sunlight.

The real scar on the other side of Kuang's face, though, was a clear reminder of Kuang's willingness to fight and ability to survive. Yuan remembered Ga having asked him if the mere sight of Wu markings took away a man's courage. *Kuang's creature could! Ga must have been scared witless.*

"You are a Chu soldier – my sworn enemy," Kuang said gruffly to Yuan. "Give me one reason I should spare your life?" He held out his hand, and the Squad Leader stepped forward, then turned over Yuan's sword.

Fu-kai pointed the arrow at Yuan and blurted out, "There is no reason for this enemy to live, Brother."

Yuan asked, "May I speak?"

"Yes," Kuang said.

"Chu is now my enemy as well." Yuan delivered the line just as he had rehearsed while on the boat – stamped with certainty. "King Ping executed my father and brother. He ordered the death of the Prince I served. And he offers a reward to anyone who returns my head to Ying."

"Then let's collect it," Fu-kai shouted. Laughter erupted from a few of the warriors. "Maybe, Brother, his presence in Wu is no coincidence. The boy makes a good cover story for an assassin. I'd wager he knows something about *this!*" He shook at Yuan the arrow that had almost ended Prince Kuang's life.

Yuan glared at Fu-kai. "What you are talking about?" Yuan scowled, reflecting for a moment on what the news meant for Sheng. He calmly stated. "I know nothing of this."

"Sure you do," Fu-kai chided. "I say it was you that let this arrow fly toward my brother."

"No!" Sheng cried out, "he can't hit anything with a bow."

This sent Fu-kai howling.

Interesting words from a boy, Kuang thought. *He doesn't have the maturity to so quickly cover for Yuan.* He held up his hand to stop the dialogue's path. "Why did you come to Wu?" he asked.

"To save Sheng," Yuan gestured with his head toward the boy. "We fled Chu with Prince Chien and the boy's mother. My chariot team provided escort. We thought it best to seek refuge among an enemy of Chu. And the Northern Alliance made sense because it exists only to defend its members against Chu.

But we found Sung in revolt, and later, Chien was duped into a plot by Jin against Cheng. Only Sheng and I escaped."

"Everywhere you go, eventually, men want you dead!" Fu-kai jabbed.

Yuan ignored the dig. "I could not trust another Alliance member to provide a safe haven for Sheng. My best soldiers gave their lives fighting to save the boy. I brought him here knowing you would still see me as your enemy. I understand my fate, but consider the wisdom of letting Sheng live. He is no threat to Wu, and as Chu Royalty, he will one day be a useful ally to you."

"Our spies have already confirmed some of your story," Kuang said but appeared unmoved. "You were at Chi-fu when we last fought."

Yuan cocked his head, taken aback by the statement. "Yes. Your plan was ingenious, and your warriors executed it flaw-lessly. I had to get over the sting before fully appreciating what you accomplished." It felt odd to compliment a man who was on the verge of ending his life, but Yuan had always regarded his enemy with both hate and respect in order to stay objective in battle. "Commander Wei Yue was no match for you."

Not once has he shown deference, yet my enemy compli-ments me without fawning like a coward, interested in saving his own life. Prince Kuang let his curiosity simmer, then asked, "Do you know what led me to devise that plan?"

Yuan's mind darted to the battle – Kuang coaxing the Dukes of Hu, Shen and Chen into pursuing a feigned retreat, entrapping their soldiers, then driving them all like livestock into Ts'ai and T'ang. "You used the constrained battlefield to neutralize our greater numbers. Our strength and the narrow battlefield worked to your advantage."

"Yes, tactically, but there is more," Kuang said evenly. "My spies have watched you for years. You probably don't know that."

Yuan allowed a knowing smile. "Actually, I have always suspected there were traitors amongst our ranks, but banishment to Chengfu prevented me from determining for certain who they were." He reflected a moment. "But you said they watched 'you'. Did you mean *me* in particular?"

Prince Kuang nodded. "You made your presence known to me during a battle years ago when you led a charge General Yang Gai did not order. Do you remember?"

Yuan knew exactly what Kuang was talking about. *My first fray with Wu.* It had ended with no clear victor. "Yes, your warriors were in transition, which opened a weakness in the flank. I commanded a company and attacked."

"We were exposed only briefly, but you recognized it and acted decisively. For your charge to have been successful, Yang Gai would've had to order support higher on the flank. But he didn't see our weakness in time, and we adjusted, thwarting your attack," Kuang added.

"I remember that day well – and the sharp rebuke General Yang Gai gave me afterward for acting without orders," Yuan recalled.

"Once we learned that you were only seventeen at that time, I knew you reacted out of instinct, not experience. I wanted to know more about you, so my spies went to work. We have watched you develop, combining experience to match your instincts and fearless spirit." Kuang looked westwardly, in the direction of Chi-fu, then back to Yuan. "Yang Gai was sure to bring you with him to Chi-fu. I was certain of it." Kuang wagged his finger toward the Dabie Shan. "Yang Gai and I have much history on opposing sides. And his death favored Wu not only for Chu's loss, but because the wrong man was chosen to succeed him. Yang Gai should have ignored politics and made sure you ascended as Field Marshal." Kuang poked the air toward Yuan. "The fight would not have gone so well for us, I think, had you been in charge." Kuang paused to let the message sink in.

"I value your praise," Yuan allowed.

"You are right about the 'why' of my battle plan. But do you know the 'who'?"

Yuan shook his head. "I don't understand the question."

"I chose which States to lure into the trap based on you. With you engaged in the battle, the States would follow your leadership in the field no matter what Wei Yue ordered while perched safely away. I wanted to prevent you from entering the fight. Duke Chao, our spies learned, had no confidence in Wei Yue and no stomach to contest me. He was likely to stay put and not fall for our trap. And without Chao's forces entering the battle, you were blocked from the fight. That's why I lured Hu, Shen and Chen away from Chu's defensive line, then drove them into Ts'ai." Kuang paused, allowing his compliment to resonate, then made a decisive face. "So I cannot let an enemy with your talents live."

Not in spite of the praise, but because of it Yuan was not surprised by this pronouncement. Indeed, he'd known since escaping Cheng that stepping foot on Wu soil would mean the end of his life. Images of Sheh and his brother, Shang, surfaced. He pushed them back. *Kuang has fed to me deep praise on a platter of death.*

Kuang drew Yuan's dagger-sword from the scabbard. He studied the blade, spun the hilt in his hand, then whipped the air with the weapon, crossing a downward slash with a back-handed slice. "We have spent much effort getting to know you from afar because I respect you as a soldier." He nodded toward Sheng, while still looking at Yuan. "What you have done for the boy is admirable. You are both a worthy opponent and a virtuous man. That will be your legacy. I'll spare the boy's life – for now – but you must meet your ancestors, here and now, so that I don't face you in battle again."

"Soldier to soldier, will you grant me one request?" Yuan asked.

"What is it?"

"That is bold of him, Brother," Fu-kai scoffed. "Don't listen to him."

Yuan squarely met Kuang's gaze and said, "Use my sword to kill King Ping. That will avenge the deaths of my father and my brother, fulfilling my pledge."

Prince Kuang didn't respond immediately and remained silent for a long time. "I have a better idea. . ." he gave a brief hand signal to the Squad Leader. An instant later the warrior's knife cut Yuan's feet and hands free. Kuang stepped forward, handed Yuan's weapon to him and said, "You do it."

Yuan was astonished. This moment spoke volumes to him along with the look they exchanged. He need only swing the blade in an arc to cut the throat of his mortal enemy. Kuang was risking his own life to test Yuan's trustworthiness and devotion to a shared cause. If Yuan was on a mission to kill Kuang, if Yuan truly wanted Prince Kuang dead, he could make it happen here and now.

He wrapped his fingers around the hilt. Yuan marveled, *What an ingenious test of my veracity to discover where my loyalty truly lies . . . at the cost of his own life if he guessed wrong.*

What Yuan didn't know was that Kuang hadn't risked his life. Two archers were hidden in the trees, behind the chariots, with bows drawn from the moment Yuan had arrived. They remained ready to the let their arrows fly were Yuan to make any aggressive motion at any time.

But for Kuang, the gamble was minimalized by his understanding that a soldier's dying wish would come from the heart, for anything otherwise would curse him and his ancestors for all eternity. By seeking help to carry out his vow of retribution, Yuan said the one thing that could save his life.

Yuan bowed, and with his head still lowered in fealty, he turned the sword around and offered it back to Prince

Kuang, hilt first, and intoned, "With my sword, I pledge my allegiance."

Kuang accepted the weapon, taking Yuan's word as genuine. He bounced the weapon in the palm of his hand. "You may one day have the opportunity to avenge your family, but it won't be with this inferior weapon." He tossed it to the burly warrior standing next to the executioner's block.

The warrior drove the sword's tip into the stump, planted his foot in the middle of the blade, then pulled on the hilt until the green-copper weapon bent.

Kuang turned to Yuan and said, "You want revenge on Nang Wa."

It wasn't a question, but Yuan responded emphatically. "Yes!"

"If you are to be my ally, you'll need a real weapon!" He glanced over at a warrior, who stepped forward and handed Yuan a newly cast sword.

Yuan could not believe the turn of events. His thoughts bounced from believing he was doomed, to recognizing that Kuang had given him sanctuary. He brushed aside the swing of emotions and stepped forward. He reached for the weapon, accepting the gift, and bowed, holding the bend, then said, "Prince Kuang, you are unique, and your generosity is unequaled."

"Go ahead. Inspect it," Kaung said with a smile.

Yuan's eyes fixed on the design of the hilt, which resembled the creature marked on Prince Kuang's face. He slowly drew the blade from the scabbard, looking closely at the details.

"The blade was forged at Metal Mount," Kuang boasted. "And it's more than twice as long as the hilt. It's a true sword, not the stubby short sword Chu soldiers carry."

A wave of gratitude overcame Yuan. The feeling had as much to do with knowing he and Sheng would live as appreciating the opportunity Prince Kuang had given him to redress the wrong inflicted on his family. "The craftmanship is marvelous," Yuan acknowledged. But his steadfast manner held. "No swordsmith in Chu can duplicate this quality." He shook his head. "Chu's metal is too brittle for this length."

"I know you will put it to good use." Prince Kuang placed a hand on Yuan's shoulder.

Yuan was dumbfounded. *He must have contemplated this path for us all along.* The two shared a look, both appreciating the surprise fate had just delivered, one that could never have been orchestrated.

Kuang nodded to the warriors who restrained Sheng. They released the boy, and he darted to Yuan's side.

Yuan wrapped his arms around Sheng. "We made it! We're safe!"

Prince Kuang watched their relief take hold and grinned, but didn't dwell, turning instead to his next course. *How do I convince King Liao to keep them alive?*

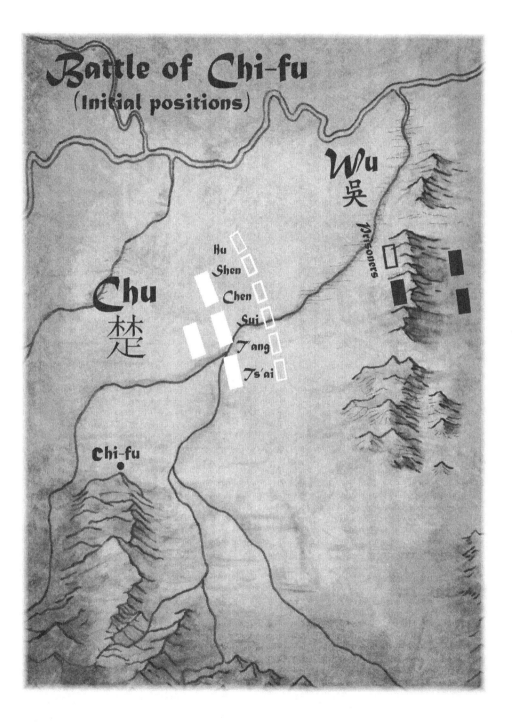

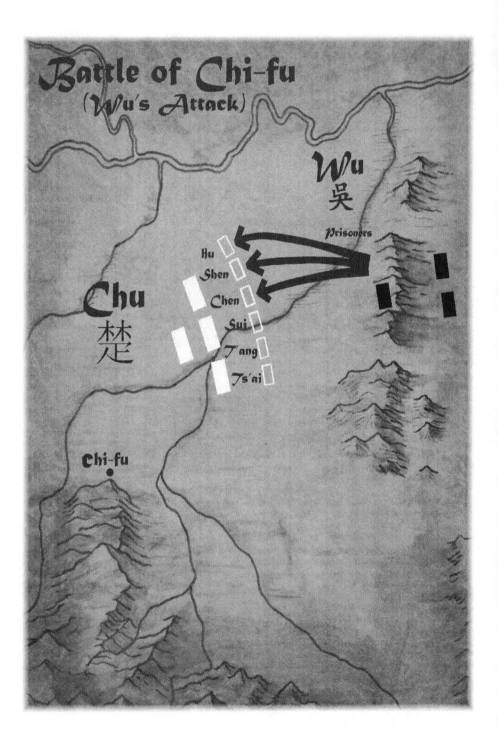

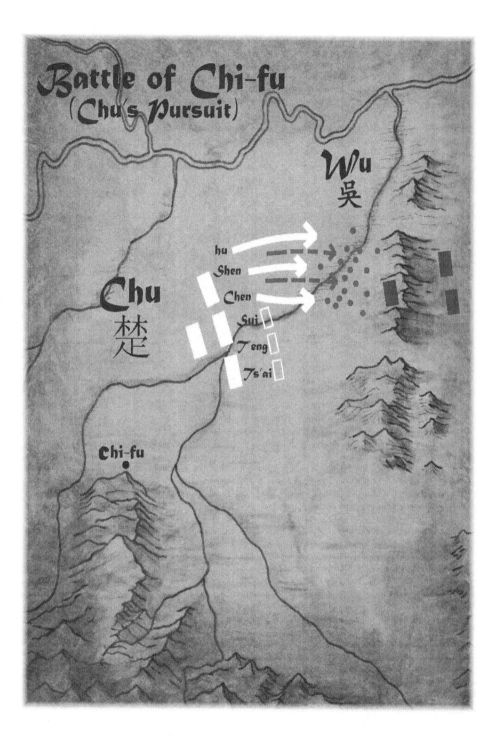

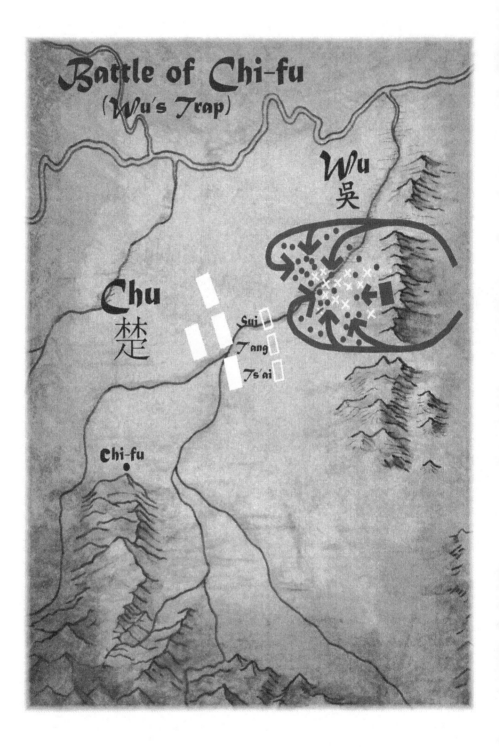

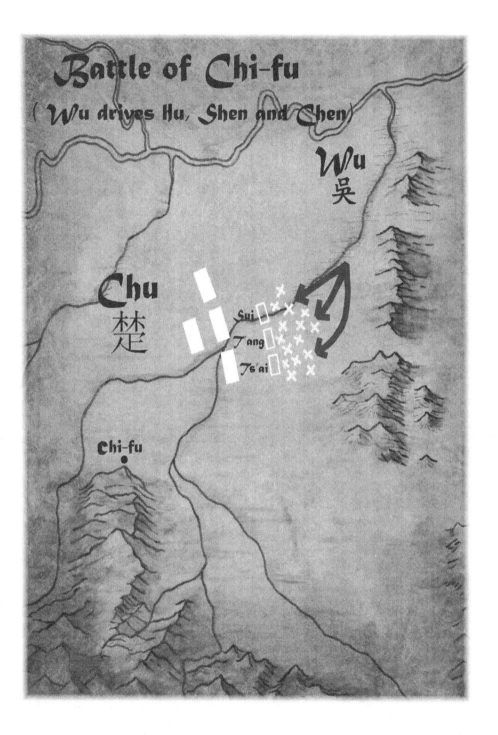

ACKNOWLEDGMENTS

*A*s a debut author, stepping into the publishing world with no knowledge of how to maneuver through it, I am fortunate to have assembled a team of professionals who provided seasoned counsel. A common theme among them has been the practice of telling me what they think even when I preferred to have heard differently.

My first task, after writing the manuscript of course, was to hire a strong editor who could provide sound technical advice as well as improve my storytelling where needed. I found that person in Cliff Carle. His guidance, helping me to fine-tune the story, was tremendous, and Cliff's wealth of experience in the publishing business was invaluable.

Stephanie Barko, my publicist, was the next addition to the team. Her platform gave structure to the PR effort and provided a roadmap to follow, with her prodding me forward at times.

Both Mayapriya Long (Bookwrights) and artist, Lee Casbeer, rescued me from the quicksand of the cover art world. The effort to create the cover, I previously thought, should have been simple and straight forward. It was neither. After failed attempts with various artists, I found and commissioned Lee to paint the likeness of Prince Kuang. He hired Jeremy Hsu, who was at the time a student at the University of Texas, to pose providing the basis of the image. My collaborative effort with Lee was tremendously positive, and although I ultimately chose not to use that work in the cover, I proudly display his art in my home and on my website. Lee also painted the Battle of Chi-fu diagrams and Map of the Spring and Autumn Period (519 B.C.), combining historical and topographical information from multiple sources. Some of his details are embedded in the cover.

Mayapriya also applied her expertise creating the book's internal design. She came highly recommended, and her work was not only superb, but a wonderful addition in my journey to publication.

Patrick J. LoBrutto applied his seasoned editorial expertise and provided meaningful guidance that helped me refine the story.

Sandra Miller Linhert (The Book Polisher) performed the final proofreading of the novel. Her keen eye caught tedious details, and her skill challenged me to reread for technical accuracies.

Ralph D. Sawyer, a prolific author on the subjects of Sun Tzu, *The Art of War,* and warfare in ancient China, is another person to whom I am grateful. I have read numerous versions of *The Art of War,* but none more important to shaping my thinking for *The Mark of Wu* series than his work. His historical accounts, analysis and period-specific details meaningfully informed aspects of this novel.

Of course, I have saved for last the most influential person to whom I must shower with praise – my wife, Lisa. She indulged, encouraged and supported my dream to write this series while keeping me grounded during the process. Perhaps at times, she had the greater challenge.

AUTHOR'S NOTES

My interest in China did not come in a single, defining moment. Rather, that part of the world has called to me, beckoning from afar, in curious whispers. The stories my father told of his experiences during WWII, planted the seed prior to Ping-pong diplomacy when information about life in China was limited. That country to me, when growing up in Wichita Falls, Texas, was very mysterious.

Dad was like many veterans of his generation. He closely guarded his darkest thoughts, choosing to share only the lighter, more humorous memories. His journey to China started before the United States entered the war. General Chenault was authorized to recruit volunteers, who later became known as the "Flying Tigers". Dad, a wiry 5'11" 135-pounder, applied. But because he was not yet 18 years old, his mother had to grant permission. She told him: "Not only no, Harry, but hell no!"

Once of age, he joined the Army Air Corps, then was eventually assigned to the 74th Fighter Squadron of the 23rd Fighter Group, which later became part of the 14th Airforce. Coincidentally, members of the Flying Tigers, who remained to fight after the AVG was disbanded, were brought into that Fighter Group. Dad was sent to the China Burma India campaign at far less the pay he would have received had my Grandmother allowed him to have volunteered. He always complained about that pay gap, but ended the gripe with a chuckle.

He spoke highly of General Chenault, the genius behind the Flying Tigers, and admired Tex Hill for both his skills and leadership. Inevitably, Dad would turn the conversation to a comical recollection – his first taste of pickled eggs that had been cured while buried in clay pots, a drunken monkey (no, not the Kung-fu style of martial arts), or a dog (I don't recall its name) that became agitated when Japanese Zeroes were about to attack, providing an early warning signal that was more effective than the jing bough network (three ball alert system) stationed at intervals along the fly routes.

Dad described only one of the numerous raids the airbases in China, where he was stationed, suffered. He and a buddy were working on a P40 that was at the edge of the runway, caught away from others and the watchful mutt, when Japanese planes attacked, strafing the grounded aircraft. Cut off from shelter, they darted for cover in a cluster of trees. The sprint took them across a plowed field, during which Dad's friend stumbled, falling to his knees. The man finished the dash on all fours, but never lost pace. Once they reached the trees, Dad turned in time to see the Japanese pilot make another pass down the runway thumbing his nose at them – literally, thumb to nose with fingers extended skyward, wiggling.

A trip to Hong Kong gave me an up-close experience of the people and culture, but my curiosity took a new direction near the end of law school when I read Samuel B. Griffin's translation of *Sun Tzu The Art of War* (published by the Oxford University Press). It tickled my interest in Sun Tzu, the man many have ascribed the first thorough, written analysis of warfare. Years later, when Dad was going through the last stages of Alzheimer's disease, I sat with him, sometimes for long stretches, while he slipped in and out of wakefulness. To keep from losing my mind, I gathered materials to research China, during Sun Tzu's days, and dived into the details.

I continued the study, when life and logistics allowed, reading multiple translations of *Sun Tzu's Art of War*, the *Tso Chuan*, *The Gongyang Commentary on The Spring and Autumn Annals* and *The Grand Scribe's Records*, along with numerous period-specific reference materials. I also poured through the pages of *The History of Wars in China*, compiled by the Armed Forces University (published by Li Ming Cultural Enterprise Co., LTD.), which was written in Chinese, but because I don't speak, read or write any Chinese language, my review was limited to studying the diagrams of battles.

Hidden Paths is the first book in *The Mark of Wu*™ series, which is a result of my research. It begins in ancient China, 519 B.C., during the Spring and Autumn Period of the Eastern Zhou Dynasty. Contrary to the tranquil name given the period, it was a tumultuous time in which many states were conquered or annexed by stronger foes during a span of about 300 years. The exact number of the defeated states is debated, but more than 100 is often floated for academic consumption. Historians also differ on the exact dates defining the period, but it generally runs from the early to late 700s B.C. to some point in time during the 400s B.C. The Warring States period followed and is widely believed to have begun by the middle of the fifth century B.C.

The series is titled *The Mark of Wu* because the name "Wu" appears in different and interesting ways during that period. The State of Wu's accomplishments provide one example, as do the markings the Wu people tattooed on their faces to ward off water demons. Yuan's name provides another example. His surname was "Wu" making his full name Wu Yuan. Similarly,

Sun Wu, who enters the story later in the series, and who is known today in the Western world as Sun-Tzu, is another example. Individually and together, the State of Wu and its people, Wu Yuan and Sun Wu left their "marks" on history, and *The Mark of Wu*™ tells that story.

Primary sources are extremely limited for the Spring and Autumn Period, which is understandable given the lapse of time, and when delving into this era, historians often cite the *Tso Chuan* as China's earliest narrative source. Probably during the first or second century B.C., Ssu-ma Ch'ien, who is also referred to as "The Grand Historian" or "The Grand Scribe", rewrote the *Tso Chuan*. Those writings were not strict recitations of historical fact but embodied the authors' perspectives, which is always the case. The body of work in modern times, providing analysis, has grown, and not surprisingly, each translator and historian present details with their individual viewpoints and nuances. Sometimes, differences in the stories are due merely to the choice of words given to a logogram, and because words and characters used 2,500 years ago do not always carry the same meaning assigned to them hundreds, much less thousands, of years later, a translator's notes often reveal pearls of wisdom as to why he chose one meaning of a passage over another. Also, details among competing interpretations may differ because of an author's reliance on sources that may help to provide context not considered (or otherwise dismissed) by those who produced competing works. All told, factual accounts of that time period are incomplete, providing fertile ground for artistic license, which I unabashedly exercised at will.

Hidden Paths presents indulgent adaptations of events in the life of "Yuan". The raw, historical account includes events and identifies specific people – sometimes unnamed – but with limited details. Over the centuries, that limited historiography has provided, I understand, the basis for Chinese folklore and literature that often tends to fill in the historical holes with melodrama. *The Mark of Wu* series trends away from the use of hyperbolic noble acts and instead, closes those gaps with details that make sense within my notions of human behavior, yet consistent with the record, keeping the goal of an easy page-turning read front and center.

The Battle of Chi-fu, as incorporated into *Hidden Paths*, provides an example of limited details in the annals of history. It is historically accurate that Chu's General (Field Marshal) died on the march to war. His name was not mentioned in three of the translated accounts I used in writing the story. The same was true for the lesser commander who assumed the mantle upon the General's death. But a fourth, rather expensive resource I acquired after writing the novel, named both men – General Yang Gai and Commander Wei Yue. So, I revised a late draft, substituting into the story the historically accurate names for the ones I had created.

Although the historical account of the battle does not specifically identify Yuan's presence, the record of his life makes his participation plausible and, when considering the overlap of his life and the State of Wu, placing him at the battle is conceivable.

For the military history buffs among you, the diagrams of the battle of Chi-fu are adaptations of drawings contained in the *History of Wars in China* and *Sun Tzu The Art of War*, translated by Ralph D. Sawyer (published by Barnes & Noble with arrangement by Westview Press) as influenced by Sawyer's narrative translation of the account of the battle. I must give significant credit to Mr. Sawyer, whose collection of remarkable work is filled with historical nuggets and period context that inform not only my rendition of the battle, but also the story *The Mark of Wu* series tells.

History is important, and the study of it inspires healthy

and scholarly debate. This series, however, is fiction, grounded in historical facts, but a tale, nonetheless, that is meant to entertain. *Hidden Paths* includes the subtle and sometimes generous exercise of artistic license where appropriate for the flow of the story. Deviations from historical melodrama, as described before, provide examples, but there are geographical turns as well and even deviations in the use of certain names. For instance, the use of "Yuan", "Sheh" and "Shang" in the series does not include their surname "Wu" because they are from the State of Chu, and I wanted to avoid confusion with the State of Wu. Also, differing translations of the relevant chronicles have produced competing alternatives for names that identify the same person, and for *The Mark of Wu* series, I used spellings consistent with pronunciations more familiar to an English-speaking audience, rather than adhering strictly to Wade-Giles, Pinyin or other systems of translation. The character "Yuan", for example, is also known in the record as "Yün", "Wu Yün" and "Wu Tzu-hsü", yet I chose to spell the name closer to the phonetic pronunciation - "Yuan".

The recorded narrative surrounding King Liao and Prince Kuang, both from the State of Wu, provides other examples. One author named Liao, "King Handsome", and referred to Kuang as "Prince Light". The stories, though, are unmistakably the same irrespective of how those men are identified.

The use of alternate names is also true for places. For instance, the primary battle of Chi-fu is named after a nearby town that existed during that time. Scholars who have used Pinyin as their mode of translation have spelled the name "Jifu" or "Gifu". There appears to be no limits to the differing translations – authors don't even agree on the names of resources. *Tso Chuan*, for instance, is also labeled *Zuozhuan*.

These notes do not attempt to provide an exhaustive list of the challenges encountered when researching and writing about ancient China, but simply draws the reader's attention to examples of the types of choices made during the creative process. For more information about the lives and culture of the mosaic people who lived during the time in which this series is set, you are invited to visit my website at www.themarkofwu. com.

ABOUT THE AUTHOR

*P*rior to becoming a serial novelist, Stephen M. Gray worked as a corporate attorney on complex litigation. Early in Gray's career, his travels to Asia fueled a thirst to learn about China's history. His extensive research into the teachings of Sun Tzu for application in today's business world led to his fascination with 6th Century B.C. China. There, Gray discovered folklore about the abuse of power and privilege, and the noble effort of a few brave warriors who fought against tremendous odds for their survival.

Hidden Paths is Gray's first of five books in The Mark of Wu series. He lives in San Antonio, Texas with his wife of 26 years.

www.themarkofwu.com